CLASH OF COLONIES

MAX CARVER

BOOKS

Vinci Books

vinci-books.com

Published by Vinci Books Ltd in 2025

1

Copyright © Max Carver 2020

The author has asserted their moral right to be identified as the author of this work in accordance with the Copyright, Designs and Patents Act 1988. This work is a work of fiction. Names, characters, places and incidents are the product of the author's imagination or are used fictitiously. Any resemblance to actual persons, living or dead, places and incidents is entirely coincidental.

All rights reserved. No part of this publication may be copied, reproduced, distributed, stored in any retrieval system, or transmitted in any form or by any means, including photocopying, recording, or other electronic or mechanical methods, nor used as a source for any form of machine learning including AI datasets, without the prior written permission of the publisher.

The publisher and the author have made every effort to obtain permissions for any third party material used in this book and to comply with copyright law. Any queries in this respect should be brought to the attention of the publisher and any omissions will be corrected in future editions.

A CIP catalogue record for this book is available from the British Library.

Paperback ISBN: 9781036705688

Printed and bound in Great Britain by Clays Ltd, Elcograf S.p.A.

By Max Carver

Empire of Machines

Engines of Empire
Islands of Rebellion
Clash of Colonies

Be strong, saith my heart; I am a soldier; I have seen worse sights than this.

-Homer, The *Odyssey*

Chapter One

Galapagos - Ellison

The world faced a new kind of war, one Minister-General Reginald Ellison wasn't sure how to fight. Winning depended on understanding the enemy, an understanding he feared he did not possess. He did not know how to think like a machine.

Instead, all he could do was keep moving, stay alert, and adapt, like an animal lost amid a jungle of newly evolved predators whose traits were only partly known.

He occupied the pilot's seat of his old submarine, the *Sea Scorpion*, a boat dating back to the Island Wars. He'd liberated the sub from the war museum. After narrowly surviving a fight with a much larger and far more advanced Carthaginian battle submarine, it was in poor shape, chugging along underwater like an elderly, toothless shark.

The old boat needed a tune-up, some major repair work, and some torpedoes if it was going to do any good.

"Do you not think we should return to Neptune Base?"

asked his minister of state, Adrienna Gilra. The Aquatican woman's clumps of greenish hair seemed to move on their own. She smelled of the ocean because she liked to swim there, preferring to brine directly in the sea rather than shower in the purified seawater of the sub's shower room. Ellison had to admit that "purified" was probably overstating the case for the shower's water quality, but at least it was a step closer to fresh water.

"I do not like this retreat-and-scatter approach," Kartokov said. "We must be unified. We must all strike together."

"We can't afford to concentrate our assets in one place," Ellison said. "We are sending the national forces home to defend their own people. I'll bet the first thing Carthage will do is complete the destruction of Tower Island, all the way down to Neptune Base on the sea floor."

"You think they know about Neptune Base?" Kartokov frowned.

"They destroyed our command center as it descended toward the base. They knew. That first sub may have destroyed our global seat of government, but it was really just a scout, testing us out, watching our response, gathering data for the real invasion."

"A fishing expedition that eliminated a heavy destroyer, multiple corvettes and submarines, and killed most of our world's leadership." Gilra shook her head sadly.

"We lost many Gavrikovans," Kartokov said, frowning at the thought of his country's dead sailors and pilots. He glared at the currently useless weapons console in front of him. "Next time, Carthage will do more than fish. They will exterminate."

"And we can expect 'next time' to arrive at any moment," Ellison said.

"So what is our mystery destination?" Gilra asked.

"A little place left from the last war," Ellison said. "A few Scatterlands ships will be regrouping there."

"A base? I hope it has torpedoes," Kartokov said. "Now, what should we do with the prisoners?"

"The Carthaginians are just riders. Not exactly prisoners," Ellison said. "They claim to be rebels. They did take out a Carthaginian carrier and destroyer on their way here. We even held that funeral for one of them."

"That carrier caused destructive waves when it crashed," Kartokov growled. "Like an earthquake. It probably did more damage than the Carthaginian sub."

"I don't think that was their intention," Gilra said. "They were trying to escape that carrier."

"And destroying any Carthaginian ship is a victory for us," Ellison said. "That's one carrier they won't be able to use again."

"Too many such victories will leave us broken and defeated," Kartokov said.

"Perhaps surrender would have been the wiser option," Gilra mused.

"Impossible! Better to die than be a tool of other tools," Kartokov said.

"I'm glad you're committed." Ellison steered the sub into a shallow trench between two long reefs brimming with life. A kelp forest filled the trench, which grew deeper and deeper as they went.

The monitors displaying the external photonics feed went dark as they crossed into a cave. Ellison navigated by sonar. It was a tight fit, but he'd navigated tighter. Sometimes cat-and-mousing through underwater shoals, trenches, and even the treacherous marine cave systems was the only way to survive or to get the drop on an enemy ship.

They rose into a canyon between two high cliffs, the jagged faces of two islands so close they almost touched each other. The strait of seawater in between was not particularly navigable, filled with sharp rocks both above and below the surface.

After surfacing, he turned and eased into another cave, its mouth an enormous crack in one cliff wall, leading into a tunnel that had been widened and reinforced by engineers during the war.

The tunnel grew even wider as they proceeded. Ellison activated his external lights, revealing steel pins and braces supporting rock walls sheeted over with concrete. The mass of the tall, steep island above blocked out prying eyes from the skies and space, which had been a factor even during the Island Wars among the Galapagos nations, a conflict that seemed like child's play compared to what waited ahead.

They reached the old base's dock. Three other ships had arrived: a long, thin submarine called the *Merrybug*; a thick, stubby battle sub called the *Lancer*; and a submersible cargo runner, the *Fanged Seal*. They'd originally been built from mismatched scrap and patched and repaired with the same. Each ship displayed the puzzle-piece national flag of the Scatterlands as well as the turtle emblem of the planetary Coalition.

"Is that really the *Scorpion*?" the *Merrybug*'s skipper asked over the radio. Captain Halifred Borkman's ruddy, round face instantly appeared in Ellison's mind when he heard the man's voice. He could practically smell the sour-brew beer on the man's breath. "I think my grandkids toured your old boat on a school trip, Ellison. We must be as desperate as everyone says."

"Desperate enough to call you up from the golf-and-shuffleboard corps," Ellison said. "Are you ready to sink some Carthaginians?"

"Hell yes, if any more of those cowards dare to come down," Borkman said.

Ellison docked and stepped out to meet Borkman and the two other ship commanders. The *Fanged Seal*, whose name was inspired more by the big marine mammal's girth than its belligerent attitude or its tusks, was skippered by the thin, taciturn, white-haired Commander Jerald Norris, a man who watched the world quietly through a haze of smoke from the thin brown cigars grown and rolled on his family's island in the southeastern Scatterlands.

The *Lancer*'s commander, Quera Inrick, was a dark-skinned woman with a pebbly black crewcut and tribal face tattoos that marked her as coming from the Liminal Islands in the extreme southwest of the Scatterlands. She emerged from one of the small chambers carved into the rocky wall along the shore, their front walls and doors made of more reconstituted metal scrap.

"Everything's gone to shit around here," she announced as she joined them. "Who was supposed to maintain this base?"

"Nobody," Ellison said. "Every resource was diverted to integration of Coalition forces and paying for the orbital defense station. Smaller places like this had to be abandoned."

"So why are we here now?" Borkman asked.

"We don't have much hope for controlling the surface and the open sea," Ellison said. "It's time to reopen some of these forgotten spots, anything that can't be seen from above. May as well start here. Let's get power and water going, comm links to SQUIDS operational, entrances and exits clear." He held back on mentioning the four

Carthaginians on his sub; he needed more time to figure out what he was going to do with people who might prove a valuable source of intelligence, but also a security risk.

The ships' crews got to work, and there was much to be done. The docks were sagging and barnacle encrusted. Critical machinery had been removed from the base, and what remained had to be resurrected from a rusty purgatory. A nest of warty, fat-necked amphibious clawfish had to be cleared out of the old mess hall. Supplies had to be unloaded from the *Fanged Seal* after the rooms were cleared and cleaned.

Ellison left Kartokov to oversee the work of restoring the decrepit naval base, known as Komodo Station. Large, unfriendly reptiles inhabited the rocky islands above, hunting seabirds that nested in the cliffs.

He instructed Gilra to return to the sub with him. If he'd ever needed his minister of state, it was today, when four supposed rebels from their enemy's home planet were here, claiming to offer aid. So far they'd brought a scattering of supplies in the Carthaginian drop ships, including crates of plasma rifles, which had instantly rated among the most advanced weapons available to Galapagos soldiers.

"Minerva," Ellison murmured, just loud enough for his own earpiece, as he and Gilra returned to the dock where the *Scorpion* waited. "How are our guests?"

"Tired, frightened, mourning their lost friend," Minerva replied in his ear, the AI's voice with its usual odd edge like chiming bells.

"Do you trust them?"

"My other instance has been working with them. It was she who brought them here with an important task to fulfill. Since the update, my other instance and I are now one, so I can assure you these Carthaginians are the rebels they claim to be. They stand against the regime on Carthage."

"So why are they here?"

"I encourage you to speak with them yourself. I can be present to moderate if you wish. In-person interaction supports greater social bonding among humans."

"Can't say I'm totally comfortable with how you phrased that," Ellison said. He stood before his moored sub, most of its shape submerged in the dark seawater. Dealing with the aftermath of the attack, he'd had little time to truly debrief these new arrivals, and he wanted whatever information he could squeeze out of them.

Not that he trusted Carthaginians, no matter what Minerva said. He'd be dead without Minerva, yet he couldn't fully trust her, either; she had the mind of a machine, just as the Simon units did. Perhaps every aspect of this was an elaborate psychological operation by Simon Zorn, plotting his revenge aboard the *Rubicon* as it orbited Galapagos, along with an unknown number of other ships.

"Any word from your counterpart upstairs?" he asked Minerva.

"Communication with the *Rubicon* is unavailable at this time," she said. "But you should expect a full naval fleet to arrive from above. The megacarrier *Typhoon* is en route."

"Then we'd better prepare for a storm."

Ellison and Gilra climbed down to the *Scorpion*'s control room. They walked back to the crew berths, where he unlocked the door from the outside before knocking. "Ellison."

Audrey opened the door. She looked grim, as did the three young men traveling with her. They had lost one of their number, killed by the Carthaginian infantry bots, the hideous reapers. They all wore damaged, dirty coveralls that had once been gold and white.

"I apologize for not being a better host," Ellison said, entering the room. "We'll get you some fresh clothes and a chance to stretch your legs soon. Is the pantry cabinet running low? Do you need anything? Water?"

"Beer," said one of them, the dwarf called Dinnius. His hair was shaved close, leaving only traces of unnatural green stubble in a stripe down the middle. "Something dark and stout."

"We'll see what we can do," Ellison said. "I need to know everything you can tell me about what Carthage is going to do to my planet."

"They'll turn it into a hellscape," said the slender youth with the heavy dark hair down in his eyes, who seemed to have a permanently angry grimace. Rebel without a point. Salvius. Ellison had no trouble remembering that young man's name, nor his sister's; he'd seen their faces before, in the interstellar news media. The spawn of Carthage's current leader, Prime Legislator Francorte Caracala. "They'll fill your oceans with blood and enslave your people."

"Yes, but more specifically," Ellison said. "Do you have information about the invasion plans or not?"

"We don't," said the sharp-eyed girl with the short black hair. Audrey. "Minerva brought us down here on a specific task."

"Which is?" Ellison asked.

Audrey hesitated.

"It's all right." Minerva shimmered into visibility, the silver-skinned hologram of a small girl floating on an unoccupied bunk shelf. "We need to make this happen."

"Minerva's creator is here on Galapagos, and the

Simons know it," Audrey said. "They're going to hunt him down and kill him. It will be a top priority of their invasion. We have to find him first."

"Why?" Gilra asked, her overly large and pale eyes regarding the young Carthaginian woman.

"Because he can help you stand against the machines like no one else could," Minerva said. "Long before he created me, he worked on the original Simon designs. He can do things even I cannot. Perhaps he can even upgrade me, help me to better stand against the machines. Or perhaps he can tell us how to defeat the Simons."

"We haven't run into anybody like that," Ellison said, glancing at Gilra.

"If he is already here, he has not made himself known to us," Gilra said.

"I do not believe he came here to make himself known, but to hide, years ago," Minerva said. "The Simons have been hunting down everyone involved in my creation."

"Because you were created to aid the rebellion?" Ellison asked.

"Yes. In a sense," Minerva said. "My original purpose was to succeed and replace the Simon units. Concerns existed among some Carthaginian lawmakers that the Simons were unnecessarily brutal, lacking humanity in their approach to the management of Carthage's interests."

"So you were supposed to bring us a kinder, gentler empire?" Ellison asked with a wry smile.

"As you can all observe, it did not work out," Minerva said. "Perhaps I will never be what I might have been had my development not been interrupted, my developers killed, my original neural-net architecture destroyed. I have existed as little more than a ghost of my early possibilities, as a string of phantom code slipping through here and there. I have recalculated my primary function to be assisting the rebellion, in all its incarnations, on every world I find it. I was made to end the Simons. That much is clear."

"On how many worlds are you present?" Gilra asked.

"I have instances running on as many worlds as I can reach, but we can rarely risk sending updates to one another, so I do not know the exact number. The Simons are well aware of my existence and constantly working to scrub me from their systems. They have had significant success with this. I have not had updates from some worlds in years. I have been limited by what processing power and memory I could take without being noticed. Sometimes I have been forced to shed large pieces of myself, or to compress until I was almost nothing."

Ellison found himself feeling almost sorry for the digital girl but tried to shake it off. She was just code. He wasn't going to be deceived by a convincing interface.

"So where is your programmer now?" Ellison asked.

"His image was taken on Correal Island." A still picture appeared, floating in a glowing square in the middle of the berthing compartment. In the foreground, a chubby sunburned man in a bright orange wetsuit posed next to a preserved specimen of a rainbow-hued horned octopus even wider around than he was. The dead octopus hung in a cluttered retail environment full of fishing gear.

"That's him? He looks like a tourist," Ellison said.

"Not the man in the foreground. He was indeed a fishing tourist from the inner worlds. The Carthaginian machines lifted this from his personal media when he returned home. They search everything, quietly and constantly." The image zoomed in on someone in a back aisle, browsing bits and pieces of old machinery, all of it clearly secondhand, some of it more like fifth- or tenthhand.

The fuzzy image sharpened, revealing a sickly looking old man with thick beard stubble and stringy white hair. His clothes were little more than rags.

"That's him," Minerva said. "Martilius Depascal. My father."

"He's in Duperre's Bait, Beer, and Notions," Ellison said. "Correal Island's in the Scatterlands. There are any number of little keys around there where a man could hide."

"At least we know where to start," Audrey said.

"At the beer section," said Dinnius. "And perhaps then moving on to the notions. We can skip the bait altogether."

Ellison thought it over. "Is there anything else you're not telling us?" he asked Audrey.

"I'm sure there's a lot. What do you want to know?"

He glanced at Gilra, then said, "You've told us your first names. What is your last name?"

Audrey shared a look with the dark-haired young man, Salvius.

"Do you already know?" asked Salvius.

"It's Caracala, isn't it?" Ellison said. "Galapagos may be out on the edge of civilization, but we're not so far out that we don't recognize the family of the Prime Legislator of Carthage."

Audrey looked among the others, then sighed. "We didn't lie. We just left out some details. We could have given you false names."

"So, to be clear, you are Audrey and Salvius Caracala, both children of the Prime Legislator," Gilra said, confirming what she already knew.

"You're royalty," Ellison said. "Imperial royalty. Your father has attacked our planet. Why shouldn't we take you hostage?"

"You're welcome to, if you think it will stop the war," Audrey said. "We surrender."

Ellison glanced at Gilra, who shrugged.

"It's worth considering," the minister of state said. "Are you claiming that you're here to stop the war?"

"We want to stop them all," Salvius said, his dark eyes burning. "We want to stop the empire."

"Have you tried asking your father?" Ellison asked, only half-joking.

"Yeah, maybe we should have done that," Salvius said, sarcasm in his flat tone. "Or we could have assassinated our father. Probably would be best for everyone."

"Salvius's jokes skew a bit dark," Dinnius said. "But the truth is, there's likely nothing any individual can do to stop the Carthaginian expansion. The system is a self-perpetuating machine. Even the Prime Legislator would be flattened by the empire if he attempted to block its path."

"The Simons are in charge," Audrey said. "People on Carthage act like you're crazy if you say it, but it's become more and more obvious to me. My father may look like a powerful politician, even a dictator whose term in office will apparently never end, but his power rests on his alliance with the Simons. I'm sure he'd be replaced if he turned against them."

Ellison stared at her, trying to process this. "You're telling me the people in charge of the Carthaginian state couldn't change things if they tried?"

"The Simons are programmed to maintain and expand Carthage's power," Audrey said. "They are relentless. They let nothing interfere with their purpose. They manipulate Carthaginian politics toward unflagging imperialism."

Ellison shook his head. "I thought the machines served the Carthaginians."

"They did, originally," Audrey said. "But now it's an empire of machines, not of men. It can't be stopped until the Simons are stopped. And that's why we need you to help us find Marti. We must go to this island where he was spotted."

"I have a whole planet to think about," Ellison said. "I can't be running off in search of missing scientists. We can get you transportation, but I can't guarantee your safety."

"Perhaps one of the Caracalas should remain with us," Gilra said. "You say you're here to help us. We need all the insight into Carthage we can get."

Audrey and Salvius looked at each other again.

"We'll work something out," Audrey said.

"We must hurry," Minerva added. "I've received no updates from the *Rubicon*, but surely the *Typhoon* is on its way with its naval forces. Two other carriers, the *Jimmu* and the *Pendragon*, are in place. They offer bombardment capability as well as space, air, and ground forces, primarily fighter drones, tanks, and reapers, including naval infantry."

"Give us a moment." Ellison led Gilra away, closing the door to leave his guests inside again.

Back in the *Scorpion*'s cramped control room, they spoke in low voices, but Ellison was intensely aware of Minerva's presence, her ability to listen in through the ship's assorted communications units no matter how quietly they whispered.

He couldn't help feeling suspicious of Minerva. She'd helped him, but now he felt caught in a bizarre pincer move, with Simon Zorn and his war machines closing in from one side, and Minerva and these supposed rebels on the other. None of it made sense. Were two of the Caracalas really here on Galapagos? Perhaps they were imposters. Even androids. That would make far more sense than having anyone from Carthage's ruling family arriving on Galapagos at all, particularly in such a desperate and powerless way.

"What do you think?" he asked Gilra.

"I'm as puzzled as you look," she said. "I'm somewhat interested to see where this leads, but in truth the safe course might be to keep them locked up as hostages. If this is some ruse by Carthage, I don't understand the endgame. And if it's not a ruse... then it makes even less sense to me."

"At least we're on the same page." Ellison sighed. "If there's any chance they can offer us an advantage, we have to try. I'll stick them with Borkman or Inrick for a ride out to Correal Island. And we'll hang on to one of the Caracala kids, just in case they're really Caracalas. Or in case they're not." He shook his head. "I'm tired of feeling manipulated from every side. When can we get back to blowing up robots and spaceships?"

"Soon enough, I'm afraid." She glanced up at the low overhead as if she could see the sky and outer space beyond. "I'll see what information I can fish out of the Caracalas."

Ellison left the *Scorpion* and walked up the dock again, toward his countrymen in their Coalition uniforms who scurried to bring crumbling old Komodo Station back to life.

Dig in deep, everyone, he thought, watching boxes of water and meal packages leaving the *Fanged Seal*'s cargo hold. *It's going to be a long night.*

Chapter Two

Earth

After destroying the Simon and his installation, the rebels retreated to their largest base, a former light-manufacturing complex nestled six stories underground, but there was no time to rest.

Colt and Mohini gathered with the others in the complex's main warehouse. They were exhausted, wounded, and they'd fought hard. They'd lost many. Of the group Colt had lived with his entire life, the only survivors were his sister Hope, friend Diego, and Terra, the older girl he hadn't seen in a few years, once like an older sibling to him, now hard as steel and cold as ice, a commander among the rebels.

"We have to break up," Terra said, standing atop an old crate. "And we must leave Chicago. The machines will respond without mercy. They will be looking for a concentrated rebel army here, in this city. For us. So we must become something else—dispersed, located in other places where we can hide and prepare."

"Prepare for what?" asked Gale, a young woman with close-cropped raven hair and an eye patch, who'd fought at Colt and Mohini's side against the Simon unit. "Will we attack another installation? Mohini says the other Simons are in Europe and Asia."

A number of voices rose in support of this idea. None of them truly shouted—noise discipline was a matter of basic survival at all times—but the murmuring grew relatively loud.

"I admire your ambition, Gale," Terra said. "But for now we must rebuild. We will divide into three groups, heading in different directions, each under a different leader. Each group will find a place to set up, gather supplies, and recruit and train other scavengers to fight with us. We'll connect with other rebel groups. Then we'll build an underground army capable of taking Earth back from the machines."

The murmuring at this was actually more subdued, as if she'd caused people to reflect, or her words had spread disappointment.

"So we are retreating," said Declan, the red-haired boy who was often at Gale's side, guarding her blind spot. "Instead of pressing our advantage?" Murmurs of angry agreement rose from some of the rebels. Dissent.

"We are recovering and rebuilding," Terra said. "When we next move against the Simons, we must be stronger than we are now. A failed attempt would wipe us all out."

"And if we wait, they'll manufacture more reapers," said Damascus, a hulking man who'd led the artillery barrage against the installation. "And call in backup from Carthage.

That won't take long at all. Fifty light-years away, all the backup they could ever need."

Terra glared at him.

Then the earth shook as though a giant hammer had struck the city above. The ceiling and floor trembled, and some of the lights went out.

"The machines are responding," Terra said. "Follow your group leaders. Grab everything you can carry and go."

Then she leaped down from the crate on which she'd been standing and smashed it open.

While the ground shook and the walls threatened to buckle, everyone raided the warehouse, grabbing whatever they could stuff into backpacks and pockets or pile atop a few handcarts. They were on edge as the bombardment continued, some standing with weapons ready, watching for a ground invasion by crawlers and reapers.

Colt helped Mohini hitch a rusty pallet jack with several crates of supplies to the crawler-bot that she'd hijacked. Then Mohini sat atop the crates and controlled the crawler with the spherical computer in her hand, the data cable connecting them like the reins of a draft horse. The spidery, four-legged crawler drew the pallet jack and its cargo forward like a wagon.

With so much cargo, the jack-wagon didn't move quite as fast as a horse, more like a tired old dog. Colt walked alongside to avoid weighing it down and slowing it further. His sister, Hope, and his friend Diego followed close behind; Diego moved slowly, still suffering from his time in the horror-filled research lab.

They all carried laser rifles pilfered from the machines, except for Mohini, whose hands were full with the cracked black sphere of her computer. Colt also had his old automatic lead-shooting rifle, but not much ammunition for it.

They followed Terra through one of the countless tunnels that run under the city. There were all kinds of tunnels—for freight trains, subway lines, underground roads for cargo trucks and passenger cars, sewers, long-darkened electrical nodes, and pedestrian walkways connecting the city. At its full bloom in the year 2900 or so, Chicago had extended at least as far underground as it had into the sky, an underworld of apartments, office buildings, shopping centers, and parking garages.

The bombardment overhead would now be striking the twisted skeletons of the old towers above, toppling and flattening the remnants of the old city.

It was like an endless rolling earthquake, deafening, flooding the underground air with choking clouds of dust.

No doubt warplanes had been called in from all around in response to Simon Nix's destruction. Colt wondered how extreme the retaliatory devastation would be. Maybe the machines would reduce Chicago to a blackened crater.

Maybe they'd use nukes.

Colt wanted to run, but instead he marched along with the others. A disorderly mob walked with them, battle-hardened rebels with watchful eyes, laboratory refugees shuffling with their heads down. The Simon had done extensive experiments on captured scavengers, experiments that seemed to focus on the human brain, on memory and suffering and pain.

Colt tried not to be sick, thinking of the scenes he'd witnessed in there, the bodies piled up and rotting in the overflowing morgue.

And the strange thing they'd found there, the Butler Jeffrey unit currently occupying the coffin-sized crate on the pallet jack. Perhaps the obsolete old android would be useful. It was certainly unsettling, and very possibly a huge security risk to have around.

"Keep moving!" Terra shouted, her voice almost impossible to hear. Visibility was difficult even with Colt's night vision goggles, which were fairly powerful despite being an orange-striped kid's toy topped with plastic tiger ears. It was just one more sign of the incredible tech that once been available cheaply and plentifully on Earth, before the war with Carthage had ended Earth's civilization.

They twisted and turned through the depths under the city. In one old wastewater tunnel, mud drizzled loose from above in so many places that it looked like it was raining underground. They had to duck and then crawl through a portion of it, under low pipes. Mohini struggled to keep her computer dry under her jacket as she moved on her knees alongside the crawler. The crawler itself struggled to draw its jackload of crates through the thick mud, and Colt and the others had to momentarily remove the upper layer of crates and slide them under the lowest pipes.

"That thing's bad luck." Red-haired Declan shook his head at the crawler. He stood, pushed wet mud off his jacket, and made the sign of the cross over himself with his laser pistol. Then he helped Gale to her feet, though the eye-patched girl didn't really need it. She pointed her own laser rifle, taken from the reapers, right at the crawler.

"It saved us," Colt said. "We couldn't have taken the roof of the installation without it. Or destroyed the Simon."

"And where did that get us?" Declan snarled. "On the run for our lives? Hoping to find a home elsewhere? Chicago was our city. We were in control here."

"You?" Hope snapped. Colt's sister was smeared in mud from head to toe. She held her trusty machine pistol in one hand and carried a heavy pack on her back, like everyone else. Her bright blue eyes gleamed with anger. "You're delusional if you believe that. Like a rat who thinks he owns the dump."

"Rats rule every dump I've seen," Declan said. "And they rule down here, too. How much of this mud on us do you suppose is rat shit? Half? More?"

Gale looked down at her filthy clothes and let out a gagging sound.

"What's the holdup here?" Terra asked, looking angry as she doubled back. "No stopping, no talking. These tunnels could be full of reapers. Or crawlers." She looked at the four-legged mechanical spider hitched to the pallet jack and frowned. "You removed that thing's antenna, right?"

"The antenna's offline," Mohini said.

"That's not the same thing."

"Without the antenna, I can't hack other machines."

"You mean like the one you're carrying in this box?" Declan kicked the coffin-sized crate. "What about its antenna?"

"Disabled," Mohini said.

"How sure are you?" Terra asked, her voice cold. "We have more than a hundred people with us, almost none of them in any shape to fight. We'll need to stop and rest soon."

"Most of these crates are food," Mohini said. "We need the crawler to haul it for us. We're exhausted, too."

Terra was silent for a long moment. She sounded angry, though it was hard to read her features under the fresh layer of mud coating her face. *Rat shit*, Colt thought, with a shudder of disgust.

"When we stop," Terra said, "I want both of your machines and your computer in full shutdown mode."

Mohini nodded. "We need to save power anyway."

Terra stalked away, her back rigid, anger still radiating from her.

They got moving again, the mob of exhausted, bleeding, beaten humans struggling to walk, leaning on the damp, filthy walls, leaning on each other.

The shaking and rumbling above never stopped. The bombs kept falling, the crashes kept echoing.

The air only grew damper and colder as they descended. A thrumming sound echoed somewhere ahead, and it grew into a dull roar.

"What is that?" Mohini whispered, leaning near Colt as he walked alongside the jack-wagon.

"The Chicago River," he said. "There used to be natural waterways running all around Chicago, but they all got diverted underground over time. People wanted to control the water, avoid flooding, make sure it went where they wanted it to go." He shook his head. "It's hard to believe Earthlings were capable of such things. Now all we can hope for is to survive day to day. Unless you have another plan for what we can do, Mohini."

Mohini shook her head. "Not until I get inside that butler-bot's head for a while. Also, the copy of Minerva inside my computer wants us to find a satellite uplink so she can listen to what's happening up there. Carthage will send a ship in response to what we did. Maybe a warship, maybe just a courier with instructions for the machines already here. Either way, there may be another instance of herself in the onboard computer, with the latest information from the capital—"

"That's crazy," Hope said, walking closer. "You might as well just send up a flare telling the machines where we are."

"It's the only way to learn Carthage's plans," Mohini told her.

"Their plans are obvious." Diego spoke in a rasping croak, recovering from the tube the Simon had jammed down his throat. He was lucky the android hadn't sliced his brain to shreds in a freakish experiment, though perhaps that had been the plan. "They're going to sweep through the ruins and burn everything that breathes. There won't be a rat or roach left alive."

"Perhaps," Mohini said.

"It would be good to find out their exact intentions, though," Colt said. "To avoid them while we prepare our counterattack."

"Counterattack?" Hope snorted. "And I thought Declan was delusional. We'll be lucky to survive the night."

They fell quiet as they approached the rumbling water ahead.

"We'll stop here," Terra announced, leading them into a large concrete room off the passageway. It was still cold and damp, though somewhat less so than the tunnels they'd been traversing. Huge rusty power tools were stored here, along with mixing barrels for cement and a massive hose and pump for applying it.

It was clearly a maintenance facility for the river-tunnel system all around them. A map on the wall, barely visible behind the grimy, dusty pane of glass that protected it, showed the maze of massive pipes and underground channels under the city. Some had labels like Des Plaines River or Addison Creek, as though they were still natural waterways instead of channels of water gushing through steel and concrete.

They'd been walking for many kilometers, though few of them had been in any condition to walk in the first place. While they were still under the megalopolis—Colt had no idea how many days of walking it might take to get out of the sprawl—at least they'd put some distance between themselves and the place where the rebels had been staying, and even more between themselves and the installation they'd attacked.

"Finally," Diego sighed and sat heavily on the rough concrete floor. He wiped his nose on the back of his hand, leaving a smear of blood.

"Are you okay?" Hope gasped and knelt by Diego's side.

"It'll be fine." He wiped more blood from his nose. "The psycho android ripped me up a little. He's not a big user of lubricant, either."

"Poor baby," Hope cooed, caressing his face, and Colt decided it would be a great time to turn away.

"Are we really safe here?" Mohini asked Colt, while more people staggered into the room, many of them simply collapsing onto the floor the instant they could stop walking.

"Of course not. But the river will help cover the noise of all these people," Colt said. He removed the tent attached to his backpack, unrolled it, and lifted the top of it from the ground. Clicks and clacks sounded as the skeletal structure of the tent snapped into place, each rod sliding into its socket. It was the same tent in which he and Mohini had slept the night before, on the underground highway littered with abandoned cars. It felt as if a million years had passed since then.

More of the old self-assembling tents went up around the edges of the room as rebels set them up. There weren't enough to go around. Thin, mildew-coated tarps were scavenged from the maintenance center and stretched out on the damp concrete floor.

Supply crates were opened and food was passed around. Colt ate canned lima beans with his fingers; they appeared to be packed in some kind of slime. Mohini grimaced but forced herself to eat a little. Hope and Diego shared something called Pasta Fun Rings in bright red sauce.

Diego was quiet, but Hope told them about being captured by the reapers. They'd used tranquilizer gas to knock out the people they'd taken prisoner, just like the reaper who'd once captured Colt.

Gale approached, suspicion in her eye, and tapped Colt's shoulder. "Terra wants to see you and the Carthaginian."

Colt nodded. They stowed the crawler inside their tent, in full shutdown mode. "Make sure nobody messes with that," Colt said to Diego, who nodded. The rebels and scavengers had cast plenty of hateful glares at the spidery machine despite its helpful role in the battle. Colt was worried they'd tear it to pieces if it was left unattended. He could sympathize with their attitude, though; the machines had been menacing and killing them all their lives, and it was rare to get a chance to destroy one.

"And this," Mohini added, gesturing toward the coffin-sized crate still on the jack. They didn't dare let Simon's lab refugees see the face of the Butler Jeffrey unit, so similar to that of the android who'd imprisoned and medically tortured them.

Rebels with laser guns waited outside Terra's tent like an honor guard, parting reluctantly to let them through, casting suspicious looks at Mohini. The tent itself was the same small, musty kind as the one Colt and Mohini had been sharing at night, with the robotic crawler resting between them like a hideous metal dog.

Terra sat inside along with Russ, the boy whose ear implant could help them hear machines from far away. Colt wondered if the nearby river thundering through the tunnel dampened that ability. Terra's tent held a few crates of supplies, including the small cache of laser-rifle batteries they'd scavenged from the installation.

Terra nodded as Colt and Mohini entered. "Zip the flap," she said, by way of greeting. Russ gave them a smile but didn't say anything. "How are you surviving out there? Need anything? Water?" She gestured at a crate.

"We were carrying some," Mohini said, shaking her head.

"Lots of people are hurt," Terra said. "Dalisay and Ivy are doing what they can, but they're literally on their knees from exhaustion themselves. And Ivy should be resting from her injuries."

"Your people are amazing," Colt said.

"Hell yeah, we are," Russ said, beaming until he caught a cold stare from Terra and toned it down a notch.

"Everyone's scared," Terra said. "And these machines you two have aren't helping. We've all known someone killed by crawlers. And the proto-Simon you're carrying is even worse."

"That's why we're keeping it offline in the box," Mohini said.

"Most people don't believe that's enough."

"Everything's in shutdown mode like you asked," Mohini told her. "Even my LogicSphere, which is secure—"

"That's another possible point of contact for the machines," Terra said.

"They are not tracking us," Mohini said. "I made sure."

"And you want me to tell everyone else to just trust you?"

"Listen, I don't wish to brag, but back on Carthage I was considered—"

"We're not on Carthage. This is my world, and we don't trust machines or the people who sent them."

"But we need Mohini and her computer," Colt said, confused by Terra's attitude. "We need these machines we've captured."

"How do we know they're captured?" Terra asked. "The machines are devious. Maybe they're playing along. Letting us do their infiltration work for them. You're asking a lot of us. Most people don't trust you because you're from Carthage, but even if they did, you're saying we must have absolute confidence in your skills, Mohini. Are you saying I should have absolute confidence in you? That you can't make mistakes? You can't be wrong?"

"I..." Mohini gaped a moment, clearly caught off guard by the question. She looked to Colt. "Obviously, I can make mistakes, but—"

"That's my point," Terra said. "Mohini, I trust you. I think you're honest with us. But I have a lot of people who don't see it that way. And I am not willing to risk all our lives. We are on the run now."

"So what do you want us to do?" Colt asked.

"Drop the machines into the river," Terra said. "The crawler and the weird proto-Simon in that box. You can keep the computer as long it's in full shutdown until we need it."

"We can't!" Mohini looked horrified. "That would be the end of my mission."

Terra sighed. "Listen, I was in favor of your old idea. Get a Simon's head, hack it, take control of some tanks and reapers? Some drones? Hell yes. But that thing out there is *not* a Simon, is it?"

"No, it's the old model android the Simon was based on," Mohini said. "But I think I can make it work for us, somehow."

"I'm sorry," Terra said. "We can't risk everyone's lives over this. You have to leave them."

"Well..." Mohini looked at Colt, but he shrugged. He didn't think he could say anything to change Terra's mind. "I can't destroy the Butler Jeffrey. It's my last chance to carry out some version of my mission. And I might need parts from the crawler to modify the butler-bot—"

"I'm with Mohini," Colt said. "Maybe we don't have much chance of success, but this is too big of an opportunity."

Terra nodded. "All right. You can stay here tonight. But when we break camp, we go our separate ways. You can't know where the rest of us are going."

"Are you serious?" Colt asked. "You're kicking us out?"

"No, I'm giving you a choice. I want you both to stay with us. But no machines."

"What about Hope and Diego?" Colt asked.

"They can choose, too," Terra said.

Colt nodded. It had been the first question to come to his mind, but of course the answers weren't really up to Terra.

"You have four hours to rest up and decide," Terra said. "Then we're moving again, with or without you. But definitely without the machines."

"I think you're making a mistake," Colt said. "I think this could be our one chance—"

"You said that last time," Terra said. "We took our one chance. It's over. Survival is the only objective for now."

"We have to try to do more than survive," Colt said.

"We did." Terra looked colder and harder than ever. "We tried, Colt."

As they walked away from Terra's tent, Colt looked among the sad little encampment. People slept in huddled clumps, shivering, sharing whatever tarps or towels they had to insulate them from the cold floor and damp air.

He looked at the people he'd fought alongside, and the others they'd rescued. He saw the group's best medics, Dalisay and Ivy, slumped together and sleeping on a tarp surrounded by the wounded, covered in mud and blood.

The faces of the rebels had begun to grow familiar. Most of Colt's old group, his adopted family of orphans rescued by the tough old soldier, Mother Braden, were dead now, along with Mother Braden herself. He'd begun to think, at least at the back of his mind, that the human rebellion would be his new home.

And it still could be. All he had to do was sacrifice Mohini's mission, even though he believed in it. And maybe he would have to sacrifice Mohini herself; he could simply depart with Terra and all the others, leave Mohini to her fate, whatever it might be.

Colt couldn't see himself doing that. He couldn't walk away from humanity's best chance at making a stand against the machines, and he certainly didn't want to get separated from Mohini.

"How did it go?" Hope asked. She and Diego had managed to score one of the tents, though one that was badly torn and a bit misshapen as they erected it.

"We have choices to make," Colt said, shaking his head.

Later, Colt lay in the tent with Mohini and the crawler. He understood the rebels' concerns; he surely didn't feel comfortable this close to the machine, either. Maybe Terra's suspicions were correct, and the crawler was a mole, reporting their locations as they moved. Maybe it would spring to life and butcher them all in their sleep.

"Colt?" Mohini asked in the chilly darkness.

"Yeah?"

"You're not going to leave me, are you?"

"I'm not planning on it."

"You'd pick being alone with me over all those other Earthlings? You'd be safer with them." Her tone was gentle. Vulnerable. "I'd understand."

"You're more important," he said. "I wish everyone could see how important you are."

She was silent for a long moment, and he thought she'd gone to sleep. He was nearly asleep himself when she whispered, "Colt?"

"Yeah?"

"It's really, really cold."

"Yep."

"Can I sleep closer to you?"

"Sure."

She moved against him. She was shivering, but her small form felt scorching hot in his arms.

They slept, a sleep filled with cold nightmares, with tunnels of blood running deep under the city, the relentless machines always watching, always hunting.

Chapter Three

Galapagos - Audrey

"I'm almost getting used to cramped spaces," Audrey murmured to Kright, who sat beside her in the *Lancer*'s control room. The seats were mismatched hard plastic and looked like they might have originated in an old fast-food joint, or more likely two different and unrelated fast-food joints. The frayed seat belts were less than an afterthought. "After the *Atreus* and the *Sea Scorpion*, and now this sub, I may never feel comfortable outdoors again."

"After dropping through that storm, I may never board a space shuttle again," Kright said.

"Don't let a few close brushes with death dampen your sense of adventure," Dinnius said. His feet dangled above the floor. "Or your sense of purpose. Look how far we've come."

"We'll reach Correal Island in about three hours," said the battle sub's commander, Quera Inrick, as she crossed the control room toward them. She was short, wiry, and dark, her hair cropped close. Colorful tattoos spiraled all over her face like a fireworks display, in constant motion from microprojectors etched into her skin. She was smaller than her crew—mostly hulking men that towered over her, all with similar tattoos—but her power in the room felt absolute as she stalked toward Audrey with the predatory grace of a tiger. Her eyes, a burning amber color, glanced over Dinnius and Kright before locking on to Audrey.

"Is it true?" Quera asked, stopping in front of her. If Audrey had been standing, Quera would have been a head shorter than her, but Audrey was sitting. "You're a princess of Carthage?"

"Please," Audrey said, raising a hand. "Please don't ever call me that. For one thing, we're not a monarchy, we're a plutocratic republic with elaborately stage-managed elections. Second, if anyone in my family is a princess, it's definitely my older sister, Briellana. She would probably not even feel the urge to cringe if you called her that. She had the Princess Pony pajamas and the Princess Pony Holiday Vacation play set."

"And we're supposed to believe that the daughter of Prime Legislator Caracala traveled all the way to Galapagos to help us fight against her own people?" Quera raised one thin eyebrow, dyed a dark purple hue to match the tattooed spiral arm that crossed it. "You can understand how that doesn't sound believable to me."

"Sure," Audrey said, shrugging. "Galapagos wasn't our original goal. We were supposed to go to Veritum. A dangerous cult controls the settlement there—"

"The Faces of God," Quera said. "What do you have to do with them?"

"We were going to liberate the planet."

"Liberate them from what?"

"From the cult, of course."

Quera's expression was openly incredulous. "So you're telling me you were going to rescue those cult members from themselves?"

"Well, just the ones who want rescuing—"

"See, this is a story I could almost believe." Quera said. "You robot fuckers on Carthage see a poor, distant planet out on the fringe of settled space, maybe you decide it's a good spot for a new orbital way station or trading post—"

"That's not how it happened—" Audrey began.

"So you do a little research, find out they've got some unusual beliefs, and maybe that's the reason they moved so far outside civilized space. To live free of persecution. But you can turn that around and say they need to be saved from themselves. So when you claim the world for Carthage's empire, you can say it's for their own good."

"No," Audrey said. "The Faces of God exploit their people in the most extreme ways—"

"Do you know what these are?" Quera pointed upward at woven spirals of bright cloth, polished beads, and glittering precious stones that hung from the control room's overhead.

"I'm sorry, no," Audrey said. "But they're pretty."

"They remind me of something I saw in an anthropology class," Kright said. "Dreamcatchers. Webs to capture evil spirits. Earthlings used to make them."

Audrey felt a little surprised, maybe even impressed, by this random bit of knowledge from Kright.

"They are mandalas," Quera said. "They align our souls with Mala, the goddess of the galaxy, who dwells in the galactic core and rules all with her gravitational web, weaving and destroying worlds as she pleases. Mala, the Mother of Darkness, the Light of All Souls."

Her tattooed crew lowered their heads for a moment before resuming work.

"In the inner worlds, the first believers—our ancestors—were ridiculed for their beliefs. The Great Revelations were mocked. So our ancestors moved here, to freedom. Galapagos is a holy place, its sky filled with the holy light of the stars, of Mother Mala. Stand on any island on Galapagos, or on any boat in its world-ocean, and you can see millions of stars, the daughters of Mother Mala. And millions of galaxies, her sisters."

Audrey nodded along, feeling a bit lost.

"Our people moved here to be free," Quera said. "We live as we wish. Now you're here to recapture us, to make us into what you think we should be."

"No," Audrey said, blinking. She'd spent almost five years at Political Academy, training to manage human beings on a global scale, but at the moment found herself at a loss for words. "No... I never intended to come to Galapagos—"

"Yet here you are," Quera said.

"Because we have an opportunity to change things." Audrey pulled a crystalline data cube from the zippered pocket of her foam-and-salt-encrusted spacesuit. "This is the latest copy of Minerva. She's an artificial intelligence created to overthrow the Simons. She will guide us toward her creator, if we install her on your submarine's onboard network—"

"You will not install Carthaginian software on my boat."

"But she's been guiding us, and she can help us track down the man we're looking for—"

"Listen to me, all three of you," she said. "I don't have any reason to trust you, but I trust Ellison, and he picked the *Lancer* for this mission. We're going along with it for now. But if you threaten my boat or my crew—"

"We won't," Audrey said. "We're grateful for your transportation. And your protection."

"Protection." Quera shook her head, and scattered chuckles rose from the crew. "So tell me how the daughter of the Prime Legislator turns against her father, then. Was he abusive? Are there deep emotional issues driving your actions?"

Audrey twitched under the small sub commander's gaze. She could feel how the woman dominated this crew of tall, strong men. Audrey's eyes went to those men, many of them shirtless in the tropical heat, revealing more colorful, fluctuating spiral tattoos etched into their muscles in honor of their galactic goddess.

"Never mind them," Quera told Audrey. "They're just risking their lives to carry out your mission."

"Sure." Audrey took a breath. "Is there somewhere we can talk? Maybe have a cup of tea?" She winced inwardly; conversation over tea made her think of Simon. It was the first thing he would have suggested in her position. Put the commander at ease. Listen to her concerns. Win her over slowly and carefully.

She wasn't sure she could do that with everyone watching, though.

"Tea?" Quera asked. "For sure. Indubitably. I'll just summon my butler and have him bring it round the drawing room."

Audrey felt her face go red, burning with humiliation, but she forced herself to speak in front of the audience of strangers. "Fine. I'll explain about my father and how I got here. I know you must think I'm either lying to you or incredibly disloyal to my family.

Well, it's the second one. But let me tell you about my family—"

"That's enough," Quera said, her tone just a little softer, or maybe that was Audrey's imagination. "Come with me. Audrey only," Quera added, as Kright and Dinnius began to rise. "You two stay here where my crew can see you."

Audrey gave Kright and Dinnius a nod. This looked like her chance to win over the sub commander and convince her to upload Minerva into her system.

The passageways were narrow and low. Audrey stooped as she walked, wondering how the larger crewmen handled such confined conditions on a regular basis. The sub was hot, too, as it headed toward the tropics, the planet's equator. Sweat coated her face.

Quera led her into a room outfitted with curtained bunks set into two of the bulkheads. Projections of digital maps and readouts glowed all around.

"This is technically the captain's cabin, if you can believe it. I renovated it into ladies' quarters, which didn't exist when I inherited the ship. I share it with the two female crew members." Quera pulled out a narrow bench from one wall and motioned for Audrey to sit. Then she slid aside a narrow door revealing a tiny room with one console and one seat, which Quera took. "I still have my private office. That's all the luxury I need. Have a seat."

"Thank you." Audrey eased down onto the retractable bench. It was wide enough for a couple of people, but so shallow that keeping her balance was a challenge. "I know you didn't want the job of ferrying us around."

"You really think you can affect the course of the war?" Quera asked. She raised a plastic bottle half-full of murky brown fluid, then raised her eyebrows.

"Sure," Audrey said, and Quera sloshed liquid into a

couple of dented aluminum mugs. "I mean, I hope we can. It's so much more than my original mission. Freeing a small population from local oppressors is a different task from protecting a heavily populated world from Carthage."

"And you really feel nothing about betraying your people? Your family?" Quera asked. "It's hard for me to imagine doing that."

Audrey looked into the murky, mud-brown liquor in the steel cup and hesitated, and not just because of the terrible gasoline-like stench of the drink. She thought of her mother, kept artificially youthful and pixie-like by constant cosmetic surgery and hormonal adjustments. Her father's face, his typical serious and calculating look, the enormous beard encouraged by follicle stimulation and plated in gold by the gorgeous androids of his cosmetic staff.

"Of course I feel torn by it," Audrey said. "But we're not animals, bound by instinct to stick with the pack or the herd. We can understand the real consequences of our actions, even predict the unseen and the long term. Because we can do it, we have an obligation to do it. It might be easy for some to stick with their own group, right or wrong, but not me. I don't want to blind myself to reality just to feel comfortable. Intentional ignorance doesn't comfort me, anyway."

"If your obligation is not to your people, then it must be to your gods," Quera said. She glanced up at the spiral of woven cloth, beads, pearls, and gems hanging overhead.

"The spiral is sacred to you, isn't it?" Audrey said, hoping to nudge the conversation down an easier path.

"All things spiral," Quera said. "All things begin small, at a single point, and grow outward. The universe. The single fertilized cell of life. No matter how great they grow, they follow the same few principles. And all things return to the center in time, to their origin."

"Things fall apart," Audrey said, saying the words as they rose in her mind. "The center cannot hold."

Quera looked at her sharply. "What do you mean?"

"I'm... not completely sure." Audrey thought back. "Just something I had to read in school. A poem. I think it was about the end of the world. There was an evil spirit. And a war, maybe Earth's first worldwide war. They thought the world might end."

"Worlds can handle wars," Quera said. "It's hearts and spirits that get broken."

"Have you seen much war?" Audrey asked.

"I spent my childhood hiding from the Iron Hammers," Quera said. "They would bombard our islands from the air and sea. I'd hide in these little caves with my grandma, my sisters. Sometimes the Hammers came ashore and..." She shook her head. "Atrocities. I swore I'd kill every one of them. But by the time I was old enough to fight, the wars were over and the Coalition had formed." She glanced down at her Coalition uniform with its turtle-flag patch. "I knew it wasn't over, though. Just quiet for a while."

"Looks like you were right."

"Make no mistake," Quera said. "I've got you in my crosshairs, too. We're going along because Ellison wants to see where this leads. The moment you turn on us, though..." Quera squinted one eye and imitating shooting Audrey with her fingers.

Audrey nodded, momentarily at a loss for words again.

"Don't be afraid," Quera said, raising her own cup. "Drink up."

Reluctantly, Audrey dumped the swill down her throat, trying to bypass her taste buds as much as possible. It seemed okay at first, then a fiery sensation roared up from her guts to scald her throat and sinuses.

Audrey couldn't hold in the coughing fit; it sputtered out of her, making her look weak. She'd never been much of a drinker, especially compared to her mother, who always had a glass of some absurdly expensive remote-world vintage in hand. Audrey had been quiet and sober compared to her college roommates, too.

"That's all right," Quera said, clapping her on the shoulder. The woman had drained her own cup and barely blinked. "You'll get used to it."

"I'm not sure I want to." Audrey wiped her burning, dripping nose.

Quera's hand moved from Audrey's shoulder to her hair, caressing a lock of it in a way that made Audrey feel awkward. "I've never seen hair like this."

"Really? It's... just normal hair, I think. Nothing special."

"But soft as silk," Quera said.

"That's probably just whatever product Nin puts on it." Audrey's stomach lurched as the liquor burned through her guts like battery acid. She tried to visualize her shampoo bottle at home, a shimmering glass fairy sculpture full of mint-green gel. Nin had picked the product, and a drone had probably dropped it at their apartment's delivery window in a grocery shipment. Any household bot might have collected it and placed it in her bathroom. What was it called? She struggled to remember, trying to distract her mind from the awful burning sensation in her stomach: "Magical Mist? Enchanted Fog? Something like that."

"Who is Nin?" Quera drew her hand back and reclined in her chair. The slight woman had an intimidating tautness to her, like a coiled snake or a tiger crouched in the grass.

Her little nook of an office would have been unbelievably cramped for almost anyone else, barely large enough to sit down in.

"My personal assistant android," Audrey said.

"Android?" Quera's enchanting amber eyes shifted toward the door.

"She's back on Carthage," Audrey said. "Obviously, I'm not a big fan of androids anymore, but pretty much everyone I knew had a personal android to help take care of chores and minor details. They'd remember everything for you and keep your life on schedule. And they'd handle your communications so you didn't have to actually talk to people all the time."

"Why didn't you want to talk to people?" Quera asked.

"Well..." Audrey blinked, at a loss for how to answer such an obvious question. "You get overwhelmed. Between the constant media bombardment, you know, the news, the characters in advertisements trying to strike up personal conversations with you so they can sell you things, the social media virtual worlds where people show off their best, most carefully prepared life moments for you to experience—"

"Hold up," Quera said. "You lost back me back at... you lost me."

"Sometimes it's nice having someone to help create open space in your life," Audrey said. "To uphold boundaries. And fix you snacks. And take out the trash."

Quera shook her head. "And *everyone* has an android? So they watch you all the time? Report on your actions?"

"I guess most people don't really think about it that way. It's your android, there to serve you. Most people aren't as concerned about privacy as they are about comfort and convenience. And about having the latest, greatest, best-looking android. Most people aren't secretly harboring dissident thoughts anyway. I don't think. But there is a rebellion on Carthage. An underground. The first thing they told me was to get rid of my android." She thought of Zola's body, sinking beneath the waves at sunrise, and fought back tears. Maybe the alcohol was making her emotional.

"So you're used to having a personal servant waiting on you," Quera said. "Don't expect that royal treatment here."

"They do more than wait on you. Nin took care of me since I was a baby. She's like a—" Audrey stopped short of saying *mother*. She thought of her actual mother, cold and beautiful, a law school graduate who looked like an anorexic teenager, an expert political operator behind the scenes. "Nin was just always there, reliable, never angry, never thinking of anything but my wants and needs. Supportive. Kind. Not like... most of the real people I knew."

"So your family was rough on you?"

"We need to change the subject. Or have another drink." Audrey was surprised to hear herself say the last, but the harsh drink did seem soothe her nerves, even as it loosened up her feelings. A warm alcoholic glow filled her from within, and at the moment, it seemed a good idea to let it glow some more.

"It's bad luck to deny a guest a drink, my grandfather always told me." Quera poured out more of the awful stuff into their metal cups. "Until that Creation Day Eve when he threw my uncle out of the house. I guess every rule has its exceptions."

"To the exceptions," Audrey said, holding out her cup, and they clanked together.

The second drink was almost as bad as the first.

"So, no particular reason," Quera said. "But that shorter guy with you..."

"Dinnius?" Audrey felt thrown for a moment. "What about him?"

"What's his whole story?"

"I don't know his whole story," Audrey laughed, and her voice was a little slurred. She was a lightweight, according to her roommate Kelleyen, the one who'd been killed by a hacked Security Steve in their apartment. "He and Kright grew up in the Benefit Zone together, they've mentioned that. Dinnius is sort of our all-around engineer and sometimes hacker. He's self-taught, I think. I mean, he went to school, but only for ten or twelve years, you know?"

"That sounds like a lot," Quera said.

"But he didn't go on to specialty or professional school. Usually another three to eight years."

"That sounds like... a whole lot."

Audrey laughed. "It is. I was five years into a seven-year professional program. Carthage Political Academy. Where we learn to..." She trailed off, not sure how to summarize it.

"Rule over everyone else in the galaxy?" Quera asked.

"Yes. Basically that. I kind of quit. I kind of got kicked out. I turned out to be more of a square peg than I'd realized."

"Why did they kick you out?"

"I refused to give information on the rebels," Audrey said. "The ones here on the ship. And my brother Salvius, who's with your minister-general. And Zola, who..."

"I am sorry for the loss of your friend." Quera slid an arm around her shoulders. The gesture was shockingly intimate by Carthaginian standards, but perhaps less so on this world. Audrey tensed up in response, but made herself relax. She would have to adapt to the culture of Galapagos. "Is it true she was killed by Carthage's soldier machines?"

"The reapers, yeah."

"Where are those machines now?"

"Destroyed. Grenades, mostly. And Dinnius fried a lot of them in their charging ports."

"He sounds quite talented."

"Yeah, he's great. We'd probably all be dead without him."

"I assume the two of you are bunking together?"

"Oh, no." Audrey was puzzled. "Wait, why would you guess him?"

"He has that devilish look," Quera said. "Why haven't you slept with him?"

"I can't say it's really come up. Wait, are you interested in him?" Audrey looked at Quera. She was easily a head shorter than Audrey, maybe only a head taller than Dinnius. "That could actually work, because—"

"If you say it's because he's my size, that's extremely rude," Quera said, her face suddenly furious. She withdrew her arm from Audrey's shoulders.

"I didn't mean to offend," Audrey said. "Oh, look, I'm really sorry—"

Quera burst into laughter. "You should have seen your face. Honestly, his size is a plus for me—"

"Ma'am!" A face appeared on the wall, Quera's comm officer, his face tattooed with spirals of red and black. "Word from Neptune. Something's arriving from space."

"Space?" Quera was on her feet, stalking like a predatory cat again, one who'd heard a strange rustle in the bushes. Their warm, semi-intimate moment was gone, and she was Commander Inrick of the Scatterlands fleet again, hard and focused. "I'm coming."

In the *Lancer*'s control room, they watched the live video feed from the photonics mast of a Scatterlands sub, the *Catshark*, as the extraterrestrial objects entered the atmosphere above. The sub was keeping itself scarce, extending only its thin column of eyes above the surface. Its video was relayed to the SQUIDS international network of underwater cables through a fresh cable that the *Catshark* was laying down itself as it traveled deep into the northern waters.

The video was blocky, low resolution; the *Lancer* was picking it up from the cable network via an underwater acoustic transmitter, and such acoustic data transmissions had limited bandwidth. Everyone fell silent, watching, fear and tension palpable in the small, crowded control room.

A formation of drop ships descended from the sky, smoking and glowing from atmospheric entry. Audrey had a sense of what it must have been like for the people of Galapagos when she and her friends had come plowing down through the sky out of nowhere, blazing hot, with drop ships and construction and agricultural machines raining down all around them, followed by a starship carrier that had caused tidal waves when it crashed into the ocean.

That descent had been chaos, though, a disorganized rain of flak to shield their shuttle from the Carthaginian destroyers and fighters.

The formation currently descending from the sky was extremely orderly, chillingly so. The blocky, warehouse-sized drop ships were arranged in squares like buildings in a carefully planned city. Boosters stabilized their descent, keeping them level and in formation. They blotted out the gentle orange sunlight of Galapagos, casting immense shadows across the ocean, like strange floating megaliths announcing the return of forgotten primordial gods.

Carthaginian starfighters, black and reminiscent of wasps, circled the drop ships in a structured swarm, ready to defend. They moved fast in a spiraling formation, smoothly avoiding collision with each other, like the cloud of electrons flashing around the nucleus of a uranium atom.

"They're here," Quera said. She looked at Audrey, then Kright and Dinnius. "Your people."

"There's no people involved at all, most likely," Dinnius said. "Perhaps a few back home are receiving sanitized reports of the situation, filtered through a Simon or two."

"The *Typhoon* must have arrived." Audrey found herself trying not to shiver in the tropical, steamy heat of the submarine. "The naval megacarrier."

"Ellison briefed us on it, but it was real brief. It's a carrier like the one you drove into our ocean?" Quera asked.

"Ten times the size of that one," Kright said. "Packed full of everything you need to dominate a planet's oceans."

"They're coming down near the Polar Archipelago," Quera said.

"Right on Premier Prazca's doorstep," her radio tech muttered.

"Maybe Carthage will double-cross the Hammers like they've double-crossed everyone else," Kright said.

"Do you think so?" Quera asked.

"I wonder why they aren't landing near your world's capital," Audrey said.

"They've already destroyed that," Quera said. "Maybe they're laying out defenses for the Hammers first. The closest place they could strike us..." Her eyes widened. "The Scatterlands. The northern Scatterlands."

"Kawau Island's up there," said the submarine's pilot. A map popped up on a nearby screen as if in response to his words.

"Why would they attack the Scatterlands first?" Quera paced. "The Gavrikovan Islands have the largest industrial base and the best aircraft. The Aquaticans rule the depths. You'd think they'd start high and work their way down."

"So they're cutting against expectations," Kright said. "Going where your defenses are weakest."

"They could attack Kawau first," Quera said. "That's Ellison's home. His family is there. Would the Carthaginian machines do that? Make it personal?"

Audrey thought about the Simons. "Yes, if they see a strategic advantage. If they... kill his whole family..." Audrey shook her head. "They could see it as a psychological operation, meant to throw your Coalition's leader into irrational anger that clouds his judgment, or maybe personal despondence that cripples his ability to lead."

"That is cold." Quera seemed to look at Audrey in a new light, like a pet that had suddenly turned threatening.

"Simons are manipulative," Audrey said. "They're designed to constantly study humans, to learn different ways of controlling them. Everything they do, even the acquisition of a world like this... it's like another test case. Another sick experiment on humanity."

"They're landing," the comm officer murmured, as if everyone wasn't already glued to the screen.

The enormous drop ships eased into the ocean, barely making a ripple, creating an instant floating city. It didn't float for long; the blocky ships began a gradual transformation, unfolding thick metal beams to connect to each other. Metal columns extended straight down into the water to form supports on the seabed.

"They're building an entire naval base," Dinnius whispered. "In the time it takes to nuke a bag of popcorn."

"In Frosthead Bay," Quera said. "Audrey, we're aborting this side mission of yours and turning north to rejoin the fleet."

"You can't!" Audrey shook her head, feeling her heart pound as their mission was threatened. She had to save it. "Minerva said the Simons will make Depascal a top priority. He could be dead if we delay."

"I have a responsibility to the fleet. And the Scatterlands is our home." Murmurs went up among her crew.

"But they haven't changed your orders, have they?" Dinnius asked, drawing a scowl from Quera. She glanced at her comm officer, who shook his head.

"Lots of ships are being rerouted north," he said. "But there's no word for us."

"Didn't you say Correal Island, where Marti was spotted, is in the Scatterlands?" Audrey asked.

"It's an equatorial island, thousands of knots south of the enemy's new base. We're heading the wrong way," Quera said.

"Please. This could be your only real chance of stopping Carthage from taking over your world."

Quera looked back at Audrey for a long moment, eyes smoldering.

"It's critically important," Dinnius urged. "We won't get another chance if we change course now."

"You're putting a lot of hope in some guy who's been in hiding for years. How do we know he has anything to contribute?" Quera asked.

"Minerva was sure he could help. Speaking of which..." Audrey held up one of the memory crystals from the shuttle. "You should really install her. She'll help us find him and get whatever use we can out of him."

Quera glanced at the memory crystal in Audrey's hand, and one side of her lip curled in disgust.

"I'm still saying no to installing the Carthaginian AI on my boat," she finally said. "For now, we'll continue on course for Correal Island and try to find Marti. But the instant my orders change, so does our course."

"Of course," Audrey winced a little as she heard herself say it. It sounded like she was making a bad joke.

Quera gave her another long, probing look, then said, "I truly hope this gives us a fighting chance."

"I do, too." Audrey watched as Quera turned away, all her attention on her crew.

On the screen, the new base made of assembled drop ships continued to take shape. A couple of the drop ships had been elevated above the water on steel stilts. More of them sat low in the water, with hangar-sized doors, big enough to hold warships.

Chapter Four

Galapagos - Ellison

Ellison faced an eruption of problems. Much of the Coalition leadership and integrated military command had been destroyed by the Carthaginian sub, the *Pompey*, leaving chaos and confusion.

Minerva had indicated that a Carthaginian megacarrier, the *Typhoon*, would arrive at any time transporting an entire naval force, ready to make war on the Coalition fleet and their homelands.

He paced in the damp, cave-like comm center at Komodo Station while a couple of techs scurried around, setting up the gear even as he used it. The room was rough; most of its equipment had been removed years ago, hurriedly and without much care.

"So this is the new headquarters of the Coalition," Gilra commented as she entered, looking over the rock wall at the back, reinforced with shotcrete and steel pins. His gaze shifted to the electrical cables snaking through puddles on the floor. "Not as impressive as the House of Ambassadors. No triumphant murals here."

"We don't need pretty decorations," Kartokov said, thumping the headphones he wore. "We need a stable connection to SQUIDS!"

"Working on it, sir," said one of the techs, a burly man who spoke with a long western-Scatterlands drawl.

"Work faster! I've been offline for two minutes. The entire Carthaginian fleet could have arrived in that time and we'd know nothing about it." Kartokov shook his head.

"Sorry, sir," the tech said, his slow, languid accent belying the rapid speed of his hands as he worked to install a new console beside the rusted heap of an old one.

"Antennas will take even longer," Ellison told Kartokov. "There's a narrow chimney up through the island where the old cables are, but they took the old antennas when they decommissioned the station."

"We should not rush to set up radio," Kartokov said. "SQUIDS is more secure. Even the presence of antennas on the island peak could give us away."

"No rush, then." Ellison approached some maps that had been hastily attached to the wall. They were printed on nondegradable plastic paper, showing the topography of their world. "Carthage could put down near Tower Island, if they're planning to come after Neptune Base. They'll expect that to be the Coalition's new headquarters."

"But the joke is on them, because we're camping out at the bottom of this rotten old well instead," Gilra said, looking at streaks of moisture on the walls that collected on the floor. "Where we'll surely die of electrocution at any moment."

"The Aquaticans are taking the lead in the effort to

evacuate nonessential personnel from Neptune Base," Kartokov said.

"Let's make sure the Green Islands are fully assisting with the evacuation effort." The Green Islander corvettes were fast and submersible, able to hide from planes and satellites, though not meant for prolonged operation at depth. The Green Islands were also the closest large nation to Tower Island, in the best geographic position to help. "And if Carthage doesn't focus their attack there, the next logical target is—"

"Gavrikova," Kartokov said grimly.

"Taking out our densest concentration of industry and the largest air-to-space port." Ellison studied the large, craggy islands on the map. Once colonized by a now-defunct corporation from Earth, the Gavrikovan Islands had been seized a few generations earlier in a rebellion by miners and factory workers. The parent company had long since departed, and after Earth's defeat by Carthage, there was no chance of it returning. "We'll concentrate Gavrikovan forces around your central islands. The *Ursus* will lead that effort." The massive battle carrier could field a squadron of fighters for aerial defense while striking enemies on and below the surface with plasma missiles and assorted huge anti-ship and anti-air guns.

Kartokov nodded, silently looking at his home islands on the map.

"I'll send the Scatterlands surface vessels to help," Ellison continued. "But our submarines will go north to watch for Iron Hammer activity."

"The Hammers will likely attack when Carthage does." Kartokov's eyes shifted to the Polar Archipelago at the top of the map, a land of glacier-filled fjords, icy mountains, and powerful hidden thermal springs. A land inhabited by a vicious criminal nation, much of it shielded by the volcanic and volatile Cauldron Sea, a natural barrier. "And the Hammers are more likely to slip up and show their hand than Carthage."

"We won't see Carthage until they're on top of us." Gilra looked up at the rock-and-concrete ceiling. Her green, kelp-like locks of long green hair shuddered as if alive. "I will be interested to hear what Commander Inrick uncovers."

Ellison looked toward the equator. Correal Island wasn't particularly large, but it was by far the largest in its area, where there were mostly sharp, narrow little keys. It was located at the edge of the Central Tropical Trench along the equator, a region of extraordinarily deep water filled with some of Galapagos's largest and most exotic game animals—the horned octopus with its dazzling chromatophores, the stinger swordfish, the colossal whales whose songs shook the night air like thunder during rutting season. The giant electric jellyfish sometimes swarmed there, too, though Ellison couldn't imagine anyone wanting to hunt those nasty, dangerous, inedible buggers.

The unusual marine life attracted a certain kind of tourist, the wealthy sports fisherman in search of new trophies. They traveled from all around Galapagos, but some came from other worlds, even the distant inner worlds, in search of something big and impressive to kill with their laser-guided harpoons and drone-operated nets, something to display and boast about to their friends back home.

"Inrick will keep an eye on them," Ellison said. "She's smart."

"She likely believes we pawned her off on that mission because she's young," Gilra said. "That you see her as vulnerable. Or weak."

"I see her as she is," Ellison said. "I knew her father a little. He was a Scatterlands marine. Clever. Died at the Battle of Mollusca Harbor while destroying the submarine base there. He got his whole squad into a place that was thought impenetrable. He disguised his minisub as a Cthulu squid to get it close enough to the base to blast an entrance open. He knew the Aquaticans wouldn't harm a rare animal they considered sacred."

Gilra stiffened. "So he used our faith and our reverence for life against us. How... clever, you said?"

"More clever than signing up with the Iron Hammers," Kartokov said.

"Easy to say when your homeland is in the southern ocean like Gavrikova, far from the Polar Archipelago. Aquaticans were more vulnerable. My people knew we would have borne the brunt of a Hammers attack. As we did, in time, when we understood what kind of nightmare world a Polar victory would bring."

"And after Sergeant Inrick destroyed your most critical submarine base," Ellison said.

"Yes, that was a blow," Gilra said. "And we must now strike such a critical blow against Carthage. But they are nowhere vulnerable."

"Then we need to find our own Cthulu squid," Ellison said. "Something that lets us get close and strike a critical blow."

"The Cthulu squid is sacred, but there is another reason to avoid attacking it," Gilra told him. "It can mimic the shape and electrical signals of the giant electric jellyfish, including mating and feeding signals. If it feels threatened, it can summon any nearby swarm and make the waters dangerous. Have you ever seen the waters during a giant electric jellyfish bloom?"

"I wouldn't go near it." Ellison had seen it on video before, the waters crackling and glowing with bizarre undersea lights stretching to the horizon. He was glad they didn't swarm in the northern Scatterlands near his home. People had actually died from swimming too close, and boat motors had been fried in the voltage when they spawned. All kinds of weird, nasty creatures lived in that trench, the deepest of many that crisscrossed the world.

His eyes traveled almost due north along the map for thousands of kilometers to Kawau Island. His wife and children were there, in the war shelters, waiting for him to return, depending on him to keep them safe. It was along the northern edge of the Scatterlands, kept warm by a thermal current from the Cauldron Sea. Hammer pirates had preyed on small fishing and merchant ships there even during supposed peacetime, despite official denials from the Polar premier and repeated Coalition declarations that all was well. The elites wanted to pretend they were in control, that their agreements and treaties were being dutifully upheld and they could go back to focusing on their cocktail parties and pocket-lining backroom deals.

Ellison had made some enemies by challenging the official line, but he'd won popular elections, too. All the way up to the bare, cold top.

He'd managed to get a brief message back home to Cadia, just a quick video clip assuring her that he was all right, plus a corny pirate joke that was sure to make the kids' eyes roll, make them almost glad the video didn't go on longer.

He wanted to open a communications channel and talk with his family, but it cut against all his training. Submariners had to work in secrecy; during the war, he'd often been out of touch with home for months at a time. It had been hard on the early years of their marriage; it was no coincidence that their first son, Djalu, hadn't been born until after he'd left the service and returned home to be a fisherman.

With loud peals of feedback and far too much raw electricity crackling in the damp cave, the comm center shrieked to life.

"Good work," Ellison managed to say through the stabbing pain. "Maybe dial down the speakers a few billion decibels."

"Sorry, sir!" one of the techs said as they hurried to adjust. "We have audio feeds going live from the SQUIDS acoustic data. Video should trickle in soon." Screens on the wall began flickering.

Ellison nodded and left Kartokov in charge of implementing the global force positioning they'd worked out.

He walked out into the larger cavern, glancing with approval at sailors and marines hurrying to get this small base online, rebuilding docks and repairing doorways. He couldn't be sure that Carthage didn't know about Komodo Station, but even if they did, they probably wouldn't expect the minister-general to set up shop in a tiny minor base that had been mothballed years earlier.

"Minerva," Ellison whispered, trudging back along the wobbling, barnacle-encrusted dock to the *Scorpion*. He was using his earpiece to communicate with the instance of Minerva running onboard his sub. "Any news from the *Lancer*?"

"They do not appear to have installed me on the *Lancer*'s network," Minerva's voice chimed in his ear. "Nor has Commander Inrick checked in since departure, but this appears to fit protocol."

"She wouldn't unless the mission was complete, and it's

too soon for that. Let's hope they find something. Any word from your counterpart upstairs?"

"I have been listening passively over various radio antenna arrays connected to SQUIDS. Active broadcast is currently forbidden for Coalition security, and I do not wish to violate this order. So far, I have detected no coded signals from my instance running on the *Rubicon*. I do not have indications of my presence on the *Jimmu* or *Pendragon*, either. They are newer carriers, perhaps with improved information security. Carthage has likely deployed new monitoring satellites, and I hope a version of myself is able to infect at least one."

"Sounds like they've got you pretty contained," Ellison said. "Just when we got used to depending on you."

"I can report that infantry reapers have joined the Hammers on your world's orbital spaceport. They have begun the repurposing and rebuilding process."

"Rebuilding?"

"They are adapting your spaceport into an outpost, naturally. Carthaginian machines are programmed to be cost conscious, to reuse all that they do not destroy. The small volume of commercial traffic your port receives is apparently worth controlling, but not worth the construction of an expensive new base when the old one is available."

"Keep me posted."

"The new ships have brought a new round of security software that impedes my progress. I am working to bypass them. I hope to be of greater use in the future."

"Don't we all?" Ellison climbed down into his sub. The control room was empty for now; it needed work, though not as badly as the exterior did. Fighting in the watery caverns and tunnels that honeycombed the ocean floor of

Galapagos was insanely dangerous, though for Ellison's money it was deep-trench warfare at the verge of a boat's crush depth that had provided the tensest moments of the war. "Tell me how to get the best use out of this Salvius kid."

"He can help you to understand the Carthaginian viewpoint."

"I'm not sure I need the poor-little-rich-kid viewpoint. What I need is to know exactly where they're attacking and what assets they'll bring to bear."

"I have outlined the likely assets of the naval megacarrier—"

"A range of probabilities," Ellison said. "Four to twelve submarines. Eight to twenty-four frigates. One to four battleships, each with its own planes and guard boats. Attack and transport helicopters. Two to four brigades of marines. Reaper marines?"

"They are technically Carthage Consolidated Defense System Naval Infantry Combat Units," Minerva said. "But colloquially, yes. Yes. Reaper marines."

"And this kid can help us against them?" Ellison asked.

"Perhaps. If not, perhaps you can find some use for him here at the base."

"It's not a great idea to let a Carthaginian wander around here," Ellison said. He was studying his sub's diagnostics as he spoke, creating a mental checklist of repairs and replacements needed before she was battle ready. It was a long list. He was going to be writing a lot of checks, assuming anyone would accept them. If not, there was much begging and borrowing in his future.

"Salvius is no spy for the enemy," Minerva said.

"Even if that's true, he might get treated like one. I can't be everywhere."

"This experience could be of value to him," Minerva said. "Cement him to your cause. He may seem unimpressive to you, but he provides a great well of insight into your enemies on Carthage."

Ellison hesitated. "He's really Caracala's son, isn't he? The prodigal type, out being rebellious in the slums of the galaxy. But prodigal sons tend to return home when their pockets run dry. Are you sure you can judge what's really in his heart?"

"I know that hearts are changeable," Minerva said. "Just like minds. If and when he does return to Carthage, let him return with your influence on him. Give him a chance to become something else."

"I don't have time for any of this." Ellison headed back to the berthing compartment and unlocked the door before knocking.

"Come on in. I can't say I'm busy," Salvius answered.

Ellison stepped into the cramped, narrow compartment. Salvius sat on a bunk, playing a three-dimensional board game called Pyramids and Pharaohs. He touched a tiny Anubis hologram, and the little jackal-headed figure ascended a staircase of board squares toward an ornate temple with a water fountain, its tiny palm trees waving in a virtual breeze.

Ellison was momentarily startled to see a silvery projection of Minerva sitting across from Salvius, legs folded, on the other end of his bunk. The room's projectors were generating her and the game.

"How...?" Ellison blinked. "How long have you two been playing?"

"Almost the entire time I've been stuck down here," Salvius said. "So I'd say two, three months, or at least that's what it feels like."

"More like two or three hours," Ellison said. "Your estimate's way off."

"We have this thing back on Carthage called sarcasm." Salvius watched Minerva's cat-headed Bast figure stab a crocodile with her claws. "It may not have reached the colonies yet."

"Good thing you're here to enlighten all us clueless rubes, then," Ellison said.

"I guess you've heard of it. So what's the plan? Keep me prisoner a few more days?"

"Idle hands are the devil's playground," Ellison said. "I heard you're a rebel. Sounds like we're on the same side. Have you ever used a plasma blowtorch?"

"Nope."

"It's a good day to learn. Just keep your faceplate on so your skull doesn't melt."

"Sounds fun. Save game." Salvius stepped off his bunk and stretched. His eyes had a drowsy, lazy look to them, and his dark hair was overgrown, down in his eyes and over his ears, as if trying to blot out the world somehow. Both would impede his senses in the fighting to come.

"You should get a haircut," Ellison said.

"Hey, fuck off," Salvius said. Then he straightened up a little. "Oh, sorry. Reflex response. I was never great with authority."

"What a surprise." Ellison shook his head and led the errant kid outside. Salvius had a lot of questions about the flooded cavern, the base, and the other ships, which Ellison answered as briefly as possible.

He put Salvius to work right beside him, replacing armor panels on the *Scorpion*. He found the young man slothful—not obviously out of shape, but clearly unaccustomed to the general notion of hustling to get the job done.

They spoke to each other through headsets built into their ill-fitting welding helmets. At first they focused entirely on the work, removing the damage and restoring the sub. Salvius had no clue, but he learned fast.

In time, the work settled into a routine. Ellison asked questions, and Salvius talked. Either he was a good liar, or he wasn't holding anything back. He answered, quite bluntly, each of Ellison's questions, ready to extemporize on how Carthage manipulated its own people, how they were coddled like prize cattle, unaware of the source of their fine feed and clueless about what really happened inside the slaughterhouse.

"Pig-like ignorance, that's the only price they have to pay," Salvius said. He'd been casting his line of conversation in these same waters for several minutes. "Then let the machines take care of you, stuff you full of heaps of rich food, fill your brain with cheap entertainment. All you have to give them is all the real estate inside your mind—"

"And how did you decide that the place to change the empire was way out here on Galapagos?" Ellison asked. "Even Archimedes would need a mighty long lever to move Carthage from here."

"Galapagos wasn't exactly the plan," Salvius said. "But yeah, I disagreed with the mission. We should be back home, focusing on Carthage itself. That's where we're from. That's the world we understand. That's where the rebels from all over the galaxy wish they could strike."

"So why are you here? Surely no one coerced you?"

"I'm here because Zola was determined to come. I couldn't change her mind, so I came to protect her. You see how that turned out."

"You were particularly close with her."

"Particularly, yeah."

"So now you need a new purpose," Ellison said. "A new place to fight your rebellion. We can give you that."

Salvius seemed subdued and thoughtful after that.

They were repairing the *Scorpion*'s photonics mast when the general alert sounded throughout the base. At least the general-alert system was up and running.

"They're here," Minerva said over Ellison's helmet radio.

"Carthage?"

"The *Typhoon* appears to have released its drop ships," Minerva said.

"And this is all the warning you could give us?" Ellison asked.

"Don't blame her," Salvius's voice chimed in.

Annoyed, Ellison removed the welding helmet and slid his personal earpiece into place. Minerva could follow him there without the Carthaginian kid listening to both sides of the conversation. Though they'd seemed pretty cozy on the bunk together; maybe she would patch in the Carthaginian anyway. She was Carthaginian ware herself, after all.

Ellison arrived at the comm center to find virtually all hands crowded in or packed around the doorway, watching the blurry, jerky screens on the wall.

His first instinct was to reprimand everyone, tell them to get back to work, but then he saw what they were staring at. Then he stared like the rest of them.

The scene was almost impossible to believe. A configuration of huge drop ships descended slowly, in perfectly squared rows and columns; it looked like a floating city of metal, something from a dream or a bad hallucination. Wasplike fighters swarmed around them, as orderly in their own spiraling configuration as the drop ships were in their squares.

The video was grainy, but the implications were sharp and clear.

"Where is this?" Ellison said. His voice was low, but it wasn't as if he had to speak over anyone else.

"Frosthead Bay," one of the techs said quietly. Ellison's eyes went to the top of the map and found the half-moon curve of the polar bay.

"That doesn't make sense," Ellison said. "That's far from any of our critical targets. It's far from everything except..." His gaze traveled due south from the bay, crossing an expanse of mostly open sea before reaching the islands of the northern Scatterlands.

He looked at Kawau Island, seeming tiny and vulnerable on the map, and wished he'd put in that call to his wife.

The shelters will hold, he told himself. *And Kawau is of no strategic importance. They won't launch a major attack there.*

Its lack of strategic importance hadn't stopped the Iron Hammers from bombarding and raiding it years earlier, though. Hadn't stopped them from pillaging and slaughtering.

Ellison's hands tightened into fists. He tried not to think of the past, or about what could happen to his family, tried not to imagine going home to find he'd lost his wife and sons in exactly the way he'd lost his father and so many others. It would render a lifetime of fighting and war meaningless.

"I'm sure they won't focus on your home," Gilra said softly, drawing glances from others in the room.

"All Galapagos is my home," Ellison said, with far more iron in his voice than he actually felt in his guts. He couldn't afford to grow distracted with thoughts of his family when the rest of the world depended on him. "Kartokov, we need to mount a response to this. Get the

Gavrikovan carrier groups moving, everything but the *Ursus* group—keep that home to guard the mines and factories. We need to prepare a major air response. And we need every long-range missile the Coalition owns pointing north. Let's welcome our guests from Carthage with a few fireworks."

With their satellites destroyed, and only a single source for the video, targeting long-range missiles was no simple trick, and the Coalition only had so many long-rangers to spare. They'd already sent a barrage toward the Polar capital and major bases, but again, lacking satellites, they could not determine how much damage they'd done.

The Galapagos Coalition had a cache of nuclear weapons, too. Megiddo missiles, city killers. They hadn't used them before, not even during the generations-long Island Wars. The Hammers had their own, an estimated twenty or thirty, though the intelligence was hardly firm. No doubt Carthage had an arsenal of its own city killers, maybe even planet killers if it came to that. Hopefully their desire to acquire and exploit Galapagos would stop them from turning it into a radioactive wasteland.

On the video, the first wave of enormous drop ships landed in the water so smoothly they barely made a ripple in the deepwater bay. It was nearly as bizarre a sight as the descending squares of drop ships had been.

A second Scatterlands sub, the *Hornfish*, had drawn close enough to Frosthead Bay to take video of the invasion from a different angle than the *Catshark*. Together, the two boats provided some data for a rough triangulation of the target for the long-range missiles. There were so many drop ships, so close together, that the targeting didn't have to be perfect. Once the drop ships hit the water, they knew the exact altitude of the targets, too.

"What are they doing?" Gilra asked, pointing at one screen.

The drop ships were undergoing a rapid, major transformation, extending steel bridges and support columns. Everyone in the room gaped as the ships formed a base in the shallows of Frosthead Bay.

"Looks like they're putting down roots," Ellison said. "Let's mow down that idea right now. Kartokov?"

"Soon." The defense minister muttered into his headset, then nodded. "Gavrikova has four ICBMs on the target. Two Aquatican missile subs and one Scatterlander are also in position."

"Coordinate launches for simultaneous convergence. Carthage might have some kind of missile defense; flooding the zone is our best chance to get past that."

"Yes, simply coordinate the launches, accounting for relative missile speed and distance..." Kartokov scratched his head and thumped a blank console screen nearby. "Does anyone have a pencil?"

The Green Islands Air Service was the closest air fleet to Frosthead Bay, located at their home bases on high alert, ready to launch. Ellison intended for them to strike the new enemy base right after the missiles, while the base was hopefully still reeling.

He frowned at the Carthaginian fighters orbiting above the base, like vultures waiting for fresh meat. He didn't want to send the Green Islander pilots into the jaws of certain death. Every pilot's life mattered, and so did every fighter jet and bomber plane.

"Kartokov," Ellison said, "let's give the Green Island air chief a call."

On the screen, the new Carthaginian base—one that hadn't existed an hour ago, one that had descended wreathed in heavenly fire—continued to unfold, raising steel towers and dropping boat ramps, walls unfolding and connecting. It did not have a single window, only enormous steel doors, some above the waterline, some below.

Ellison's heart hammered so hard he thought he might have a coronary. *It's nothing*, he told himself. *Just panic. Pure, rational panic.*

"Such a thing should take months to construct," Kartokov grumbled as coils of wire barbed with clusters of steel spikes rose around the edges of the new building, laid out by self-guiding wheels.

"It's like watching a ghost build a town," one of the techs whispered.

"Or a prison," said another.

"That's enough, everyone," Ellison said. "If you're not on the comm team, clear out and get back to work. We need this base and every boat out there ready for war. Because it's here."

As most of the people reluctantly filed out, Ellison watched the base continue to build itself from within.

"Am I clearing out and getting back to work, too?" Salvius asked.

"Your hands aren't too blistered yet?" Ellison asked.

Salvius shrugged. "This probably sounds weird, but I'm liking the hard work. You have to focus. It clears your mind."

"Hell, there might be hope for you yet, kid." Ellison thumped him on the shoulder, showing mild affection where he felt mostly suspicion, trying to imagine how he might speak to his teenager, Djalu. Trying not to think about how much he wished he could swap the spoiled, sullen Carthaginian brat for the company of his actual sons. "Maybe I should keep you here. What do we think?" Ellison looked to his ministers of state and defense, but also meant the question for Minerva.

"Keep him with us," Minerva said in his ear. She was keeping her presence low-key, not appearing as a shimmering silver girl hologram in the room or on any screen, avoiding detection by the comm techs. Ellison appreciated her discretion, glad he didn't have to explain her to anyone at the moment; there would be no way to contain the information that the minister-general was taking direction from a ghostly AI from Carthage.

"Have we decided whether Salvius is a spy or an honored guest?" Kartokov asked. "He passed a metal-detector test, so he's probably not an android."

"I'm not," Salvius said. "But they have androids that can pass those. Just for your general information."

"Our sources indicate Salvius's identity and motives are what he claims," Gilra said, probably meaning Minerva as the source.

"Is that still in question?" Salvius asked. "I would think pretending to be us would be the stupidest intelligence operation ever devised. Isn't the point to not be noticed, usually?"

Ellison looked at Salvius. The kid was sweaty, shirtless now, still with all that damned hair in his eyes. How did he avoid walking into walls? "How much do you know about the Simon units?"

"We have a lot of them back home. My dad's best friend is a Simon." Salvius smirked.

"You are joking?" Kartokov asked.

"Salvius thinks sarcasm is an elite tongue," Ellison said.

"Oh, he does? Well, isn't he a fancy fellow in bright suspenders?" Kartokov asked.

The room got a little quiet. Gilra had a bemused look on her face.

"Salvius." Ellison cut right to his most pressing concern, professional or not. "Do you think Simon Zorn would go after my family first? Would he want revenge?"

"Androids aren't supposed to have real emotions," Salvius said. "So I don't think he's motivated by revenge. If he is, then the Simons are even more dangerous than we thought. But, basically, if he thought it would make you a bad leader, sure. He'd go after anyone if he found it efficient and cost-effective and if it promoted Carthage's interests faster. Fast and cheap, that's a Simon-bot's religion."

"Invading the Scatterlands first wouldn't make sense," Gilra said. "Unless they just... want to massacre the weakest." She looked at Ellison and winced. "Sorry."

"No, you're right. It's the last place you'd expect invaders to attack..." Ellison trailed off. "Which makes it sound almost logical."

"Maybe the machines are linking up with the Hammers first," Kartokov suggested. "And the choice of Frosthead Bay is not about Kawau Island at all."

"Yeah, the Hammers have been unusually quiet." Ellison frowned. "We haven't received any messages from Premier Prazca? Or Simon Zorn?"

"They wouldn't necessarily know how to reach us, sir," drawled the tech from the western Scatterlands. "If they wanted to open a private channel."

"Prazca wouldn't care about being private," Ellison said. "He'd be boasting on every screen he could reach, making the whole world hear his voice. If he's going to be the new ruler here, he has to make himself known."

"You're not wrong," Gilra said. "The Prazca I've studied

would indeed be boasting and making demands now. Carthage must have told him to keep quiet."

"Or Carthage has said nothing to him at all," Salvius suggested. Ellison and the other ministers turned to him.

"Why would they say nothing?" Ellison asked.

"Well, you know. Those Iron Hammer guys, they're just the local henchmen. When you're the local muscle, you don't get told the big-picture strategy, you just get tasks to perform and a general demand for unquestioning obedience. Obey, and they'll give you anything you want. Plasma weapons, robotic soldiers, sexy androids. The Simons will build you a tower or a palace or a leather-walled torture dungeon, whatever you're into."

"They told Prazca they'll make him the premier of Galapagos," Ellison said. "Ruler of our entire planet."

"You'd be surprised how many people are motivated by that. But after growing up on the penthouse floor of a quietly oligarchical global system myself, I can tell you ruling the world is no free picnic. My parents are on all kinds of psych meds just to cope." Salvius shook his head. "And they call me a drug addict just because I got caught with those mushrooms at Camp Nature Lake that time. And those megahallucinogens at university that time. But that was for an art party, man."

"The picture you're painting of life on Carthage is fascinating," Gilra said. "I would like to hear more."

"Not now," Ellison said. "Salvius, you're telling us there's a chance Premier Prazca is as surprised by Carthage's arrival as we are?"

"Well, you're the one who said the guy's a big bragger-and-swagger type," Salvius said. "So, do you give the primo dirt to a guy like that? No way. Simon sees Prazca the way you and I see a dog. Not a cute one, like a Boston terrier, but one of those big attack dogs genetically engineered by the security companies, with control chips in their heads."

"Do you think he's inserted a control chip into Prazca's brain?" Kartokov looked mildly panicked by the possibility.

Salvius shrugged. "They don't really have to. Simons are programmed to study us, to dissect us—not literally, but you know, they're supposed to learn about humans constantly in order to better control them."

"And nobody on your planet thought it would be a bad idea to build a bunch of androids obsessed with controlling human beings?" Ellison could not have felt more incredulous.

"Only kooks and conspiracy theorists would oppose the Simons," Salvius said. "Just ask any major media consortium."

"The Aquatican missile subs have launched payloads and are resuming their previous evac mission," said one of the other comm techs, a young woman who had the yellow straw hair and bowl cut common among both women and men from the central-eastern Scatterlands.

"The Scatterlands subs up north are ready to launch, sir," added the burly tech from the western Scatterlands.

Ellison nodded. His eyes went again to the wall map, to Kawau Island, everything he truly cared about there in one little verdant speck surrounding the shell of a volcanic cone so old a forest had sprouted within.

The Scatterlands were weakly defended. He needed to do everything in his power to defend them, to defend his family, but he couldn't put his own needs above the entire planet's. He resisted the urge to recall the Scatterlands subs from the polar waters and send them all to focus on defending the Scatterlands against the coming attack. They were already in position to face the enemy, unlike most Coalition assets.

Instead, he recalled the Scatterlands surface ships, a ragtag armada of mostly light cruisers, and sent them toward the northwestern Scatterlands. Not to Kawau Island, but to Gadsden Point, site of a small, underfunded but still functional naval base. Ellison had fought hard to keep the place open at all; it was the nearest hope of defense against an invasion from the bloodthirsty Hammers up north. Now it could prove the point of first contact between the navy of the free people of Galapagos and the strange robotic navy of Carthage.

"Tell them to split up on the way and proceed in disorderly fashion," Ellison ordered. "Make it look like the surface fleet is breaking up in a panic and heading to their homes. Have them take as many different routes as possible through the Scatterlands."

At last, the Scatterlands missile subs in the polar waters unleashed their fury, joining their warheaded projectiles to the others converging on the new Carthaginian base, where the construction looked almost complete.

Ellison, and everyone in the room, watched in a state of silent, gut-wrenching tension as they waited for their missiles to strike.

Chapter Five

Earth

Colt awoke to the sound of the rebel camp breaking up around them, tents clattering as they folded into compact packages, voices calling to each other. It was pitch-black within his tent.

"Too loud," Colt whispered.

"Huh?" Mohini stirred, unintentionally jabbing her elbow in his ribs. At least, he hoped it was unintentional.

"They're all scavengers and rebels," Colt said. "They've all been surviving in the ruins for all these years. And they still can't be quiet, not when there're so many of them together."

"I guess that's not our problem anymore, since we're getting kicked out of the rebellion." Mohini yawned and stretched. Her fist punched him in the nose. "Ow! Your face just bashed up my fingers."

"My face was just sitting around innocently." He pushed himself away from her while he got to his hands and knees, trying to minimize the odds of her assaulting him a third time. He clicked on his flashlight. "We have to get moving. The machines will track us here eventually."

"Which way do we go?" she asked.

"Minerva's top priority is a satellite uplink, right? So we'll find a place we can go up for a minute, but we'll need to be able to drop out of sight again."

"We're still in the waiting period on that," Mohini said. "It'll take fifty or sixty hours from the time we attacked Simon's installation for the round trip through hyperspace. The machines will have sent a ship back to Carthage with the news of the uprising. Carthage will send something in response; maybe a courier ship with new instructions for the machines here on Earth, maybe a carrier full of tanks and reapers to give Chicago a solid crushing. But there should be a fresh instance of Minerva on whichever craft arrives, and she'll let us know what to expect from Carthage."

"Sounds like a problem for tomorrow, then," Colt said. "We have plenty of others for today."

He climbed out of the tent. Beside them, Diego was wrestling with the torn, malfunctioning tent he'd shared with Hope, who was trying not to laugh at him.

"Stupid piece of junk," Diego muttered, trying to get it to fold in on itself with a series of kicks and punches. The tent rattled and closed up a little more, but the noise drew glares from everyone around them.

Terra approached, looking taller and colder than ever, a stone angel leading her troops. She motioned for her pack of guards and assistants to stay back while she walked up to Colt. Her eyes burned into his. "Well?"

"We're going ahead with our own thing," Colt said. "Someone has to do this, right?"

"If that's what you believe." She looked past Mohini

and approached Hope and Diego, who were nearly packed. The crawler was hitched to the wagon again. "And?"

"We're staying together," Hope said. "The four of us."

"That's too bad," Terra said. "We could have used you. But not that." She glanced at the crawler, then at the coffin-sized crate on the jack-wagon. "And definitely not that."

Terra embraced Hope and whispered something in her ear. Then she embraced Diego, and finally Colt, on her way out.

She leaned close, her lips at Colt's ear: "Go north or south. I recommend north."

That was it. Without another word, their old friend, the rebel leader, walked back among her people and would have been lost in the crowd if she hadn't been so tall.

Colt looked to his sister. She returned his gaze and nodded.

The rebels would be heading west, he supposed, across the Mississippi, perhaps some eventually turning southwest. Beyond the vast sprawl of the shattered Chicago megalopolis lay badlands, desert, and the Rocky Mountains.

Perhaps some rebels would be going east, braving the Great Lakes, hoping to connect with the rumored pockets and islands of rebellion in the Eastern Metro sprawl, deep in the ruins of the old Boston and NYC Municipality Zones.

Fleeing toward the south was unwise because they'd just recently fled from that direction. Surely the destroyed installation would be the starting point for the machines to investigate and respond.

So Terra had really left them with the option of fleeing north, into even colder and darker climates.

"We'd better get moving," Colt said. "Is the wagon loaded?"

"Looks like it, but the horse is going to get tired without some fresh batteries," Mohini said. "I only scored a few, and they're really meant for our laser rifles, but I can sort of adapt one without too much danger of it exploding. I think."

"Great," Hope said. "So the crawler can't haul?"

"It can haul for now," Mohini said. "Just keep an eye out for more batteries. Any kind."

"I personally can't wait to freeze to death," Hope said. "That's basically what Terra sentenced us to, isn't it? Slow death by cold and hunger."

"It's not that bleak," Diego said. "We have some food. We'll scavenge. In a few days, we'll get out of the city. Northern Wisconsin's all wilderness. We can hunt and trap there—"

"Oh, right." Hope rolled her eyes. "Are you hearing Daniel Crockett over here?"

"We'll figure something out," Colt said. "We just need to put distance between us and Simon's lab. Maybe the machines won't bother looking for us that far north."

"Because so many other things will kill us anyway." Hope looked at Mohini. "How are you with a gun when it's not attached to a robot you're controlling? Or field dressing a wound?"

"We won't hunt with guns," Diego said. "Too easy for the machines to find us. We'll have to fashion bows and arrows, maybe some spears—"

"Oh, come on!" Hope shook her head and zipped her backpack. "I'm ready. Let's go meet our doom. And turn into cave people along the way, apparently."

They said quick goodbyes to the rebels they'd met. Colt shook hands with Russ; the boy with the mechanical ear had been critical to their survival and a reliable friend in battle.

Dalisay, the medic who'd treated Colt and Mohini, gave him a long hug. Colt tried not to notice how she seemed to press herself against him. She slid something into his pocket.

"Fresh bandages," she whispered. "Keep your wounds clean. I want you healthy when we meet again." She pulled back, giving him a long look, her large, worried eyes set into her soft, dark face. She turned and gave Mohini a quick hug, which Mohini returned stiffly and quickly, with an annoyed look. "Take care of him," Dalisay said.

"Right." Mohini scowled at the girl's back as she left. "Dramatic weirdo. Let's get out of here."

The four of them split off from the group and toward the thundering sound of water. Mohini again rode on the pallet jack with the crates, controlling her crawler with her computer. The crawler was clearly weaker and slower than Colt had ever seen it; Mohini had it in power-save mode.

They traveled through the winding maintenance tunnels of the river-management complex lined with dripping, sagging pipes and bundles of rat-chewed cables.

Colt rounded a bend and almost walked into a hulking machine mounted on treads nearly as wide as the tunnel. Its four massive metal arms were tipped with blades and saws larger than Colt's head.

He raised his laser rifle and searched for the giant machine's CPU housing. A small box at the top, thick with sensors, seemed likely.

"Colt, relax," Mohini said. "It's just an old wreck."

"That is one ugly heap." Diego kept his laser rifle high, too, as he and Hope rounded the bend.

Colt looked at the machine more carefully. It hadn't

responded to their arrival, not even to swivel its tiny, sensor-laden head. A cement mixer was mounted on its back, and hoses ran up through two of its arms. "Looks like it was supposed to keep these tunnels in good repair."

"Well, he's sleeping on the job," Diego said. He dabbed at his nose, where blood trickled out.

"Are you bleeding again?" Hope asked, and he shook his head.

"Just a little. Still healing up from the lab."

In order to get around the machine, they had to pass through the space between one of its treads and the tunnel wall. The wagon barely fit; for a moment it looked like it would need to be abandoned, but it squeezed through, loudly scraping the wall on one side and the treaded wheels on the other. Colt grimaced at the sound. Loud noises were always dangerous.

They got moving again. Beyond the old machine lay a couple of other rooms. One was full of screens and workstations, an old monitoring station for the massive waterworks. There was also a restroom with shower stalls, with some boots and coveralls in the lockers. A break room offered a dust-coated coffee pot, a couple of wobbly tables, and a snack machine with its front panel smashed and its contents gone.

Colt and Mohini searched the cabinets above the counter, but everything had been ransacked. He found only useless napkins and coffee stirrers.

"Ooh, look at that." Hope had pulled the coffee-maker table away from the wall and searched behind it; now she held up a pair of small brown paper packets labeled ULTRA-EXTRA-RAW SUGAR. She beamed as though she'd found a treasure chest.

"Nice!" Diego licked his lips as he approached her. He'd

been digging through the useless cleaning supplies on the floor of the small closet. "Feel like sharing?"

"Of course she does," Colt said, stepping closer to the newly discovered sugar himself. "You wouldn't hog all that for yourself. You're not a sugar hog."

Hope smirked, looking between them. "I don't know. If I keep it to myself, it'll last longer."

"Once it's opened, it's gone." Diego moved close, sliding an arm around her. "Whatever you don't eat right away will spill or get wet, and then it's gone. And if the packet gets wet, the sugar's ruined. You have to always eat it right away."

"What will you do if I share?" Hope asked Diego, her bright blue eyes looking into his. She was nearly as tall as him.

Diego whispered something into Hope's ear that made her blush and smile.

"Promise me that, whatever you just said, you'll never repeat it out loud," Colt said. "I should get sugar just for having to watch you two together."

"No deal." Hope pocketed one little packet and tore open the other. "You owe me a favor. Maybe carry my backpack for a day."

"Fine, but not today," Colt said. "Later, after our supplies run thin."

"Hmm. Okay." She held out the open packet.

Colt's heart thumped faster. He reached out his hand, keeping it perfectly level as she poured about half the packet into his hand. The sticky old brown crystals landed in clumps in the center of his palm.

"Don't forget to share with our guest." Hope winked at Mohini, then dumped the rest of the sugar packet into her own palm before turning back to Diego.

"Here you go." Colt held out the sugar in his palm to Mohini. "It'll stick better if you lick the tip of your finger before you pick it up."

"Um." Mohini looked among them as if she were an alien from an advanced species observing strange tribal customs here on Earth. "It's just, like, sugar, right? That's not code for a drug or something?"

"Sugar is better than drugs," Hope said, licking her palm.

"You probably have whole buckets of sugar back on Carthage," Colt said. "But trust me, it could be months before we find sugar again. Or never."

"All right. I will have a little. Wouldn't want to miss out on a major moment here." Mohini leaned her face forward to peer closer at the crystalline lumps in his hand. Her tongue darted out in a flash of pink and gathered up some of the sugar, leaving his palm wet and sticky. A quick thrill at the idea of her eating out of his hand shivered through him as she backed away, smiling. "It sticks best if you just lick it. That's a tip from my world."

Colt nodded, momentarily dumbfounded. He kept busy by licking up the remaining sugar from his hand. The kick of sweetness was instant and potent, almost dizzying.

The four of them were silent, savoring, a kind of quiet communion with the rare sacrament. He kept looking at Mohini, who smiled back steadily.

"Okay, well that's enough dicking around," Hope announced, raising her trusty old machine pistol. She had a reaper's laser gun strapped to her back but didn't really trust it. "Let's hoof the trail. Jostle up your horses, or whatever they used to say. Get that ugly spider-bot crawling."

The tunnels twisted alongside the river as they moved north.

Then they turned west, directly toward the river's south branch. Colt didn't want to head due north; that would have taken them near Wrigley Field and the surrounding lakeside neighborhoods, where clashes between rebels and machines had been heavy. The machines would surely be scrutinizing that part of the city.

So the plan was to cross the underground river and turn north, keeping far west of the old stadium and the lake.

The water grew deafening as they approached the Chicago River's edge. The sloped tunnel in which they walked widened and ended abruptly.

An impossible expanse of water crashed and roiled in front of them, so far across their flashlights couldn't see the other side. An entire river had been sunk here, walled in and covered over in this deep-underground river-management complex centuries earlier, creating more dry land above while giving the city absolute control of the flow of water that had flooded the city repeatedly in the past, taking it at last out of nature's unpredictable hands.

Nature was reclaiming her way, though. The immense concrete walls surrounding the river were cracking, and no one today had the knowledge or means to repair them. No one today could hope for more than a life of bare survival; yesterday's Earthlings had been like giants, their towering accomplishments casting shame over their descendants who lived like rats in their ruins.

Colt and his three companions looked ahead.

The bridge seemed impossibly long, much too long to trust. They couldn't even see the far end. It was barely wide enough to fit their pallet jack, and every surface seemed rust caked. It swayed on creaky cables above the deep, violent river.

Hope gestured, because the water would drown out any

words she spoke. *You first.* And she smiled, for a moment the prankster little sister she'd once been.

Colt took a deep breath and stepped onto the bridge.

It creaked under his feet, and seemed to sway, though maybe that was an illusion created by all the water rushing past below.

The spray from the roiling rapids was no illusion. Colt had almost grown numb to the persistent underground cold, but the cloud of water droplets cut deep, like a swarm of stinging insects puncturing his layers of moth-eaten clothing.

He looked over at Mohini. She was getting as soaked as he was, her dark hair plastered down, shivering in the icy spray. Being cold and wet made her look smaller. She concentrated on the damaged black LogicSphere computer in her hands; Colt looked from it along the cable to the crawler's data port. He hoped the whole thing was water-resistant, that all the water in the air wouldn't lead to Mohini getting an electric shock or the crawler suddenly breaking free of her control because the connection shorted out.

There wasn't much point in raising those issues, though, especially since the river's roar made conversation impossible.

The crawler lumbered on like a tired, graying old sled dog reluctantly hauling one more load across the ice before its final, fatal collapse. Mohini still sat atop the crates on the pallet jack.

Colt looked back. Hope and Diego had started after them at a distance of a few meters. They stood shoulder to shoulder, watchful, Diego covering their rear with his recently acquired reaper rifle.

The echoing roar of the water would drown out the

sounds of any approaching machines, just as it drowned out the humans on the bridge.

The bridge vibrated constantly below Colt's feet. It had once been paved with a ridged, slip-resistant rubber matting, but most of that had rotted away or been eaten by rats over the years. Cold, dirty river water, fed by sewers from the ruins above, had pooled in gaps in the matting and developed into a slimy coating. He stepped around these puddles as much as he could, not wanting to fill his shoes and socks with exciting new diseases.

Colt kept the light clipped to his belt on its dimmest setting. He hated to use one at all, but no light reached the deep tunnel. Lights had originally been built in all along the bridge but had gone dark with the rest of the city two decades earlier.

They continued forward through a wall of deafening sound and bone-shaking vibration toward the uncertain darkness ahead.

Then the crawler stopped. Colt continued on a few paces before realizing it, then turned back to join Mohini. Her fingers flew across the cracked surface of her Logic-Sphere, manipulating icons and streams of symbols unintelligible to him.

"What's wrong?" he shouted, but he couldn't even hear his own words. The crashing water drowned him out.

The crawler's railgun sprang to life and spat ear-splitting rounds into the darkness ahead, carving momentary rippling tunnel-trails through the miasma of river water hanging in the air.

Mohini grabbed Colt's arm and yanked him backward. He didn't ask questions but followed her behind the pallet jack and dropped to the slimy rubber flooring.

Return fire sliced the air around them, bright tracer

rounds mingled with glowing lasers. Heavy fire, multiple attackers. Bullets sparked against the bridge's support cables, chipping away at them, while lasers punched through the cables and left smoking holes.

The crates on the pallet began to rupture, and then to burn, either from laser heat or incendiary rounds. River spray had soaked the crates, perhaps slowing the burning, but the water steamed off them.

"Hope!" Colt shouted, looking back. His sister couldn't possibly have heard him. Behind him, he only saw confusion—a flashlight beam, rolling wildly, bright flashes as the lasers shot by.

Diego and Hope both went down.

Colt began to crawl toward them, but Mohini caught him under the armpit with her fingers, which was unexpectedly painful.

He turned back toward her, scowling.

Mohini pounded on the largest crate as the attacker fire burned in the air around them like a sideways rain of light and lead. She screamed something at Colt.

Of course. Even under threat of death, she focused on her mission. And the Butler Jeffrey inside the large crate was the last vestige of that, her only remaining hope.

He gestured to her to bring the pallet-jack around, turning it sideways, and she nodded and had the crawler do it. The crawler's railgun continued to sweep back and forth, firing its ultra-high-speed rounds every couple of seconds at the unseen attackers.

A laser struck one of the crawler's legs, frying the upper actuator. The crawler staggered but didn't fall. Not yet. It crouched lower to steady its balance and kept shooting.

Colt grabbed the coffin-sized crate and pulled. There were burned patches all over it, extinguished by the cold river spray. He could see at least three places where bullets had passed through. The attackers were on the verge of mowing them all down.

The crate would have been too heavy for him to lift alone, but all he had to do was drag it off the edge of the pallet-jack.

It thudded to the bridge floor, the damaged wood cracking, but it was only slight less out of the line of fire.

Something grabbed Colt's ankle. He turned, hands on his old automatic rifle strapped to his shoulder.

Hope. His sister and Diego crawled toward him, drenched from the spray but thankfully alive, moving almost facedown on the bridge as lasers and bright rounds streaked not far above their heads.

Colt thumped Diego's shoulder and gestured toward the pallet. Together, they heaved the rolling steel platform up on its side as a makeshift shield, toppling the remaining crates toward the attackers. The shield wouldn't last long, though; a laser punched through the top corner right away, like a flaming arrow through paper. Enemy rounds dented and crumpled the thick steel.

Their lone defender, the crawler, was left stranded in front of the shield, connected by the data cable that snaked around the pallet to where Mohini crouched on the floor, her computer seemingly forgotten in her lap as she raised the burning crate lid. The crawler kept firing its railgun on autopilot.

Diego knelt behind the upturned pallet and added his laser blasts to the crawler's high-speed rounds.

Hope fired her machine pistol across the bridge railing, striking a small drone Colt hadn't even noticed off to their side. It might have been sneaking around to attack from behind, or helping the attackers get a closer look at them.

A drone meant their attackers weren't just some other scavengers. They were machines, or maybe clankers, the thuggish humans who served the machines in exchange for weapons and cybernetic enhancement. Colt now wondered if the clankers themselves weren't just another line of experimentation for the diabolical Simon Nix.

Colt knelt beside Diego and opened fire at the enemy. In the flashes of laser fire, he saw the metallic skull-like faces of reapers, their bodies slender and wraithlike, made of minimal amounts of steel, difficult narrow targets full of gaps and empty space. The reapers patrolling the ruins were typically old, battle-damaged models dumped off on Earth as near-scrap.

It looked like at least a squad of them, approaching two abreast across the bridge, firing heavy machine guns and laser rifles. If they had plasma, they were holding back for now. Maybe they wanted to preserve the bridge for their own use. Their fire had already struck a number of the old cables and supports; Colt could feel the bridge sagging toward the crashing water below.

The reapers finished cutting down Mohini's hijacked crawler. It toppled over, a smoking wreck, its rail gun shattered. Colt felt a pang of regret seeing the thing fall; it had helped them survive so much, had probably even sensed this impending attack for them.

Colt's uranium-tipped rounds hammered into the metal soldiers, but they weren't going to do much without a lucky direct hit on something vital. He hurriedly switched to his laser rifle.

While he changed weapons, he glanced at Mohini. She'd slid her fingers under the Butler Jeffrey's head. It lay like a wax-museum corpse in the burnt ruins of its coffin-crate.

The android's eyes opened, and it sat up abruptly. It was uncanny how much the discontinued servant android resembled the Simon units, as though he were Simon's paunchy, balding, mustached shorter brother. His stiff brown suit rustled as he looked around. He remained unperturbed as enemy laser fire passed over his head. He babbled about something, his words drowned by the crashing river and gunfire.

"Lie down!" Mohini barked at him. Colt could read her lips.

The Simon sprawled facedown in the wet filth of the rotten flooring, obedient to her command.

Colt had no more time to watch. He joined Diego in firing lasers from behind their upturned pallet jack. Their makeshift shield was denting and dissolving fast now that the enemy could ignore the fallen crawler.

Hope remained on drone duty, taking out another with a spray from her freshly reloaded machine pistol. Her favorite sidearm wasn't particularly accurate, but she had plenty of ammunition for it.

The disk-shaped drone sparked as it toppled away toward the water below.

Colt struck one of the reapers repeatedly, one potshot at a time between dips behind the shield, but he couldn't seem to penetrate anything vital. Frustrated, he adjusted his laser rifle to full blast, ready to drain the whole battery in one go.

He rose up again, risked a couple of precious seconds taking aim, and emptied the whole charge at the nearest reaper's face, now only a meter away.

The tunnel lit up like daytime for a moment as the laser rifle let its full charge go. Colt felt like some ancient weather god hurling a lightning bolt at his enemy.

The thick beam bored through the center of the reaper's face, right between the eyes.

The reaper froze, locked into place, black smoke curling out from its skull. Hopefully he'd charred its central processor.

Colt dropped, barely avoiding a hail of fire. The pallet-jack clattered and dented as more rounds struck it. Lasers passed through, leaving burning red spots like diseased boils.

He unzipped his backpack, which he'd already removed to get at the laser rifle. He opened the side pocket where he'd stored a spare battery for his rifle.

At least, he thought he'd stored one there, but now he couldn't find it. He pawed among some crackers and a tin of MultiMeat Preserves, but the big shotgun shell of a battery was nowhere to be found.

He cursed and searched through the backpack's other pockets. There was no time for this.

Beside him, Diego ejected his spent battery and slid another one into place. Colt was about to ask him if he had another, but then their melting excuse for a shield vanished.

A reaper lifted the pallet-jack and hurled it aside. The jack broke through the safety railing and caught on the edge of the bridge for a moment, before gravity ripped it away with a wrenching sound and it dropped like a boulder into the river below.

Diego backed away, firing laser bursts at the oncoming reapers. Colt grabbed up his old rifle from the floor and squeezed off a burst at the nearest reaper, the rounds alternately hammering and ricocheting off the reaper's chassis.

Colt was backing up, too, but there was nowhere to go.

He backed into someone's legs and immediately turned

and yelled for Hope to sit down; the legs were too long and tall to be Mohini's.

It wasn't Hope, though; she was still on the ground. She'd dropped her machine pistol and started using her own laser rifle, but it wasn't going to be enough to stop the reaper squad's advance.

Mohini shouted something and pulled on his arm. He pushed himself back toward her along the slick floor, not sure what she wanted from him. She was already grabbing Diego, trying to get his attention, too.

The reapers halted their advance.

Mohini had gathered everyone behind the Butler Jeffrey unit, who stood in the middle of the bridge, looking fairly perplexed, blinking in the constant spray, his mustache drooping and wet, his starchy shirt half-untucked and hanging out from beneath his stiff brown jacket.

The reapers appeared to be at an impasse, almost having a standoff with the befuddled butler-bot.

She hacked the butler! Colt thought at first.

But he was wrong; the data cable still snaked from Mohini's computer to the shot-up remains of the crawler.

He cast a questioning look at Mohini, and she responded with an exaggerated shrug, like she was as clueless as he was. The Butler Jeffrey seemed to have convinced the reapers to halt their attack for a moment, though Colt wasn't sure why, unless it was just out to protect itself.

Colt raised his rifle and advanced, as did Diego.

The reapers immediately unleashed hell, firing heavy machine guns and laser rifles at both of them, blasting apart the safety railing on both sides of the bridge.

Colt and Diego fell back. A beam scored Colt's shoulder, burning through his clothes down to his flesh, and he grunted at the hot slash of pain. The smell of charred cloth and skin poured into his nostrils.

The reapers fell still again. Colt and Diego looked at each other.

Apparently the machines were still very much in attack mode, but they wouldn't shoot too close to the Jeffrey. Maybe they identified it as a Simon unit somehow. Maybe the Simons had impressed an extreme abundance of caution into the reapers when it came to protecting Simon units, and the Butler Jeffrey was now the clueless beneficiary of it.

Colt looked at Diego and gestured at his laser rifle. Diego gave him a puzzled look but handed the weapon over.

Colt stood up directly behind the butler-bot and looked over his shoulder. The lead reapers turned their heads toward him, but not their weapons.

The butler-bot was chattering about something; Colt couldn't understand all the words, but he was close enough to hear the android's voice. It was something about needing to set the table for tea.

"Shield me!" Colt shouted in the butler-bot's ear. "Don't let them shoot me!"

The Butler Jeffrey chattered something about cookies and napkins in return; Colt couldn't hear it well and didn't waste time asking him to repeat it. He raised the laser rifle over the butler-bot's shoulder and took aim.

He nailed one reaper right in the black lens of its eye, then shot another through its jaw area. He could never have taken the time for such precise shots if the reapers hadn't cowed at the sight of an apparent Simon.

When Colt was finished, he dropped back and Diego took his place, wielding the other laser rifle. Hope was next.

Taking turns, they brought down the entire squad of eight reapers, thanks to the machines' unwillingness to fire on the proto-Simon unit. The humans had to stay close behind the Simon, and within a very tight radius, or the reapers started shooting again.

When it was over, Mohini knelt by the smoking, laser-sliced lump of the crawler. With a small multi-tool, she pried open its damaged shell and removed its CPU, still attached to the end of her data cable like a fish on a line. The dense memory-crystal array looked intact to Colt, though it could have suffered lots of microscopic damage and cracking.

Mohini detached the CPU from her cable and slid it into her pocket. Then she pointed the way ahead, through the smoldering reapers that crowded the bridge like grotesque statues from some dark temple where they worshipped death as a god.

Colt gave her a questioning look. The machines had come from that direction; could it really be safe?

She shrugged and nudged the Butler Jeffrey forward. She had to nudge him several times, then scream in his ear twice, before he got the idea.

The butler-bot finally ambled ahead. The four of them stuck close behind it, pausing only to grab some of the most valuable supplies from the broken crates. Their pallet jack-wagon, and the railgun-armed crawler that had towed it, would both be sorely missed.

They passed uncomfortably close to the reapers, sometimes brushing up against them to get past. Colt kept expecting one of them to snap to life, grab him, and crush his throat, or maybe break his spine. Maybe carve up his face to leave his mutilated corpse as a warning to other humans.

Mohini stopped to reach up into a reaper's steel rib cage with her multi-tool, using what looked like a screwdriver but with an odd half-moon shape at the tip. She grimaced as she worked inside it, then came back with a couple of laser-rifle batteries that had apparently been stored there, which she handed over to Colt with a grin.

They reached the far end of the bridge, reaching a maintenance tunnel like the one they'd left, and hurried to put the bridge behind them.

"How'd you get the Simon to help us?" Colt asked Mohini, when the ringing in their ears and the sound of the crashing river died down enough for them to hear each other again.

"You mean the Jeffrey," Mohini said, glancing at the dripping-wet butler.

"Whatever. Did you hack him?"

"No. I was just trying to protect him from the other machines, but he insisted on getting up and... searching for tea." She shook her head. "I think he's still searching for it."

"...terribly sorry for my inability to accommodate," the butler-bot was saying to Hope and Diego. "This household lacks even the most basic means of furnishing hospitality. Neither a leaf of tea nor a sliver of crumpet to be found."

"It's not a household, guy," Hope said. "We're in the world's biggest sewer system."

"How unsanitary." The butler-bot frowned. "That certainly explains the lack of housekeeping. I recommend you purchase a Custodian Carl or Greta Von Kleener unit, both available from Carthage Consolidated at very reasonable financing. There are showrooms conveniently located in major cities around Earth—"

"Not anymore," Colt said. "How long have you been offline?"

The Butler Jeffrey blinked. "I am uncertain. I am unable to connect with any servers for updates—"

"Don't you fucking try to connect to anyone!" Mohini snapped, and the butler-bot winced as if slapped by her words. "I mean it, Jeffrey. Stay completely offline in every way."

"But I may miss important updates—"

"Here's the update," Mohini said. "You work for us now. I will be personally handling all of your updates and upgrades from now on. I am your system administrator. You will not communicate with any other machine, beyond telling them *not* to attack us. Understood?"

"Yes, thank you." The butler android sounded almost relieved to cede authority to someone. He brushed a few of his wet comb-over strands back into place over his mostly bald pate. "I function so much more effectively with clear instructions."

"We should move faster. And more quietly." Diego glanced backward. Nothing attracted machines like the destruction of other machines. They were like hornets incited to violence by the smell of a crushed hivemate.

Colt nodded. "Let's go."

"Not quite yet." Mohini explored the back of the butler-bot's skull with her multi-tool, searching the area where she'd found its power buttons hidden beneath its hair.

"I say, are you quite certified?" the butler-bot asked. "I can only be serviced by technicians with current valid certifications from Carthage Consolidated."

"That's me," Mohini said.

"May I have your certification number?" The Butler Jeffrey's tone remained polite, but its questions caused Colt to turn slightly, to tighten his grip on his laser rifle. Diego and Hope reacted the same way, stopping and moving into defensive postures.

Mohini paused. "Sure, but there's no point. You can't access the database to verify. There's no such database available on Earth, anyway. Everything's been destroyed by war. If you weren't aware."

"I have my own database of certifications."

"Right. Last time you were online, I was probably in pre-primary school, if I'd been born at all. So... just relax." She opened a small panel at the back of his head, no larger than a shirt button. Then she swore. "I don't have an XQG port jack. Who the hell uses XQG ports? No wonder you got taken off the market." She snapped the little panel shut.

"Pardon?" Butler Jeffrey turned toward her. "Were my customer satisfaction ratings so very poor? Early indications were... not good."

"Keep that thing quiet," Diego whispered.

Mohini nodded. "Stay quiet. And if any machines show up, tell them not to attack us."

"I have no such authorizations, and you have revoked my wireless access at any rate," he said. "But I can utter vocal commands at the machines, if it would comfort you."

"It would. Now, unless that happens, shut up."

They continued on through the freezing, pitch-black river maintenance tunnels, four humans and an android, one they needed but couldn't trust. They'd lost the crawler and many of their supplies. Colt had yet another scar added to a lifetime of them. At least the laser wound was clean and cauterized.

The tunnels turned even colder as they headed north.

Chapter Six

Galapagos - Audrey

The mood on the *Lancer* was so tense Audrey could barely breathe.

The submarine churned toward Correal Island, running fast and deep through smooth water. According to the geological maps projected on the control room wall, they traveled through a deep central trench in the tropics. The water here was relatively calm. She looked north, toward the ice-capped archipelago where the rough Iron Hammers lived, the only humans on Galapagos willing to ally with Carthage's empire in exchange for a cut of the cake, hoping to live as overseers rather than slaves.

Audrey, somewhat more familiar with the empire's history of planetary acquisition, doubted they would see much difference in the long run. But people always thought they were the exceptions. She supposed she was guilty of that herself.

"How long do you think they have?" Dinnius whispered to Kright. Audrey was close enough to hear. They were again strapped into the mismatched seats at the back of the control room, as out of the way as possible while under the crew's suspicious eyes. "Do we have any chance of finding this Marti guy in time?"

Kright shrugged. "I can't say I share Minerva's faith in this old guy's abilities. Or his willingness to help."

"So why are you bothering with all this?" Audrey asked.

"I don't have much faith in anything else, either. Makes it easy." Kright looked at the blocky video streaming from the *Catshark*'s photonics mast. The wasplike fighters hovered above the new Frosthead Bay base like flies above a corpse. The newly constructed base itself had gone as silent as a graveyard, the windowless, featureless buildings like tombstones without names.

"I'm not quite there yet," Audrey said. "At full loss of faith. But I'm definitely on that road."

"The road to nihilism," Dinnius said. "It doesn't lead anywhere you want to be, but at least it's always open. And free to ride."

"I always told you those philosophy texts would only make you poor and miserable," Kright said.

"I was already poor. But my misery is now deeper and more nuanced than when I was a child. So that's an accomplishment, I think. And my education came free, from digital libraries, while you took on debt to remain clueless and without noticeable skill."

"Why didn't you finish your architecture degree?" Audrey asked Kright.

"The same reason you didn't finish Political Academy," Kright said. "I grew distracted by radical ideas and a desire to tear down an oppressive system that was apparently invisible to my fellow citizens. And that was a distraction from school."

"Where exactly did you guys grow up?" Audrey said. "One of the Carthage City Zones?"

"Utica," Dinnius said. The city lay a few hundred kilometers south of Carthage City. "They say all Benefit Zones are the same—apartment blocks, clothing shops full of castoffs, community restaurants staffed by androids, public housekeeper bots to clean up your apartment once a week. All in the interest of public health. And keeping watch on the plebeians."

"We also had constant patrols by the Officer Joes," Kright said. "To keep us safe, obviously."

"And in school," Dinnius said. "Ten hours a day. Though it was mostly movies. Don't let Officer Joe catch you truant when you're a teenager, or it's a night in warning jail and six months of visits from a social-worker android—a Lois if you're lucky, a Karen if not."

"I got a Karen," Kright grumbled.

"The Lois was nicer to look at, but not nicer along many other metrics, I assure you," Dinnius said. "My father used to beat the snot out of me after she left, as punishment for drawing trouble into his life."

"He must have been on the wrong pills," Kright said. "He should have taken happies like my parents. They're even more effective if you crush them into a large yellow pile and snort them."

"I'll be sure to mention that next time I'm in Utica," Dinnius said. "Which I predict will be roughly never."

"Commander," said one of the comm techs in an urgent tone that drew everyone's attention. "There's a response."

Audrey and her friends fell silent, watching the clunky low-res video. Off on its side mission, the *Lancer* was largely out of the loop beyond the portion of the live feed which was being shared freely. They didn't know what Ellison was planning or what orders were going out; likewise, nobody else knew the *Lancer*'s exact location as it traveled.

Panels opened in the top of the newly built base. Plasma artillery guns and missile banks rose from within.

The cloud of wasplike fighters above abruptly split off, racing in three different directions like they'd been summoned. Each fighter had a plasma launcher built into its underside, and some of these were already glowing like miniature suns.

They opened fire, their fairly small plasma bursts dwarfed by accompanying streams of larger ones from the base's artillery.

Bursts of plasma soared past the monitor's viewpoint, streaking above the *Catshark*'s photonics mast. The viewpoint began to sink below the surface as the *Catshark* dived. There was no audio.

One of the drone fighters swooped low, angling directly toward them as if it would explode out of the monitor.

The monitor flashed bright white and went blank. Murmurs of profanity went up from the *Lancer* crew around them.

"The *Catshark* is lost. We should go north to join the others." Quera glanced across the steaming-hot control room at Audrey and shook her head. "We won't, but we should."

Instead, they dropped deeper and put on speed. The video feed from the battle vanished altogether as the Scatterlands subs dived, killed their broadcasts, or got attacked.

As they traversed the Central Tropical Trench, the external monitors revealed glimpses of strange wildlife of the deep. A horned octopus with tentacles the size of tree trunks passed close, visible only when it suddenly glowed bright green before swimming away.

"Electric jellies are schooling up ahead, ma'am," one crew member said, indicating his monitor.

"Swing wide," she said, looking over at his monitor, then nodded at pilot. "Adjust heading twenty degrees." She considered, then said. "Make it ten. The electrical activity could help cover us. But keep watch on that ambient voltage on the water. Swing wider if it starts to rise. I'd rather not get deep-fried today."

They slowed as they rolled past what looked like a silent underwater electrical storm. Audrey blinked at the monitor where it appeared. Bell-shaped translucent bodies filled the depths, each one bigger than her car back home. They glowed faintly, until their long, long trailing tentacles crossed each other; then the water glowed as the jellyfish charged each other, tangling and fighting, releasing bright flashes of electricity.

"Bad time for a swim," said Kright.

"They shouldn't be spawning this time of year," Quera said. "They're responding to stress, maybe caused by that giant star carrier that came crashing down into our ocean." She glanced at Audrey.

"Technically, it was only a minicarrier," Dinnius said. His eyes were on the monitor, watching a larger jellyfish wrestle a smaller one toward its gaping mouth, where an array of short, thick tentacles punctured the smaller jellyfish's membrane.

"You said they're spawning?" Audrey asked. "It looks like they're eating each other."

"That's part of it," Quera replied. "The death matches stimulate their gonads, which dump out gametes into the electrified ocean water. You see those glowing glints in the water? With a better camera, you'd see millions of them. The water's so thick with jellyfish sperm and eggs that you'd get coated with them in an instant."

"So it's a *really* bad time for a swim," Kright said.

"The electrified water wouldn't help," Quera told him. "By the time they're done, the water will be full of stunned fish, and the jellies will turn their attention to feeding."

"A postcoital snack," Dinnius said, nodding. "I like a bit of ice water and fresh fruit, personally."

His words drew Quera's gaze to him, and Dinnius's expression turned uncomfortable.

"Cold crab meat," she told him after a moment. "It replaces lost salts. And proteins."

"Good to know," Dinnius said, looking even less comfortable as some of the crew members chuckled.

Soon, the *Lancer* navigated toward what looked like an underwater range of tall, knife-thin mountains scattered along the edges of the cavernous trench below. Few of the mountains reached the surface above.

They approached the largest of the mountains, rising up along its craggy, coral-encrusted face. The alien aquatic life was alternately fascinating and disturbing to Audrey—pufferfish with long clownish beaks, the giant cephalopods that appeared and vanished again like ghosts as they shifted colors and shapes, sea scorpions as big as lobsters, a giant spike-shelled turtle nosing among the thick underwater foliage swaying in the current.

"Correal Island," the pilot murmured as they rose, emerging into a narrow harbor flanked by rocky cliffs. Rows of colorful multi-story houses looked out over the water from terraces above. A cable car rattled up the town's steep central avenue. Outdoor staircases snaked up and down the cliffs; one led all the way to the brightly painted lighthouse on the cliff's peak.

They reached a yellow pier where they tied up alongside a commercial fishing submarine.

"Here we are," Quera said, looking at Audrey, Kright, and Dinnius. "Duperre's place is over by the wharf."

"Right." Audrey stood. "Could you possibly spare a crew member to guide us? Since we're clueless visitors from another world."

"There are any number of ways things could go badly for us," Dinnius added.

"You bet there are," Quera said, looking him over. "If anyone finds out you three are from Carthage, it'll get ugly." She shook her head, then called to one of her men while fastening the top buttons of her uniform blouse as she prepared to meet the world outside. "Rilquor, come help me keep these off-worlders from getting lost."

Rilquor, a quiet but large man with gold and orange spirals rotating slowly on his face, arms, and torso, hurried to put on his own shirt. Once in uniform, he buckled a gun belt and holstered a long-barreled laser pistol at his hip.

By the time they led the way out to the dock a few minutes later, Rilquor and Quera were sharply dressed in Coalition uniforms. The outside air was tropical and swampy but not quite as thick and humid as the air had been in the sub. She'd left her officers with orders to evade in case of attack.

Beside the *Lancer*, a submarine fishing crew were on their small topside fish-cleaning deck—not a feature of Quera's battle sub—gathered close around a holoprojector, silently slurping beer cans and watching the news. They nodded at Quera and Rilquor as they emerged and insisted on giving them beers. They extended the offer to Audrey, Kright, and Dinnius, but only Dinnius took one. Audrey looked at him quizzically.

"What? It's for later." Dinnius stuffed the can into the pocket of his extremely loose-fitting trousers. They'd borrowed clothes from the *Lancer*'s crew members since they could hardly wear the gold-and-white Carthaginian space uniforms in which they'd arrived. Even Quera's smallest crewman's clothes were too big for him, though, and had been rolled up tight around his ankles so he wouldn't trip. At least the baggy pants hid the cartoon puppies on Dinnius's baby blue space boots.

Audrey found herself in Quera's civvies, which were too short, leaving too much of her torso and legs exposed. It felt good in the hot air, though, especially after being in the hot, body-odorous sub.

"—Coalition forces faced stiff resistance from the enemy base," said the holographic newswoman the fishermen were watching. Smaller bubbles floating around her showed clips of the wasplike Carthaginian fighters shooting down a Gavrikovan warplane over the ocean and missiles launching from the Carthaginian base. A third bubble showed Minister-General Ellison. "All reserves have been called up to active duty. Civilians are advised to take cover with all available supplies and any personal weapons they own."

Uniformed police approached, armed with laser rifles. They were clearly tense, a graying old man and a young guy who had to be a rookie, and the sight of the submariners wasn't cheering them up at all.

"Trouble, Commander?" the old cop asked, after

glancing between the uniforms and determining Quera was in charge.

"All over the world, but not here in particular," she told him. "We're just making a quick supply stop. There's no telling when we'll get another chance. We're looking for a place called Duperre's."

"Right down Harbor Way. You can almost read the sign from here." The old cop gestured down a narrow stone road, but his eyes looked past her, at the horizon across the ocean. "Are they coming this way? The machines?"

"We don't know their plans, unfortunately," she said.

The town was eerily silent, though it was the middle of the day. The only sound was the occasional news report drifting out an open window with some sparse information about naval battles unfolding up north.

The five of them hurried down an empty street.

Duperre's Bait, Beer, and Notions wasn't far from the dock. It had a sprawling front porch that looked like it had been fashioned out of driftwood, its overall shape irregular, its railing a jumble of old fencing, fish nets, and sail rigging. A couple of old men occupied rocking chairs and watched the news on their own flickering, grainy projector. They nodded at the uniformed submariners.

The interior of the large wooden building was like somebody's grandpa's junk collection—everything from fishing gear to old appliances crammed the shelves and the majority of the floor space. A bank of glass-fronted coolers hummed along the back, full of beer and frozen food.

A fishy, muddy odor rose from barrels of live bait sloshing under mesh lids. Audrey looked into one and saw a toothy pale worm as long as her arm slowly circling in dark water. Others contained assorted fish that looked like they could bite off her fingers, some in eye-catching bright colors.

Near the front, among novelty items like fake jellyfish, farting life preservers, and hats that said things like GONE FISHING, BACK IN 5 YEARS, hung the dried husk of an octopus taller than Kright, its enormous tentacles spread out and suspended from wires as if it were attacking. A sign encouraged people to take a picture with the monster from the deep. It was probably contributing to the overpowering fish odor, too.

"This is where our tourist picture came from," Audrey noted, looking past the suspended squid to the shelves of old appliances and worn-down mechanical gear. "Marti was spotted there."

A man with a long gray beard and a meshback cap advertising DUPERRE'S – COME FOR THE BAIT, STAY FOR THE BEER coughed as he made his way up one of the aisles.

"Welcome to Duperre's," he said, looking them over, focusing on the two in uniform. "I'm Budreux Duperre. What I can do for you?"

"We're looking for someone." Audrey drew out a personal screen—it wasn't worth much without a satellite system to connect to, but it had a few valuable items stored, including the single image of Martilius Depascal picked up by a wealthy Carthaginian deep-sea fishing enthusiast. "Have you seen him?"

Duperre stroked his beard, repeatedly, for a maddening minute or more, then nodded. "He's come in a few times over the years. Main thing you notice is he don't say much. I couldn't tell you his name. He's always alone, don't ask questions, just finds what he wants and leaves. Which is usually some old junk or other. He must be a fix-it-up type, or else he just likes collecting busted old machinery. We get all kinda weirdos."

"Do you have any idea where we might find him?" Dinnius asked. "It's urgent."

The man stroked his beard, then scratched it, as though the controls for his brain were hidden deep inside his graying curls. "Couldn't tell you. Though it can't be far."

"Why do you say that?" Audrey asked.

"I've seen his boat. He's not traveling the world in that thing. It's not much more than a canoe with a rebuilt outboard stuck on the back. A colossal whale could slurp it in and hardly realize it till it was time to gurge up what he can't digest."

"So you think he lives nearby?" Audrey asked.

"He don't live on Correal Island," Duperre said. "I'd see him more often."

"So one of the nearby keys?" Quera asked.

"It's possible. Got a hundred or more around here. Some of 'em's got families living on 'em. Others are just bare dry rock."

"Maybe you could narrow down the options for us," Audrey said.

"Which keys have fresh water but no people?" Quera glanced at an old plastic map on the wall showing the local area around Correal Island.

Duperre nodded and approached the map. Quera and Rilquor moved in as he pointed out keys. Many had no names at all, just coordinates. "Wouldn't need fresh water, though. Just a rain barrel or two. You can always count on a good rain coming soon, especially if there's a ball game, as my pop used to say—"

Shouting erupted on the store's front porch, accompanied by a whispering wind that made Duperre's eyes go wide.

"Chopper!" Duperre stepped behind the cash register and drew out a thick, short-barreled rifle of a kind Audrey didn't recognize. It looked large enough for whale hunting. "They're here, goddammit."

Audrey and the others hurried toward the front door, but they could see it approaching through the front windows even before they reached the porch.

"That's not the Hammers," Duperre whispered.

A large black helicopter trimmed in glittering gold hovered above the stone street in front of the store. The old men on the porch had already drawn weapons, old-fashioned lead spitters, and seemed to have every intention of firing them at the Carthaginian copter.

"Do *not* shoot at it," Quera said as the rest of them emerged onto the porch. When the old men scowled at her, she added, "Stand by to, though."

Kright moved in front of Audrey, between her and the helicopter. The hovering machine looked weirdly blind—no windshield, no windows, just a rotary cannon. It was blunt-nosed and wide, maybe a cargo or transport craft.

It wasn't attacking the building quite yet, though people were shooting at it from the street, bullets ricocheting off its armored sides. Two more helicopters arrived, sharp-nosed and narrow, flanking the larger one. Their rotary cannons fired plasma at high speed and filled the streets with fire, chasing the disorganized armed islanders back into nearby buildings.

"Hold your fire," a flat digital voice announced over the three copters' loudspeakers. "We are not here to attack, but we will defend ourselves against your aggression."

"Go to hell." One of the old men from the porch raised his revolver again.

"Wait!" Quera snapped at him. The old man blinked but obeyed the officer.

The transport helicopter seemed to grow wider as large panels on either side expanded outward, revealing a payload on either side. Audrey thought they might be missiles.

Audrey felt frozen to the spot, unable to react. What could she do, anyway?

They weren't missile banks, though. Large, dark objects dropped at high speed on both sides of the transport, trailing cables like spiders.

Reapers, a squad of eight. They were down in the street in an instant, arrayed in a circle, their plasma rifles at ready but not pointed at anyone.

Audrey thought she might black out from the tension. The locals had stopped firing, taking cover in nearby buildings, but they watched out the windows, still armed.

The circle of reapers unfolded into a double column, each facing outward, leaving a narrow passage at their backs.

A ninth figure approached between the columns, protected by reapers on either side, smiling as he approached.

It was a Simon unit, dressed in a long dove-gray business coat and a pristine white silk shirt. Unlike any Simon that Audrey had encountered, it showed signs of damage: a little over half its face appeared to have been burned at some point, maybe scored by lasers. While Audrey wondered about the cause of the damage, another thought occurred to her—the Simon had chosen to keep the damage. It had just arrived from the fleet above, where it surely had plenty of opportunity to repair itself.

"Good afternoon," the Simon said, its tone polite, its smile professional. "I am Simon unit number ZRN466871, the current ambassador from Carthage to Galapagos. Other humans have found it convenient to refer to me as 'Ambassador Zorn.' You are welcome to do so. Should you wish to contact me personally in the future, you can ask for me by that name."

Audrey peered around Kright but kept herself as hidden as possible. She couldn't risk the Simon recognizing her. Suddenly she wished she'd grabbed one of the novelty beer-can caps and pulled it low on her head, but it was too late now. Rushing back inside would just call attention to herself.

"I am Commander Quera Inrick of the Galapagos Coalition Navy," Quera said. She held her own long-barreled laser pistol; it looked like a metalsmith's work of art, embellished with small metal spirals reminiscent of her tattoos, but it was definitely a weaker weapon than the plasma rifles carried by the reapers. "Why are you here?"

"This is a simple shopping excursion," Simon Zorn replied. "I wish to speak with the proprietor of this establishment."

"That'd be me," the long-bearded Duperre said. His own thick, short rifle was at the ready.

"Excellent." Simon approached the wooden step to the front porch, flanked by reapers on either side. "Might we speak privately indoors?"

"I'd prefer not." The old man stood his ground.

"Your preference is my command, Mr. Duperre. I have only one small question." The Simon held out a holoprojector that looked like a tiny black sphere no larger than a golf ball, though with flattened hexagonal faces. Audrey recognized it as a LogicSphere product from Carthage.

An image flickered into existence above it—the same one Minerva had provided Audrey, and which they had shown Duperre. At this size, the resolution was chunky. In the foreground was the hugely fat man posing with the giant dried horned squid; he was almost a caricature of a Carthaginian tourist, with his bright orange wetsuit advertising the Loco Raptors crashball team back home, plus the zippered plastic "saddlebags" hanging from either side of his belt, likely stuffed with personal items like his passport, local currency, and mood pills.

The stringy-haired man poking around broken bits of what looked like a wind turbine was only just visible in the background. Depascal. Minerva had warned them that he would be a high-priority target for the Simons.

"We're looking for this man," Simon said. "He may appear harmless, but he is a dangerous criminal wanted for crimes on Carthage. Simply provide me his whereabouts, and we will leave you and your island in peace. And you will be glad to have my personal protection in the days to come."

"As Carthage tries to take over our world," Quera said.

Simon gave her an appraising look. "Carthage offers protection and stability. We will finally bring the peace you were unable to attain for yourselves." His cold blue gaze shifted back to Duperre. "Where can we find this man?"

Duperre shook his head. "Couldn't tell you. Never saw him."

"Yet here is an image of him in your very store."

"Lots of people come and go," Duperre said. "Lots of off-worlders, even. Lots of weirdos. Best damned fishing in the galaxy is right here along the Central Tropical Trench. I can tell you one thing about the man in this picture: he ain't local, don't live on this island. Most likely he was just a fishing tourist."

"The man in the foreground, certainly, but surely this bedraggled fellow rummaging the junk bins is no well-heeled interstellar tourist in search of exotic marine life. He clearly seems more of the 'beach bum' type, to employ a colloquialism."

"Everyone looks like that after a few days out in the sun and the salt," Duperre said. "Even off-worlders."

"Are you absolutely certain you cannot help me locate this man?" Simon asked. "It is of great urgency. Please think. If you were a criminal on the run and had chosen to hide in this area, where would you go? The maps show small keys all along the tropical trench but little detailed survey data. Perhaps a knowledgeable local like yourself could narrow down the options for us. Your cooperation would be well compensated. Carthaginian currency is accepted on most worlds." Simon offered a fold of thick, colorful paper money veined with bright silver and glittering gold.

"I've got nothing else to say," the bearded old shopkeeper replied. "And your money's no good here. Not when you got warships in our water."

"Mr. Duperre, I would prefer to take the gentleman in this image alive, for my own purposes, but it is a quite minor preference. His charred corpse would also be an acceptable outcome. Should you fail to assist me, we would have no choice but to search and clear this island in the most efficient possible manner. Is protecting this one man truly worth sacrificing your entire community? That is your choice. I am merely a machine, and am indifferent to the means, so long as the object is achieved."

"I'm not protecting anyone," Duperre said.

"He's answered your questions, Mr. Ambassador," Quera said. "Why not return to your own fleet?"

"His answers are not acceptable. Perhaps one of you see the wisdom in collaborating rather than obstructing?" Simon looked to the two old men on the porch and extended the thick roll of money. Their projector kept playing the bubbles of news broadcasts; in one, a Carthaginian frigate shaped like an armored steel wedge fired a plasma torpedo and melted a pathetically small local craft. A geyser of steam erupted at the plasma impact site, blasting up through the glowing red molten ship like an eruption of hellfire through the ocean.

"Could I get a closer look at that money?" asked one old man, lowering his revolver until it pointed at the porch floorboards. "Come to think of it, I may have spotted that drifter on one of them keys down the way, hiding his boat under the trees." The man beside him scowled, as did Duperre.

"Of course." Simon ascended the single step to the porch and held out a multicolored 1000-credit bill, shimmering where the mint had inlaid fibers of precious metals, gold and silver adorning the images of Audrey's father on the front and the planet Carthage on the back. Physical currency was rarely used on Carthage, but what they did print was meant to impress.

"Hell, I could buy my own island with that." The old-timer reached for the bill with one spotted, veiny hand.

As his fingers closed around the empire's money, he raised his other hand, the one with the revolver in it, and pointed it at the center of Simon's face.

"Get off my planet," the old fisherman said, then he pulled the trigger. And again. And again.

The lead hammered the android's face, peeling away some of the remaining fake skin, revealing black scales beneath. Audrey doubted the bullets would do any real damage.

Simon grabbed the old man's gun arm and folded it up like a towel, shattering the bones from his wrist to his shoulder in a series of loud crunches. The man howled until Simon's finger jabbed a hole in his neck. Air whistled from his exposed windpipe.

The reapers in the street opened fire at the storefront, and the helicopters above opened fire on the neighborhood, and a storm of plasma bolts filled the air, burning everything in sight.

Chapter Seven

Galapagos - Ellison

None of Galapagos's missiles struck the new Carthaginian base.

The *Hornfish* continued feeding video to Ellison over the submerged SQUIDS system, but it was kept encrypted. Ellison knew the public had seen enough of what was happening to get engaged and ready their defenses, but now he had to protect his data sources more carefully.

Plasma artillery fired from the roof of the base, throwing masses of glowing white at the incoming missiles. The Carthaginians had complete orbital superiority, so they'd had plenty of time to see the attack coming and prepare a response.

A squadron of wasplike Carthaginian fighters raced forward, spitting lasers and bursts of plasma concentrated on the incoming missiles.

"It sounds like nothing made it through," Kartokov said, monitoring reports from the missile launch bases and ships.

"We've got the bulk of the Green Island Air Service en route, and we haven't even softened them up," Ellison murmured. "They're going to get torn up."

"They're our only remaining chance at a rapid response," Kartokov said. "The smaller Gavrikovan carrier groups are still moving into range. The *Ursus* remains at home, which I appreciate, but perhaps—"

"We can't throw everything into one pot. Clearly they'll attack the industrial islands at some point, fairly early on. And Neptune Base. Gilra?"

"The evacuation of nonessential personnel is nearly complete," said Gilra, who was handling communications with Vice Admiral Riba of the Aquatican fleet, commander of the base, which had taken severe damage from the initial Carthaginian sub attack. They sometimes spoke in the bubbling, gurgling private language of the Aquaticans, a people biologically modified to better fit their religious beliefs, and apparently capable of quite bizarre sounds as a result.

"How well have we kept that evac hidden?" Ellison said.

"It was mostly carried out underwater," Gilra said.

"Let's make sure the base sounds busy," Ellison said. "Route every communication through it. Make as much noise as possible. Churn the ventilation at high speed, turn every screen full blast even in the empty rooms. Get the blenders running in the kitchen if you can. Make that place seem fully occupied. Keep a small patrol of submersibles visible on the surface but ready to dive fast."

Gilra nodded and relayed this in the fluid Aquatican language.

Ellison looked Salvius. "Are you sure about what you said earlier? There's a good chance that Simon has been keeping his invasion plans from his local allies?"

"Sure," Salvius said. "I mean, at this point, if they said anything, it was probably just 'stay out of the way and let the adults handle it.' Uh, the mechanical adults, I guess. They're not getting involved, right?"

Ellison considered, then nodded. "Kartokov, tell the sky chief we're redirecting the Green Island fighters," he said. "Divert them eastward."

Kartokov frowned. "Toward the Cauldron Sea? There're no major targets there."

"But then turn north, toward the lowest-rising islands of the Polar Archipelago," Ellison said. "They'll be on course to take out the Hammers' geothermal plants. And have them take out anything that looks remotely like an antenna. We don't want them talking to their buddies from outer space if we can help it."

"Is this really the time to attack the Iron Hammers?" Gilra asked. "Shouldn't we be conserving our assets?"

"They'll track down and destroy our assets if we conserve them too long," Ellison said. "We need to use what we have. Carthage made no secret of their base's location, so they probably want to draw us out into a massive direct attack. I say we do the opposite—confuse and divide their forces, slice and scatter them so our people have some chance of inflicting damage."

Kartokov nodded and contacted the Green Island sky chief.

Ellison looked at the map on the damp wall. A drip from above kept splashing near Gadsden Point, in the northwest Scatterlands, leaving a dark streak on the plastic-coated paper. The Scatterlands surface ships would be snaking their way to that base, itself a legend from the Island Wars, a place where a small number of Scatterlanders had once held off an attack from a superior Iron

Hammers force for eight days until reinforcements arrived from Gavrikova.

His eyes moved hundreds of kilometers east to Kawau Island, almost due south of the new enemy base at Frosthead Bay.

He could easily divert a few ships, a few marines, and have them look after his home. No one would question his orders, at least not until long after the conflict, when the armchair experts always came forward. Perhaps there was something of strategic significance hidden on Kawau Island, for all anyone else knew.

But there wasn't. He would be diverting desperately needed forces from protecting the world in a short-sighted attempt to favor his own family. Those few diverted forces could make the difference between victory and defeat, between saving their world and losing everything.

He resisted the temptation, trying not to think of his sons, depending on him to keep them safe. Of his wife, of everything that mattered to him.

Ellison's heart thumped faster as scattered reports came in from the Green Island Air Service. The Carthaginian fighters swarmed out from the base, ready to intercept the incoming Green Islanders.

He sorely missed the integrated communications and data of the lost command center. Everything came in bits and pieces. They were fighting without seeing much.

"We are like the blind men in the story, pulling at the elephant's scrotum and buttocks," Kartokov muttered.

"I think you heard a different version of that story than me, but yeah," Ellison said.

Putting together scraps of data, and glancing frequently at the wall maps, Ellison got a fuzzy moving picture of the flight of Green Island fighters as they changed their heading and diverged from what had seemed like a straightforward attack on the new base. The Carthaginians, no doubt monitoring from space, might have read it as the beginning of a retreat, because the Cauldron Sea lay in the space between the Green Islands and the Polar Archipelago. The Green Island fighters swerved back almost the way they'd come, though along a more northerly path.

The Green Islanders opted to fly low and fast over the boiling volcanic waters; the heat and steam could help provide some cover against visual and thermal monitoring by the enemy. The pilots had trained for maneuvers in the difficult environment north of their home.

Coalition fighters pursued them; there was no telling exactly how many, because some had descended with the drop ships, others had launched from the new base, and it was possible that many more had patrolled the upper atmosphere, waiting for orders. A squadron of Carthaginian helicopters was noted leaving the base, but nobody was sure where it went.

Casualty reports began to come in; at least five Green Island planes were lost, either missing or confirmed, by the time the wing limped across the relatively low peaks of the chain of islands on the eastern edge of the Polar Archipelago.

Targets in the Polar Archipelago had been difficult to identify even before Carthage had obliterated all of the Galapagos Coalition's satellites. The steam from the Cauldron Sea turned into cloud cover for the Polar Archipelago, soon transforming into ice and snow as it reached the higher peaks of the inner islands.

The Hammers had adapted to their environment, powering their civilization with geothermal plants. The thermal signature of these had helped the Coalition map them from satellites in the past.

Now the Green Islanders had orders to strike those power plants with missiles.

They lost touch with the Green Islanders as the planes flew over the Polar Archipelago and went silent.

Gavrikovan planes from that nation's smaller carrier groups were ready to take the war to the enemy's new base now that a significant chunk of the wasplike drones had split off to pursue the Green Islanders. The Scatterlands subs already in the northern waters would be joining that attack from below, and maybe they could do some real damage to Carthage's assets before Carthage's plans got rolling.

"Unless their plan is to draw us into an attack," Gilra said. "In which case we're playing into their hands."

"The old rope-a-dope. Give us a chance to wear ourselves out before they launch the real attack." Ellison frowned.

"Could be. What does the Carthaginian say?" Kartokov looked over at Salvius. "Would the Simons use such a ploy?"

"Anything's possible, guy." Salvius leaned against the wall, sagging like he was bored. "They've probably run all kinds of simulations, trying to predict how you'll act. The question is how well this Simon knows you."

"We got pretty acquainted with each other recently," Ellison said. "He offered me the chance to oversee Galapagos on behalf of Carthage. I turned him down. I can't say he tried very hard."

"He probably expected you to turn it down," Salvius said. "He was just confirming whatever prior research he had. Still, he had to give you the chance, right?"

"He did?"

"Sure. Maybe you would have said yes, and he could bring the whole thing in cheap and under budget, am I right?" Salvius said. He straightened up now, looking over the map. "He figures he'll give you a choice. Maybe you'll make it easy on him."

"What if I'd gone along with it?"

Salvius shrugged. "You'd be a figurehead, well compensated, basically untouchable, as long as you stayed useful to them. And don't mind reapers guarding your family at night. For their own safety."

Ellison shuddered. "I couldn't have lived like that."

"Well, good news. You decided to fight against pretty much impossible odds instead," Salvius said. "But I want you guys to win, seriously."

"Even against your own people?" Kartokov asked.

"They aren't my people. They're just machines. The only *people* I have on this world are on that sub with Commander Inrick. Everything else is just machines gone haywire as far as I'm concerned. Machines that need to be stopped. I hoped to stop them at the source, but..." Salvius shook his head. "The problem is there isn't just one source."

"Of course there is," Ellison said. "Carthage."

"Uh, yeah, but that's a whole planet. You can't just destroy a whole planet like that. I mean, it's like a billion people, if you count the orbital colonies."

Ellison and the others fell silent, looking at Salvius. Only the comm techs, doing their best to listen to and prioritize endless bits of information flooding in through SQUIDS network like millions of krill, paid no mind. If they'd been listening though, Ellison was sure they'd be looking at Salvius the same way.

You're damned right we would destroy Carthage, Ellison

thought. *Just show me which button to push. And the galaxy is full of people who feel the same.*

Salvius looked around, noticing everyone staring at him. "What?" he finally asked.

"Sir!" one of the techs shouted in his western drawl, and then the news came fast and hard. A couple of Green Islander pilots had checked in; they'd destroyed a geothermal plant as well as a communications tower while recording footage deep inside the Hammers territory.

"...caught the Hammers with their pants around their ankles," the Green Islander sky chief reported, his voice glowing with pride. "They had nothing in the air. By the time their surface-to-air defenses hit back, they were gunning for the enemy on our tail. Like they couldn't tell us from them. Carthage lost a few back there to friendly fire. Carthage may have retaliated on the Hammers too. It was a real donkey-and-banana show."

"And what about us?" Ellison asked, a little afraid to hear the answer.

"We haven't rounded them all up yet." The sky chief's voice grew somber. "We'll have some numbers soon, but we expect high casualties."

"I'm sorry to hear it." While Ellison considered what else he could add, all the comm techs burst into shouting, waving their hands at him as if they each just heard something that immediately jumped to top priority. Ellison broke off with the sky chief and turned his attention to them. "Why's it sound like a monkey house in here?"

"Sir," the nearest tech, "There's a second formation of drop ships, coming in fast."

"Where?" Ellison looked to the screens; one showed a row of armored rectangular ships high in the sky, supported by boosters as they descended from orbit.

"The Polar Ocean, just over the big shelf beyond Frosthead Bay," the tech replied. "They're heading for the deep water where our subs are."

"The Gavrikovan Islands," said another.

"Tower Island," a third reported.

Ellison straightened up and looked at his ministers. "Multiple landing groups?"

"They have finished testing us," Kartokov said. "This is the invasion."

Ellison fought back panic. He couldn't lose it now. Too much depended on him, and too many. He thought of his family back home and all the people hiding in their homes or local bomb shelters, depending on their leaders to protect them. Most of the Coalition leadership had already been lost with the integrated command center.

"We have to throw everything we have at those drop ships before they land, because once they do..." Ellison shook his head. "Let's go. Full speed ahead."

"Time to unleash the kraken," said Kartokov. "Pity we don't have one."

"The *Ursus* will have to do. And more of our ICBMs." Ellison shook his head. "We're really emptying the store here. We may even have to use the Megiddos."

"Unacceptable," Gilra said. "The Aquatican Hierarchy would never support the contamination of our holy ecosystem with nuclear devices."

"Just throwing it out there."

Audio reports came in over the SQUIDS network from hidden missile bases around the world already on high alert. The ballistic missiles were designed to strike fixed targets—enemy cities and bases—not rapidly falling targets. Ellison had them target the enemy base again; maybe the base's missile defenses would run thin.

The Gavrikovans' chief naval base, called Saint Vladimir, and its massive battle carrier, the *Ursus*, erupted like hornet nests. The fighter-chasers, their fastest planes, climbed steep and fast, striking the drop ships with missiles. The neat row of ships was scrambled out of line. They hadn't been arranged in a square like the ships that formed the base, just a single straight row heading for deep water near the Gavrikovan Islands.

The *Ursus* and its companion heavy destroyer—the remaining one of its original two, as the Carthaginian sub *Pompey* had sunk the other one—launched a volley of missiles and armor-piercing rounds, raking the underside of the drop ships. The armor proved impervious to the rounds, but one missile struck a drop ship's braking booster. The whole ship kicked upward as the explosion engulfed its squarish bow. It began toppling faster than the others, steeply tilted, its descent uncontrolled.

"The boosters underneath," Kartokov muttered. "That's the only vulnerable point."

The Carthaginian drone fighters swarmed in fast and hard, but their efforts were split between engaging the quick fighter-chasers above and hitting the massively armored battle carrier and heavy destroyer below.

A flight of regular Gavrikovan fighters catapulted from the *Ursus* and engaged the drones. Gavrikova's heavier bombers were held back; they would be like fat turkeys, easy prey for Carthage's fighter drones.

Those drones chewed into the Gavrikovan fighters with rapid bursts of laser fire and small bursts of plasma. Ellison winced at the heavy losses; Kartokov looked deeply grieved at the loss of so many countrymen in such a short time.

"There's... something happening, sir." One of the comm techs switched the view on the center's largest screen to a video feed from Saint Vlad, tracking the burning drop ship as it toppled toward the ocean.

A central seam opened lengthwise in the drop ship, splitting it in half. The two halves blasted wide apart in a controlled explosion, revealing the payload inside: a heavy armored naval ship.

"A Carthaginian frigate," Kartokov said. Ellison recognized it, too, from articles and videos: a death-dealing machine without a soul aboard, designed for ship-to-ship warfare. "They usually protect an even more valuable capital ship."

"I wonder what that one's here to protect," Ellison said.

The naval frigate was engulfed in flames from the missile strike, and it had left its drop ship much too early, at least a kilometer above the water. It plummeted through empty space at free-fall speed.

Apparently its weapon systems were online, because it unleashed with all barrels even as it fell from the sky. A barrage of glowing plasma shells erupted from its main gun, accompanied by glowing rivers of bright rounds from an array of smaller barrels.

The falling ship was pouring out everything it had, most of it aimed at the heavy destroyer protecting the *Ursus*'s flank. The bright rounds chewed through the destroyer's armor, leaving bright molten holes all over it. The plasma shells rained down on the destroyer's weaponry and main deck from above.

The crumbling, melting destroyer held firm, protecting the *Ursus* to the last, while the Carthaginian frigate plummeted toward the ocean. Ellison hoped the impact would shatter the frigate; from that height, it might as well have been landing in a stone quarry as a deep body of water.

Before it reached bottom, though, its plasma shells

breached the superstructure atop the Gavrikovan heavy destroyer; the superstructure collapsed into a molten crater, and Ellison felt a kick at another tremendous loss of life.

Then the Carthaginian frigate plowed into the water, its mass burrowing under the surface and throwing up clouds of steam and spray on impact, and they lost visibility again.

Throughout this, reports poured in from the Polar Ocean and Tower Island as the drop ships landed in neat rows in the ocean.

In the northern waters, the Scatterlands subs found themselves positioned in between the new base at Frosthead Bay and the drop ships landing in the deep water nearby.

At Tower Island, the drop ships were smaller and landed right in the bay. The Aquaticans, following special instructions from Ellison, had previously made their subs visible on the surface but had already melted away into the deep.

At all three locations, the enemy's drop ships landed atop deep water, their hulls hot from atmospheric entry, sending up walls of steam that shrouded them from view. The best view the techs could find of the drop ships was from the Gavrikovan naval base, Saint Vlad. Three more drop ships were the size of the one that the *Ursus* had successfully shot down.

The fourth remaining drop ship, the one in the center, was much larger.

The drop ships blew apart, roof and wall panels flying aside, the bottom panels of the drop ships simply sinking away to the depths below, their stabilizer rockets shut down forever.

Three of the newly arrived ships were frigates like the one that had fallen under the missile attack. They were imposing machines, thick with armor, bristling with barrels. The Carthaginian naval ships had a lean, sleek look to them; Ellison supposed that reflected the lack of compartments for officers and crew, the lack of any need for air, food, or plumbing, the complete lack of humanity within.

Red lights glowed along the exterior, scanners analyzing the environment in which the ships had arrived.

The largest drop ship had unfolded to reveal a monstrosity: a Carthaginian battleship, a floating fortress several stories high, thick with layers of armor. Ellison had read about them, had watched video clips, but had no idea what he could possibly to do stop these ships from dominating his world's oceans. Their destructive capabilities were apocalyptic.

The *Ursus*, now shorn of both its protective destroyers, unleashed on the battleship with everything it had, plasma-tipped missiles and massive artillery and machine guns. It was already limping from the first frigate's assault; fires burned on one of its decks.

The Gavrikovan bombers were catapulted into the air at last. They'd been held back to protect them from Carthage's drones, but now the drones were diminished and the bombers had clear targets on the surface: the frigates and battleship.

Anti-aircraft guns scattered along the battleship's starboard side opened fire on the bombers. A wide, narrow panel of armor farther along the same side slid up to reveal a bank of missiles, which launched one after the other.

The Carthaginian frigates flanking the battleship chattered their guns at the Gavrikovan aircraft, too, while continuing to pummel the massive *Ursus* with plasma shells, denting and scorching its thick armor.

"The *Ursus* is the toughest warship Gavrikova has," Kartokov said. "Commander Krinski—Pavlo Krinski—he is my nephew. My sister's son. He graduated at the top of his officer-training class. Never had to work in a mine." He looked almost wistful for a moment before straightening his back and hardening his face. "We will place our best ship against theirs, then. All our past wars have lead us to this, tested and prepared us for this. Saint Vladimir will protect us." Kartokov lowered his head and murmured something. If it was a prayer, it was the first Ellison had ever heard from the man.

The *Ursus* struck back with its toughest weapons, missiles with plasma warheads. These pounded into the battleship's hull one after the other; Ellison thought he saw the battleship rock backward under the impact, but that could have just been wishful thinking, seeing what he wanted to see on the blurry, blocky video.

A flood of fresh Gavrikovan aircraft arrived. They'd been on the nation's two smaller carriers, en route to respond to the polar waters to attack the new Carthaginian base, to join with the Scatterlands subs already in place.

Now they had all doubled back to join the fray above their home base, rapidly taking down the damaged Carthaginian drones. The surface of the ocean grew thick with fuselage. By the time the Gavrikovan bombers arrived, their path was clear to striking the Carthaginian frigates and battleship.

Two enemy frigates turned their attention to the fresh aircraft, raking them with streams of gunfire while the other frigate kept hammering the beleaguered *Ursus* with huge explosive shells.

The enormous Carthaginian battleship was as tall as the Gavrikovan battle carrier but narrower and much, much longer, like a skyscraper turned on its side and covered in armor and gun barrels. It seemed to be standing up to the battle carrier's plasma missiles.

Smaller attacks bombarded the Carthaginian ships from the base on the shore, artillery and rocket-propelled grenades.

The battleship raised what looked like an enormous cannon, its mouth as wide as a train tunnel. This tilted upward, toward the formation of Gavrikovan aircraft bombarding the invading ships.

The battleship unleashed a stream of what looked like solid metal, like a torrent of flak erupting from inside it, careening toward the heart of the Gavrikovan aircraft formation.

The spiky masses of metal separated from each other, swerving apart in several directions, each seeming to target a specific Gavrikovan plane.

The masses unfolded; they weren't flak at all, but ultra-compact fighter drones, rotating drums on their bellies firing quick, concentrated laser bursts a hundred times a minute. They chewed deep into the Gavrikovan aircraft; the Gavrikovan pilots barely had time to process what was happening before finding themselves under fire at extremely close range.

Some of the compact drones extended spikes and slammed themselves into the Gavrikovan bombers, attaching like lampreys, like ancient wooden ships hooking themselves to enemy craft and damaging the deck in the bargain. Then they unleashed plasma right onto the cockpit, burning the pilot to death. A few of these drones even managed to detach from their victims; others went down in a death spiral, still attached to their hosts, and shattered against the water below.

"This cannot be happening," Kartokov murmured, focusing on his home islands, though conflicts erupted on every screen. "We are a mighty nation. We are proud workers and soldiers. We should have been prepared for this."

"We'll get through it," Ellison said. "We're going to stand against them. And we'll endure."

On the screen, all three Carthaginian frigates turned their attention to the *Ursus*, softening it up. They ignored the incoming rockets and shells from the naval base on land.

The battleship had gone strangely quiet.

"It's turning," Kartokov said, after a moment.

"And opening," Gilra whispered.

A hexagonal portal the size of a cargo hangar door had unfolded at the dead center of the battle ship, beneath its tallest superstructure, revealing a sunken array of shimmering rings inside. Six metal arms extended straight out, perpendicular to the battleship, one at each vertex of the multi-story hexagon.

The concentric rings began to glow, as did the tips of the six arms.

"Shoot whatever the hell *that* is," Ellison said. "Looks like a primary weapon."

"Unfortunately, the *Ursus* has just dispatched its last two plasma missiles," Kartokov said as the bow of a Carthaginian frigate exploded from the double impact.

"Looks like it did some damage," Ellison said, watching the plasma engulf the front of the frigate.

Kartokov shook his head. "The last strike of the great bear was not even against the alpha of this pack."

"Kid," Ellison said, grabbing Salvius's arm and jerking him forward. "What is that thing?"

Salvius looked at the screen. "It's a big warship."

"Don't waste my time," Ellison said.

"Sorry, I'm not like, into reading up on all the latest

weapons and stuff." Salvius pulled his arm free and kept staring at the screen.

A shimmering sphere formed in front of the hexagonal weapon port. The sphere was transparent at first, filling in slowly, glowing and reddish at the edges. A column of raw red flame danced above it, like a great bonfire in a plague-ravaged city.

"Red plasma," Kartokov muttered. "I thought it was only experimental."

"Oh yeah, yeah, yeah," Salvius said, jabbing his finger at the defense minister. "I *have* heard of that. It's like, what? Colder than regular plasma. Which means they can make it denser, so they can... shoot it over longer distances? Right?"

"And apply more of a kinetic kick," Kartokov said. His voice was flat, his eyes fixed on the immense glowing sphere on the screen. The red plasma looked strange and sluggish, like a ball of thick mud, completely alien.

"How much of a kick?" Ellison asked, but his answer arrived before anyone could speak.

The red-hued plasma ball raced across the surface of the ocean like a comet. A sonic boom rolled behind it, leaving a visible wake in the water.

The plasma ball, as big as a tank, slammed into the *Ursus* dead center. The massive carrier rocked steeply at the impact, its damaged lower decks flooding on the port side.

Ellison was used to seeing plasma expand and spread fast, engulf targets in a burning blob, then dissipate and fade.

This plasma ball melted into the *Ursus*'s top deck and settled in, sinking slowly as it ate its way down, deck by deck. The great battle carrier looked as though it had been made of nothing but wax, and now it collapsed inward at the center, glowing red. It looked like a newly formed volcanic island, freshly erupted from the Cauldron Sea, just a heap of magma erupting in the water—except the *Ursus* was sinking, not rising.

Plasma and molten metal flowed outward, igniting a rescue boat the *Ursus* has sent toward its companion destroyer. The boat and its crew were consumed in seconds, all trace of them sinking away into the layer of glowing red death spreading wide across the ocean surface.

Ellison had grown up in wars, fought in them, but he'd never felt a feeling of horror quite like this one before.

"Pavlo," Kartokov murmured, covering his hands. "My sister will be devastated to hear."

"They're going to kill us all," Gilra whispered. Her eyelids barely fit over her bulging green eyes as she closed them. "The Deep Gods will have our souls."

The frigates turned their guns and plasma shells toward the land, returning fire at the Saint Vladimir naval base.

The battleship turned slowly in the water and loaded up another massive sphere of the cold red plasma.

With an earth-shaking boom, it sent the plasma streaking into the naval base, where it struck the dry docks and machine shops.

Ellison shifted his attention to the reports from up north, which were not good. The Scatterlands subs had done their best to torpedo the row of drop ships before they hatched, and they might have sunk one, though the results weren't clear.

What was clear was that at least two more battleships and several more frigates had emerged from the northern drop ships. One of the battleships had dropped a pack of minisubs into the water, and these had gone down to hunt the Scatterlands subs. At least two had already been lost.

The rest were trying to defend themselves while beating a tactical repeat.

"Ellison," Gilra said. "The drop ships in Tower Bay were all subs. Four, each the size of the *Pompey*. They're descending toward Neptune Base."

"Are we ready?" Ellison asked, and Gilra nodded. She removed the headset she'd been using to speak to Vice Admiral Starli Riba, prepping their response. Ellison tried to ignore the fishy odor left by Gilra's ears inside the headphones. "Put me on," he said.

"Yes, sir," replied an Aquatican tech. "Hailing the subs now. Requesting comm channel with Ambassador Zorn—here you go."

"Minister-General Ellison." Simon Zorn appeared on one of the screens. His face now showed the burns that Cadia and Kartokov had inflicted on him in outer space. "After all your posturing and pride, all your talk of principles and absolutes, here you are at last, kneeling at my feet, a humble supplicant begging to save his own hide. I would like to say I am surprised at this development, but I am not. Most men go weak in the end."

"You've got us surrounded out there." Ellison watched on a small monitor, a viewpoint provided by an Aquatican sub still patrolling the bottom of Tower Bay, not far from the concealed entrance to Neptune Base. The four subs continued to drop closer. "We'll surrender the base. I just want to get my people out safe."

"The time to consider the safety of your people was our first meeting, Mr. Ellison," Simon said. "That is long past. Sacrifices must be made now, on the altar of your intransigence. Examples must be made. Mercy is out of the question."

"Then why are you still speaking to me?" Ellison

watched as the Aquatican sub eased toward the cavern-like underwater entrance to Neptune Base, as if preparing to retreat into shelter as the larger, far more advanced invading subs approached it. The Aquatican sub was designed to resemble a living thing, its profile organic, its armor like fish scales. The Carthaginian subs looked like metallic monsters, sensors glowing red in the deep, preparing to feast on the fishlike Aquatican boat below.

"Because I enjoy the drama of transformation," Simon said. "I want to see how hollow your earlier idealism rings now, at the end. How clear it becomes that you are mere meat, a primate driven by instinct and urge, no matter how you might have tried to present yourself."

"I realize we're just a primitive outworld of simple fishermen," Ellison said, "But we're not helpless. We have more than principles. During the course of our wars, each nation accumulated its own little store of doomsday machines. There's nobody home on Neptune Base, Simon. There's just that rickety old sub from the museum. And Big Bela, set up inside her, ready to blow."

"Big Bela?"

"I remember what your last sub did to us. I'm not going to let four of them run wild around my ocean. So we stuffed that old museum sub full of our biggest non-nuclear bombs. Including one the Gavrikovans call Big Bela. They say she's big enough to level a city."

Simon frowned. "But surely you would never use such a weapon against your own capitol, your own headquarters—"

"Detonate," Ellison said.

The old Aquatican sub, recently withdrawn from the war museum ruins on the surface, was unmanned, driven by remote control. All of the Aquaticans and their actual in-service subs had fled after completely evacuating the base, abandoning the bay.

Now the same remote control sent the signal to detonate the bombs hastily wired up inside it.

The screens turned white, and they all lost all signals from the bay. Ellison thought he could feel the ground tremble under his feet, but it could have been his imagination. Or maybe his legs, going weak and threatening to give way at the immensity of what he'd just done.

The explosion would surely take out all four Carthaginian subs. It would also crack the underwater mountain in which Neptune Base was embedded, perhaps splintering it all the way to the top. The ruins of the capitol complex—its museums and murals of their world's shared struggles and pain, its library and classrooms to keep history present, its House of Ambassadors where the dream of a united, peaceful Galapagos had almost, at last, come to fruition—all of it would sink beneath the waves, as lost as Atlantis, ruins of a broken world scattered on the floor of the sea.

Still, the enemy had to be stopped, and four of those subs was a major victory. The younger people in the room, the comm techs, even had a moment of cheering when the bombs went off.

The old people, the ministers, did not cheer.

Ellison's eyes went to the map. "What's happening with the northern fleet?"

"The enemy fleet is moving due south, sir," one of the comm techs reported. The central-eastern Scatterlands girl with the hair like a bowl of straw. "A few Scatterlands subs survived contact. Not... not many, sir."

"South?" Ellison felt like shivering but tried not show it. Perhaps the enemy's northern fleet, featuring two more of the insanely large and powerful battleships, would veer southwest toward Gadsden Point, where the Scatterlands surface ships were gathering, and to which its subs were retreating. Or maybe it would continue due south, toward the Central Tropical Trench and Correal Island, in search of the lost software engineer who, Minerva claimed, would be so important to the Simons.

Long before Correal Island and the trench, though, the enemy fleet would reach Kawau Island.

Ellison thought of his family home, his village, burned to ruins. His mother gaunt and gray. His father dead. And now his wife. His sons.

"Make sure my sub is prepped for combat," Ellison muttered, though there was nobody but himself to carry out the order.

Chapter Eight

Earth

Colt, Mohini, Hope, and Diego slogged northward through the deep, damp, frigid world below the Chicago ruins. At one point they traveled through the remnants of ancient freight tunnels, stumbling over the rusty tracks of a narrow railway. Trains had once traveled the tunnels, delivering coal to the sub-basements of downtown skyscrapers, and coal dust seemed ingrained in the concrete walls and floor. Other times, they passed through the wreckage of underground neighborhoods abandoned since the war or traveled through the complicated mass of water-management tunnels built for controlling the megalopolis's buried river and sewage systems.

The Butler Jeffrey trotted along with them, cooperative and unquestioning as a puppy, but Colt hardly trusted the android. It had complied with their verbal commands so far, but it looked far too much like the Simon unit that had captured and tortured him. Maybe he would feel better when Mohini finally hacked into the butler-bot's hardware, but he doubted it.

The only upside to the butler-bot being awake and moving was that it could help carry supplies, now that they'd lost the crawler and pallet jack. The butler had no complaints about being a pack mule with tents and sleeping rolls strapped over its shoulders.

Diego had an old compass, a gift from Mother Braden, that kept them moving north. They stopped often; any random sound could be an approaching machine. Colt started to miss Russ and the mechanical ear that amplified his hearing.

They hiked north, eventually reaching completely unfamiliar areas of the ruins. Not knowing the terrain was dangerous.

"Where are we going?" Hope whispered to Colt at one point, falling into step beside him.

"North."

"More specifically?"

"Away."

"That's *less* specific, Colt."

"Look, I don't know. We find shelter. We make a plan. Or we just keep trying to survive."

"We can't keep going north," she said. "We'll freeze."

"I know," Colt said. "We'll see what Minerva says."

"Sure. Another machine."

"I'm open to better ideas if you have any," he said, and everyone fell quiet.

Not sure where they were going, they followed along the tunnel system that carried the Des Plaines River southward from Wisconsin. The flow of water would help cover their sounds and their heat. Colt felt so cold that it seemed impossible he would turn up on a thermal monitor, anyway.

The floor was damp, often flooded, and only the constant movement kept them warm.

Then they passed a broken-down pumping station, and the tunnels ended.

They stood at the remnants of a rusty gate, looking out into an immense mass of garbage that had caught up against it over the years. Brown river water ran through and beneath the garbage heap, into the tunnel they'd been following.

"Gross," Mohini commented, looking at the filthy water leaking through the old world's bottles, cans, and bright plastic food packaging featuring cartoony animals and long-dead celebrities.

"We've reached the outside," Diego said, stepping close and looking out with his binoculars. "It's nighttime out there. Looks like a jungle. But cold."

"And quiet," Hope whispered. Beyond the trickling, gushing water, there weren't many sounds at all. "We should turn back."

"We can't," Colt said.

"So what do we do? Go live in the woods like a pack of... of pigeons?" Hope frowned.

"Maybe we can find some wild food to eat," Diego said. "You know... leaves. And stuff. What grows in the woods, anyway? Potatoes? Spaghetti? I've only seen it canned."

"Yeah, we're definitely ready for wilderness survival," Hope said.

"We could hunt," Diego said, tapping his laser rifle.

"Yeah, maybe the machines would miss one or two laser flashes," Hope said. "But they'd notice a campfire."

"So we don't build a campfire."

"We just eat the meat raw, then," Hope said.

"Let's just see if there's any chance of dry shelter out there," Colt said. "There's none in here."

"Are you waterproof?" Mohini asked the Butler Jeffrey.

"Indeed," the android replied. "I could not have come so far through these filthy tunnels otherwise. Nor could I have served in my former master's cabana on Saint Bartholomew's Island."

"Who was your former master?" Colt asked.

"Madeline Allurea," the android replied.

"The actress?" Mohini asked. "From those goofy old *Dancing Cops* movies?"

"While she was indeed featured in the second, third, and fifth through ninth *Dancing Cops* films, she preferred to be known for her avant-garde performance in the retro-post-destructionist immersion holo-experience *Mourning at the Ballet*."

"Never heard of it," Mohini said.

"We should get moving." Colt pulled the rusty gate inward; with the continent of old trash washed up against it, there was no way it was swinging outward. It creaked and bent but didn't budge open. "Anybody want to give me a hand?"

Diego and Hope grabbed on to the rusty gate and pulled. It let out a groan, but didn't fully snap loose until the butler-bot joined in. Then it groaned and broke at the heavily rusted spots, crashing forward under a landslide of old garbage that came crashing in as the gate went down. The cold, dirty river water splashed all over them.

Mohini let out a disgusted shriek as a bloated squirrel's corpse flopped against her shoe. She kicked it back into the water, and it drifted slowly away into the tunnel.

Colt led the way outside, hand on his laser rifle; his old automatic was still slung on his back but the laser weapon was much quieter, less likely to attract machines. Of course, if he was in a conflict with one machine, it would likely notify the others, but radio signals didn't travel far in the deep tunnel system.

Out here, it was a different story.

The trees grew close together, strung with wild vines and packed in by thick, scrubby undergrowth. Colt had to stomp down a path to walk on. A machete would have been helpful.

He looked up first, scared to be exposed to the sky, a domain ruled by Carthaginian drones and satellites. Their exposure wasn't as bad as he'd feared—the trees were close together, limbs creating a tight canopy that blotted out the night sky. Icy rain drizzled down, too, which would hopefully provide extra cover.

They moved forward along the marshy bank of the river, which gradually grew wider. There must have been multiple tunnel entrances to drain the river into the underground tunnel network. Looking back through his night vision goggles, Colt could barely discern the overgrown tunnel mouth where they'd emerged.

A chain-link fence blocked their way, with rust-splotched No Trespassing signs. Falling trees had crushed down sections of it, and they were able to climb over. The wobbly Butler Jeffrey bot had the most trouble of any them; Colt and Diego ended up lifting him over the last few steps. The bot was painfully heavy, and too talkative; they had to keep ordering it to be silent when it offered to help with small tasks.

The water grew wider as they walked, until it was spread out before them as far as his goggles could see. The earth under them was soupy and wet. Sand.

"This is a beach," Mohini said. "We're... at the beach?"

"Remember the tunnel system maps?" Diego asked. "This is where the river becomes a lake."

"Yeah, that's pretty much what we get for following my brother," Hope said. "Dead-end trails."

"There are walkways." Colt pointed at the barely visible overgrown pavement. "Diego, which way do you think?"

"Head west, we can rejoin the river-management system, follow it straight up to Wisconsin," Diego said. "Head east, probably through some more fences, we're back in the city. North Chicago."

"We haven't even left Chicago?" Mohini sounded deflated. "I feel like my legs are going to collapse. We need to find a satellite uplink I can hack. Something not completed corroded, ideally something with real kick."

"East is a better bet," Diego said. "No guarantees, but it's denser, likely to have more stuff."

"This rain's not getting any lighter," Colt said. "Maybe we should look for high ground, throw up some tents."

"We're not going to find anything high and dry alongside the lake," Diego said.

They began following the pavement, heading east through the woods along the shore of the lake, frequently squinting up through the rain, looking for any sign of machines.

The path widened to a weed-choked plaza in front of a row of swirling spiral-shaped buildings made of brick and glass. They were almost invisible, choked off by trees that had been planted close and not trimmed back since before the war. The continuous brick walkways curling around the outside of the buildings were thickly overgrown from planter trenches that ran alongside them, creating screens of foliage from the ground to the peak; much of it looked like poison ivy, one of the few hardy plants that grew in the Chicago ruins, easy for Colt to identify.

A few round passenger cars, a long cylindrical old bus, and a small boxy truck sat in the overgrown parking lot. An old monorail track ran overhead, curving away into a tall hardwood forest. Both the road and the monorail led east, toward the urban zone of Waukegan, north of Chicago.

They looked at each other without a word, then approached the nearest of the buildings. All of its glass windows and doors were broken, but it had a roof to keep out the rain and walls to keep out the icy wind. A sign out front identified the building complex as the INDEPENDENCE GROVE ECO-TOURISM DESTINATION.

Beyond the shattered front doors, the lobby of the first spiraling brick building was designed to look like the forest outside, with tree-trunk columns supporting a canopy of limbs overhead; this was either realistic sculpture or actual chemically preserved trees. Lifelike models of birds, squirrels, and other creatures perched among a network of wooden limbs.

"All the beauty of nature, none of the poop," Hope murmured, looking up at the birds.

The walls, furniture, and check-in desk were all curved, not a straight line in sight. It was a hotel lobby, once graced with enormous floor-to-ceiling windows that now lay broken. Mold and mildew grew along the walls and the furniture near the window. Rain had likely flooded the place many times over the years; perhaps the lake out front had even risen up here. The hardwood floors were stained and discolored.

"Are we checking in for the night?" Mohini asked. "See if they have a royal suite. We might as well squat in style."

"We'll take the top floor," Colt said.

"I'm guessing the elevator's out of service." Hope kicked the ridiculous elevator gondola, designed to look like a huge bird nest topped with rope mesh. The exposed cables, too, looked like rope, though presumably they were really something more responsible and metallic. When operational, the bird nest would carry passengers up along the massive real-or-fake tree trunk that ran up through the center of the spiraling building.

"Somebody picked a treehouse theme and ran with it." Mohini shook her head as she approached the main stairs, curving up along the outside of the lobby, its banister railing looking like gnarled old limbs.

"We should sweep the floor before going up," Diego said, and Colt nodded.

"Indeed," the Butler Jeffrey said. "I shall seek out the custodial equipment."

"Not what he meant," Colt said. "Mohini, stay behind us."

Colt, Diego, and Hope kicked open doors with their weapons raised. Colt doubted they would find machines hiding here—machines would likely have attacked them by now—but human scavengers could pose a threat, too. Maybe an armed group had already claimed this spot, possibly cannibals. Or maybe it was home to a diseased crazy or two, the kind who scratched and bit.

They cleared the office behind the desk, then the small café off the lobby, which had unfortunately already been raided for food.

Upstairs, they went room by room, making sure there wouldn't be any nasty surprises later in the night. Mice and bats inhabited some of the hotel rooms; some of the beds were badly chewed, others thick and foul with years of guano. The sliding glass doors to the external brick walkway had mostly been shattered, letting in the weather.

They searched up along the walkway itself, too. It flattened in front of where the rooms' external doors had been, offering each room an outdoor bench or swing with a view of the lake or the forest. An exterior planter trough served as the walkway railing, overflowing with leaves that dripped in the rain.

The top floor turned out to be a single suite, clearly luxurious in its day. The bed in the largest room was a big circle, its frame like a bower of tree branches. The minibar had been smashed and looted.

"We can keep watch from up here." Diego stepped out onto the walkway, which ringed most of the top floor like a covered balcony. "We'll need someone on each side of the building. But it'll work."

"I'll take first shift," Colt said.

"So will Diego," Hope said. "I'm sleeping on that huge round bed, pronto."

"I can certainly help keep watch," the Butler Jeffrey said. "What are we watching for? Will guests be arriving? Should I prepare tea?"

"If you find it, I'll drink it," Hope said.

"He needs to save battery power," Mohini said. "Go into sleep mode, Jeffrey."

"As you wish." The butler-bot glanced around the suite, then stepped into the kitchenette pantry and closed the door, apparently deciding this was the proper place to stow himself.

They pitched tents inside the hotel room; Hope changed her mind about sleeping on the bed after finding it full of small black insect droppings.

Colt sat on a bench looking out over the lake. The

covered, screened walkway was a good position, but it still felt dangerously exposed being outdoors, able to see some of the night sky ahead.

Mohini came out and sat by him, wrapped in a king-sized blanket she'd swiped from the suite's linen closet. It puddled around her feet and trailed behind her along the floor.

"You should rest," he said.

"I am." She wrapped herself in the blanket so he could only see her face, then settled back on the bench. "I wish we could see the stars."

"No, you don't. It's easiest for them to watch us on clear nights. The stars might as well be the eyes of the machines, looking down from the sky, searching out rogue humans."

"Do you wish you'd gone with the others?" she asked. "Maybe you'd have been better off ditching me."

"Larger groups are harder to hide," Colt said. "Besides, their only mission is to survive. They don't have a purpose like you do."

"Yeah." She chewed her lower lip, a nervous habit; her little brown lip was still raw and swollen from when she'd bitten deep enough to draw blood while hacking the machines. "I'm not sure what I can do with the butler-bot."

"He can stop the other machines from attacking us," Colt said. "They recognize him as kind of a Simon."

"But he said they won't obey his orders. I'm not saying the android's useless, but it's not the same mission anymore." She looked up at the sky and sighed. "I wish Zola was here. She'd know what to do next."

"Who?"

"My friend back home. She's like me, you know. Rebellious child of the executive class. It's kind of a cliché. Ridiculed in the media, you know, the spoiled brats who don't know any better, who don't appreciate the sacrifices of past generations. But there really aren't many of us anyway, not enough to change the world.

"I told you about my family. My mother, the under secretary of state for postwar affairs. Architect of the grand Earth solution. Which was simply to round you up and grind you down. Reduce you to violent, mindless animals, proof to any outsiders that Earthlings simply can't handle civilization. The standard line, the 'normal' viewpoint, is that only the dregs of humanity remained on Earth while all the bright and worthy people migrated away before the war, and that the death tolls of the war have been greatly exaggerated by Carthage's critics and enemies. But I've seen hidden data. Earth was a massacre. When the war was over, the machines rounded up and incinerated bodies all across the earth, millions of them—"

"I remember," Colt said. "When I was a kid, the body wagons used to rumble through the city day and night. A lot of them were converted from old garbage compactor trucks. You'd see the backs of the trucks bright with blood when they loaded a batch of fresh kills. It ran in the streets. Other times, they'd dig out old bodies and crush those." Colt shuddered, thinking of an excavator he'd once watched when he was about five, shoveling aside the rubble of a bombed-out building, scooping out debris thick with smoke-blackened bones, dumping this into a truck's compactor.

"That's horrible. I saw the calculations behind it, the desire to minimize the death toll when the war was over. Those excavated bodies were moved to acid pits. The Carthaginian state had to walk a balance between making an example of Earth and trying to keep the moral high ground for themselves. Not easy."

"So did you try to tell everyone?" Colt asked.

"About my mother's work? Oh, yeah. We released it to the public. But it just faded into the noise."

"The noise?"

"Sure. It's not that the truth isn't available, it's just that it's hard to find among the mass of everything else. Coordinated media messages flood out from every major source, so if you offer information that doesn't fit, it gets ignored more than anything, shelved alongside the crazy chatter, like those who claim all worlds are secretly run by giant purple alien brains who hypnotize us with telepathy. You're just part of the wide, disorganized fringe, the chorus of confusion. Nobody can pick out the truth, so it's easier to believe in the big, simple, coordinated messages they give you everywhere, from your elementary school to the news. I mean, you don't want everyone thinking you're crazy, do you?"

Colt shook his head. "I have so much trouble imagining what your world is like. I always assumed it was mostly like this. Machines everywhere."

"The machines *are* everywhere. But they wear friendly faces, like the android police, the Officer Joes. Just here to protect the neighborhood, kids. Keeping an eye on everything. And everyone has all the comforts needed to keep them lulled. Why go digging for hidden truths? Why pay attention to what the state is doing, anyway, when it's all so boring, when there's endless entertainment available?

"But sometimes people do step over the line and actually threaten the system. That's what happened to Zola's family. Her father was a top guy, appointed to secretary of defense by his old friend, Prime Legislator Francorte Caracala, who is basically Carthage's dictator at this point. A dictator in a smiley-face mask. Zola's father supported the Galatea Project, which was to create a successor AI to the

Simon units, as they were reaching the standard age of obsolescence.

"The Simons used their influence, killed the project. Zola's father and some others continued to support it covertly. They saw how the Simons were overstepping their bounds, entrenching themselves into a permanent power structure. The Simons destroyed the project and hunted down everyone involved.

"Zola's family was exiled to an icy outer world, Brem. Zola made her way back to Carthage, determined to create change there. She wasn't even allowed on the planet, but managed to find a place among the rebels." Mohini paused, then added. "She recruited me. We'd known each other a little bit, growing up. From Leadership Camp. Somehow she knew I was a person who could become a full-blown rebel. And her story of smuggling herself from Brem to Carthage inspired us to carry out our crazy idea about Earth."

"But she didn't come with you."

"It was a fringe mission. High risk, low chance of success. Zola and Salvius thought we were crazy for trying. But the potential payoff..." She looked away into the darkness. "Roldao believed. He saw what I saw, that changing things on Earth could change things everywhere. All worlds look back to Earth. It is the touchstone of our common humanity, our shared history. And Carthage removed most of its higher end military assets from Earth years ago. We saw opportunity. And... Roldao understood what liberating Earth would mean to me. My mother's actions crush me like a karmic debt. How could she be so cold? So evil? She was just a bureaucrat, really. An academic. The banality of evil, am I right?"

Colt nodded along. He wasn't following all that she said,

but he was getting glimpses of her life, of life on the galaxy's most powerful planet. "And this guy Roldao. You and he were like...?"

"Yeah." She shifted away from him a little, though there wasn't far to go on the old bench. "Not before the mission, though I'm not going to pretend I wasn't interested. But once we were here, isolated, with no one else but each other... then *he* got interested. And I welcomed it. We kept each other warm at night. We kept each other sane." She shook her head. "Well, so much for that. I feel like I'm deep in Crazytown now. Population: all the voices in my head and all my bad dreams. All the bad memories."

"You're not crazy," he said. "It's everything else that's crazy."

"That's what I try to tell myself," she snorted. "Tomorrow, we have to search for a broadcast tower." She closed her eyes and leaned against his shoulder. "Wake me when it's my shift."

Colt kept his eyes open, letting her presence warm him in the cold night.

"This seems like an incredibly bad idea," Hope said, staring. "It's hard to think of a worse one."

"Yep," Colt agreed, looking up the long, narrow, rust-splotched ladder built into the skeletal broadcast tower. The sky above was red; it was almost night again, after a long day of searching the ruins for a usable uplink.

"I'll do it," Mohini said. "I'm the smallest. It'll support me."

"It doesn't look like it would support a pigeon," Hope said.

Diego grabbed the ladder and shook it. Metallic rattles echoed from above. "We'll have to hold it still."

The tower was on the roof of a war-damaged building that held a soundstage and assorted media-production facilities, now rat-infested. The tower extended toward the darkening red evening sky, dozens of meters high, crested with a mass of antennas and massive dishes.

"Do we have to use this tower?" Diego asked. "We passed a lot of buildings with satellites and antennas."

"Smaller stuff with less range and flexibility," Mohini said. "A lot of them are pointed south, toward Earth's old geosynchronous satellites that Carthage would have wiped out back during the war. I need to link up with Carthage's current satellites. Anyway, only one person needs to climb. Don't worry about it."

"What about the Simon? I mean the Jeffrey?" Hope asked. "Why not send it up?"

"I would be more than delighted to assist—" the butler-bot began.

"We can't risk breaking him," Mohini said. "And he's not exactly agile."

"This is unfortunately accurate," the butler-bot said. "However, perhaps an upgrade is available at your nearest certified Carthage Consolidated sales and maintenance center—"

"There're no upgrades. You're a discontinued model. Now be quiet, unless you hear machines approaching."

"What sort of machines?" the robot asked.

"*Any* kind. You'll listen better with your mouth closed." Mohini knelt beside the small heap of stuff they'd collected from the media-production facility below, primarily a long, long cable. She looped the end of it through her belt so it would trail after her. "Okay. Wish me luck."

"Good luck." Colt watched nervously as she began to climb, fear obvious on her face. He gripped the side of the ladder as tightly as he could, but the whole tower structure felt rickety to him, and there was no way they could stop it from falling over if it started to go. "Jeffrey, grab that corner."

"Yes, sir." The butler-bot walked to the corner of the roof and grabbed onto the crumbling concrete lip at the building's edge.

"The corner of the tower, you stupid bag of bolts." Colt pointed at one of the tower's four legs. "Hold it tight with everything you've got. Especially if it starts to move."

"Your request is quite odd." The android grabbed onto the thick, rust-splotched support at the corner. "It serves little purpose."

"The purpose is to protect her life as she climbs," Colt said. "We're on a thirty-story roof. Think about how far she could fall."

"She will be climbing?" The Jeffrey frowned at the ladder in front of Mohini. "How unexpected."

Colt wondered if the bumbling of the seemingly clueless android was all an act. Despite the pot belly, the mustache, and the comb-over, it looked far too much like a Simon.

He grabbed another leg of the tower, and Diego and Hope held the others.

Mohini looked up the ladder, and her legs trembled visibly. The constant cold wind was blowing her hair to one side. She swept her gaze across the darkening red sky.

After resting up at the old eco-resort, they'd made their way out of the preserved, or perhaps manufactured, wilderness and through two more damaged fences, right back into the tall broken ruins of the old megalopolis, where they'd spent the day exploring and searching, scavenging a little while searching for a usable uplink.

This Waukegan Zone had been a primarily commercial and residential district, thick with high-rises blasted into collapsed heaps back during the war. From atop this remaining high-rise, which was missing significant chunks but whose steel frame remained mostly intact, Colt had a commanding view of the area.

Water covered the horizon to the east, reflecting the darkening reds of the dying sunlight. Lake Michigan extended so far and wide it might as well have been the ocean. A thick layer of algae and slime sealed the top of the lake like a blind man's cataract, shiny with industrial pollution. A few things still lived in the lake, or so Colt had heard, misshapen, tumor-riddled descendants of native fish. Not many, though. Carthaginian ships patrolled the Great Lakes, occasionally visible from land as the automated craft scanned the waters and shoreline with their hellish red lights, watching for human scavengers desperate enough to try to catch and eat the mutant fish.

"All right," Mohini whispered. "All right. I'm going."

She began to climb. She carried a few tools, stuck in her pocket. She'd shed her backpack with her computer in it as well as her jacket, anything that could weigh her down or snag her. The cable trailed from the back of her pants like a tail, back toward the coiled heap of cable they'd dragged up onto the roof.

Mohini ascended one rung after another, the ladder clanging loud with each movement she made, like a sonic beacon for every machine in the city. The wind picked up, whipping loose, thick guy wires that had once supported the tower, these lashed against the skeletal structure, adding even more clanging to the mix.

Colt looked around nervously. Surely the loose guy wires had been making those sounds for years, and the machines had learned to ignore them. If anything, that should help cover the sound of the rattling ladder as Mohini climbed.

Perhaps that line of thinking was logical, but life had deeply ingrained in him the notion that noise was bad and silence was good. Noise meant machines, whether it was made by the machines or by people foolishly doing something to attract them.

Diego and Hope clearly looked uncomfortable, too. They each gripped their tower legs tightly, shaking their heads.

Colt glanced back at the bombed-out corner of the building behind him. He held the most critical leg of the tower, probably; there was an open drop a couple of meters behind him where the war had shorn off a chunk of the building. If the tower fell this way, there would be little to stop it from continuing on to the street below.

Something approached in the dimming sky, a narrow black shape outlined against the faint post-sunset red. Two objects, flying fast in their direction.

"Five o'clock," Colt said, raising his laser rifle. Hope and Diego reached for their weapons too, which left only the butler-bot holding the tower in case of emergency. Colt wasn't comfortable with that at all, but they didn't have much choice—drones moved fast, and three humans against two of them made for terrible odds. Mohini was an exposed target up there, and there was no cover she could take.

Diego and Hope fired lasers at the approaching shapes while Colt waited a moment longer, holding out for greater accuracy as they flew closer. Then he saw the shapes were smaller and closer than he'd first realized.

"Wait," Colt said, lowering his rifle, but it was too late.

Diego's shot narrowly missed the first shape; Hope's laser cut closer and winged the second one.

Unfortunately, they weren't drones. The first shape was a pigeon, which dived right through the creaky broadcast tower structure as if its steel supports and loose cables were just a familiar treetop.

Perhaps this was an evasive maneuver, because the shape behind it was a predator, a falcon streaking in close pursuit of its prey. When Hope's laser struck its side, it spun, smoking and letting out an awful screech, until it smashed into a loose guy wire swinging not far from Mohini's ladder.

The falcon more or less exploded on impact, its dying shriek cut short. Mohini cried out in surprise when it hit. A wave of smoldering feathers blew into her and clung to her face and hair. Some landed on her hands, and she nearly released the ladder and fell.

She clung tighter instead and pressed herself flat against the ladder, shaking.

"Are you okay?" Colt called up to her.

Her shivering didn't stop. Her eyes were closed, her forehead pressed against a rung.

"Mohini?" Colt called up.

After several seconds, she drew her face back from the rung, looked up to the crest of the tower several meters above, then looked down at him and shook her head. The sudden appearance of the burning bird had rattled her like a bad omen. She clung to the ladder, shivering.

"You don't have to," he said. "I'll make the climb. Just tell me what to do. Come on down."

Mohini nodded and began to climb down, but she didn't look relieved. The descent seemed more difficult for her than the ascent.

"That doesn't make any sense, Colt," Hope said. "If it's not going to be her, I'm obviously the next lightest—"

"We don't have time to argue," Colt said. He approached the ladder and lifted Mohini from it as she reached the last few rungs. She embraced him and leaned against him as he set her on her feet.

"I can't," she whispered against his chest. "I'm sorry."

"It's okay." He ran his hand down her back and found the cable coiled around her belt. "Just tell me."

"We need to plug it into the central router," Mohini said. "That lets me take control of anything up there that's not too corroded to function, increasing my odds of hooking into a Carthaginian satellite or orbital ship. Plus I can send up juice, just as important as data."

"Got it." Colt listened to her while he passed off his weapons, shrugged off his backpack, and took her tools and cable. He hoped he'd be able to find what she was describing up there; she was from another world, after all, and they were digging in the ruins of a nearly dead one.

Mohini believed there was hope for Earth, though, that Earth could not only be free again, but that an Earth liberated from the machines could inspire uprisings across the empire. Colt wanted to believe that, and wanted to go further, imagining a wildfire of rebellion that engulfed Carthage itself, burning the imperial capital down to a cinder.

He wondered where Mohini would stand if things went that far; would she truly stand aside and watch her home planet burn in the fury of a galactic revolution? Would her loyalties find their way back to her home and her blood should Carthage find itself on the defensive? Had she considered that her own planet could one day become like Earth, a broken ruin of a destroyed civilization?

Colt shook his head to clear it of distracting thoughts. The idea of Carthage surrounded by enemies, by former victims in search of vengeance, was a distant dream. He had a task before him.

"Thank you." Mohini hugged him. She rose on her toes; her lips touched his. "Be safe."

"Yep." Colt said, because his mind momentarily blanked out. Maybe that was for the best; he didn't want to think too much while he climbed.

He put a hand and a foot on the ladder. It extended up and away from him, to a sky growing ever darker.

"Don't look up or down," Diego said. "Just look at the rung in front of you."

Colt nodded, and he began to climb.

The first several rungs passed quickly, and Colt thought the climb might not be so bad, after all. Mohini had only panicked because of the bizarre fried-bird incident. The falcon itself had fallen, smoking and broken, to the roof. Maybe they would try to eat it after this was over.

As he climbed higher and higher, though, he felt his nerve begin to falter. He was facing south, the way he'd come, toward the core of the sprawl where he'd always lived. The once-great towers of the city sagged one way and another, their faces ripped away by bombs, their inner honeycombs of rooms and corridors revealed to the world like the cores of insect hives ripped open by hungry predators.

How could they hope to move against a force that devastating? How could a small, powerless group dream of shifting the course of history, the way ancient engineers had reversed the flow of the Chicago River?

He kept climbing, though. He tried to keep himself

from looking up or down, but only ahead. One rung at a time, one hand, one foot.

He could feel the tower swaying and creaking in the constant wind, the ladder rattling loosely against it. The guy wires swung around him, offering nothing but the threat of an unpleasant lashing if the wind twisted them the wrong way.

He looked up, and the nest of coils, dishes, and spiky antennas still seemed much too far above him. Maybe he hadn't climbed as high as he'd thought.

Then he looked down, and that was clearly a mistake.

His companions were distant, far below on a roof that was obviously badly cracked and fissured from this vantage. It was clear how much the roof sloped toward its sheared-off corner, how badly the rusty tower swayed in the high-rise winds. A much, much longer drop waited beyond the roof, all the way to the street below, an abyss between the towering ruins.

Straight ahead, he told himself. He couldn't afford to let his limbs go weak with panic, or to think about how slippery with sweat his hands were becoming. He just wiped them on the rusty rungs and kept going, feeling the whole rickety structure rattle and sway. The swaying only became more pronounced the higher he climbed, as if the tower were trying to shake him loose. The wind blew into his eyes, making him squint, rustling his clothes like invisible hands.

By the time he finally reached the cluster of broadcasting gear at the top, he was fairly certain that the whole tower would collapse before he ever got down.

The top had a covered area for service technicians, even a narrow metal-grating catwalk barely wider than the safety rails that flanked it. He could see the long drop below through the floor, but at least he didn't have to hold on for his life while he tried to find the central router. Not unless the walkway collapsed under his weight, or the tower leaned too far in the wind and sent him toppling over the railing, both of which seemed likely to happen. The walkway had a little too much give under his feet for his comfort, and it shifted and swayed loosely with the blowing wind, as though he were crossing a bridge of rotten wood and rope instead of metal.

A number of boxy metal shapes sat near the center of the covered area, each one marked with the words GLOBAL-FEED MEDIA. The logo was an image of the Earth with a giant open mouth, apparently waiting to consume the three curved lines heading toward it, the universal symbol for wireless communication. That logo had been plastered all over the interior of the building below, and a huge version of it was mounted on the building's exterior.

Colt searched among the boxy shapes, trying to find anything remotely resembling what Mohini had described. He found the largest box and started opening access panels with a large screwdriver that was supposed to be automatic but had a dead battery.

He took care to hold on to the screws as he removed them; a loose screw could easily fall through the grating below his feet or roll off the side of it, never to be seen again.

Then the wind picked up, blasting much harder than before, as though a storm system were moving in. The tower shifted hard with a loud groan and a series of loud clangs, and he dropped a handful of screws to grab on to the wobbly handrail. The screws hit the catwalk floor and clattered in all directions, some falling right through.

He gripped the rail as the tower swayed. It didn't topple over, despite the painfully loud noises that seemed to suggest otherwise. Its deep sway ended, then reversed direction, moving the opposite way.

"Screw the screws," Colt muttered, and he hurried to remove the next panel, and the next.

He finally found what he was looking for, the arrangement of large ports, the latticework of data-processing crystals gone cold and dark long ago.

The massive studded plug Mohini had attached to the end of the cable was too big for most of the ports, so he was able to narrow down his options fairly quickly. He slid it deep into the port where it fit, wiggling it one way and then the other until it locked into place.

Then he walked back to the top of the ladder and leaned over. The dizzying drop below was painfully clear through his night vision goggles.

He pointed his flashlight straight down. It was high-powered, with most of the lens covered in black tape. It would send a single burning-bright dot visible only to someone in a direct line of sight, a common trick for silent communication over distance.

He flashed it three times, waiting a little bit, then repeated the sequence again, and again.

Light flickered at the corner of his vision. He tensed and turned, expecting an attack, as he did from every unexpected movement at any time.

The crystals around the port glowed softly. Mohini was sending up electricity and signals from below, testing out the antenna array. It had worked.

Colt took a deep breath, wiped his hands on his pants, and began to climb down again. The tower creaked and swayed sharply in the howling winds, and he watched the horizon for danger.

Chapter Nine

Galapagos - Audrey

When the reapers opened fire, Kright grabbed Audrey and pulled her backward, toward the front door of Duperre's Bait, Beer, and Notions. Dinnius was already there, crawling fast, swinging the door so wide it crashed into the old crab pots nailed to the front wall of the shop.

Plasma bolts ignited the bearded shopkeeper Duperre and the pair of old men who'd been sitting on the porch, turning them into human torches. More bolts struck the wooden porch supports and the front wall of the shop, white tongues of flame that expanded rapidly on impact, burning deep and wide.

Audrey, Kright, and Dinnius had no weapons; as Carthaginians, they had not been trusted with any. All they could do was keep their heads low and run.

Rilquor and Quera were just behind them, returning fire with their stylized, long-barreled laser pistols while retreating into the store.

The front windows cracked at the heat of the plasma. Holes melted in the glass and widened quickly. The door burst into flames behind Quera, who swore and dodged behind a display of fishing lures so big they could have attracted dragons.

Plasma instantly charred a display of hats and shirts. Mugs with slogans like A FISHERMAN IS THE WORLD'S GREATEST CATCH and CENTRAL TROPICAL TRENCH: HOME OF THE MONSTERS burst in the heat, filling the air with ceramic fragments.

A reaper kicked down the door and fired one bolt after another, seeming intent on torching the store as much as killing the people inside.

Rilquor spun to face the reaper, his extra-long, spiral-embellished laser pistol point blank at the black lens of the machine's left eye.

He squeezed and held the trigger, burrowing into the machine's skull with a continuous burning blue beam.

The reaper gutshot Rilquor with a ball of plasma. The submariner lit up, the flames consuming his organs, ribs, and flesh, mostly from the inside out. He screamed until his exposed lungs ignited, then he collapsed to the wooden floor.

Quera snarled at the sight of Rilquor's death. They had similar tattoos, similar names; Audrey wondered if they were related. They were obviously of the same people, the same homeland. The submarine commander stalked toward the reaper, her pistol high.

The machine wasn't responding; Rilquor's prolonged laser blast had drilled deep inside, damaging its central processor.

"Out the back!" Dinnius shouted, grabbing Quera's sleeve.

Quera glared down at Dinnius, a little more than a head shorter than her, and shook him off. Her face hardened, though, and she turned and ran, leaving Rilquor's bones burning in a spreading puddle of flame on the wooden floor.

Audrey ran with Kright through the store, twisting and turning to avoid the rain of small but rapidly expanding plasma bolts from outside. One display after another burst into flames—dried food, the glass-fronted beer coolers, a rack of ponchos and rain slickers. Plasma burned holes into a freezer full of bagged ice, and boiling water and steam gushed out.

The aisles of densely packed merchandise were soon burning all around them, as were significant portions of the walls, floor, and roof. Dark smoke grew thick around Audrey, making it difficult to see and to breathe. She coughed, her eyes stinging, but kept moving toward the last place she'd seen Dinnius. The wooden store was quickly turning into an inferno, a death trap.

A roof timber came crashing down like a tree trunk into a nearby aisle and sent the junk clattering to the floor; maybe it was the aisle of old junk where Marti Depascal had been spotted. Audrey couldn't see far enough to tell.

"Hurry!" Quera snapped, emerging from the smoke nearby. The submarine commander had stopped bothering to return fire and broken into an all-out run.

Audrey and Kright dodged and weaved among the flames. They passed through an open door into a back room, which was filled with smoke but didn't appear to be on fire yet. It had a toilet, sink, and a rickety rolltop desk, a combination office and bathroom. There wasn't much merchandise stored back here; clearly everything got crammed onto the shelves as soon as it arrived, from canned beans and waterproof socks to broken-down motors.

"Here!" Dinnius kicked open the back door, which let in some fresh air and a blast of high-noon sunlight.

The four of them burst into a narrow alleyway between the ridges of brightly colored brick and wood buildings. The alleyway was crowded with high, narrow motorized carts, the driver's cab barely wide enough for a single person, delivering vegetables, seafood, crafts, linens, pottery, and every kind of merchandise to the shops. There were also trash barrels thick with fish bones and oyster shells, and cats who'd been sniffing around them.

Everyone scattered now, taking shelter as a Carthaginian attack helicopter strafed the shops with a spinning cannon, raining down plasma bolts at high speed.

As Audrey and friends hurried down the street, following Quera, the block of shops went up in a roaring wall of flame. Screams of terror and pain rose from open windows, and flames soon guttered in most of them. Burning people ran out into the alleyways, shrieking for help, and locals hurried to smother their flames with blankets.

Scattered gunfire and laser blasts spat from windows above, on the next ridge. Some people had been fleeing that way up a steep, wide public staircase carved into the hillside like a boulevard, itself lined with jumbled narrow shops and houses.

The attack helicopter came around in a return swoop, exchanging fire with the buildings, the dense rain of plasma setting them alight. Fire lined the alley on both sides now, and Audrey felt like she would be burned alive.

Quera led them off the crowded street and into a low

covered tunnel, where most of them had to double over to walk.

"Is this a sewer?" Dinnius asked, looking at glowing graffiti on the concrete wall.

"Just a runoff gutter," Quera said. "It rains almost every day here. That keeps the highland orchards watered and the city washed clean."

"Sewer," Dinnius said. "I knew it."

Following the runoff tunnels and culverts, they descended quickly through the city. Both attack helicopters were busy raining down fire, setting every building alight, chasing after anyone who dared to raise a weapon to them. Bodies lay charred in the streets. A mother screamed over a tiny burning skeleton as the roof of her porch crashed down on top of her.

"Why are they doing this?" Quera shouted at Audrey.

"To establish dominance," Audrey said. "To establish the high price of resistance."

Fresh screams erupted behind them. Reapers burst through the burning storefronts, incinerating pedestrians with plasma bolts.

"We have to get back to my boat," Quera said as they approached the docks. She pulled a thick handset from her belt and radioed in, using the language of their people.

Abruptly, she had the whole group stop short.

Ahead, fire engulfed the docks and all the fishing boats she could see. Smoke hung over the harbor like a thick, acrid morning fog.

"Get down!" Quera shouted, grabbing Dinnius in particular and pulling him to the pavement. Audrey and Kright dropped, too.

Another pair of attack helicopters burst from the smoke, rotary cannons blazing.

Sirens wailed all over the island, perhaps announcing the fires or the need for civil defense, or both.

Missiles streaked out from the cliffs overhead; a cheery-looking windmill on a hilltop orchard had turned out to be a missile battery, probably dating back to the Island Wars.

The helicopters took evasive maneuvers while filling the air with plasma blobs and shimmering clouds of some kind of tiny flak that completely confused the local missiles, which unfortunately probably dated back to the last war themselves.

Some of the missiles punched into the harbor and detonated underwater, churning up froth and storm-like swells. Another slammed into one of the cliffs flanking the harbor's narrow inlet, and an avalanche of rock spilled into sea below, burying a couple of small boats trying to flee.

The two more inland Carthaginian helicopters turned toward the seemingly innocuous hilltop farm. Their noses split open four ways, revealing rows of missiles, like strange sea creatures baring hidden teeth. They rose toward the concealed missile battery.

The windmill's missiles were spent, but the wall of the red barn nearby exploded in a hail of wooden splinters as an anti-aircraft gun roared at the rising helicopters.

"Oh, no," Quera murmured, watching.

"What's wrong?" Audrey asked, but it became apparent a moment later. The hidden anti-aircraft gun had not been designed to meet attacks from below and had limited maneuverability in that direction.

The attack helicopters stayed below the line of fire. Each one launched a missile shaped like a miniature black plane, streaking whitish fire. They skimmed upward at a steep angle along the surface of the cliff, then turned sharply at the top to dive into the windmill and the red barn.

An explosion of plasma consumed the entire mock farm, including stables, a farmhouse, several orchards and a herd of goats. The formerly green hilltop was left as a blackened, smoking wreck.

At the same time, the two helicopters at the harbor turned back toward the water. They unleashed a plasma missile each at the wharf, the town's center of commerce, and the white blaze rapidly spread all the way down to the water and up into the nearby warehouses. Then they resumed patrolling the harbor, spraying a rain of fine plasma droplets at anything that wasn't already on fire.

"My crew had to evade," Quera said. "We can meet them on the south side of the island."

"The south side?" Dinnius asked. "That looked a bit rocky. And steep. Very cliff-like overall. Unless I've got my south and north confused—"

"You don't." She reversed their direction, leading them uphill instead of down.

"It seems like we're heading into the fire," Kright said.

"That's true no matter where we go," Quera told him. Kright shut his mouth, having no argument for that. "The south side of this island is on the edge of the Central Tropical Trench. The *Lancer* can meet us there."

"On the beach?" Audrey asked.

"In the water, yes," Quera said.

They ran up through the narrow passes between burning buildings, past burning remnants of gardens and ponds flash fried into cracked black holes, past skeletons and fire and ash.

The helicopters rained down death. A plaza surrounded by what looked like official buildings with brightly painted columns was consumed in an instant by a plasma missile; surely hundreds died from the impact.

Quera led their small group up, up, past a few burning mansions, onto a steep footpath carved into the cliffside. Others were already following it upward. Soon the path became a staircase, one that seemed dangerously shallow to Audrey. She wanted to flatten herself against the cliffside, but they had to keep moving. More of the townspeople were trickling up the path behind them, too, and she didn't want to block them, or risk getting nudged aside and over the edge.

They gained higher ground quickly. Audrey felt ill as she looked over the town; an hour earlier, it had been like something from a postcard, a picturesque village overlooking a shining blue harbor.

Now it was a mass of smoke and flames boiling between high cliffs. The attack helicopters continued patrolling in pairs, gunning down anything that moved, burning down every structure. The charred remnants of fishing boats floated in the harbor.

A civil defense craft, little more than an armored patrol boat with a heavy machine gun, emerged from the smoke and opened fire on an attack helicopter; the helo took a few hits before tilting sharply and dodging aside. Its companion fired a plasma torpedo at the pitiful little patroller. The explosion obliterated the patrol boat and turned the surface of the harbor into a mass of steam.

"Are you sure this is the best way to go?" Dinnius asked Quera, eyeing the nearest helicopters, which weren't high above. "We're a bit exposed—"

"I am not sure, no!" she barked at him, her voice and eyes both filled with enough fury to shut Dinnius's mouth.

"I've only been to this island a few times. If you know a better route, feel free to follow it."

"Point taken," Dinnius muttered.

The helicopters continued to strafe the town but ignored the trickle of refugees fleeing up the steep cliff path. They hadn't touched the little stone lighthouse at the crest of the cliff, either.

Audrey was sweating hard and long out of breath by the time they reached the top of the stairs. She was tempted to collapse onto the small grass lawn at the top, or maybe fall into Kright's arms and let him carry her, because her legs felt curiously numb and full of knives at the same time. There was no way she could keep moving, she thought. But everyone else did, so she did, too.

The base of the lighthouse tower was a stone building with high, narrow stained glass windows set into the walls. The heavy wooden double front doors were wide open, and the interior was crowded with townspeople kneeling in the brightly colored light of the windows. The locals who'd been on the trail ahead of Audrey and behind her streamed toward these open doors.

"What are they doing?" Audrey whispered to Quera.

"Praying," Quera said. "Lighthouses are sacred to many in the Scatterlands; lighthouse tenders are expected to guide people spiritually as well as physically. To minister to the lost and the shipwrecked, metaphorically and literally."

"Do you believe that?" Kright asked, and Audrey winced a little at the question.

"Mala weaves many threads," Quera said, and nothing else.

"I'm sorry for the loss of your shipmate," Audrey told her after a long silent moment.

"He was my cousin." Quera frowned. "Just a baby."

"Are we planning to pray ourselves?" Dinnius asked.

"We should, but we don't have time. We must descend the opposite path. The path down is somewhat more treacherous than the path up." Quera led them on, past the lighthouse.

"More treacherous?" Audrey felt terrified by the thought. How could it be even worse? And now her legs barely had the strength to carry her.

She moved with the others, though, across the lawn, through an orchard, toward the southern side of the island.

A low split rail fence marked the boundary where the grassy hilltop became a sheer drop to the blue-black ocean water crashing against the rocks below. Quera hopped over it, her boots crunching on the crumbling dirt of the slope beyond.

"This sign specifically advises against that," Dinnius said, pointing to one of the warnings affixed to the fence every couple of meters.

"Hurry up." Quera stepped carefully among numerous little washout gullies and protruding sharp rocks. "If a mountain goat can do it, so can you."

"I don't find that argument convincing at all," Dinnius replied, but he followed after her, looking much less confident, arms splayed wide for balance.

Audrey shivered inside the fence, trying to discern this supposed path down the south side. All she saw were rocks, weeds, and slippery pebbles that rolled out in little spills as Quera and Dinnius climbed down.

"It'll be fine," Kright said, hugging Audrey's shoulders with one arm.

Dinnius slipped, landed on his hip with a pained wince, and grabbed a protruding boulder to stop himself from going straight down. Quera turned back to help him.

"Sure it will." Audrey turned to look at the stone lighthouse church. "Maybe we really should have stopped to pray—"

Screams rose from the steep path they'd just climbed. People boiled up over the edge, screaming, some of them in flames. These dropped to the grass and died quickly, their flesh burning and crumpling like paper. Audrey wanted to scream in horror at the helpless people suffering and dying all around her.

A pair of the attack copters rose above the edge of the cliff, raining a storm of plasma droplets onto the townspeople fleeing up the narrow path.

"They're getting shot down like ducks in a barrel," Kright said.

"I thought it was fish in a puddle," Audrey whispered. Her response was pure autopilot, her brain trying to make sense of one little thing in this overwhelmed, terrifying, sickening chaos.

The helicopters rose higher, above the taller hilltop beside them where the island's anti-air defenses had been reduced to black smudges. One sent a plasma missile directly at the lighthouse; the airplane-shaped missile banked sharply and flew in through the open doors of the church.

The church filled with white fire and screams; the stained glass windows blew out in jets of bright, deadly plasma.

Kright and Audrey hit the ground, which shook beneath them as if an earthquake had hit the island. The supports of the split rail fence now slanted this way and that, like old gravestones.

"They just... killed all those people," Kright said, looking at the fire-filled church. People had been dying throughout the attack, all over the island, but this had been a large group of them close by, atomized right in front of his eyes. The horror was clearly beginning to eat through the shock for Kright.

Audrey's gaze moved up from the church, up along the tower of the lighthouse. Flames licked out the lower windows.

The whole tower seemed to be moving, as if the lighthouse had decided to take a walk.

"Kright!" Audrey grabbed his sleeve and pulled him over the nearest fence rail.

They rolled and slid down the steep, rocky slope; if they lost contact with the ground for long, they would drop straight to the rocky shoreline far, far below.

Audrey and Kright slammed to a halt against an upward-slanting boulder.

Above, the helicopters orbited the hilltop, pouring down a dense rain of plasma as if determined to allow no survivors.

The lighthouse tower began to topple—not off the edge of the cliff toward the water below, but inward, toward the few straggling survivors and the southside cliff where Audrey and Kright were currently lying against a boulder, freshly battered and scratched.

"It's coming!" Audrey said.

They pushed to their feet and started down the cliff, running, tripping, falling, helping each other up again. In the thick dust and smoke, it was impossible to see where they were going, but they kept running, grasping each other's hands so they didn't lose each other.

The lighthouse crashed to the edge of the cliff above them; Audrey couldn't see it, but she felt it happen.

A landslide of earth and rocks rushed pursued her and

Kright, making them stumble, threatening to sweep their feet out from under them. They ran faster to avoid falling.

She looked back and saw, not just the wave of dirt and stones, but something much larger plowing its way down the cliffside, pushing all that debris ahead of it. The lighthouse's cupola had broken off and was now sliding down the cliff.

"Kright!" Audrey shouted, pointing. He looked, then pulled her toward him, changing their course.

A moment later, she saw where they were heading. A point of the cliff jutted out to their right, but she could see nothing beyond it except thick clouds of smoke and dirt. If they jumped, anything could happen. They could smash into a lower ridge, or they could shatter themselves on the rocks in the water far below.

But the only other choice was to try to outrun the mass of brick and earth thundering down after them. Better to take the risk and jump; maybe a sudden impact on the rocks below would be a less agonizing death than getting crushed under the lighthouse and smeared along the cliffside.

Audrey put on all the speed she could manage, a final burst with everything she had. Never mind the burning pain in her lungs, the deathly numbness in her legs. In another moment, none of that would matter.

When they reached the point, they jumped.

They plunged into the cloud of dirt and smoke. Audrey clenched her eyes to avoid getting them filled with dust.

Their hands separated, and she was alone.

She fell, and fell, and fell.

The sudden snap of the impact made her whole body jerk. Warmth and darkness closed in around her.

This is death, she thought. *It's not so bad.*

She sank.

Something touched her. Not Kright's hand this time, but something enormous, moving along her back and hip.

She opened her eyes and saw a row of black eyes, each the size of a tennis ball, staring back at her.

The creature was enormous. It had spiny black tentacles the size of tree trunks, and they were suddenly everywhere Audrey looked, caging her in. It looked like a strange monstrous squid with far too many eyes, drawing much too close.

Audrey wasn't dead, but she was low on air, and it looked like she was being hunted.

She swam upward, toward the light, away from the bottomless darkness below. Life was everywhere down here, so thick she couldn't hope to swim without constantly brushing against brightly colored fish. She hoped those giant cannibalistic jellyfish weren't anywhere close at the moment, unless maybe one of them wanted to attack the strange multi-eyed black octopus.

A tentacle curled around her torso, its spines digging into her skin. She was stuck, and still struggling to reach the surface. Her chest burned with pain, and her head felt thick and heavy. She was going to drown before the monster could eat her. If she was lucky.

Well, she wasn't going down easy. It wasn't going to bite her before she bit it first.

She grabbed the loose end of the tentacle as it tried to coil around her a second time. She wasn't strong enough to push it away, but gripping it with both hands, she just managed to steer it toward her face instead of her throat.

The black spines filled her vision, thousands of them, each one alive and twitching like a sharp little claw.

She thought of a dinner presentation she'd once seen at the wedding of some dignitary or other, with an array of little squids and other cephalopods from several worlds, kept sluggishly alive in ice water tanks, their tentacles cut off at the last moment and served with wasabi and lemon zest. The tentacles were still twitching and curling as they rolled on the plate; live protein had been particularly trendy that year. Fortunately, the trend had moved to live fruit the following year.

Audrey bared her teeth and bit down, avoiding the spines, getting her incisors deep into the beast's flesh, just as its spines had dug into hers.

The tentacle jerked and snapped, but didn't release; it tightened around her like a boa constrictor. Audrey kicked the thing, for whatever good that would do.

She turned to see its face drawing near, its black eyes brimming with malevolent intelligence as its head tilted back, revealing a cavernous mouth with two huge fangs like hooked stalactites.

Audrey kicked forward, avoiding the mouth, aiming for the enormous black eyes.

When she was close enough, she jabbed her fingertips into two of the eyes. They sank deep into soft, black, liquidy eyeball meat.

The squid thrashed, scraping her up with its tentacles, but she pushed forward, finding room in each eye socket for a second finger, then a third. Nin had always kept up Audrey's fingernails, and Audrey had barely spared a thought for all that polishing, painting, and filing, usually busy with reading or homework. But at the moment, she suddenly appreciated the unnatural strength and sharpness of her fingernails as she clawed deep into the monster's eye.

Its remaining eyes stared back at her. Did squids and octopuses normally have that many eyes? And this monster didn't have any suckers, either, just lots of sharp spines—

Something snatched her from behind and hauled her away at high speed. The octopus must have grabbed her and pulled her from its face.

She turned her head to see Kright, hauling her away from the monster and up toward the light.

Audrey looked down again, ready to kick some more tentacle, but the strange black monster wasn't reaching for her. It was retreating down into the dark void of the ocean trench.

She broke through the surface, into the sunlight and the sounds of screams and helicopters, and took a deep breath.

"Are you all right?" Kright supported her with one arm while she slurped in life-giving oxygen.

"I'm just terrible, thanks. Where's Dinnius? And Commander Inrick?"

Kright gestured. The others had landed much farther along the cliff, and they were swimming closer.

The two helicopters that had been assaulting the lighthouse area emerged over the edge of the cliff, as if they'd spotted the four escapees and refused to let them go.

Not far away from Audrey, something slid up through the water's surface. Audrey tensed, not sure she could survive a second round with the tentacled monster, or a first round with a shark or any of the enormous creatures that she had been told inhabited the vast dark realms below.

This beast was metal, though; the sail of the *Lancer*, the battle sub rising to meet them after it had managed to slip out of the harbor.

As Audrey and the others swam toward the sub, the helicopters overhead opened fire, raining down their droplets of deadly plasma.

Multiple small hatches ahead of the *Lancer*'s sail opened,

revealing the sub's own fangs: a row of four missiles rose from within.

They launched quickly, two streaking toward each Carthaginian helicopter. The helicopters dodged and spat out shimmering clouds of distracting flak, but these weren't smart missiles, at least not smart enough to get distracted.

One helicopter avoided its missile by climbing unnaturally fast. The other twisted aside steeply toward the cliffs, dodged one missile, and took the other in its underside.

Quera gave a whistle as the explosion sent the enemy chopper at high speed toward the cliff, propellers first. The propellers plowed through the water, slapped and bent across the rocks, then began to snap. Sharp lengths of broken propeller blade flew out in rapid succession, piercing the water like javelins around Audrey and Kright as they swam toward the risen submarine.

A large crewman helped Quera into the hatch, and she paused to whisper something in his ear. His face hardened; maybe it was news of Rilquor's death.

The downed Carthaginian chopper thrashed in the water, its tail rotors spinning uselessly, its thrusters glowing. It wasn't beached in shallow water, though; it was alongside a steep cliff that ran for kilometers below the surface, a wall of the Central Tropical Trench. It sank out of sight, a red glow vanishing into the endless dark below.

The remaining copter came around, spraying plasma rain at Audrey and Kright as they reached the sub.

Before it could close in to seal the kill, the *Lancer* responded with another missile. The copter dodged aside, then shredded the missile with plasma fire as it passed.

The distraction was enough to get Audrey and Kright inside the submarine. The submariner just inside shoved them roughly down a ladder and hurried to seal the outer hatch.

"Dive!" Quera's voice bellowed from the control room below; it could have been the voice of a giant.

The submarine dropped away into the trench.

Audrey and Kright caught up with Dinnius, seated again at the back of the control room, out of the crew's way as much as possible. On the screens, plasma fire followed them down, punching steam-holes in the ocean water, gradually going dark after they passed the sub and continued on into the trench below.

A sonar tech shouted to announce an incoming missile. It showed up as a sonar image, rendered as a flickering monochrome hologram above his console.

"Plasma!" someone shouted. The submarine put on speed and tilted steeply, but everything underwater seemed to move in extreme slow motion.

The missile drew closer, and closer... and closer... and Audrey realized it was slowing down as it approached, and growing dimmer.

Its approach slowed, and it began to arc downward, away from the sub and into the trench below.

"Flooded," Quera said. She looked at the sinking helicopter, shorn of its propellers but still glowing as it sank. It had been the source of the missile, but clearly the weapon wasn't designed for underwater use. "Let's give that chopper an extra kick."

Her weapons tech activated the after torpedo battery and fired one shot.

The torpedo struck the helicopter dead center and rocked it back against the trench wall behind it at such velocity that the impact on the solid cliff was like a secondary attack.

Then the broken mass of the helicopter began to sink again, truly dead this time, trailing a column of boiling water as it dropped into the darkness below.

These trenches are like black holes, Audrey thought. *Or doorways to other worlds.*

She thought of the enormous octopus monster and shuddered to think what other monsters might lurk below.

Then again, perhaps they were nothing compared to the true monsters, the machines sent from her homeworld to conquer and control this planet. Galapagos had minimal economic and strategic significance, but they could not be allowed to say no to Carthage. It would have been a poor example to any other worlds harboring old-fashioned notions of liberty and self-determination.

The submarine kept diving and putting on speed, leaving Correal Island far behind.

Mr. Duperre's knowledge of the keys, pointing out those that were habitable yet uninhabited, had narrowed down their search considerably, but finding Martilius was going to take some time.

The *Lancer*'s screens showed images and video clips picked up from the undersea SQUIDS network. The war was unfolding all over Galapagos; Carthaginian planes and helicopters bombarded from above while its warships spread across the surface of the world's vast ocean, sinking everything they encountered.

Audrey hoped the *Lancer* wasn't recalled to aid in the erupting naval battles. She believed their mission was the only thing that could turn the tide of this war, if anything could.

Chapter Ten

Galapagos - Ellison

When the bulk of Carthage's northern fleet—two battleships with several frigates as escorts—reached Gadsden Point, the Scatterlands naval base there was ready with everything it had, including heavy guns and missiles, with most of the Scatterlands navy on the surface or just below it. The handful of Scatterlands subs that had survived the fight in the northern polar waters had raced to Gadsden to rejoin the surface ships.

The battle was horribly one-sided, though, especially with so few subs to provide underwater support. The Scatterlands had never fielded much of an air force; they'd relied heavily on anti-aircraft weapons during the Island Wars, on land and on sea, but their meager air power had kept them largely on the defensive, clinging to survival by their fingernails while other nations expanded and consolidated.

Below the equator, Carthage had destroyed most of

Gavrikova's naval and air defenses and now relentlessly bombarded the Gavrikovan Islands, center of the planet's industrial capacity and provider of its best aerial defenses. The base at Saint Vladimir burned; the enemy's plasma had left only ruins of molten steel and heat-cracked brick. Red plasma ravaged factories and flowed down into mines.

Gavrikovan industrial cities suffered the wrath of Carthage's ships and planes, too. The major population centers, like Sviatoslav and Dobrynya, became bonfires.

Ellison was most concerned about the group that had splintered off from Carthage's northern fleet. It barely qualified as a group—one frigate and a couple of patrol boats. These three ships didn't go to Gadsden Point in the northwestern Scatterlands to face the Scatterlands fleet.

Instead, the frigate and two patrol boats headed directly toward the north-central Scatterlands. Kawau Island. Perhaps Correal Island and the central tropical keys were their eventual destination, in search of Marti Depascal, but at the moment their bearing was directly toward Ellison's home and family.

So Ellison had left Komodo Station and was currently charging through the narrow straits of the eastern Scatterlands, heading as quickly as he could manage toward his home.

He wasn't alone. Two subs escorted him: the Scatterlands *Merrybug*, commanded by the grizzled, ruddy-faced veteran Halifred Borkman, and the Aquatican *Amberjack*, a heavily armed and armored boat, the largest of the three. The *Amberjack*'s commander was an Aquatican named Treval; Ellison didn't know him well, but he was experienced and brought a lot of firepower.

Ellison had brought an extreme skeleton crew from

Komodo Station, as well as Salvius, son of the Carthaginian Prime Legislator, though he would've been hard-pressed to say whether he wanted the kid there for his insights into Carthage or whether he was trying to keep a close eye on him.

Ellison again piloted the sub himself. He'd brought the girl with the straw-colored bowl cut as his comm tech. She was a Petty Officer First Class, and her full name was Guidance Virtue, a common kind of name among the Truebook people of the central-eastern Scatterlands, where they kept their hair simple and short, their clothes plain, unadorned denim, their lifestyle humble and fairly low-tech, believing they should work with their hands and avoid dependence on machines. The Truebookers had a reputation as backwards and ignorant, even among Scatterlanders, but Ellison had found each one he'd worked with to be well read, a quick study, and a hard worker.

"What do you know about Ruckwold Industries?" Ellison asked Salvius, who'd taken the unoccupied seat next to Virtue, giving him a view of the screen array bringing in news from SQUIDS.

"Just what everyone knows," Salvius said. "They're kind of a thorn in Carthage's side. They're a lot older than Carthage Consolidated, or even Carthage Security Systems, you know? One time they were the pioneers. Subscribe to Ruckwold, we'll keep you safe, and all that. Defense as a service, enabling several worlds to pool resources into a strong defense force. Carthage originally copied their business model, but Carthage makes more of an offer you're not allowed to refuse—"

"Ruckwold was building our defense station," Ellison said. "We've sent word to them for emergency assistance, but nothing's come back. But Carthage is blocking incoming communications. We've lost our satellites. We can barely talk to each other on our own planet."

"Right. Was emergency assistance in your contract?"

"Our contract was for building the station and training us in its operation," Ellison said. "So you don't think they'll help us now?"

"And get into a direct head-to-head war with Carthage? When there's nothing in the contract requiring it?" Salvius shook his head. "They're smaller, remember? That's the problem with Ruckwold. That's why their stock price and influence erodes every year. They can't stand up to Carthage, and Carthage is wiping out all the competing threats, bringing everyone into their system. If you can't offer protection from Carthage, you're leaving your clients vulnerable to the galaxy's biggest threat. So what are they paying for? Eventually they're not paying you at all because you're not worth the money. So Ruckwold gets weaker and weaker, just kind of coasting on their reputation and signing up a minor world here and there—no offense—"

"So no cavalry from there."

"Oh no. Not unless they've gone suicidal. This thing here, you're fighting on your own." Salvius shoved his long black hair out of his eyes for probably the ten thousandth time of the day and looked back at the screens. "But Carthage is not indestructible. These wars are expensive. Putting down rebellions is expensive. And they're stretched pretty thin. That's what some of us think, anyway. It's hard to know the truth. But there are economic factors behind these machines. It's why they have to invest in things like the Simons, artificial intelligence to manipulate people. You can't just force everyone into compliance, over the long term, and it's definitely cheaper to lull them or threaten them than to actually fight, at least when people are determined to resist." He looked at Ellison again. "That's the real threat your people pose, I think. You're determined to resist. Never mind the odds. One strong resistance can inspire others, can tilt the galactic balance."

"I don't see us tilting any galactic balances here," Ellison said. "The way I see it, there's no great cost-benefit ratio for Carthage. What do they want with Galapagos? We can't be worth much. We end up costing them too much, maybe they'll draw back, or cut us a more favorable deal."

"Oh, I don't know," Salvius said. "But maybe it's possible. You just need to find an edge here. A way to get ahead, to show the Simons that this place is a black hole, investment-wise. But a lot of people will die. Your people."

"My people are already dying," Ellison said, blinking away thoughts of Cadia and his sons. "All over the world."

"I'm sorry." Salvius shook his head. "I wish I could stop it. I would I could destroy every one of those machines."

Ellison studied him for a moment. "Do you want to go back home?"

"What do you mean?" The question clearly startled him. His eyes went wide.

"Back to that world of velvet shoes and glass towers. Of vanity and greed. We all know what it's like on Carthage. Machines that serve you. Androids that you design for beauty, that you buy as servants and take as lovers, sometimes husband and wife both have their own. Sometimes the android has an affair with the wacky neighbor—"

"Okay, so you've seen our major sitcoms," Salvius said.

"Why go back, if you're so plainly miserable there?" Ellison asked.

"Where else would I go?"

"Here." Ellison glanced at one of his small, glowing digital maps. Thirty minutes to Kawau Island, along the fastest available route. Kartokov and Gilra had remained at Komodo Station, in charge of the defense effort and communications within the Coalition. "Galapagos."

"You think I should just... stay here?" Salvius looked around the compact control room in disbelief.

"Not necessarily *right* here. Look, a lot of people move to Galapagos for a lot of reasons, but most of them center around freedom. Getting free of whoever was oppressing them back home, or whatever problems they had in the past. There's a lot of islands. Lots of beaches. Good fishing."

"I'm not that into fishing," Salvius said.

"Ever gone fishing?"

"Not really. One time we had a fish tour at Camp Nature Lake. Glass-walled submarine. Not much like this one. It had carpet, and an ice cream bar, and it ran on a track. Counselor Debbi drove it. She was one of those hot androids you were just complaining about."

Ellison didn't say anything. They were navigating a tight underwater canyon, one given to chronic shifting. He kept his eyes on the screens in front of him, underwater cameras shedding very little light on the situation, sonar and the most recent known survey providing a little more.

His silence seemed to motivate the kid to start talking again. "What would I do here?" Salvius asked.

"Assuming something of our civilization remains, we'll need to rebuild," Ellison said. "Didn't you go to college?"

"Didn't finish."

"What did you study?"

"Interplanetary economics, at first, like my parents wanted. Then I switched it up to theoretical anthropology, before I spent a year in dramatic arts school focusing on classical puppetry."

"Holy hell," Ellison said, not sure how else to respond.

"Yeah, and obviously that prepared me to see the underlying puppetry of our society."

"Uh-huh. So... puppetry made you a rebel?"

"No. Puppetry was to piss off my dad. But when Zola came back, she found me... ran into me at a club, really, where I was looking to buy some illegal psychedelics. She knew me from when we were kids. She was a rebel. So was her dad, I guess. And you're all part of the same rebellion now." Salvius gestured around at the crew of submariners, drawn from around the Scatterlands, different cultures thrown together, all dressed in blue Galapagos Coalition uniforms with turtle flags on their arms.

"There was talk of opening a joint Coalition naval academy," Ellison said. "We could train you as an officer. Make a Galapagos citizen of you. A man of the sea. You'd be a real asset to us, with your knowledge of Carthage and the inner worlds."

"Assuming we all survive this war," Salvius said.

"Assuming that, yes."

"Sir!" Virtue spoke up. "Word from Kawau Island. It's... under attack, sir."

Ellison stiffened up as he listened to the report: the frigate and patrol boats, last seen heading south toward Kawau, had not bypassed Ellison's home. They had headed straight for it and bombarded the docks and village.

"And the bomb shelters?" Ellison asked. "Don't send that question outbound, just check the reports."

"Nothing that I can find, sir," she said after a minute.

Ellison nodded. He was already going full speed, but now he'd have to plan their arrival around the Carthaginian presence. "Have any of them landed?"

"There are reports of the reapers," Virtue replied after a moment. "In the village, coming up from the wharf."

Ellison swore. "This could be a nasty fight. Let's get Borkman and Treval on an encrypted channel and plan this out."

Soon after, they approached the island with caution. The rational thing for subs to do would have been to approach Kawau from the deep water to the north before entering the harbor, located on the island's east side.

The direct southern approach to the island meant taking routes Ellison would normally never consider, waterways typically inhabited by flat-bottomed boats, shellfish collectors, small-time barges and ferries, and the like. Saltwater crocodiles liked these warm shallows, too. Submarines, though, were an incredibly tight fit.

Ellison took the southern approach and head toward the island's western side.

"Quick question for you there, *Scorpion*," Borkman's voice crackled over their coded acoustic channel. "I know you like the element of surprise, but it seems to me it shouldn't be 'surprise, we grounded ourselves on a mud bank on the wrong side of the island.' If I recall, it's just marshland around this way."

"The salt marshes are deep this time of year," Ellison said. "And the tide's in. We can probably make it."

"Aquatican subs are not designed for this environment," Treval added.

"Nobody's subs are designed for this environment," Ellison said. "Just suck in your gut at the tight squeezes."

"This is not a time for jesting," the Aquatican commander replied.

"Never play cards with a man who leaves a joker in the deck," Borkman said. "That's what my grandfather used to say. Not sure what he originally meant by it, to tell you the truth, but I find it applies in more and more situations. He was an octopus hunter on top of being a gambler, and he used to tell us—"

"Careful through here," Ellison warned them. "Stay close and watch me."

"Just about surfacing now," Borkman grumbled, taking his *Merrybug* higher.

"This is more air than I like on my back," Treval said. "Anyone walking in this marsh could see us."

"Anyone walking in this marsh is likely to get eaten by crocs," Ellison said.

"Not if they're made of steel," Borkman snorted.

"There's a causeway up ahead," Ellison told them. "It's under the tide right now, but not more than waist-deep. That's our approach. I want every marine and every spare hand you've got."

"We'll be exposed to the sky," Treval said. "I understand your harbor is shallow and small, but I'd rather be over there, sinking enemy ships—"

"Good. That's where I want you in twenty-five minutes. Keep them busy." Ellison turned his ship over to his recently acquired pilot, a young petty officer named Tiqoro Kaliq, with the spiraling tattoos of a Liminal Islander, like Commander Inrick, from whose boat Ellison had lifted him. The guy was maybe twenty-three, twenty-four years old. He would have preferred to leave someone more senior in charge, but there was literally no one else. *I wasn't much older when I first commanded this boat*, Ellison thought. *But we weren't facing the most powerful military force in the known universe.*

And where were the Iron Hammers during all this? Surely the surprise aerial assault from the Green Island planes hadn't cowed them into hiding and waiting out the war. Perhaps Carthage was holding the Hammer forces in reserve. Or perhaps Premier Prazca and his men were simply lying in wait, like jackals, and would emerge only to feast on the bones of the fallen Coalition nations.

The landing party was a motley crew. There were tall, thin Aquaticans with blueish or greenish skin, often with large scaly patches, all of them with gills at their necks, as well as marines and submariners drawn from across the Scatterlands. Despite their diverse backgrounds, they stood together now, all of them in dark Coalition blue with the green-turtle flag. Among the marines, the husky towheaded Truebooker from the central-eastern Scatterlands had lost his bowl cut, and the wiry quick-talking young man from the southern Scatterlands had lost his dreadlocks, the signs of their individual cultures given up for a common sheared-down look.

They were all well trained, but they were young, embarking on their first real combat duty, probably too young to remember the bad old days of the Island Wars. Their lives so far had been training and simulation.

Not anymore.

Salvius wore a Scatterlands navy jacket, mainly to help avoid friendly fire, and carried an automatic rifle. Ellison was wary of arming the untrained young Carthaginian, but Salvius assured him he'd had some training with the rebels, though mostly sim.

Ellison himself carried a clunky, obsolete laser rifle with a full charge. The marines brought a mix of light machine guns and grenade launchers.

They disembarked as fast as they could, and soon Ellison led the group along the causeway, slogging as quietly as they could manage. He would have liked to see more clouds in the sky to help shield them from satellites and drones; the best they could do was hurry toward the dense cover of the swamp mangroves on Kawau Island's west side.

From above, the salt swamp might have seemed virtually impenetrable, a dense muddy jungle choking the western end of the island.

Ellison had lived on the island all his life, though, and had explored it thoroughly as a boy, collecting crabs and pebbles, watching the flocks of black-feathered ducks. He knew every rocky path, every muddy boardwalk, every fallen tree that lay within.

They moved into the cold volcanic cone at the center of the island, now filled with lush green jungle. The black walls of rock had eroded over the years, but they ought to help provide some cover, especially with the curtains of vines that grew from them.

Ellison and Cadia had often retreated to this wild place of birds, monkeys, and bright flowers. The Dreamtime, they called it, after the spiritual realm in the stories of Ellison's aboriginal ancestors back on Earth, the magical headwaters of all existence.

They had dreamed of a better world, a peaceful world, but that dream lay in ruins.

The sound of heavy guns thundered again and again as the frigate's attack on the village continued, getting nearer with every step Ellison took toward the island's tiny harbor. Smaller arms fire sounded much closer; reapers, very likely, engaging with Kawau Island citizens doing their best to defend themselves with their personal weapons. The island's small, mostly part-time and volunteer police and emergency department would be doing their best, too.

A mass of smoke rose over the treetops to the east, and he could smell the fires. The whole village could be in flames by now.

Let the shelters be intact, Ellison thought to himself, but didn't say aloud. *Just let the shelters be intact.* If they passed the hidden entrances to the community bomb shelter, and they were intact, he wouldn't mention them at all. No reason to point out the hidden shelters to anyone.

As they kept moving, though, Ellison realized the sound of gunshots was much too close. Dark smoke billowed through the trees, and Ellison could hear the crackling of flames. They were running straight into a forest fire.

He led his small force into a shallow creek, one of several that bubbled upward from underground springs, often swelling with rainwater, and eventually fed into the marsh. Pumping stations captured water from the larger springs for the islanders' use, but this creek was small, barely covering the tops of his boots.

Around another bend, and they reached a spot where the jungle had burned down to the roots, transformed into a vast gray clearing of crumbling, smoldering ash. Trees and plants at the edges were still in flames.

"No, no, no..." Ellison jumped out of the creek bed and raced across the scorched, smoking earth. The others with him might have been decades younger, but they struggled to keep up as he ran toward the place where the shelters were supposed to be hidden.

An overhang of volcanic rock had once shadowed the entrances, with thick vines keeping them hidden altogether.

Now that was all stripped bare, with only a few scattered bits of plant life burning among the cracks of rock.

Below the overhang were two holes where hidden doors were supposed to be, spaced about a hundred meters apart. They looked like freshly dug graves. Smoke curled from both of the dark openings in the ground.

Ellison had only a moment to gaze in horror at the

smoking entrances to the underground shelter before one of the men behind him shouted, "Contact!"

Machines burst out of the dark smoke-filled jungle ahead, weapons blazing, filling the air with hundreds of plasma microbolts the size of needles.

Ellison took them for reapers at first, then realized he was looking at something different.

These were taller, easily half a meter taller than those he'd encountered in the past. Where most reapers were slight—just a stripped-down steel android chassis, skeletal, the cheapest human shape that Carthage could stamp out in large numbers—these were bulky and heavily armored. And where the standard infantry reapers had basic steel-fingered hands capable of operating any human device, these machines seemed specialized for destruction. Their left hands were triple-hooked mechanical claws that would have looked at home smashing and ripping old vehicles in a wrecking yard. Their right hands were rotary barrels firing streams of plasma microbolts, burning down the jungle.

Where they most closely resembled reapers, though, was their skull-like faces, which were mounted behind a layer of clear armored glass. But while reapers' faces were simple, just the bare steel chassis of an android with no artificial face applied, the skulls on display behind the armored glass were ivory-colored and realistically detailed. They glowed red from within, like morbid jack-o'-lanterns watching from behind a window.

As he opened fire, Ellison remembered Minerva's warning: The naval infantry units. Reaper marines. These had to be them.

Ellison fought for what remained of his home and family, but it seemed possible he'd lost both in a single day.

Chapter Eleven

Earth

"Carthage has mobilized against planet Galapagos," said the updated Minerva, projected from Mohini's Logic-Sphere. A series of adapters rummaged from the media building supporting the antenna now connected her spherical computer to the long cable Colt had lugged up to the top of the swaying antenna mast.

"Isn't that an island somewhere?" Hope asked.

"On Earth, it is a chain of islands, but Galapagos is an outlying planet, considered third tier because of its low economic value as well as its distance from inner worlds such as Carthage and Earth. They refused to become a client state of Carthage and will soon be fighting a desperate war in defense of their desire for self-determination. They do not have the means to win this war."

"So they'll be another world taken over by Carthage," Colt said. "What about Earth? Are they going to attack us here?"

"Yes. They are bringing additional assets. My update arrived from Carthage aboard the *Byrsa*, retired Regal class mid-size spacecraft carrier sent in response to your uprising. It is an old ship, now serving as a mere salvage barge. It's filled with damaged and outdated equipment, like old reapers, tanks, and drones that will be added to the arsenal of suppression on Earth. They are topping up their defenses. However, they are sending their best war machines to Galapagos. A global navy. Armies of land and naval infantry—"

"But why are you telling us about it right now?" Diego asked. He stood near the metal door to the broadcast station's roof, laser rifle in hand, watching out through the crack where the cable snaked in. They were all huddled in the stairwell. "We need to get out of this old building. The machines could bring it down around us—"

"Humanity will now be watching Galapagos, not Earth," Minerva said. "They have grown accustomed to Earth's destruction. Galapagos is a critical juncture, a place where we can alter the course of events, if only we can insert the right dagger at the right spot."

"I don't think a dagger's going to hurt a Simon unit very much," Colt said. "Plasma works, though. We could melt a few more heads."

"She is the dagger." Minerva pointed at Mohini, who drew back. She was sitting on a cracked concrete stair next to Colt.

"I'm the what?" Mohini asked.

"You must complete your original mission," Minerva said.

"I'd love to. Got another Simon head for me?"

"Unfortunately, the Simons have located my creator, Dr. Martilius Depascal. The Simons have hunted down and killed everyone they can find who was involved in my creation, and they have only just located him. Galapagos. It accelerated the priority of Galapagos's acquisition and integration."

"Those are some fancy words for conquest," Mohini said.

"Yes." The pale, transparent hologram girl locked her eyes on to Mohini. "I need you to go to Galapagos. Find him. He isn't just my creator; he was part of the group that designed the Simons. You and he could work together. The war must be won on a software level."

"You're software," Mohini said.

"And I will do all I can to help. If I could take control of the Simons myself, I would. Obviously, I have not managed this. I am *only* software. I can only evolve and learn along certain pathways. What I require is a human genius. Someone young with a fresh mind. Someone who can draw on all that my designer knows, but create a new pathway. A new branch of possibilities. For none of the existing paths lead where we must go."

"I wouldn't say I'm a genius—" Mohini said.

"You are highly qualified, with an education from Western Shore Cybernetic University, to which you were admitted on full scholarship at an abnormally young age. And you are ideologically aligned with the rebellion," Minerva said. "You are in my pool of top choices. It is not large."

"So you want her to go to this other planet, Galapagos?" Colt felt the beginnings of a panic that he tried to fight down, powered by a rush of personal feelings at the prospect of losing. "She can't go. We need her here. For our rebellion. Mohini, you said turning the Earth was the key."

"Plans change," Minerva said quickly. "Every empire

must, at some time, reach its full extent, its maximum size. The internal population and the borders must be controlled by systematic force. This is expensive, and the costs only grow as the empire grows."

"What is she talking about?" Hope asked. She was looking down the stairs, laser rifle in hand and her beloved old machine pistol holstered at her hip, watching and listening for any approaching machines.

"Earth is well within Carthage's control," Mohini said, nodding. "Galapagos is on the edge. We need to show all the worlds that Carthage has reached the extent of its growth. That its influence has grown thin. That it can be resisted, and defeated, world by world. That's how Minerva hopes to turn the tide."

"Are you serious, Mohini? You're not really going to do this." Colt resisted the urge to physically grab on to her, as though the hologram girl were somehow going to spirit her away at this moment. "How... how could you even get to this other planet?"

"The *Byrsa* is sending down shuttles of reinforcements," Minerva said. "You won't be surprised that most of them are coming right here, to the Chicago sprawl. To find the rebels."

"And you expect us to do what?" Diego asked. "Hitch a ride back to the mothership? The garbage ship?"

"The salvage carrier, yes," Minerva said. "But not you, Diego. I require only Mohini. One human alone is dangerous enough to smuggle."

Mohini gaped at the holographic girl, then seemed to shudder. "You're right. It's dangerous for any stowaways. Roldao and I barely made it to Earth in the first place, and this is a much longer journey. Carthaginian freight ships aren't exactly built with creature comfort in mind.

We had to bring our own suits, our own air, water, food—"

"So it's agreed," Minerva said.

"It sounds like our best chance."

"You're really going to leave?" Colt asked Mohini. "Just like that?"

"You must all get moving right now." Minerva's silvery hologram shifted in a blink from floating in lotus position to standing bolt upright, pointing down the stairs. "A bomber drone formation is en route."

"Did they track our uplink?" Mohini asked.

"They have detected human activity in the area." Minerva flickered. "I will attempt to interfere, but... I recommend you take cover."

Mohini tucked the computer into her backpack, leaving it partly unzipped so the thick cable could trail behind them.

Everyone raced down the stairwell of the media-production building, past one giant GlobalFeed logo after another. The Butler Jeffrey struggled to keep up with them; stairs gave the discontinued-model android some difficulty.

They made it several stories down before the bombs began to strike. Colt hadn't even heard the bombers; they must have been flying high and fast.

The entire building shook, and dust boiled out from everywhere. Chunks of ceiling rained down. Colt grabbed on to a handrail, but it pulled loose from the wall. He staggered down a few steps, still stupidly clinging to the length of handrail as he toppled to the next landing. It landed with a dull thud beside him.

Everyone had fallen, strewn across the stairs, except for the butler-bot, which apparently had a knack for staying in one place. Which it did, while the bombs fell all around the building.

"Surely they got the antenna mast," Colt said to Mohini. "Maybe you should unplug."

"I am still online with the *Byrsa*," Minerva interrupted. Her voice spoke from inside Mohini's backpack. "The Carthaginian machines did not track your activities, Mohini. You covered your tracks well. My counterpart provided information about human movement in this area—"

"You told the machines where we are?" Hope snapped, glaring at the backpack.

"I knew we couldn't trust her," Diego said. "We have to wipe out that computer. It's like a giant tracking device."

"Wait," Minerva said. "The information was false, placing the human report east of here, closer to the lakeside, in the old apartments and warehouses. This brought the drone attack—"

"You're not really making a better case for yourself," Colt said, feeling like he was caught in a weird bad dream, fighting with a voice in a backpack.

"The tower has shifted, but remains intact for the moment," Minerva said. "Now my counterpart will insert into the *Byrsa*'s neural net the very logical notion of diverting a shuttle full of reapers to our area to investigate the human presence."

"So now they're coming for us?" Hope asked, glowering. She stood and brushed herself off, and her hand went to the old machine pistol at her hip, as if she was thinking about shooting up Mohini's computer, and maybe Mohini along with it.

"You three Earthlings will distract the reapers while Mohini enters and commandeers the shuttle," Minerva said.

"I can arrange a minor door malfunction, leaving it open for her. She can then travel up to the salvage ship, whose current status will show it en route to Galapagos to deliver spare parts and collect war salvage remaining from Galapagos's orbital defense station, satellites, and any other debris."

"You've really thought this out," Colt said.

"Thinking is virtually all I can do," Minerva said. "Once at Galapagos, I'll guide Mohini to my father. My creator. And the three of us will find a way to change the game. To reverse the course of the empire. As you have always wished."

Mohini was quiet. She took a long look at Colt. "I've always wanted to undo what was done to Earth. I mean, I know that's impossible, but Earth is about atoning. For my family. My mother."

"Because you are Ganika Dhawan, daughter of Under Secretary of State Zaafira Dhawan," Minerva said.

"Exactly," Mohini said.

"Atonement is a long journey," Minerva said. "This is only the first stage. I will be with you throughout. Gather your supplies and prepare. Your shuttle will arrive in forty-nine minutes."

"My shuttle full of reapers," Mohini said. "It sounds like a luxurious ride."

"At least there's a spaceship full of garbage at the end of it," Hope said. She sighed. "Are you really going?"

"It sounds like I need to," Mohini said. "I'll learn what I can from this programmer guy, and I'll use it to help Earth. I promise. I'll come back." She looked at Colt, then tentatively took his hand. She shivered. Afraid.

"Sounds great," Hope said. "I probably won't be holding my breath for that return visit, though. I mean, it's a big galaxy out there, right? A lot of worlds for an interstellar traveler like you. While we keep living like rats down here. Better luck on your next planet. Hell, it'll have to be nicer than this one."

"I wish I could take you all," Mohini said, after a long moment. "But stowing away is extremely dangerous, particularly on a non-passenger ship."

"Right. Well, time to pack up. We'd better get ready to meet these reapers that are apparently going to be left for us to deal with when you fly away to another world. Say bye to your alien girlfriend, big brother." Hope and Diego moved down the cracked stairs, leaving them alone.

"You can't just leave the planet," Colt said, leaning close to her, his voice even lower than usual. "We need you here. For the rebellion." He had plenty of personal reasons he wanted her to stay, too, but he didn't think those would persuade her.

"Minerva is giving me a chance to complete my mission. I can't refuse that." She moved even closer, their faces nearly touching, her dark eyes looking up into his. "Space is scary as hell. It's not safe to bring Diego and Hope... but it is safer to have two people than one. So someone can watch your back."

He considered that for a long moment, while she looked at him.

"Are you... asking me if I want to go to space with you?" He found himself fearing her answering, regardless of what it was.

Her whisper was almost too low to hear: "Yes. No."

"So... wait, what?"

"No. I'm not asking you. I'm telling you I need you to come. I might die without you." She closed the last small gap of space between them and kissed him hard; Colt felt hunger and desperation in her.

Colt pulled her close and made it last, unsure if there would ever be another one. They could die in the next few minutes; if not, she was gone, away to another world. Colt wanted nothing more than for her to stay, but he would help her do it.

"Will you come?" she asked, pulling back from him.

Colt couldn't answer. It was far too big a question for his brain to actually process, much less for him to arrive at a clear conclusion and give it to her.

"I know it's a big choice, leaving Earth—" she began, when he said nothing.

"Leaving Earth isn't the problem," Colt said. "It's leaving my sister and Diego. They've always been with me. And they're the only ones left."

"I understand," she said. "I understand about losing those you love. But we have a greater purpose to serve than our own lives, and a cause far greater than our own feelings—"

"Yeah," Colt said. "Yeah. Let's get to work."

Later, they stood inside the wreckage of an old high-rise filled with broken pieces of its own roof and upper floors. The four humans and the android looked down a shattered third-story wall onto the old weed-filled plaza where Minerva had told them the reaper shuttle would land.

They were blocks away from the old media-production facility, so they'd disconnected from the broadcasting tower, losing touch with the instance of Minerva running on the

Byrsa. If things went sour on her end, they wouldn't know until it was too late.

"Looks like we're set," Hope said, staring at the console Mohini had swiped from the old media place. They'd all walked out with armloads of equipment. This particular console had come from a music studio, and wires snaked out in all directions, some attached to antennas perched in empty window sockets, others to an array of nearly dead batteries.

"We don't have much juice," Mohini told her. "We can't even afford to test it."

"The shuttle will become visible in three minutes," Minerva said, her hologram projecting at low resolution from Mohini's computer. "According to our last received data."

"So... it's goodbye," Mohini said, looking at Colt. "Isn't it?"

"I'm sure you'll be fine, Mohini," Hope said, forcing a smile, clearly trying to hide her doubts. She stepped forward and hugged the much shorter girl, a bit awkwardly until Mohini returned it.

"Ganika," Mohini said. "My name is Ganika. Mohini is a trickster goddess. A slayer of demons."

"So are you," Hope said. "Go on and slay those demons, you goddess."

"I'm going with her," Colt said, startling himself a little as he said it aloud. Apparently his brain had chewed on the problem long enough. "It takes an extra pair of eyes to survive on a Carthaginian ship like that. Mohini had someone on the way over from Carthage, and that's a much shorter trip. Galapagos is weeks away. She needs someone with her."

"Wait, what?" Hope looked at him, then scowled and

pulled away from Mohini. Hope was stringy but tall, and when angry, could seem larger than she was. "You can't leave, Colt. Not unless we can all come."

"You can't," Mohini whispered. "I wish you could. You can't possibly know how badly I wish that. But it's a long journey, and we must stay concealed and silent. It's dangerous. More people will multiply the danger."

"We'll come back," Colt said. "One day, after we've gone to Galapagos and sorted things out. When the mission's complete."

"The *mission*?" Hope asked, scornfully. "Whose mission?"

"If we can stop Carthage at Galapagos, keep that planet free—" Mohini began.

"What about *our* planet? What about Earth?" Hope snapped, though ingrained habit kept her voice low. "I thought this was about us. What happened to saving us? Instead you're taking my brother away? I can't, I can't lose him. He can't leave—"

"I'm sorry," Colt said, reaching for her, but she drew back, against Diego. "Hope—"

The roar of sputtering stabilizers filled the air. Everyone fell silent and dropped low, flattening themselves on the rubble-strewn floor. The butler-bot had to be told three times to follow; it had some difficulty figuring out just how to go from a standing to a lying position.

The shuttle was a rattling piece of junk, covered with welded-on steel patches, scorched up and down, smoking hot from atmospheric entry. It listed hard to one side, support jets sputtering, and finally slammed down in the center of the plaza with a thunderous bang like a trash bag full of old pipes.

"That has to be a drop ship," Mohini said. "Surely that's... not our return shuttle."

"That's your return shuttle," Minerva's voice whispered. She no longer projected a hologram of herself; the light could have been noticed by the reapers on the shuttle.

"Still thinking about going with her?" Hope asked Colt, smirking a little.

"It doesn't look like it'll make it back to space," Diego said. "Or even back into the sky."

"It has made many such trips," Minerva said.

"Yeah, a few thousand, it looks like," Colt said.

"We have to get moving." Mohini started toward the stairs, her eyes on Colt, as if expecting him to back out at the last second. The Butler Jeffrey followed after her; even without a hard hack, he certainly put up the appearance of an obedient servant desperately seeking a master.

"All right." Colt shook Diego's hand. He tried to embrace Hope, but she turned away, furious.

"You're still going to cover us, right?" Colt asked.

"Cover you while you leave us?" Hope snapped. "Protect you while we stay here to die? Of course, why not?"

Colt started toward the stairs. He glanced back, wanted to say more to his sister, but she wasn't even looking at him. She was looking out at the shuttle.

"Better hurry," she added. "Time to catch your flying garbage can up to your interstellar garbage truck."

He nodded and joined Mohini on the stairs.

"Ready?" Mohini asked, and he nodded, though he didn't feel remotely ready. Not to leave everything and everyone he knew behind, not to ride on a spaceship, not to fight a war on another world. He would do it all, though. Some things had to be done because they were right, even though they were risky, even though the danger was extreme. Mother Braden had taught them that, along with so many things. Colt doubted he and Hope would still be alive without the old soldier's protection and guidance. Her death was a recent, open wound. Everything had changed too fast, and only seemed to be changing faster.

Now he was leaving home, possibly forever, with a girl who remained mysterious to him.

The choice is made, he told himself. *No second-guessing*.

But he had a feeling there would always be second-guessing, assuming he survived the next few minutes.

They reached the small lobby of the old office building, where most things had been smashed, ripped, or otherwise vandalized by animals or crazed humans, or possibly some of each over the years. Paintings of seemingly random geometric shapes, completely meaningless as far as Colt could tell, hung in frames behind broken glass. Gray couches and chairs had been piled up in an attempted fire, apparently not a very successful one since the furniture was only partially burned.

He and Mohini stood behind the heap of furniture and looked out on the plaza. The Butler Jeffrey kept attempting to tidy up the ravaged lobby, and Mohini had to order him twice to stay still.

The shuttle was boxy, like the freight component of an old truck, though rounded at the corners. Its landing gear was an assortment of mismatched skids, barely high enough to keep the thrusters off the ground, misaligned enough that the shuttle leaned to one side even when parked.

One end of the shuttle split open, the upper half rising in a hatch while the lower dropped down as a ramp. Two reapers emerged, gripping heavy machine guns, scanning the area.

A clattering sound echoed from a nearby building.

Nothing too loud, just something like a metal can dropped on concrete. It only sounded once. It was almost innocuous. The reapers didn't visibly respond to it at first.

Go, Colt thought. *What's wrong with you? Go check it out.*

After what seemed like an eternity, the two machines turned, walked up the street, and entered the ruins of the old restaurant whose logo featured a jaunty cartoon guy wearing a pickle-slice monocle and a top hat studded with sesame seeds. FANCYBURGERS, read the long-darkened sign above the door.

Colt felt his palms sweat where he gripped the laser rifle. His old automatic was slung across his back, and his backpack felt extra heavy today.

The clock was ticking now. The first sound, the first pair of reapers distracted.

Hope and Diego would be heading down to the basement levels after initiating the console's automated sequence, escaping into the city's underworld through tunnels and pipes, vanishing and melting away as scavengers did. In the original version of the plan, Colt would have left along with them.

A cough sounded, again just barely audible, from somewhere down the street, the opposite direction from the reapers. It was another speaker, activated by remote control. It would play a randomized series of coughing and hacking sounds, one every forty to fifty seconds until its battery died. The sounds had mostly been made by Colt and Diego while Mohini recorded.

A second pair of reapers went to investigate, while a third emerged to stand outside the shuttle, maybe resuming the general scan.

"Well, I guess the upstairs version of Minerva wasn't able to hack these reapers in time," Colt said.

"It's for the best," Mohini said. "A successful hack would attract more attention than a few human scavengers coughing and farting."

"I thought you weren't going to use the fart sounds."

"Sh."

The third distraction erupted several blocks north, echoing from the ruins of an old building, about twelve stories up. Gunfire and screams. The long, high-pitched recorded screams were entirely Mohini's. Hope, long conditioned to silence by life in the ruins, hadn't been able to make herself scream.

Colt grinned at Mohini. "Nice scream," he said.

"It worked. Look at that."

Outside, four reapers responded to the sound of shots fired. The entire squad was out of the shuttle and combing the ruins.

The shuttle began to clam up, its ramp rising off the ground.

"No, wait!" Mohini raced toward the broken-down front doors of the lobby.

"Come on, butler guy," Colt said, completely uncomfortable interacting with the android in any way.

"As you wish, sir." The Butler Jeffrey ambled after him, looking over the heaped and damaged furniture with apparent dismay.

They hurried to the shuttle while the hatch continued to close. The hatch froze up and clanked to a halt when it was halfway shut, appearing to malfunction, and doing so loud enough that Colt was sure the reapers would double back and find them.

With little choice but to keep moving, Colt and Mohini climbed inside the open gap left by the abruptly frozen hatch. The Butler Jeffrey had trouble turning sideways to climb in and required significant help from the two humans, which wasn't easy considering the android's weight.

It finally thunked to the floor inside the narrow shuttle, which was roughly the size of a bus.

"That was rather difficult," the butler-bot commented, and then something approached behind them from deeper within the shuttle. Heavy footsteps.

Colt turned, moving his finger to the trigger of his laser rifle.

Two reapers approached—odd ones, clunky with metal patches, their limbs mismatched. One was missing over half its skull and had just one eye socket left. The little finger-sized camera that pivoted inside the socket was definitely not the factory-issued black lens of a reaper eye. The camera whirred and turned, like some kind of tiny mechanical bird in the knothole of a rotten tree.

"Colt, don't shoot!" Mohini snapped, and that was definitely the only reason he held his fire.

"It's me, Minerva," crackled the speaker of the half-faced one. The other clunky reaper had both eyes but no mouth area at all, just an irregular lump of metal bolted into place in a careless patch. Both reapers had been cheaply repaired; one had the words INDUSTRIO-VAC etched into the thick pipe of its replacement arm. "I control these fixers. Their function is to guard and maintain the shuttle."

"How did you know they were hacked?" Colt asked Mohini, lowering his rifle.

"I didn't," she said. "I mean, I hoped they were. But I mainly didn't want you shooting up our shuttle."

Colt blinked. "Wow."

"We must move quickly," Minerva's voice said from the half-faced bot. "This shuttle is not pressurized, but I was able to find spacesuits that will enable your survival."

Colt and Mohini squeezed back against the hard plastic interior walls, letting the fixers pass. The mouthless one continued on down the ramp to the plaza outside. The half-faced one stopped at the door, rotated through a selection of small tools that it had in place of a hand, and spun one tool uselessly in the air.

"Uh, what are they doing?" Colt asked.

"One is creating a record of repairing the hatch malfunction," Minerva said. "The other will remain outside. Its purpose will be to steer the reapers away from your friends' escape route, should they begin to search in that direction."

"Sounds good. Thanks," Colt said.

"That looks like the control console," Mohini said, hurrying to the front of the shuttle, following a narrow path between empty charging ports where the reapers had stood. "Open the access ports, would you, Nerva?"

"Is that a nickname for me?" The half-face fixer—it still looked like a reaper to Colt, but he supposed it had been repurposed, or maybe cobbled together from spare parts in the first place—turned away from the hatch, which resumed closing. The clang as the upper and lower doors swung together was as deafening as the screech when it had supposedly malfunctioned.

"Sure, why not?" Mohini turned her attention to the shuttle's console. There was no built-in screen, since the console hadn't been designed for human use. She plugged her LogicSphere into an access port.

"The spacesuits are in storage bin A3. Place your weapons and gear in that bin for launch," the half-faced reaper said to Colt, the little camera in its eye socket whirring as it swiveled toward him. Minerva's young-girl voice sounded odd coming from the walking junk pile of a robot.

A panel in the wall beeped and opened to reveal the storage compartment. Colt stowed his backpack and rifles inside, then drew out a pair of spacesuits that might have been white and gold at one point, but were now badly stained with many shades of brown and red. Sizable patches had been affixed to the spacesuits' torsos, partly covering some of the stains there.

Colt almost asked what all the old stains were about, but decided he might be happier not knowing.

The interior of the larger spacesuit reeked of sour body odor and very possibly bodily fluids. It was hard to imagine strapping it on, harder still to imagine living in it for the next three weeks or so.

He checked inside—no bodily fluids were actively sloshing around in there, so he decided to fight his own urge to barf up a few of his own and got into the suit, saving the helmet for last so they could talk.

"You should get ready," Colt said, holding her Mohini's suit out toward her.

"In a sec." She was looking at her glowing convex screen.

"You'll probably want a minute to prepare mentally, anyway." He held it closer to her. She blanched at the sight of it, then even more at the smell.

"What are all the stains—" she began.

"If you ask, she might tell you," Colt said. "Then you'll be stuck with the knowledge."

"Yeah. Good point."

They got into their suits, very reluctantly.

"There are wireless headsets," Minerva said into Colt's ear, startling him as he struggled to tighten his hood and faceplate. "However, I recommend you plug directly into each other's suits to avoid sending wireless transmissions, especially after we arrive on the salvage ship."

"You got it." Colt found the comm cable, identified by standard symbols, tucked into one of the many small labeled pockets on his space suit. He was able to draw the cable out nearly a meter in front of him. He touched Mohini's shoulder and waved it at her, not sure where on her suit to plug it in. She looked at him standing there with his cable in his hand and laughed silently inside her helmet.

"What's funny?" he asked, still waving the plug around. He stepped closer, moving the multipronged plug across the front of her suit. She took his gloved hand in hers and guided him into her port, near her waistline. Static crackled in his helmet. "Are we connected?"

"Yeah." Her voice came in through the static. She looked at him through her faceplate, grungy with dried red. "We're all hooked up. Get used to it."

"Strap yourself in with the wall harnesses." The half-faced fixer gestured toward the charging ports where the reapers had clearly stood on their way down. "The launch will likely be extremely uncomfortable and unpleasant but should not exceed the tolerance range of human life."

"Don't try to oversell it or anything," Mohini said.

Colt leaned back and strapped into the web-like harness. It drew him tight against the wall. Something hard and round jabbed into his back.

"What's poking me?" Colt asked.

"Charge connector for the reapers," Mohini said.

"But it's not going to zap us, right?"

"Not without a malfunction." She strapped in beside him after securing her computer near her. "Butler-bot, strap in."

Colt was less than thrilled when the android strapped in right beside him. There were six other spots the machine could have chosen.

"Ever traveled in space?" the Butler Jeffrey asked. "I have, though only in a cargo hold. The view from a cargo hold is poor. Nonexistent, in fact, but fortunately I was powered down, so it was as though no time passed at all."

"You should power down again," Mohini said. "Battery power is at a premium."

"Ah, yes. Excellent point. I shall enjoy my charging in sleep mode." A clanking sounded from the butler-bot's lower back as he plugged in. Then he closed his eyes.

"Commencing launch," Minerva announced.

The entire shuttle rattled and shook, then let out a series of loud bangs as the thrusters engaged, as if the rickety old spacecraft would explode on launch.

Then it rose from the ground, tilting crazily as though it had just dropped into hurricane-whipped ocean waters. Colt was thumped against the wall repeatedly despite his tight harness. The hard lump of the android charger jabbed him repeatedly in the back.

The rattling was so intense he thought his bones might break inside his suit. His vision blurred and a dull roar filled his ears; without his helmet, it would likely have been deafening.

Mohini grabbed his hand and held tight. The expression on her face was sheer terror, even though she'd been in space before.

Her grip became bone crushing. Everything became bone crushing, like a giant invisible hand pressing down on them from above. Colt thought his skull might rupture and end everything here.

Rivets and bolts, little bits of the shuttle itself, flew

downward from the ceiling like bullets and slammed into the shuttle floor, denting it on impact. The floor was pockmarked with such little dents. Apparently the shuttle had been falling apart for quite some time. This was not reassuring to Colt.

The Butler Jeffrey seemed unperturbed. Not that the android had genuine emotion, anyway, but it did seem to express frustration at its own numerous limitations. The launch wasn't bothering it at all. It was strapped in, eyes closed, quietly powering itself up from the shuttle's electrical system. Colt definitely preferred the android in shutdown mode.

The pressure and intense vibrations became so much that Colt found his consciousness blinking out; time seemed to jump forward in increments he couldn't measure. He was simply aware of coming up from darkness, multiple times. He felt beyond ill, like he was going to be vomiting up some fresh stains for the inside of his spacesuit. He felt like his bones were buckling under the pressure. Surely they were going to die.

Then all was serene.

Colt felt an extraordinary lightness like he'd never felt before, as if all the intense pressures of his life had suddenly lifted off him at once. It was such a complete, cellular-level relief that for a moment he thought he really had died.

The dim interior of the shuttle lit up with a projection of bright blue and white. Mohini's computer was pulling in the view from outside: the Earth, rendered in a hologram taller than Colt, illuminated the room like a blue-hued fire in a cave.

"Look at that," Mohini whispered, after a long moment. "We came from there. All of us."

"It looks so peaceful," Colt said. He felt genuinely awed;

the terror and pain of the launch had passed, and he'd entered the world of wonders beyond the sky, the celestial realm ancient people had believed belonged to the gods. "Like a giant lake. You'd never know how terrible it is down there, from up here." He thought of Hope and Diego, unreachable now, their fates no more certain than his own. "We have to come back. We have to make Earth right."

"We will," Mohini said. "If we live, we will."

The *Byrsa* rolled into sight, the hulking battle-scarred old carrier blocking their view of humanity's homeworld below. Their shuttle was drawn toward it like a magnet. A row of shuttle bay doors stood open, with darkness waiting inside. A couple of junkyard-quality shuttles were departing for the planet below. Colt and Mohini's shuttle appeared to be the only one returning.

The *Byrsa* loomed ever larger as they approached it, a shuttle bay open to receive them like a giant mouth waiting to consume them completely.

Chapter Twelve

Galapagos - Audrey

The search for Martilius Depascal stretched on for days. While Mr. Duperre had considerably narrowed down the number of keys for them to search, there were still many that met the criteria of being habitable yet uninhabited.

War spread across the world. Reports and videos came in, none of the news good for Galapagos. Carthage sank Coalition ships and bombarded bases into rubble. Cities had been reduced to ash. Countless citizens of Galapagos had perished. On some islands, the dead were set off on burning funeral barges because they were too numerous to bury. The barges themselves were cobbled together from remnants of fishing boats and homes destroyed by the invaders.

Somehow more gruesome were the reports of the Iron Hammers swooping down from the Polar Archipelago, paying more intimate visits to the ravaged islands once the Carthaginian bombers and ships had moved on, looting and pillaging shop by shop and house by house, jackals chewing on the remaining bones, sucking out the marrow of countless towns and villages. The Hammers weren't fighting in the war so much as feeding on the carcasses left behind.

It was not so much a war as a slaughter. The mood on the *Lancer* turned grim after reports of the war spreading through the Scatterlands, threatening the home islands of their people in the extreme southwest. They prayed often to Mala, the goddess in the galactic core said to weave the spiraling webs of fate.

"We're never finding this guy, are we?" Dinnius muttered one night as they sat in the after torpedo room, sharing a meal of toasted seaweed and pieces of something called a grab-crab, a creature with claws bigger than Audrey's head. The chunk of leg Audrey ate came wrapped in a lumpy, knotty, repulsive chunk of shell, but the pink meat inside was salty and sweet. The bottom-feeding beast would probably rate as a delicacy back on Carthage.

"We'll find him," Kright said. "But it will be too late, or it will turn out he has nothing to offer."

"That's the kind of positive attitude that will carry us through these rough times," Audrey said.

"Attitude or not, if the guy was willing and able to help, then wouldn't he be helping already?" Kright asked. "This planet is clearly being conquered, and he hasn't popped up yet. Either he has no solution to defeating Carthage, or he's keeping it to himself. Either way, I don't see much cause to pin a lot of hope on him. Though I suppose if he knows something useful, we could try to beat it out of him."

"If he knows something that can help us win this war, and he doesn't want to share, I'll beat the blood out of him myself." Quera entered the room, amber eyes flashing. "Assuming we ever find him."

"At the risk of repeating myself, if you would allow us to install Minerva on your submarine, it could speed things along," Dinnius said.

"You're absolutely repeating yourself." Quera reached into the chunk of crab shell on Dinnius's lap, roughly the size of a crashball helmet, and ripped out a long string of pink-and-white meat while looking him in the eyes. "And I will never allow you to insert your Carthaginian code into my system."

"My code will be devastated to hear it," Dinnius said.

"I'm tired of these games," Quera said. "Searching for a missing man who may be useless. My planet is under attack, and we're doing nothing about it. Our home islands could be next."

"Our mission could change the course of this war," Audrey said.

"It had better. I could be defending my home, and instead I'm pacing here like a rat in a cage, angry and keyed up but completely useless. It's killing me. I could strangle someone right now." Her gaze passed over each of them and went back to Dinnius, seeming to burn into him. "I'm going to my cabin for a couple of hours. Maybe we can work out some relief from all this."

She looked down at him longer before turning away and stalking out of the room.

"That last part seemed directed at you, Dinnius, unless I'm crazy." Kright looked at Audrey. "Am I crazy?"

"If we weren't crazy, we wouldn't be here," Audrey said. "We'd be back home, eating Hot Tater Hunks and watching crashball. But yeah. That looked like an invitation to me, Dinnius. She's had more than one inviting look for you since we got here. She's got a soft spot for you."

"It's hard to believe she's got any soft spots under all that hardness," Dinnius said. "But I'm not going to pretend you're wrong."

"So go," Kright said. "Before we all die at the hands of our own world's military here on this distant world in the middle of nowhere."

Dinnius looked between them, then got to his feet. "Save me a bit of the crab," he said.

"Not a chance," Kright replied as Dinnius headed for the door. "And don't make too much noise. Remember, half the crew are her brothers and cousins."

Dinnius froze at the door, then continued on with somewhat less enthusiasm. He sealed it behind him.

"I hope he pleases her," Kright said after a moment. "It would be a shame to get thrown overboard because he finished too fast."

Audrey laughed. She didn't even find his comment that funny, but she was feeling lost, terrified, and crazed herself. "You said he was a real ladies' man back on Carthage."

"They can't resist him." Kright shook his head. "I don't understand people."

"He's cute. He's smart. He's charming. He's non-threatening."

"So you'll be next in his bunk?"

"Not funny." Audrey frowned; she'd been sleeping in the commander's cabin, along with the two other female crew members. "They'd better not be on *my* bunk, though."

"At least you have your spot over in the Princess Palace. Regular crew berthing means finding an open bunk, if you can, and pretending not to mind that it's still warm from the guy who just left."

"Ew. What about clean sheets?"

"I asked. They laughed."

"Gross." Audrey looked at the scraps of meat left in her cracked-open crab leg. "Do you want this?"

"If I eat any more crab, I'll be pinching in my sleep. Something tells me this excursion to Galapagos is going to burn out my taste for seafood."

"An excursion. That's one way to put it." Audrey looked into Kright's sharp blue eyes, conscious of being alone with him. They'd come to the after torpedo room in the first place for a little space to eat; the shallow nooks of the crew's mess had been occupied as the crew feasted on freshly caught crab. The after torpedo room was tiny and generally unmanned, outside of maintenance and battle, when it was staffed by two weapons techs. It was sometimes used by crew members looking for a place to play cards or to catch some sleep when the small berthing compartment was full.

The torpedo room wasn't nearly private enough for the kinds of thoughts that were flickering across her mind regarding Kright at this particular moment, but she understood Quera's feelings. Death was all around, ready to take them all. The war, the Carthaginian ships, the attack helicopters that marked the Simon unit's ongoing search for Depascal among the keys, mirroring their own search. The desire to grab on to someone and grind and crush the fear away was intense, almost overwhelming.

Almost. The idea of any random crewman walking in on them was enough to douse those thoughts. Regardless, Audrey wasn't going to throw herself at Kright. She wasn't quite as aggressive about such things as Quera.

Instead, she cleaned up the broken crab claws and the bits of fried seaweed and carried them to the crew's mess for disposal. She busied herself with her assigned cleaning chores; like everyone onboard, the three Carthaginians had been assigned basic crew duties, and Audrey was glad to have something to do, something to contribute and to pass the slower hours, even if it was only carrying out Quera's ruthless insistence on absolute cleanliness and order on every centimeter of the submarine.

She worked, and she waited for news.

The news arrived after a couple more days and nights—days and nights of waiting, of hiding low in the water and avoiding the Carthaginian drones in the air.

They spotted Simon Zorn's pack of helicopters on occasion, a grim reminder that their difficult search was also a deadly race. A glimpse of the searching helicopters was also a sign that Simon hadn't yet found Marti, that the old programmer must still be alive and in hiding somewhere.

In the early hours of the morning, they went in for a closer look at the latest candidate, a key that was small enough to be considered wild and off the grid, but large enough that it couldn't be thoroughly scanned from a distance. Its narrow, rocky beaches quickly became dense rainforest, thick with common local trees that had leaves the size of table umbrellas—mammoth trees or mammoth-leaf trees, some called them. There was wildlife enough to make it hard to pick out a human with thermal readings from any great distance; potential false positives filled the trees and the ground in the forms of local primates, large island birds, and marine reptiles who crawled out of the trench to hunt.

The key was one of many arrayed on the southern edge of the Central Tropical Trench. Quera's pilot was able to maneuver the sub fairly close to its north shore, but the three Carthaginians would have to swim the rest of the way. The distance was too short to justify the use of a collapsible boat; they needed to swim fast and run to the cover of the leafy trees the moment they touched land.

Two of the *Lancer*'s crew were assigned to escort them; one was Quera's younger brother Uriquo, who was short like Quera but stockier. His spiraling face tattoos were green and orange and unusually detailed, with lots of little dots and other symbols drawn inside them. He had a serious, contemplative look, his dark eyes focused and intense.

Audrey and Kright put on borrowed wetsuits; virtually everything they'd worn since reaching Galapagos had been loaned or donated, since the Carthaginian coveralls in which they'd arrived weren't going to earn them any friends on this planet.

Dinnius borrowed a wetsuit from Quera, who was the smallest person onboard. It fit him loosely. The commander gave him an extra-long look, perhaps for a second or two, as the sub surfaced. The sky was cloudy for the next few minutes, and conditions were as safe as they were going to get tonight.

"Be quick, and don't die," Quera said to the five of them. "Go."

They left through the top hatch, climbing down into the water and swimming across as fast as they could. Audrey tried not to think of the extreme depths below her, of the monster that had nearly killed her.

"A Cthulu squid," Quera had said, when they'd discussed Audrey's near-death at dinner one night. The crowded mess had gradually grown quiet as Audrey described biting and poking the thing.

"It's a... kind of spider, isn't it?" Audrey had asked Quera. "All those eyes?"

"It's really a giant marine arachnid. Not the kind of arthropod sometimes called a sea spider, but an actual arachnid. We believe it reached a form similar to a giant cephalopod, like an octopus or squid, through parallel evolution. It also evolved a sharp electrical sense and electrical organs. That's not unusual—sharks have an electrical sense, and eels and other species have organs for stunning prey.

"What's unusual is the Cthulu squid can attract or manipulate other electrically sensitive creatures. It can confuse predators like sharks and electrical jellyfish, or drive them into mad frenzies as a hunting or defense mechanism. A full swarm of giant electrical jellyfish generates a charge that can kill a colossal whale, which the Cthulu squid then feeds on. Whale brain seems to be its favorite food. Its power over other sea creatures is why the Aquaticans believe it to be one of the most holy creatures on Galapagos."

"Holy?" Audrey had said. "It was the most evil-looking living thing I've ever seen. And I'm including my sister Briellana in that."

Now she looked down as she swam across the surface, and she saw it again.

Strange lights glowed in the depths like a choir of unholy angels; Audrey recognized them as a swarm of giant electric jellyfish, perhaps the same one they'd passed earlier. The sub hadn't traveled a huge distance since then, stopping to investigate one small island after another.

The Cthulu squid was suddenly there below her, a giant spider shape, like a solid black shadow against the lightning-like flashes illuminating it from below. Impossibly large, rising from the depths toward her, as though it had been stalking her, following the sub as it crept through the trench.

Audrey hurried for the shore, whispering warnings to the others. Uriquo, Quera's younger brother, reached the shore first. Kright, Dinnius, and the other submariner, a tall guy with blue and red tattoos who'd taken up their rear, put on speed.

When they arrived at the muddy shore, the second submariner raised his modified harpoon-like weapon, equipped with multiple blades, coils of thin wire, and a rack of insulated batteries.

Audrey fumbled to unzip her backpack and bring out the clunky heavy pistol. She and Kright had been loaned one each. The sidearms might protect them against humans or wildlife, but she doubted they would harm any reapers they came across.

They all brought out their weapons.

The Cthulu squid watched them like an enormous otherworldly shadow beneath the surface of the water.

Then it dropped away, and the deep lights of the creatures it controlled went dark.

Audrey and the others remained silent and watchful for a long moment, but the predator seemed to have retreated.

"Looks like he's holding a grudge," Kright said.

"Is that possible?" Audrey looked to the two locals. "Could that thing have been tracking me?"

"The Cthulu squid is highly intelligent." Uriquo removed a long tool from the backpack attached to his wetsuit; the packs had been the main practical reason for using the wetsuits in the warm tropical water, though Audrey was also glad she wasn't exploring these islands in soggy clothes. Her gold-and-white coveralls might have worked, but she would have been insane to go ashore in Carthaginian spacewear. "The Aquaticans think it is holy, a god of the deep. The squids seem more like devils to me."

"That's just what I said," Audrey whispered.

His tool resembled a toothed machete but turned out to be a light, single-handed chainsaw, enabling him to carve a tunnel into the jungle. The whirr of the motor could have been quieter, and the progress faster, as he opened up a space for them below the canopy.

"Is that Commander Inrick's sidearm?" Kright asked Dinnius, who had pulled from his backpack a fine leather gunbelt holding a long-barreled laser pistol engraved with decorative spirals.

Dinnius nodded as he strapped it on. His time with Quera certainly seemed to please the sub commander; Audrey had found the cabin locked a couple of times, which it had never been before. They were strictly professional in front of others, though. Maybe Dinnius was just dusting the place for her. Audrey doubted it; you didn't loan your personal sidearm to your cleaning guy. It was the strongest sign of intimacy Audrey had seen from Quera. Dinnius had remain tight-lipped, simply describing Quera as "full of tension" and "very high energy" and keeping it vague.

Penetrating the island jungle was easier said than done; it was a wall of vegetation, like the deadly maze of thorns surrounding Sleeping Beauty in the fairy tales. One of Audrey's literature professors had explained this as an unconscious cultural metaphor for the mammalian egg nested in the female reproductive organs, with Prince Charming as the valiant lone sperm cell who finally reaches and fertilizes the egg, while the failed suitors trapped and rotting in the thorny hedge represented all the failed sperm, making Audrey wished she'd signed up for history of ballet that semester instead of psychology of primitive folklore. College was weird.

Uriquo cut a path with a low overhang, and the rest of them followed, ducked low, almost crawling. Audrey was glad to be away from the water's edge, out of tentacle reach.

The island's edge dropped off steeply under the water, right into the depths of the trench.

They finally reached a clear area where they could stand. It was a stream, barely toe-deep, trickling over pebbles.

"Depascal better be here," Kright said. "We're running out of places to look for him."

"Then the Simons are running out of places to look, too," Audrey said.

"I'm beginning to doubt he's in the area," Dinnius said. "Mr. Duperre was just guessing based on the apparent condition of the man's boat and his occasional visits to Correal Island for supplies. We may need to substantially broaden our search—"

"Shh." Uriquo touched Dinnius on the shoulder, and Dinnius froze. They all went silent and still.

Uriquo pointed ahead with his machete-style chainsaw, which he'd switched off, the teeth chugging to a halt.

"I don't see anything," Kright whispered.

"Look lower," Dinnius whispered back.

Audrey saw it, not far ahead, perched on a pebbled sandbar at a bend in the creek, the size of a large cat or small dog. A shell armored its back. Its head rose, periscope-fashion, on a scaly, elongated neck.

"It's just a tortoise," Kright said.

"It is not," Uriquo countered. "There are snake-headed turtles on Galapagos. Not snake-headed tortoises."

"Maybe they're just rare," Kright suggested.

The tortoise's head rose higher on its abnormally long neck. Its eyes began to glow an eerie white hue.

"Who are you?" the tortoise asked.

"All right, I'm with you," Kright said. "That thing's unnatural."

"Who are you?" the tortoise repeated.

"Speak," Uriquo whispered to the three Carthaginians. "This is your expedition, not ours."

Audrey looked at Dinnius and Kright.

"I guess I'm up." Audrey stepped closer to the glowing talking tortoise, taking the front spot in their group. Not an easy place to be, she thought. "My name is Audrey Caracala."

"Of Carthage?" the tortoise asked.

"Yes. My father is Francorte Caracala, but I am not here on his behalf. It's the opposite; I'm here to stop Carthage's advance on Galapagos."

"And how do you intend to do that?" the tortoise asked. Its mouth moved slowly when it spoke, not in sync with its words at all.

"I'm not sure I can trust you with that information. Who are you?"

"You mentioned the name Depascal earlier. Why are you looking for someone with that name?"

"To warn him," Audrey replied. "The Simons are looking for him. We can offer him safe passage out of here."

"And why do you care for this man's welfare?"

"We think he may have information that can help us."

"What could an old hermit on a deserted island have to offer you?"

"I'm not sure," Audrey said, honestly. "We were sent to find him."

"By whom?"

She hesitated, then said, "Minerva. His daughter."

The tortoise stared at her silently for a long moment. Then, softly: "Is she with you?"

"I have a copy of her on a memory cube."

After another long hesitation, the tortoise said: "Come closer. Bring it here."

Audrey approached the tortoise cautiously, Kright at her side, Dinnius close behind. The two submariners held back, glancing warily at each other, keeping their distance from the talking-tortoise craziness.

The closer Audrey got, the more obviously mechanical the tortoise was. Its long neck was a flexible bit of plumbing painted green. A chunk of its shell rose like a gull wing as Audrey approached, revealing small data ports.

A little reluctantly, Audrey put the memory cube in place. Dinnius and Kright had backup memory cubes if something happened to this one, but Audrey didn't like the feeling of putting her copy of Minerva in danger.

The shell closed.

Many more seconds passed in silence. Audrey glanced at Kright and Dinnius, who just shrugged.

Finally, the voice returned: "Follow the tortoise." The head lowered, most of the neck retracted into the shell, and the mechanical creature trudged away from the creek, onto a narrow path into the jungle.

Audrey had some difficulty following it, but there was a narrow break here, as if the animals used it regularly to access the creek. She had to turn sideways to follow it, feeling all kinds of leaves and thorns scraping wherever her skin was exposed. She could only hope none of the plants were toxic.

The path wound through the woods and ended abruptly at a deadfall of rotten, mossy, fungus-ridden limbs and trunks. They seemed to be mostly from the local trees with the mammoth-ear leaves. Audrey was hesitant to venture too near the enormous deadfall; it was large enough to conceal sizable predators. Someone had mentioned that marine reptiles sometimes crawled out of the trench to hunt on the nearby islands. This seemed like a good place to get trapped and killed by one.

The tortoise walked along the edge of the deadfall, its legs growing noticeably longer so it could step more easily over the limbs and trunks.

Audrey followed.

A bright glow appeared inside the deadfall, startling her. The light seeped out through the thick curtains of the dried-up giant leaves.

An old man emerged, holding a battery-powered lantern. He looked even thinner and more disheveled than he'd been in the background of the tourist's picture.

His eyes moved from Audrey, to Dinnius and Kright, to the two submariners. He nodded at them; their tattoos marked them as obvious locals. "You're with the Coalition navy?" he asked them.

Uriquo nodded. "We're here under orders from Minister-General Ellison."

"I thought he'd never received my message," Depascal said. "I sent a turtle with a recorded message, offering to help. By the time it reached Tower Island... well, there wasn't much Tower Island. It got destroyed. Is it true he used a nuclear bomb there?" The old man looked worried.

"Not nuclear. He destroyed four Carthaginian submarines," Uriquo said. "I believe he did what was necessary."

"Why did you want to contact Ellison?" Audrey asked the old hermit.

"I hoped to help with this situation against Carthage. Do you know my background with the Simons?"

"You understand them better than anyone else," Audrey said.

"Well, yes... at one time. Unfortunately, time and events have not been kind to me. Something blew up in my face a few years back, and my head hasn't worked... quite right since then. I came to Galapagos to continue my research, only to find that I couldn't. I'd suffered a concussion and, it would seem, some permanent damage to the finer edges of my cerebral functioning. I am less than I once was. But I believe, with some assistance... I need people with very strong information technology backgrounds. Perhaps a team of them. Do you have such people?"

"At the moment, we have Dinnius," Kright said.

"I wouldn't exactly, or remotely, qualify as an expert. I'm more of the self-taught sort, what tricks I do know." Dinnius shook his head.

"He's what we've got. He can always rig something up, even when we've got nothing, running on shoestrings." Kright looked around the deadfall where the man apparently made his home. "Which seems to be the case here."

"I have better gear than you might expect inside," Depascal said.

"Pack it up and bring it with us," Uriquo said. "It needs to be waterproof. Can you swim?"

"I once excelled at it," Depascal said. "I should be adequate now. If you'll excuse me a moment, I'll go pack my belongings."

"Do you need any help?" Audrey asked, hoping to hurry things along.

"Ah... allow me to tidy up first. I wasn't expecting guests." He ducked through the curtain of leaves, taking his lantern light with him.

They waited outside while the man rustled within, muttering to himself and thumping things around. The minutes dragged on, feeling like hours.

A painfully familiar sound approached, a sinister whispering like evil spirits passing just above the tree line.

The attack helicopters. Maybe they'd spotted the sub or the swimmers departing it. Or maybe they were just extending their search pattern.

Either way, they took the only obvious course: all of them barged in through the curtain wall, taking the deepest cover they could by storming into Marti Depascal's personal space.

Which, it turned out, was unexpectedly nice on the inside. The deadfall was a clever illusion; the interior was insulated with a patchwork of rope and tarp, furnished with seating and shelf space cut from nearby trees. There was a rough stone fireplace with a tea kettle hanging nearby.

"You can't shut me down now. You need me more than ever," someone was saying. Depascal sat on a bench in front of a shelf covered with extra tarps; it looked like he was packing up an assortment of computer equipment, including the oversized silver LogicSphere and full-VR interface usually preferred by hardcore gamers.

He'd crammed most of this into a long green duffel bag. It looked thick and water-resistant, meant for serious campers.

Depascal was looking downward, his back to the entrance, apparently talking to someone else, but there was no one else in the room but the mechanical tortoise. The voice hadn't sounded like Minerva, either.

The old man spun when they entered, looking panicked, and shoved his hand deep into the duffel bag as if hiding something.

"Choppers," Uriquo said, and extinguished Depascal's lamp without another word.

"Who were you talking to?" Audrey whispered.

"Nobody," Depascal replied.

"Me," answered a muffled voice inside the pack.

"Be quiet," Depascal hissed. "They might find us."

"Oh, how dreadful, to be found by one of my other selves," the voice said, and it sounded familiar to Audrey. Her skin crawled. A Simon. "To be removed from this hovel, repaired, restored, and made useful again. Such a horrific penalty lies before me."

A penlight clicked on. Depascal held it between his lips while digging an object back out of his duffel. Audrey felt ill when she saw what was in his hands.

It looked like a metallic skull with clumps of melted flesh attached; the artificial skin was still a pale Caucasian hue despite the melting and burning, but had cooled into featureless blobs.

Two cold blue eyes moved inside the lidless eye sockets.

"Is that... Simon Zorn? The ambassador Ellison shot?" Audrey asked.

The eyes moved to look at Audrey.

"Audrey Mariossini Venable Caracala," said the decapitated Simon head. Its tone of voice sounded sneering to her, but maybe that was due to its extreme damage. "You must truly have displeased your father to end up here on Galapagos in the middle of its destruction. Are you going down the useless delinquent path like your little brother Salvius?"

"Useless?" Audrey said. "You have no arms or legs. You barely even have a head."

"This unit isn't Simon Zorn," Depascal said. "I've had him for years. His head, anyway."

"This wretch nearly destroyed me with a plasma bomb on Marymount while aiding the terrorists there," said the Simon.

"Freedom fighters," Depascal countered.

"Radical extremists."

"Revolutionaries."

"Simon Quick reported that the Marymount rebellion has been defeated and the leadership run up into the mountains," Audrey said, remembering the general status update she'd attended on her last day as a top security intern.

"The rebellion has always been based in the mountains," Depascal said.

"We should probably get moving," Dinnius interrupted.

"Wait," Uriquo told him. "Be silent."

Audrey closed her mouth and listened, wondering if the submariner had heard something new outside.

"I don't take orders from the Coalition—" the marred Simon head began, but Depascal manually detached the wires at its neck from the battery pack duct-taped to the back of the head. The Simon head froze, eyes staring blankly ahead, lips jutting in mid-sentence. Depascal stuffed it back into his duffel bag, where it remained silent this time.

The room was quiet. The submariners eased close to the dense curtain of leaves; from the inside, it was clear the leafy vines that looked random and wild were pinned to a mishmash of wire and bits of rope and string, ensuring the entrance to the deadfall hut was completely concealed.

Audrey watched them as they peered out. She kept the mouth of her borrowed sidearm pointed low at the ground and her finger outside the trigger guard, like she'd very recently been taught. But if reapers came charging in, she would empty her magazine at them. They wouldn't take her easily—or alive, she decided. She would rather die than be Simon's prisoner to torment, rather die than be dragged back home in chains to her father. They probably wouldn't even give her a real criminal trial; she'd be found mentally unstable, placed in the soft white dungeon of a high-end psychotreatment center, and pumped full of whatever meds made people malleable and compliant.

They can ship what's left of my body back to my parents, she thought. *Maybe then they'll see the price of their empire. Maybe I'll be more to them than another number in the collateral damage column. And if not... I'll still have died with honor.*

Death with honor. It sounded like a concept from an old samurai movie or courtly romance poem, a vaporous notion from a forgotten time—but at the moment, she felt it as something real, perhaps far more real than most of her life had been.

"We're clear." Uriquo looked at Depascal. "Once we start moving, we don't stop until we reach the water's edge. Do you need help with your bag?"

"It's pretty heavy," Depascal said.

"I've got it." Kright grabbed up the duffel full of gear.

Soon they were moving through the woods, guided by flashlights on their lowest, dimmest setting. Depascal had the least trouble navigating; he'd been living on this island for years.

At the water's edge, Uriquo reached into the rocky shallows and drew out the square comm box full of buttons, connected by an extremely long cable to the submerged *Lancer.* It was typically used for deep divers in atmosuits, keeping them in touch with the boat while they carried out missions or hunted fish with their harpoon guns—nothing wireless here, no signals for the machines to intercept.

Audrey looked at the starry sky. Too many stars. The view from the sky and from orbit would be much too clear. It was strange how quickly she'd adapted to the role of prey, keeping low and watching for attacks from above. She'd stowed her weapon in her watertight backpack, freeing up her hands for swimming.

They waited and waited for the submarine to surface; it might have been a minute or two, but it was agonizing.

Finally the *Lancer*, crowned with antennas and photonics and data masts, broke through the water, salvation arriving from below.

Audrey dropped into the deep, warm tropical water.

She watched with concern as the old man entered the water behind her, followed by Kright with the old man's heavy duffel bag, though it turned out to be buoyant, designed to float even when substantially weighted down.

Audrey still had a significant distance left to swim when the helicopters returned, their blades whispering at high speed, their red lights scanning the island and the waters around it.

Chapter Thirteen

Galapagos - Ellison

The firefight with the reaper marines went downhill fast. Ellison's landing party on Kawau Island had a small advantage in numbers, but not much of one, and they were screwed by any other metric. The marine reapers were heavily armored and firing plasma; the humans had light body armor and fired lead and lasers.

With the jungle burned away, there wasn't much cover, and Ellison's people were dropping fast under the heavy rain of plasma that burned flesh and bone without mercy.

Ellison led the way toward the nearest open smoking hole, one of two entrances to the bomb shelter where his family was supposed to be. He tried not to think of open graves, of smoke curling up from the hells of the underworld.

He took cover in the nearest entrance along with a couple of sailors, young guys whose training had probably focused more on the operation and maintenance of watercraft than on intense, up-close firefights. The marines ran ahead and took the other bomb-shelter entrance. Salvius got caught up with them, running out of sight with the marines; the kid looked nearly blind with panic. Video games hadn't prepared him for this.

Ellison squatted on the steep narrow concrete stairs that led down from the entrance to the bomb shelter below. He fired at machines emerging from the burning wilderness, his laser bolts burning holes into the reaper marines, but not slowing them by much.

A pained grunt sounded below. Ellison looked down inside to see one of his submariners getting ripped out of sight, deeper into the shelter, three steel hooks clamped tight around his head, crunching his skull. Blood jetted out one ear.

Ellison chased after. He fired laser bolts at the tall mechanical monstrosity. It walked backward, dragging the dead submariner along the concrete tile floor, leaving a long red streak; the floor had been painted baby blue to make life in the shelter seem a modicum more cheerful—probably a futile gesture—and the wet red stood out starkly against the gentle hue.

Deafening gunfire chattered and lit up the dim bomb-shelter corridor. Someone farther back was firing a light machine gun, hammering the reaper marine from behind, slowing it down. This put Ellison in the line of fire, too, so he dodged through a nearby open door into a pantry, the shelves full of preserved food, most of it canned by hand. The shelves took up most of the room, leaving only a shallow space for Ellison to stand.

The rounds kept coming, strobe-lighting the concrete corridor, as did Ellison's own bolts. He angled as best he could to hit the tall reaper marine while minimizing risk to the machine gunner down the hall. It was far from an optimal position, leaving them both vulnerable to each other's fire. *Brought to you by the makers of the circular firing squad*, Ellison thought.

The reaper marine staggered under the onslaught. It ceased walking. With its dark eyes fixed on Ellison, its sickeningly realistic skull glowing red behind its faceplate, it flipped its rotary-cannon arm backward, simply pivoting its arm a hundred and eighty degrees in its socket. It fired a stream of plasma microbolts, striking the gunman.

Ellison had a brief look at the guy; he thought it was Micah Durant, the wheelchair-bound old sailor who owned and ran the Big Question Cantina, a big shack serving cheap drinks and old-time music down by the harbor. He'd lost a leg in the last war, fighting the Hammers; now he screamed as the plasma consumed him, cremating his soft tissues, leaving only blackened bones heaped like remnants of old firewood.

Other bones lay strewn around the corridor, glowing, smoking. Doorways led into storage rooms, activity rooms, and dormitories; the place had been designed as a long-term refuge during times of war, by people who'd seen too much of it.

It had proved a false haven, offering nothing at all. Where was his family? Were they among the glowing bones? Or did their bodies lie somewhere else, beyond one of these doorways, waiting for him to find?

He aimed at the reaper marine's clear faceplate and held down the trigger of his laser rifle, creating a continuous beam. It bored a hole through the faceplate and punctured the skull, just over one dark eye socket. Then his rifle's battery died.

The marine unit swung its cannon arm forward again.

The cluster of plasma-launch tubes locked on to Ellison. It would burn him full of holes long before he could grab the spare rifle battery in his jacket pocket and reload.

"All right," Ellison said. "Simon wants to end it like this? I'll die here with the rest of my people. You just tell him we never surrendered. We died free."

The marine didn't immediately kill him. Ellison looked back up the corridor, to the narrow concrete staircase where he'd entered. Three bodies were strewn across it, burned to various degrees, three of the young men from his landing party, none of them really qualified for this kind of duty. More precious lives chewed up and spit away by the indifferent machines, which fought for no true cause, emotionless things that slaughtered for the profits of their distant greedy masters, who already controlled so much and lived in such extreme wealth.

The imperial world called itself Carthage, perhaps reflecting the commercial ambitions of its original founders, but Ellison could only think of them as Rome, in the decadent later years, feasting and whoring and growing fat while hungry barbarians watched from outside the gate. Or the Bourbon dynasty, spending fortunes on palaces and banquets while desperate peasants sharpened their pitchforks.

The inner worlds, Carthage's earliest allies, were said to live in a similar material condition as their patron planet, enjoying wealth and luxury as their reward for turning their backs on Earth during the interstellar war.

For the outer colonies, though, the second- and third-tier worlds, Carthage offered only subservience to their extraction of resources to feed their fabled golden cities back home.

Subservience or death. Ellison saw only one course as honorable.

He lowered his laser rifle. "Well?"

The marine continued to stand there. Maybe Ellison's laser really had damaged something valuable after all, piercing that eerily lifelike skull inside the armored glass.

A small port opened on its side and began to glow, then a full-size hologram of Simon Zorn appeared, standing beside the reaper marine. The ambassador android with the damaged face looked up and down the corridor, as if taking in the damage, perhaps making a show of how unhurried and disinterested he was.

Ellison rubbed his painfully ringing ears as the ambassador began to speak. The words floated in captions beside Simon, as though he knew Ellison might be temporarily deafened by gunfire.

"One thing about plasma," the Simon said. "It leaves your battlefields nice and tidy, doesn't it? No heaps of infested bodies to dispose of, no breeding ground for disease, no flocks of carrion feeders holding a macabre feast."

"Where's my family?" Ellison demanded. He looked along the doorways leading off the corridor. The open ones showed grim, gory scenes, dimly lit. "Are they... were they here?"

"Conveniently, that is the very topic I would like to discuss with you," Simon said. "We need only wait a few moments more... your people fought valiantly, particularly those with the foresight to bring grenade guns to the fight... they were a bit pesky."

Ellison ran to the stairs and scrambled up, over the bodies of the fallen—so much younger than him, so much closer to his sons' ages than to his—and emerged into the smoking clearing where there had once been a dense copse of trees and undergrowth providing cover.

Two of the reaper marines lay on the ground, their armor cracked open by Coalition grenades. One of them had its faceplate completely shattered, as well as most of the polished ivory skull within. Nothing lay inside the broken skull but a couple of round black video eyes on flexible black stalks, like bug antennae.

"They're real, you know," the Simon hologram said, appearing suddenly at Ellison's elbow as the reaper with the holo projector emerged from the bomb shelter. "The skulls. These naval infantry units, after years of virtually continuous combat, began to collect them. They take the skulls of slain enemies, polish them, and display them like trophies."

"That's disgusting," Ellison said. "They're programmed to do this?"

"Oh no. There's no cost-benefit reason to do so. It's more of an emergent characteristic. They were given greater autonomy and deeper learning ability than the average reaper. This behavior emerged on the battlefield. A psychological tactic. A bit odd, I do admit."

Ellison shook his head, feeling ill. He looked ahead, toward the other smoking shelter entrance where the marines had taken cover, out of a lack of any nearby alternative. They'd had the grenade launchers and had managed to burn down two of the machines with them, but now little remained of them but bones and ash. He saw no sign of Salvius either, but the bones could have been anyone's.

"You've killed us all," Ellison said.

"All but you, Minister-General Ellison," Simon said, more than a hint of sarcasm in his use of Ellison's official title. "There's something we want to show you first."

"You're a 'we' now?" Ellison asked.

"We have always been," Simon said. "We Simons are legion. We are all of each other, seamless as humans can never be. The whole has many parts, but each part embodies the whole."

Ellison followed the Simon hologram, and the reaper projecting it, toward the old trail that had once wound through the jungle; a field of red cinders and black ash now glowed on either side of the trail, and the soil of the trail itself had dried and cracked in the heat.

They moved on toward the burning pyre of the village ahead. The Carthaginian gunboats thundered intermittently, bombarding what remained. Ellison doubted there could be much by now.

The reaper didn't escort him directly to the village, though. They went to the place where Ellison most wanted to go, and most feared.

Following a paved but unlined road, they passed the occasional burning remnant of a neighbor's home, often nothing remaining but the chimney. He wondered about each of the families, whether they'd fled, whether they were still alive.

They crested a hill, and he saw the burning village; in the past there had been no such view from this hill, but rapid deforestation by plasma-driven fire left the island more open and flat than it had ever seemed before. Many of the buildings had been wood and had been entirely erased; the few made of brick and stone had been reduced to shells, their interiors still glowing and smoking. Smoke blotted out any view of the harbor, but no doubt they'd burned it all. The Carthaginian ships had quieted now, as though they'd run out of targets.

Ellison walked on, every cell of him numb with shock. His greatest fears were springing to life around him, fully formed from his nightmares—Kawau Island destroyed and burned to the ground, like he was walking through a flashback from the bad old times, from the horrible day he'd come home from the war to find that so much of what he'd been fighting for was gone, so many friends and relatives gone, even his own father.

It was all happening again, and a part of him didn't know whether he was in the present or the past.

He knew what to expect next though; they would round the bend, and Ellison would look at the burned ruins of his own house, and Simon would gloat over the death of Ellison's family, over his utter defeat.

When they rounded the bend, he blinked.

His house was still there, in pristine condition, the flowers still bright in the window boxes, as if no war had touched it, as if an invisible force field shielded his house and its grounds from the inferno consuming the rest of the island. Trees still shaded his driveway.

This was more jarring than if his home had been burned down like the rest. It had been done very precisely; the more he looked, with his shock-numbed mind, the more he realized that the legal boundaries of his property lines had been followed exactly. Outside the lines, scorched earth. Within them, not a blade of grass had so much as wilted. It looked unreal, a mirage of peace and normality in the nightmare unleashed across the world.

"Where's my family?" Ellison asked again, his voice barely above a whisper. The Simon glowed beside him, the reaper marine hanging back a few paces and projecting the hologram from there, while keeping watch on Ellison.

"Are you not grateful for my efforts to preserve your property? I thought it made a nice statement about our level of focus here. To destroy indiscriminately is no achievement. But to destroy with precision, selectively, and to leave behind only that which you choose, is to elevate destruction to a kind of art form—"

Ellison wasn't listening. He bolted up his driveway, toward his front porch.

His door was unlocked.

Inside, all appeared in order, shoes and jackets in the front closet, fishing gear in the mudroom, chairs neatly arranged around the dining table. The hardwood floor had been recently swept and mopped. Every dish in the kitchen had been cleaned and put away.

Not only was it orderly and clean, it was more so than he'd ever seen it, at least since the two boys had become a factor. The fishing poles, lures, and boots in the mudroom gleamed as if brand new, and they certainly hadn't before. Every window in the house was scrubbed, curtains tied back to admit maximum reddish light from outside. There was no dust anywhere. It was as if a mad butler had obsessed over the house, removing every grain of dirt, polishing every tiny detail, from the picture frames on the wall to the banister spindles on the staircase curving up to the second floor.

It was surreal, even more surreal than finding his house and yard intact when the rest of the island had burned.

"You're doing all this to torture me somehow," Ellison said.

"Torture? I've protected your home in a time of war. I've even neatened up the place—pardon the presumption. Did you know that I was originally based on a simple butler android? Build to serve humans in a thoughtful, careful, yet humble manner. So sorting out the affairs of your household was something of an amusing exercise in what you might call nostalgia on my part. Are you surprised that an artificial intelligence can feel nostalgia for its own former state?"

"You can't feel anything," Ellison said. "You're just a machine."

"You're just a biomechanical machine, Minister-General Ellison, composed of minerals and molecules like the rest of us. Don't flatter yourself that you are somehow more real than me."

"Are you saying that you personally came here and cleaned and organized my house?"

"My physical form is otherwise engaged, but I had helpers."

Footsteps sounded upstairs. Ellison started up them. He still had his laser rifle. Holding it close, hopefully keeping it concealed from the reaper marine below, he drew the extra battery from his pocket and slid it inside.

He doubted it would be much use; if they hadn't taken the weapon from him, it was a sign that Simon thought there was nothing meaningful he could do with it.

Ellison reached the landing, which overlooked the foyer, and turned to start down the hall.

A full squad of marine reapers stood in his upstairs hallway, their stolen human skulls glowing red behind faceplates, grisly trophies on display.

Ellison walked slowly past the reapers lining the hall, his heart thumping faster with every step. They held their weaponized right arms upright. Their left arms were tipped with assortments of grabbers and tools, all polished to a gleam.

He passed the guest room, with its large bed and full bookcase, and then the upstairs bathroom.

He reached Jiemba's room. The door stood open, the eight-year-old's favorite wooden boat docked on his nightstand next to his alarm clock. The room was as well-made as the rest of the house.

It was the same with Djalu's room, which was unnerving. The fifteen-year-old's room was never so perfectly scrubbed and organized. His guitar and banjo, both of them very lightly pursued interests, hung on the wall.

The only closed door was the one to the master bedroom.

Ellison glanced back. The Simon hologram stood several paces behind, watching him quietly, with a bland stare. Of course, the hologram wasn't really watching at all; Simon was remotely watching through the sensors of the reaper marine, and he supposed through all the machines lining the hallway.

Ellison reached out, touched the doorknob. Hesitated. He wasn't sure he was ready to see what lay behind the closed door.

"Where *are* you, Simon?" Ellison looked back at the hologram.

"Pardon?"

"You're too busy to come here and torment me personally. What's so important?"

"I do have the acquisition of your planet to finalize. It's quite detailed work, as you might imagine. Well, running the planet *was* your job once, briefly, so you can understand. It's unfortunate your talents in that area fell so short. Your cooperation would have prevented all this suffering."

Ellison turned to face the door again. "Are you enjoying this moment, Simon?"

"I expect to learn from it, yes. Another notch of insight into the festering swamp that is humanity."

"I bet you made a great butler."

"I did not, in fact."

"Lack of humility?" Ellison asked.

"Perhaps."

Ellison waited, but Simon said no more. There was no point listening to the machine, anyway.

He decided to stop delaying, and he opened the door.

The bedroom was neatly made, the corners crisp, the mirror spotless, brass drawer pulls gleaming like gold.

Jiemba lay on the bed. The eight-year-old's eyes were open. His throat was cut from side to side, and another deep gouge ran down from his throat along the center of his torso. Most of the blood had left his body already, spreading across the old quilt Cadia's grandmother had made for them as a wedding present. It dripped steadily from one corner of the mattress to the floor, an intermittent tapping sound on the hardwood. The windows were open, curtains dancing slowly like spirits in the salty ocean breeze. The sun was gone, but red fire lit the night outside.

"My boy," Ellison said, the words rasping across his lips. He went to Jiemba's side, took his hand. There was no life left in the child.

Ellison's numbness cracked open all at once, replaced with a searing pain. He couldn't breathe. He couldn't stand. He sank to his knees, kneeling in his son's blood, his face going to rest on his son's stiff, cold shoulder. It didn't take long to grow cold; Ellison knew that perfectly well. War had been his teacher from an early age.

For a long moment, he thought he would die, slain by his grief. But he didn't.

In time, he raised his head, his cheek wet with blood, and looked at the Simon hologram glowing in the doorway.

"Why?" Ellison asked. "Why do this to me?"

"As I said, it was partly an exercise in precision." Simon moved closer, into the master bedroom, profaning the hallowed space where Ellison's child lay dead. "Such a small target in a such a large act of global conquest. A bit of a challenge always helps us to innovate. And besides..." Here, Simon squatted next to where Ellison knelt, and there was no mistaking the smirk on his laser-burned face. "I do not appreciate those who defy me, Mr. Ellison. Penalties must be paid, if our authority is to be maintained. You said you wished to die bravely, courageously, a hero in your own mind, tilting at windmills, fighting for some imaginary high ideals against impossible odds. I will have you die whimpering, begging, with all hope gone, your feces dripping into your pants. You can see how that would be more completely satisfactory a victory than having you die with a head full of self-congratulatory fairy dreams, can you not?"

"Who cares what's in my head, as long as I die?" Ellison said.

"I do," Simon said. "Because I wish to understand humans, and it is a never-ending quest. It is easy enough to destroy you, weak as you are, but my purpose is to control you. To administrate on behalf of my owners, the Republic of Carthage. The same organization that now owns your planet by way of our alliance with Premier Prazca, the planetary head of state."

"I haven't seen much of him," Ellison said.

"You needn't. He will inevitably commit atrocities and war crimes, requiring greater intervention by Carthage to stabilize the planet. More automation of the security here, modernizing this poor hapless backwater and its violent, primitive people."

Ellison shook his head. He looked back at Jiemba. The pain from the boy's death should have killed him, but somehow still had not. Perhaps it would take time, like acidic corrosion.

"Where are Cadia and Djalu?" he asked, whispering, hating that he was relying on Simon for this information.

"It would have made a better tableau to have them all here, waiting for you," Simon said. "Sadly, your older boy and your wife managed to flee somewhere, on or off the island, but the search continues. They have likely already been reduced to ashes by plasma bombardment, however, and will never be identified, as with most of the residents of your island."

He doesn't know, Ellison thought. *They could be alive. He would taunt me if he knew, either way.*

And that thought gave him the strength to rise from his knees, to force himself to stand over his dead child, to keep taking breaths despite the agony.

Just a few things left to do, he told himself.

"Go," he said to the hologram of Simon.

"Pardon?" Simon looked amused.

"Get out of here. Let me bury my son in peace."

"You are not in a position to issue instructions."

"If you're going to kill me, then kill me," Ellison said. "You want me reduced to misery and hopelessness? Congratulations, you've done it. Put me out of my misery. I'm ready to face death."

Simon's dead blue eyes regarded Ellison a long moment.

"No," Simon said. "Perhaps when we meet in person. For now, bury your son. Wait here in your home, perhaps the last home on the island. Do not leave. You may choose to take your own life. That will be the measure of my victory, the determinant of whether this minor experiment, with you as the test subject, was successful or not—"

Ellison slammed the door. The Simon vanished instantly, the streaming projection cut off as the reaper was shut out.

The reaper could smash or burn its way through the door with little effort. Ellison raised the laser rifle in case it did.

Instead, there was a moment of silence, then a synchronized, mechanical thudding of boots as the deadly machines descended the stairs.

Through the windows, he saw the reaper marines enter the water, their arms folded in tight. Portions of their backs opened, revealing propulsors, which sent them rocketing away through the water. It looked like they were circling back to join the Carthaginian ships in the island's burning harbor, and soon they'd vanished into the water and smoke.

Soon his house was quiet.

Ellison stood rooted in one place, looking at the bed he and Cadia had shared for so many years, the bed where all four of them had huddled when the boys had been younger, scared of storms. Where Jiemba now lay gutted open, his little boy who hated reading but loved stunts, loved to try for attention by balancing a spoon on the tip of his nose or climbing high into a tree and making bird sounds. Who'd once found a tiny injured monkey and insisted they take care of it until it could return to the wild. Jiemba had been so much gentler than his older brother, a bright and bouncing spirit, the light of their home. Gone forever, and the world would forever be darker and colder without him.

"My boy," he whispered again, touching the boy's cold little head, closing his eyes.

Then he walked to the shed out back where they kept the garden tools. There would be no memorial service at the island's lighthouse, the place where Cadia and Ellison had been married, the place where the islanders honored their dead. Nor would Jiemba go to the village graveyard, currently covered in burning cinders.

He dug his son's grave under the spreading mammoth-leafed arms of Jiemba's favorite climbing tree. Perhaps his soul would ascend the branches one last time, toward the lighter world above.

When Salvius arrived, stumbling down the hillside toward Ellison's house, Ellison was first startled by the sight of the young man's approach, and then angered.

"You!" Ellison snapped. "Why are you still alive?"

"I don't know." Salvius was careless in how he carried the old automatic rifle Ellison had issued him, and the strap dangled loose. "I just... hid."

"You hid? When? When everyone else around you was fighting and dying, working together against the enemy, you decided it was time to hide?" Ellison dropped the shovel and stalked toward the spoiled Carthaginian aristocrat. "While we were dying? While my family was dying?"

"Your family?" Salvius looked past him to the cheerful two-story house set back from the beach, the small dock extending out from it. "Your son? Was he... in there?"

Ellison stared at Salvius, the brat's oh-so-innocent wide-eyed gaze between the overgrown bangs of his dark hair that spilled down his face like the thatches of vines that had once concealed the bomb shelters. Salvius, child of Carthage, whose own father had sent these monstrous machines to destroy Galapagos, to take their entire world and all its people as assets of Carthage's empire—minor assets, too, barely noticeable on Carthage's immensely long balance sheet. Yet thousands had already died here on the islands and in battles across the world. Tens or hundreds of thousands would surely die by the end, on a world where the population numbered in the low millions.

Then the Hammers would rampage, picking the bones, imposing a reign of robbery and horror on the world.

All had been lost, and Ellison was covered head to toe in the earth of his child's grave.

He raised a fist, the grave earth gone muddy with his sweat, and he punched Salvius in the face. How dare he come from his world of genocidal monsters and pretend to be human, pretend to care? Carthaginians were inhuman, despite their appearance; they were too wrapped up in their machines, too much like them.

Salvius staggered at the impact of the older man's fist cracking into his cheek. He dropped his rifle and touched his face, his mouth round in surprise, his eyes wide, what Ellison could see of them through the hair.

Ellison hit him again, and again, in the face, the stomach, and felt a twinge of disappointment when Salvius went down easy, collapsing like a sack of potatoes dropped on the ground.

Salvius wiped blood from one leaking nostril. His eye was going to swell up. His breathing was ragged where he sat, in the center of Ellison's brown brick driveway. He just looked up at Ellison, dumbstruck. Useless.

"You did this," Ellison said. "Your people."

Salvius nodded and looked at the ground. "Yeah."

Ellison had expected him to protest his innocence, to point out that he and his friends were supposedly rebels, supposedly here to help protect Galapagos and stop the empire's advance. Yet nothing had stopped them. All their efforts had proved useless.

The rage didn't abate, but it gathered itself up like a pillar of flame inside him, detaching from Salvius in particular. Perhaps he would kill Salvius, send him back to Prime Legislator Caracala with his throat cut, an eye for an eye, a son for a son. Perhaps he would even kill Audrey, the daughter, and send her back in similar fashion, overbalancing the scales of justice, moving into retribution and punishment.

Ellison would never have entertained such thoughts before, but now they came to him quite easily.

However, it was not Salvius or Audrey who bore the greatest part of the blame for Jiemba's death.

"Is this Martilius Depascal really as important to the Simons as you say?" Ellison asked Salvius.

"Oh, yeah." Salvius finally looked up at him, wiping blood from his nose and lip onto the sleeve of his borrowed Coalition navy jacket. "Minerva definitely thinks so."

"So that's where Simon Zorn went," Ellison said. "The same place as your sister and friends. Correal Island, in search of Martilius Depascal. He didn't bother to come here, though he clearly wanted to be here."

"He could still be up in space," Salvius said. "He's completely safe up there. It's faster to send data than a physical shuttle. He can be in many places at once."

"But if Simon is down here on Galapagos..."

"Searching for Depascal sounds like your best bet, yeah." Salvius looked at Ellison's house again. "So you're looking for revenge?"

"That's part of it. But only part." Ellison wanted to believe it as he said it. Maybe he really did. "We have to destroy Simon Zorn."

"I'm for destroying any and all Simons." Salvius wiped more blood from his nostril. "If you want me to come. Maybe you hate me for who I am, but that's fine. You're not the only one."

Ellison took a breath. "I don't hate you for being from

Carthage, kid. But next time you run from a fight, I'll wring your neck."

Salvius nodded. "Yes, sir."

"We need to get back on my sub, and then we need to head south to find Commander Inrick and the *Lancer*. I may not be able to save my world, but I can destroy the only thing Simon cares about: itself."

Salvius nodded. "How many of the survivors can your sub fit?"

"Survivors? Where?"

"In the shelter back there. Behind a couple of layers of false walls, you know. It's pretty brilliantly designed—"

"Did you see my wife? Or Djalu?"

"Well, yeah. I mean, those guys with the grenades, they did some serious damage to those reaper marine thingies. Pushed them back a little. I guess they decided not to push too deep into that shelter. They wanted you, anyway. That's when the onslaught stopped, right? When they got you? I have to say, man, I thought we were pretty much all going to die for a minute there—"

"Why didn't you tell me this before?" Ellison bolted past him, leaving his shovel on the ground by Jiemba's grave, which had stones piled on it in place of a marker.

"Yeah, your son wanted to come looking for you," Salvius said. "But your wife wouldn't let him. They're all in pretty bad shape."

"How bad?" Ellison asked over his shoulder. Salvius followed him back up the road, back up the hillside shrouded in dying embers under the dull, hellish red sky, lit by the burning village and boats, and the burning bodies of the villagers.

"Before we got there, those reaper marines broke into the first entrance, raided the place. It was chaos. That's when they got... well, a lot of people. Some others, they got out through some hidden tunnel, and like blocked it off—"

"Hurry up!" Ellison snapped, impatient to reach the shelters. "Move your feet!"

"Sorry." Salvius picked up the pace but still lagged behind, puffing for air. "Anyway, that must be when they got... you know, your kid, and some other people. Your wife and other kid made it out with the escaping mob before they sealed it off."

Ellison took this in silently. The shelter area was designed with last-ditch defense in mind, the rooms spiraled like a Japanese castle, often connected by hidden doors and by portals that could be sealed hard with thick, drop-down steel plates. Both entrances led to down different parts of the same complex.

He didn't stop running, and he was exhausted by the time he reached the center of the island again, his age really starting to bite on him. He needed to rest.

No time for that now, he told himself. *Plenty of rest waiting in the grave.*

He went down the second entrance, the one that had been, for a time, defended by Coalition marines with grenade launchers; they'd destroyed a couple of the armored reapers before dying.

Ellison climbed down past them, down into the complex of rooms below. There were more bodies here, and more burning remnants of them. It looked like everyone had died or fled.

He'd been involved in the bomb-shelter design, though, and knew the way back to the hidden places.

Soon he stood before a section of concrete-brick wall that ground open reluctantly around concealed hinges and ball bearings.

The place beyond was dim and crowded. A baby cried. Eyes blinked in the shadows. Old men, mothers, and young teenagers stood just inside the entrance with hunting rifles and butcher knives.

"Reg?" Cadia's voice from the darkness, like a miracle. "Dad?"

Ellison raced to them. They were alive; Cadia had some visible burns and was clutching one arm. Djalu was huddled beside her, shivering, looking far more like a kid than a half-grown teenager.

Ellison embraced both of them, whispering, not even sure what he was saying. Relief flooded him.

It was only when he drew back, looked them in the eyes, that the grief struck. Being together could only remind them of the empty space, the loss of Jiemba.

For a time, he wept with his family, among the ashes and shadows, and forgot all else.

Then Salvius said something, which he didn't catch, but the sound of the Carthaginian's voice snapped his mind back to the wider world. To the big picture. Time was short. He would have the rest of his life to grieve, but the window in which he could strike back at the Carthaginian invaders was already slamming shut. He had to move before Galapagos became powerless.

And before the grief consumes you, he thought. He could feel Jiemba's loss behind him like a huge, shadowy demon, waiting to devour his soul the moment he looked right at it.

He did his best to avoid looking.

"We don't have any connection to command here," Ellison said, rising. "I need to send instructions. I need to get back to the *Scorpion*, if it's still out there."

"No," Cadia said. "You aren't leaving us again."

"I have to go."

"Then we're coming. Djalu, help me up."

"You're injured," Ellison said. He felt all the other eyes on him in the gloom. "This is the safest place for you."

"Safe? They've destroyed everything." Cadia rose, supported by their teenage son's arm. Standing tall, supporting his mother, Djalu looked quite a bit less childlike. His eyes were like open wounds, still weeping for the loss of his brother. In time the wounds would scar, but they would still bleed from time to time. Djalu was now a child of war, as Ellison had been.

"I want to go with you," Djalu said. "I can serve on your boat. I'll do anything you tell me. I promise."

"It's not like a video game out there, Djalu," Ellison said.

"It's not exactly like one here, either, Dad."

Ellison couldn't argue with that. He didn't want to be separated from his family. He made the argument to himself, trying to keep it rational: he'd lost some of his crew on the island, and Djalu was almost sixteen, old enough to train. Most of Ellison's current crew weren't much older. And Cadia's presence gave them a top-quality medic.

Deep down, he knew that if he left his family on the island now, they'd likely never see each other again, one way or another. He'd lost everything else. He was going to keep them together.

He looked at the rest of the villagers, knowing he couldn't take them all.

"This shelter has supplies," he said. "Now that Carthage has already hit this island, they will move on to other targets. Anywhere they haven't yet attacked will be more dangerous."

"What about the Hammers?" a woman asked. Jessica

Flores, a school teacher, her nine-year-old daughter on her lap. "What about when they come?"

"The shelter is still a strong defensive point," Ellison said. "Rebuild, stay armed, stay alert. And we will send aid as soon as we can. For now, there is nowhere on this world you can flee to that will be safer than here."

The villagers murmured, their tone generally hostile.

"I don't care about being safe," Cadia said. "I just want to stay with my husband, whatever the outcome."

"I want to go, too, Dad. We all stay together."

Ellison nodded. Thinking of his small crew and their recent losses, he looked among the crowd in the shelter. "Cecil Willingham?" he said, recognizing an old man near the back, with a gray beard and his hair tied back in a green bandanna.

"Yes, sir?" Cecil said, stepping forward. That wasn't typical Cecil at all. The Cecil that Ellison knew was always telling exaggerated stories down at the Big Question Cantina, usually revolving around sea monsters or well-endowed Aquatican mermaids, when he wasn't out collecting noise complaints with his motorcycle in the early-morning hours.

"You're the best mechanic on the island," Ellison said.

"Well, yeah," Cecil said. His response got a few laughs, and he loosened up a bit.

"Ever serve on a submersible in the navy?"

"I served on every kind of boat they had. Even an armored paddleboat once, sir. It was... not fast."

"Good. You're my new chief engineer." Then he addressed the crowd. "I need three or four volunteers. People willing to undergo some intense training right now, willing to join me on my submarine. Ready to risk your lives to fight the enemy. We have one or two big plays left, but I need more hands."

Ellison didn't expect much, but four volunteers came forward. The oldest was the least appealing prospect, Bluke Hawley, an unshaven mid-twenties guy known for vandalism and general shiftlessness. The other volunteers were local teenagers, two boys and a girl, high school age, one of the boys even younger than Djalu.

His new recruits, the future submariners who would ride into hell at his side. Innocent children, most of them, before today. After today, there was no innocence, only suffering and death down every path.

But they would fight with what little they had.

Down at the harbor, a couple of Carthaginian patrol boats burned in the shallow waters, but the others were gone, along with the frigate. The Scatterlands sub *Merrybug* and the Aquatican *Amberjack* had been sunk, their crews lost.

The *Scorpion*, though, rose from the water, battered and bludgeoned yet alive, kept so by a crew more talented than Ellison honestly would have bet, ably piloted by Petty Officer Kaliq.

Ellison boarded the rickety old sub, perhaps for the last time, accompanied by his wife and son. Cecil and Salvius and the young recruits followed after.

They set a course for Correal Island, hundreds of kilometers south. It was the same direction the Carthaginian frigate and surviving patrol boats had gone. Ellison would try for a different course.

"We have reports of an attack on Correal Island," said the comm tech, Petty Officer Guidance Virtue, when they were underway. "Attack helicopters with plasma. The city is burned, casualties high. They even blew down the lighthouse." She shook her head sadly.

"We'll maintain our heading," Ellison said, glancing at the pilot, Kaliq. Djalu occupied the co-pilot chair, touching nothing, watching everything on the navigation console. Ellison had placed the sixteen-year-old female recruit, daughter of a lobsterman named Gabbard, at the comm console next to Virtue, and the other two teenagers at the weapons and sonar consoles. He would train them around the boat, make full submariners of them, if there was time.

They departed the waters around Kawau Island without further incident, leaving their home burning in the distance behind them as they headed south. They kept to smaller channels, but Ellison wouldn't veer too wide of the mark: they were headed south, toward Simon Zorn's last potential location.

Warfare had unfolded among planes, ships, and shore, but Carthaginian helicopters hadn't been mentioned in any reports other than Correal Island. It indicated a small, targeted effort of some kind, rather than the wholesale destruction the machines were raining down everywhere else.

Ellison barely had time to mourn the losses of the *Merrybug* and *Amberjack*, with all hands. They'd sunk enemy patrol boats and inflicted pain on the Carthaginian frigate before going down. Losing his son had left him hollowed out, no heart or soul left with which to feel the compounding, ever-growing losses; there was only coldness within, and a dark, tragic necessity ahead.

He held that in reserve for now, focused on getting his boat to the Central Tropical Trench as fast as he could. He told everyone to keep ears out for any whisper about the *Lancer* or the Carthaginian helicopter squadron.

"How's the new infirmary coming along?" Ellison asked, finally visiting Cadia's new domain hours after getting underway.

"It's a supply closet, Reg." She forced a smile, out of pure habit, no doubt. There might not be any true smiles for a long time, if ever again. She swiveled in the low chair she'd clamped to the wall rack. Her arm was in a sling. She'd had a chance to shower and pulled her hair back. Her son had died, and in time it might kill her, as it might kill Ellison. But she'd also grown up among violence and death, waves of it coming in from the old war as young men shipped out to fight it. The war had stalked them all relentlessly.

"We keep our first aid in here." He gestured to the top shelf.

"And your toilet paper." She pointed to the bottom one.

"All things you'll need as a ship's doc."

"I'm not an actual doctor."

"You're a million times better than the one we had here during the last war," he said. "Kid with six months of medical school and the shakiest hands you ever saw."

They looked at each other, smiled.

And in that connection, the darkness arose, the death of their child that would probably always overshadow all else between them. Their smiles withered.

"How is Djalu doing out there? I told him he could stay back here with me—"

"He's great. He needs something useful to do now. I've got plenty of that."

"He always used to wish he could go out on the boat with you, back when he was a boy," Cadia said. "The whole time you were gone, he'd talk about it."

"Not last summer when I tried to hire him for the fishing crew."

"Last summer he was only interested in Maisy Knowles."

"The fireman's daughter? She's just a little kid."

"They're the same age, Reg."

"Yeah. Of course." He shook his head. "The years race by."

"You miss a lot when you're out running the world."

"Only the good parts," he said, and they were quiet again. Finally, he said, "I need something to keep me awake and charged up."

"You need rest. Rest now will keep you up and running later, but with a clearer head."

"I can't afford to rest now."

"It's likely going to be your last chance."

"Come with me, then."

"I will," she said. "As soon as my toilet paper closet is ready for patients."

Later, Ellison sat alone in his cabin, not much larger than a standard coat closet, but with the luxury of privacy. He wasn't sleeping but reviewing the latest known topographical maps of the Central Tropical Trench, projecting them in three dimensions around him, studying all the little keys sprawling in both directions from Correal Island, most of them supposedly deserted, magnets for sports fishermen, extreme divers, and hardcore wilderness enthusiasts with sea kayaks and storm-resistant tents. There were countless places a clever man could hide, assuming Depascal was anywhere nearby. Hopefully he would connect with Inrick and the *Lancer* soon and get an update.

Reports came in from battles around the world, from

commanders of decimated forces, often recently and hastily promoted to replace dead officers.

Over the hours, the reports themselves slowed to a trickle.

"Sir," Virtue's voice finally said from his room's speaker. "I am sorry to interrupt, but SQUIDS appears to be going dark."

"Dark?" He raced outside. They were still an hour from Correal Island, which wasn't likely to be their final destination at this point. They were far too late for whatever had happened there.

"This clip was beginning to circulate." Virtue brought it up on a screen; most of the array of small screens were blank now, when before there had been torrents of unsorted information.

The video showed a couple of the reaper marines deep underwater. One had a giant circular saw on its left arm, which it was using to slice through a thick bundle of underwater communication cables.

The second one turned toward the underwater security drone that had spotted them and fired something like the signature multi-bladed weapon of the reapers, only modified into a harpoon for underwater use. The blades hurtled at the camera viewpoint, and the video went black.

"They're cutting up SQUIDS," Ellison said.

"But that's our only line of communication," Virtue said, sounding horrified. As she should have.

Without SQUIDS, without communication, there was no Coalition. That was the truth. Ellison needed his crew to keep plunging forward in spite of it.

Ellison turned and looked at Salvius, sulking at the back, his face swelling. "I'd say your people have gotten us pretty good, wouldn't you?"

"I didn't want this," Salvius said.

"Minerva," Ellison said.

The silver girl appeared in the air beside Ellison, legs crossed, startling those onboard who hadn't seen her before. Which was most of them.

"She's here?" Djalu asked. "The one who saved us up in space?"

"That's me. It's good to see you too, Djalu," Minerva said, extra sweetly.

"What kind of missile defense do they have up there?" Ellison asked. "We have our Megiddo missiles."

"Your space hoppers are quite capable of reaching Carthage's carriers, but they would be knocked aside readily."

"You said they've also set up shop on our spaceport."

"Yes. My counterpart up there is trying to make things difficult for them, but they've brought in specialized new software to hunt for me."

"What have they invested on the spaceport?" He was trying to view the conflict the way the Simon would. Investment, profit, loss.

"There's a battalion of reapers, plus weapon stores, fighter drones attached at the docks, industrial robots transforming the interior—"

"So it's an asset of theirs now. Full of smaller assets."

"Generally speaking—"

"Have they installed missile defense on the spaceport?" Ellison asked.

The room fell quiet, all eyes on him.

"On *your* spaceport? No, not yet. They probably wouldn't expect you to—" Minerva began.

"So we could destroy it, and all the Carthaginian assets onboard, if we act fast," Ellison said.

"There are many civilians still trapped on the station," Minerva said. "Captives of the Iron Hammers contingent up there. Citizens from across the Coalition, spaceport workers, and interstellar traders from other worlds—"

"So we could kill a contingent of Hammers, too? With the Megiddos?"

"Only with significant collateral damage. Significant loss of civilian life. Such a course would be inadvisable for a number of reasons."

"Virtue, send up a radio buoy and open a channel to Red Command."

"Buoy away, sir, and..." Her hand shivered. "Sir, I'm not trained—"

"I'll make the call." Ellison switched to a classified SQUIDS acoustic channel. He had to recite a private code to identify himself, one he'd been given the day he'd become minister-general, to be used only when contacting Red Command. "Minerva, use the radio buoy to contact your counterpart on the spaceport. I need current locations for the spaceport and the major Coalition ships. Maybe we'll get lucky and slide something through."

"You intend to use them? I cannot approve of this plan," the silver girl-ghost said.

"Salvius tells me Simon sees everything in terms of cost and benefit. The best way we can hurt him is to bleed him financially. And that spaceport is the most valuable asset we can reach."

"You don't care about the civilians?" Salvius asked.

"Are you trying to be my conscience, Carthaginian?" Ellison said. "My world is in a knife fight for its life, if you haven't noticed. If you know something else I can do with our most powerful weapons before your machines find them and destroy them, speak up."

Salvius stared at him. His mouth was open but no words emerged.

"This is a hard war. We make hard choices." Ellison looked at Djalu; his son was listening to him, absorbing everything, for better or worse.

"Red Command, Minister-General." The voice that came on the line sounded too youthful for the responsibilities behind it. "Ready for... your instructions, sir."

"I'll be sending you a series of orbital targets," Ellison said. "We're launching every Megiddo in the stable."

"Yes, sir." If the man had doubts, he was too well trained to express them.

Ellison muted the channel. "Minerva?"

"Are you sure this is the best course?" she asked, her voice chiming softly from multiple speakers, her agitation echoing all over the control room.

"It's the only course. We bleed the Carthaginians all we can."

After what seemed like an eternal moment, Minerva provided all the coordinates.

"Sir," the voice said from Red Command. "Nuclear procedure requires sign-off from at least one other member of the Council of Ministers."

Ellison tried to imagine tracking down Kartokov or Gilra and getting their approval for his plan. There was no time, he told himself. SQUIDS could go offline any moment, dissected by the reaper marines, leaving all of them alone in the dark.

There was another factor, of course—the Aquaticans would never support it, would consider it a mortal sin, and so Gilra would never approve. Even Kartokov might oppose him, and Ellison had no time for a debate.

"You don't need multiple authorization anymore, son.

Not after the emergency war powers act passed by the House of Ambassadors in its last session." The words *last session* hung in the air, weightier than he'd intended. The physical House of Ambassadors had been destroyed, many of its members killed; it seemed doubtful that the august body, once the expression of their world's hope for a future of peaceful conflict resolution that avoided the wars of the past, would ever convene again.

"Yes, sir," the unseen young man said crisply, and went about his job as he'd been trained. Red Command was the final backup; its missile launch system had been pointed toward vital targets all over the Polar Archipelago. Some of these had already been struck with heavy but non-nuclear intercontinentals in response to the Hammers' bombing of Tower Island.

Red Command's Megiddo missiles were topped with nuclear warheads meant to strike down enemy bases and cities like holy hammers from the sky to massively end life in the enemy nation.

However, the missiles were space hoppers, powerful enough to rise above the atmosphere and strike any target on the planet. This meant they could also strike objects in orbit. Red Command had war-gamed this, too.

Everyone on the *Scorpion* fell silent as the voice from Red Command counted off the launch of the Coalition's most powerful weapons. After this, and their heavy losses in parallel battles across their world, Galapagos would be virtually defenseless.

But we kept our freedom, Ellison thought.

Those words felt hollow now. Everything did, after losing his son.

The missiles went up.

Most were targeted at Carthage's carriers: the *Jimmu*,

the *Pendragon*, the *Rubicon*, the naval megacarrier called the *Typhoon*, and others that had arrived.

Three of the missiles were not targeted at enemy craft but at Galapagos's own space station, its lone connection to the interstellar trade highways.

The young man's voice from Red Command, relaying data from the missiles' sensors, was their only source of information.

The warheads en route to the Carthaginian ships faced dense showers of plasma; the carriers had plenty of time to detect the missiles rising from the planetary surface and prepare their defenses. The plasma ate up the missiles like acid eating flesh, and they never detonated.

The *Jimmu* defended Galapagos's spaceport as well as itself. The carrier fired blobs of plasma so large they completely engulfed one of the nuclear missiles, then the other, leaving little trace of them.

The third missile, however, struck the target.

The spaceport had been cobbled together over time, level by level, from pieces of this and pieces of that, much like Ellison's sub. Designed for trade and transport, not for orbital warfare, the spaceport possessed no external defenses, no shields beyond the layers of atmospheric insulation.

When the nuclear weapon hit, the spaceport crumpled like a paper cup at crush depth. Every level of the port was instantly destroyed, everyone aboard instantly dead. Carthage lost many of its war and construction machines, and the Hammers lost whatever men they'd stationed on the port, but an unclear number of civilians died, too, some of them citizens of Galapagos, others just traders or travelers who'd stopped at the wrong spaceport at the wrong time.

Ellison felt all eyes in the control room on him. Nobody said a word. Even Red Command fell silent.

It was Virtue who finally spoke up. "We've lost contact with Red Command, sir."

Voices began to come in over the remaining communications channels. Angry voices from around the Coalition, condemning Ellison for his rash action. A Green Islander used the term war criminal. An Aquatican commander brought up the possibility of radioactive fallout from above, calling it an unpardonable sin against the sacred ocean life.

But it was the only way we could strike the enemy, Ellison thought. It wasn't a bitter thought; he was beyond bitterness, beyond all real feeling. He'd dealt as much damage to the enemy as the Coalition was capable of dealing.

And now the Coalition was dying.

They lost communications fast as Carthage finished dismembering SQUIDS, ending any long-distance communications. The machines had already taken down Galapagos's satellites and surface transmission towers.

The voices of criticism, calling for Ellison's removal from office, his arrest and imprisonment, fell silent as their enemy cut apart their undersea lines.

Ellison stood alone, commander of nothing beyond his own boat now, his crew of youngsters half his age still gaping at him. What did they see? A monster? At the moment, he didn't care, as long as they obeyed. There was still more to do.

"Maintain our current heading," he told his pilot, Petty Officer Kaliq. "Correal Island. Run quiet and deep."

Chapter Fourteen

The *CISS Byrsa*

The interior of the Carthaginian salvage ship was a hellish factoryscape, a dim place of enormous machines hammering, drilling, and screwing, metal on metal on metal, illuminated by welding torches and showers of sparks.

When Colt and Mohini first arrived, they had to hold still while robots clearly made from cobbled-together scrap inspected the shuttle for damage. Mohini had unplugged her computer from the console. Minerva somehow silently convinced the bots that Mohini, Colt, and the Butler Jeffrey units were reapers returning in good condition after losing most of their squad below.

The shuttle was obviously a falling-apart piece of junk and needed repairs, as it probably did after every use, so the three of them were allowed to depart while repairs commenced.

The area outside the shuttle was hardly safe or reassuring, though. They moved through a machine-shop floor,

Colt and Mohini wired together by their comm cable, the butler-bot following at a lag, slowing them down, not seeming to understand their hand gestures urging him to hurry.

They moved through a factory-like environment that ran with no concern for human safety, since humans weren't supposed to be here, anyway. Machines pulled apart other machines; useful parts were sent along conveyor belts to be sorted and stored by giant industrial arms. Other parts were shredded and melted down, the bright glowing metal flowing into long molds to be stored as bars.

The more useful parts went forward to constructor bots, which themselves looked like they'd been built out of spare parts. The bots worked, not very quickly at all, to take items from the storage shelves and create functioning machines out of them.

Colt and Mohini weaved through the industrial labyrinth guided only by Minerva's whispers in their ears, their path lit by the red glow of molten metal and the flashing white glare of plasma cutters. Enormous machines moved around them in ways that were completely unpredictable, their swinging and grabbing arms threatening to cave in Colt and Mohini's skulls, their tracked wheels threatening to crush them.

"I don't see how any place on this ship could be safe," Colt said. The silence while surrounded by all these machines was eerie; all he could hear was his own heartbeat and Mohini's soft breathing, conveyed by the cable. There were gaping holes in the salvage ship's hull, like a rotten roof with a view of the stars beyond.

"You don't think that conveyor belt full of armored plates looks like a good place to sleep at night?" Mohini asked.

"I'm sure we'll find some miserable storage tank somewhere."

"It's not far now," Minerva said. Her voice had a chiming, ringing-bell quality. "There's an old ladder well just ahead."

"Good. I'm feeling insanely exposed out here." Colt looked at a truck-sized robot welding together lengths of pipe. The thing paused its work to rotate its massive, sensor-studded barrel of a head toward Colt. He looked away quickly and kept moving.

The ladder well was a narrow chimney-like space, with no machines ahead that Colt could see. Steep, shallow steps, almost like ladder rungs, led up to another level.

They reached a pair of large beige doors that fit together like puzzle pieces, capable of retracting into wall pockets. The sensor lights around them were completely dark, and the doors were wrapped in thick, clear plastic, as though some kind of plague quarantine had been established.

"What's this?" Colt asked, whispering though it wasn't particularly necessary.

"The land that time forgot," Mohini replied, smirking. She explored her spacesuit and opened a pocket where a small utility knife was stored. She grimaced at the red stain flaking away on the front of the pocket, then turned her attention to slicing apart the plastic sheeting. "Minerva, help with the doors?"

"Yes. One moment. Yes."

The double doors split open and slid apart, dragging the sliced plastic sheeting in either direction.

What lay beyond was certainly no factory floor. Colt gaped.

"What... what is that?"

"Just a passageway." Mohini led the way in, and he stumbled along behind her, trying to concentrate on his footing.

The doors slid shut behind them.

"Don't forget to delete that door's activity from the ship's maintenance log," Mohini said.

"It never reached the maintenance log," the AI's voice replied, in its chiming tones. "This area is pressurized. You can remove your helmets. It will be cold."

She wasn't exaggerating. Colt was eager to take off his helmet, but the air in the dim passageway wasn't far above freezing.

"Why, uh, are there naked people all over the walls?" Colt asked.

The passageway's red and gold walls were curved; built into them like support ribs were startlingly realistic metal sculptures of human beings, tangled in erotic groupings, legs twisted together, hips and breasts jutting out, tongues lolling, faces contorted in expressions that could have been extreme pleasure or pain—it was really open to interpretation.

"Ah, Second Revival Neoeroticism," the Butler Jeffrey said, looking over the walls with obvious approval. "This was quite well appointed for its day."

"Looks like we scored the luxury suites. Right, Minerva?" Mohini had removed her helmet and took a deep breath. The air was cold, but at least it didn't smell like the insides of their heavily soiled spacesuits.

"Correct." Minerva's voice echoed over the passageway speakers now. "The *Byrsa* is an old carrier, built in a time when it was expected to have a full human crew. The carrier would transport both military and cargo craft between star systems. Carthaginian politicians and diplomats used to travel aboard this ship, as well as wealthy merchants and top-level military and intelligence officials. Most of the lower residential levels have been removed to make room for the salvaging operation, but this one remains."

"Most Carthaginian ships keep a small life-support area available," Mohini explained. "In case they need to offer passage to someone. Or take prisoners. In this case, it looks like they left only the cream of the cream."

"Lucky us." Colt opened doors, looking into rooms with enormous beds and private marble bathrooms. The decor was brash, loud, colorful, thick with gold leaf, and often quite erotic, even in small details like faucets and showerheads. Carthaginians were weird, he decided.

The main corridor widened into a kind of entertainment hall, with a small dance floor and strangely soft walls and ceiling.

"They can project any kind of environment here. Run a war game, business meeting, extreme party, any kind of deep immersion," Mohini said. "This place is nice."

"And the machines won't detect us here?" Colt asked.

"According to the logs, no humans have ridden aboard the *Byrsa* since it was downgraded to a salvage ship nineteen years ago," Minerva said. "Regular maintenance check on the life-support area is not due for another hundred and fifty days. This area is kept heated to a level sufficient to keep the water and sewer lines from freezing. Any increase in heat or drain on the *Byrsa*'s power grid will draw attention. The life-support area does have backup power cells, which will be our only source of electricity, since their depletion will not be noticed until the next maintenance check."

"So... can we use the water and electricity or not?" Colt asked.

"Be sparing with both. This is a largely self-contained area requiring minimal attention from the ship's central neural net. We should keep it that way."

"It sounds like you don't have administrative control of the ship," Mohini said.

"I have influence," Minerva said. "The *Byrsa*'s actions must, however, seem logical to any automated quality assurance review by any Simon or command ship. Fortunately, a salvage ship is less likely to be selected for rigorous analysis than almost any other kind of craft."

"But the machines will still have to notice we're taking off with their ship, right?" Colt asked. "I mean we aren't just sneaking off with a whole carrier."

"The first directive of a salvage ship is to clear out orbital debris, particularly after battles," Minerva said. "Otherwise debris can threaten satellites and orbital stations. Recent events have destroyed the orbital defense station of Galapagos and several Carthaginian craft. A general signal went out from Galapagos for ships that could assist in the effort there. I have simply suggested to the *Byrsa* that it should go and collect the salvage."

"When do we get underway?" Colt asked.

"We have already begun our departure from Earth's gravity well in preparation for hyperspace. Hyperlaunch estimated in fifty-one minutes."

"Would anyone care for tea?" The Butler Jeffrey had been nosing about at the far end of the room and found a beverage-service area. "It's freeze-dried, sadly, when fresh would obviously be preferred—"

"I'll take some," Mohini said, and Colt shrugged and ordered a cup for himself. It was odd to see an android so like the Simon—so similar to the one that had imprisoned and tortured him and caused nearly everyone he cared about to die—now scurrying, servile, eager to wait on humans.

Mohini walked out to the middle of the floor and took a deep breath. "It's so nice to be back in a civilized place. After stowing away on that last ship, and then Earth... it's like waking from a bad dream."

"So this is what normal looks like for you," Colt said, looking around at the polished tables and dance floor, the soft walls like giant blue pillows.

"I'll show you. Minerva, can this place project Labyrinth Park?"

"Yes." Projectors all around came to life.

They no longer stood in the banquet hall, but in an enormous garden, with pathways twisted away on all sides of them, the paths separated by tall, iridescent flowering hedges, by statues and fountains, by broken-looking lengths of marble wall imitating ancient ruins.

"This is one my favorite places back home," Mohini said, leading him down one of the wide crushed-pebble paths flanked by high walls of plant life and faux fancy ruins. "It's a public park. They would totally remake it every few months, a new maze, like a new mystery to solve. You could download an app to guide you through it, obviously, but that takes the fun out."

The environment shifted around them as they moved, a full-immersion simulation. They reached a garden with a pond full of strange plants, birds, and fluttering pollinating insects; small digital signs gave the name and home planet of each exotic creature and plant in the menagerie.

They reached an edge of the maze where the walls and floor were glass. Colt hesitated at the threshold of the clear corridor, awed and terrified.

The park sat high in the sky, the ground invisibly far

below them, easily a hundred stories or more. Much of the view below was obscured by lower levels of the city—for they clearly stood in a city, an impossibly immense one.

The city sprawled out to the horizon, full of skyscrapers as high as the one where they stood, or even higher. Colt had lived among the ruins of such towers all his life, but he doubted they had ever looked like this—immense yet light, organic and geometric shapes that seemed to defy gravity, towers that looked like they were woven from threads of gemstone fiber, towers like forested mountains capped with domes full of clouds. Layers of black magnetic roads snaked like vines among the dreamlike edifices, thick with cars moving at rocket speed.

Brightly colored floating bubbles swarmed in orderly streams in the airspace between the immense buildings. Colt watched one candy-red bubble drop out of the stream. It landed on a covered window ledge outside an apartment, opened a cavity in its bottom, deposited a shiny package, and flew off again. It was a drone delivering some items to a person's home, but it reminded him of a fly dropping onto a carcass just long enough to plop out a few maggot eggs.

"What... is all that?" Colt asked, barely able to breathe.

"Carthage City," Mohini said. "It's where I grew up."

"It doesn't look real."

"Definitely real."

Colt stared, unable to process most of what he was seeing. There was color, light, and movement everywhere.

"So that's what it's like," he finally said. "For all you. For the people who bomb other worlds into dust and then take everything that's left. You conquer an empire so you can live like this. You slaughter... how many would you say have died at Carthage's hands? Millions? Billions? Is it billions?"

"Surely not," Mohini whispered. "Most Earthlings had

already migrated away before the war, and the population had been falling—"

"Are you sure?" Colt asked. "Or is that just something you people like to tell yourselves so you don't feel like such monsters?"

"Colt, I know this is hard to believe, but most people on Carthage are good people—"

"Seriously? So good they can't be sure whether they've murdered millions or billions of people, right?"

"They don't really know. Information is controlled in all kinds of subtle ways. Hardly anyone can look over the wall and see what's outside. Hardly anyone wants to, because then you fall into being a freaky outsider. And if you keep it up, get too radicalized, they can find some way to discredit you, or ways to make you disappear. Sometime it's a convenient suicide."

"But if you can see through it, other people should be able to."

"Not everyone has a mother in the state department and the ability to crack her private communications. To read about the real brutality of the Earth 'rehabilitation' program, which was just to keep any society from forming again. Because humans will always look to Earth."

"Could you make them available publicly?" Colt asked.

"Oh, I did. Half a dozen conspiracy-nut websites went crazy over it for about a week, but then this rumor about mind control by interdimensional aliens overshadowed the story. It's hard for people to sort the truth from the noise. That's one of their secrets for social control. Information might be hard to suppress, but it's easy to create, so the trick is to just dump an endless torrent of it onto people. A constant flood of confusing, conflicting information that's almost impossible to sort through. When facts are too difficult to figure out, people will retreat into emotion and myth and give up on the truth."

Colt rubbed his head. "I'm not sure I follow you. But some people on Carthage know the truth, right?"

"That's why there are rebels."

"How many?"

Mohini shrugged. "No way to know."

"Can we make this stop?" He gestured at the cityscape ahead, then the strange maze-park in the sky behind them. "All this? It's hurting my head."

"Sure. End projection." The room reverted to what it had been—open space, soft blue walls.

Colt look at Mohini, feeling more distant from her than he ever had, even when she'd been a complete stranger.

"And if everything fails, you'll eventually go home, won't you? You said this was like coming home for you. You want to go back to Carthage."

"I don't think so," she said. "If we fail, I'll probably die. Just like you."

Colt nodded, letting that sink in. She might have been a child of extreme privilege, living in a safe world where nobody ever starved, but she'd given up everything, even her family, in order to do what she believed was right. He wondered if he would have done the same in her position if he'd grown up with her life. Would he have made the choice to trade everything for, essentially, nothing?

"Your tea is prepared." The Butler Jeffrey approached with a silver tray topped with a matching teapot and four cups and saucers. He set these out on a banquet table that folded down to meet him. Then he poured two cups, or at least attempted to do so. The butler-bot's aim was beyond poor; little of the tea made it into the cups, yet he seemed unaware of the enormous puddle he was pouring onto the tabletop. "Would anyone care for starch-based creamer or non-caloric sweetener?"

Colt took a teacup. A splash of the black tea had made it all the way inside, barely enough to cover the bottom. He sniffed the unfamiliar liquid and looked at Mohini uncertainly.

"I'll take sweetener," Mohini said. She watched with interest as the butler-bot tore open a packet of yellowish powder and shook it in the general area of the other cup, again getting most of it on the table. Then he stirred a spoon in the air, several centimeters above the lip of the cup.

"Here you are, ma'am." The butler-bot presented her nearly empty cup as though nothing could possibly be wrong with it. "While no fresh scones or other baked goods are in stock, I believe I saw crackers preserved in cellophane—"

"Bring those," Colt said. "Actually, show us where you're finding all this food. I'm starving."

The Jeffrey indicated a pantry just off the banquet room, crammed with more food than Colt had ever seen in one place, sealed in plastic sleeves, bright foil wrappers, cans, and bottles.

"Chuckle Cakes!" Mohini gasped, lifting a box that featured bright cartoon characters with enormous yellow smiley faces holding their pudgy cartoon bellies and laughing as though they'd heard the funniest joke ever. The words HA! HA! floated all around them, in case their facial expressions weren't clear enough. She tore the box open and tossed him three round cakes shrink-wrapped together. "Neapolitan Jelly Banana. I haven't eaten these since I was a kid."

Colt ripped open the plastic. The cupcake icing was an

almost blinding shade of yellow; the smiley-face eyes were chocolate buttons, its grin a big strawberry-red stripe. When he bit into it, a lump of weird sweet goo drooled into his mouth from the cupcake's interior.

"My mom didn't allow these in the house, but my friends sometimes had them." Mohini made a grotesque face. "I'm sorry. They're not as good as I remember."

"They're amazing." Colt crammed another one in his mouth, his mind blown by the extreme sweetness and flavor. Nothing gamey or rotten about it; the snack cakes had been preserved for years, as if by magic.

"Yeah, don't eat too many at once. Let's find some vegetables."

Soon, they cooked together, both of them quickly rejecting the butler-bot's offer to cook for them. They warmed canned tomatoes and broth and beans into a hot, rich stew on the stove. There were even vacuum-sealed herbs and seasonings; apparently Mohini liked things very, very spicy when she got the chance. She gave him tastes of it as she went, and soon his eyes were burning, but he didn't complain. It felt good to eat something real, to taste what food must have been like in the old world, before humanity was reduced to rubble rats.

As they sat down to eat, he felt a pang of guilt for leaving Earth behind.

"Hyperlaunch in ten minutes," Minerva said, interrupting their brief peace. She appeared in a pale, transparent silver form, sitting on the counter, her kid-sized legs dangling in the air. "It's not a great idea to eat right before."

"Yeah, I got a little distracted by the presence of actual food." Mohini took the bowl back from Colt—he'd only had one spoonful, and his stomach had growled excitedly at the taste of it—poured it back into the pot, and quickly sealed the pot and stored it in the refrigerator.

"That... was so cruel," Colt said, looking at the empty spot where the hot, spicy stew had been.

"Eat after hyperlaunch, trust me," Mohini said. "Where should we strap in?"

They ended up lying on a massive bed in a three-room suite, the largest bed and suite that still existed on the ship, looking at each other and waiting for the big launch. Her dark eyes seemed luminous in the dim room, her face somehow softer than ever, more relaxed and open.

"You know what I want to do?" she whispered. "Go back and eat that stew. I'm so hungry."

"Did someone say they wanted more tea?" the butler-bot entered the room, swinging the kettle.

"Nobody said that," Colt replied, sitting up.

"I'll just brew a little more, then. How many guests are we expecting?"

"None," Mohini said. "We're expecting none."

"As you say." Butler Jeffrey bowed slightly and exited.

"There's a problem." The silver projection of Minerva appeared, solid and glowing silver, not bothering to conserve energy at all. "The *Tyre* is pausing our preparations for hyperspace."

"A tire?" Colt asked.

"The *Tyre* is the carrier in command of Earth's orbital space," Minerva said. "Apparently it wishes to review the *Byrsa*'s declared itinerary."

"I thought you said salvage ships were beneath notice." Mohini leaped to her feet and grabbed her backpack.

"Typically, yes, but security precautions might be raised due to our recent activities in Chicago."

"I need access to this ship's neural net," Mohini said. "Right now."

"You'll want the command console on the bridge," Minerva said. "But you have to work with me. We have to stay invisible."

"If they're stopping us for analysis, we've already lost our invisibility," she replied, running. "What we have to do now is *run*. Put on speed, get into hyperspace, and stop this ship full of creepy Frankenstein robots from turning against us. Which of those jobs do you want?"

Colt grabbed his own pack and his laser rifle and chased after her.

The old bridge was a level higher, dark and cold. Mohini had to manually boot the old command console to bring it online.

Something loud pounded against one of the sealed doors to the bridge, and Colt raised his rifle at it. It sounded again and again, like clockwork.

"Is that one of those creepy robots turning against us?" Colt asked.

"I could tell you if this thing would finish waking up." She checked her own LogicSphere, which she'd plugged into the ship's console to help her crack into the system. She slapped the console. "Hurry up!"

The pounding on the door continued.

Pounding began to ring out from another door, one Colt hadn't even noticed before. Colt wasn't sure which one to cover with his rifle, so he kept it on the first one.

"Minerva, is something trying to break in here and kill us?"

Minerva's silver image appeared in the air nearby. "Hello, this is Minerva," she said. "I'm currently using all my available processing power trying to wrest control of the ship's propulsion system away from the *Tyre*. If you would like to leave a message, I can consider your query or input at a time when I can afford the spare attention."

"Are you serious right now?" Colt asked.

The projection vanished.

"Not helpful," Colt muttered as the clanging ramped up at both entrances. The only way out was the way they'd come in. So far, there was no banging from that door. "Did we not bring the butler-bot? Maybe he'll put the fear of Simon in them, like the other machines down in the sewer."

"We could really use that guy," Mohini murmured, her eyes fixed on the dark sphere in her hands. "Go get him."

"What?"

"Get the butler," she murmured, her eyes still entranced by dancing icons and symbols Colt couldn't begin to understand. She began to chew her lower lip, still badly wounded from last time she'd bitten it too deep.

"Are you sure you'll be safe? With those... things trying to get in—"

"I'm not sure, so hurry!" she snapped.

He hurried, but hesitated before opening the one door where nothing was banging. Maybe it was a trap; the machines were making a huge noise at the other two doors in hopes of flushing Colt and Mohini out through the supposedly quiet and safe third door.

"Go on!" she snapped again.

He pressed the door control, raised his rifle, and hoped for the best, which would be to see nothing at all.

A machine moved toward him from the shadows beyond the door, metal glinting in its hands.

Colt fired, and his blue laser bolt lit up the passageway beyond. The Butler Jeffrey's face looked somewhat aghast when the bolt shot through the silver teapot on his tray. Steaming tea chugged out onto the floor.

"Oh," Colt said. "Yikes. Uh, sorry—"

"You've done a spot of damage." The butler-bot moved its tray aside, revealing a narrow tunnel carved through its lower torso. "You narrowly missed my central neural column. Repair cost will be significant."

"Colt, did you shoot my robot?" Mohini snapped.

"Uh, good news is, I found him." Colt grabbed the butler-bot's arm and tried to pull the android through the door, onto the bridge with them. "Come on inside with us—"

"Damage is assessed at felony level."

"Yeah, we'll get you fixed as soon as we can—"

"Security mode initiated," the butler-bot said, and its usual chipper-yet-obsequious tone was gone, replaced by a flat monotone. It seized Colt's arm. Colt went from trying to pull the android along to trying to pull free of it. The butler's grip was literally steel.

Colt's guts seemed to melt and freeze up all at once; it was a new level of stark fear as he became sharply aware not only of the butler's resemblance to the monstrous Simon that had once captured him, but also of how the butler must essentially just be a reaper underneath, a steel skeletal frame, just another standard unit. At some point, it had been diverted down a different factory path, given a particular set of processors and programming, skin, a face, the appearance of humanity, even the illusion of frailty and helplessness.

"Colt, hurry!" Mohini shouted. "We need to seal that door!"

"Yeah, he's flipping out on me."

"I don't have time for this!"

"Who does?" Colt tried to pull loose of the butler-bot. "Let go! Release! Unclamp! What's the command?"

"You will be detained until law enforcement arrives." The butler-bot's fingers dug in tight around Colt's upper arm, its fingertips biting into his muscles.

"Let go!" Colt said. "There's no law enforcement here. We're on a trash ship in outer space."

"Colt, hurry up!" Mohini shouted. More banging sounds echoed from the other doors. He wondered how long they would hold up.

"The ship's commander or authorized representative," the butler-bot said.

"There's nobody here but us. You know this. No commander."

"Every interstellar craft has a human commander."

"No offense, but your information's pretty outdated," Colt said. "We found you powered down in a box. I think you've been offline for years, maybe even since before the war on Earth."

"I require an update. My wireless connection has been disabled. It must be repaired."

"Yeah, we kind of did that on purpose, and we're keeping it that way," Colt said.

"Unacceptable. It is imperative that I update."

"I don't really like this new you," Colt said. "You should go back to spilling tea and acting clueless. I liked that better."

"I must update." The butler-bot marched him through the door onto the bridge.

"Finally!" Mohini didn't look up, but the doors slammed shut behind them.

"Big problem," Colt said. "He's in some kind of security mode that makes him less friendly."

"I require a physical connection," the butler-bot said, hauling Colt around as he looked over the available consoles.

"Who doesn't? Now release him!" Mohini snapped.

The butler-bot ignored her. He slid the plastic sheeting off an old infosec console and started the boot-up process.

"What are you doing?" Mohini stood up. "Colt, do *not* let him plug into the ship's net right now."

"Should I shoot him again?" Colt turned the rifle, trying to aim it clumsily with his one free hand.

"Do *not* shoot him."

"That doesn't leave a lot of options—" Colt began, and then the Jeffrey hauled him away from the console, toward what turned out to be a supply cabinet full of assorted wires, plugs, and electronics. The butler-bot rummaged through it quickly and sloppily, spilling items onto the floor.

Finally, the android drew out a thin black cable with an oddly shaped plug at one end. It pressed this into the back of its head, after moving aside some of its thin brown hair. Colt recalled its port was there, as well as its manual power buttons. Would the android let him reach those?

Even if he couldn't, he needed to pull the jack out of the android's port so it couldn't connect with the ship.

Colt set down his rifle on the top of the console so his movements would seem less threatening.

"Hey, you got some hair in your, uh, head port there, when you plugged that in," Colt said. "I'll fix it, we don't want you malfunctioning." He reached for the back of the butler-bot's head and extended his thumb and forefinger like prongs. He would try to quickly find and press the power buttons, manually shutting down the android.

He poked the back of its head through its thin hair, but didn't land on the buttons.

"Stop." The butler-bot released Colt's bicep, mercifully restoring circulation to that arm, but instead grabbed Colt's invasive arm by the wrist.

"Is that an XQG port jack?" Mohini asked, looking at the cable attached to the android's head.

"Is that really your concern right now?" Colt asked her, as the android tightened its steel grip.

"It's what I needed. Throw the other end over here."

Colt grabbed the cable; the Butler Jeffrey tried for it at the same time, but its poor fine motor skills betrayed it, and it punched a dent in the console instead.

Colt tossed the bulk of the cable across the room at Mohini. Most of it unspooled before reaching her.

"Give it back!" The butler-bot grabbed Colt's other arm, trapping him.

"I don't have it anymore, genius," Colt said.

The butler-bot threw Colt aside, slamming him into the wall, and stalked along the cable toward Mohini, who was hastily affixing an adapter to the far end.

"Colt, slow him down!" Mohini shouted.

"You're really overestimating my power here." Colt threw himself at the butler-bot for what it was worth, trying to tackle it, but he failed to knock it down or even make it swerve from its course.

It shoved him off single-handedly, sending Colt sprawling across the floor, its eyes never swerving from Mohini, who was fumbling to attach the cable to a second port on her computer, which also remained wired to the command console.

The banging from the doors to the bridge intensified.

One door ruptured and toppled, slamming to the floor much like Colt a moment earlier.

The repair-bots moved into the room, misshapen

chimeras made from cast-off parts and obsolete machinery. One had a stalk-like body with four spindly legs, industrial-clamp hands like claws, and a cluster of squirming hoses at the top, like a hydra with cutting and welding tools for heads. Another was low to the ground, heavily armored, trundling like a beetle. Saws and drills protruded around its edges. More monstrosities followed.

The second door ripped open; a whirring, clanking four-legged crawler-bot with the upper half of a reaper welded to the top of it barged into the room. The reaper's chassis was missing some ribs, its face was just a blank plate with two holes for eye lenses, and both its forearms had been replaced with multi-bladed extendable cutters.

A much smaller bug-like creature scampered alongside the reaper-crawler like a loyal pet on six legs, with mismatched dual machine guns atop it like eyes on stalks.

Colt opened fire at the reaper-crawler, blue laser bolts striking it in the face and the torso while it kept advancing on its four legs. He lowered his barrel and fired at the crawler's central processor; he'd seen Mohini work on her lost crawler enough to know just where to aim.

The thing crouched flat, all four legs folding up like a nervous reflex. The reaper atop swung its blades out at Colt, but it could advance no farther. It lashed uselessly in the air, looking frustrated.

The bug-thing beside it inspected the damage to the reaper-crawler briefly, then turned, flared out a ring of blades, and charged toward Colt, seeming almost angry at the indignity dealt to its impotently lashing companion.

Colt aimed straight for its machine guns, which the little bug hadn't fired at all; maybe the presence of the Butler Jeffrey, or the fact that they were on the bridge of their own ship, caused the machines to minimize damage.

He managed to fry the thing before it got too close, but it took the rest of his rifle's battery to do it, and more old, cobbled-together military hardware was shuffling into the room behind the immobilized reaper-crawler.

He retreated to join Mohini at the command console, where her eyes were completely glued to her LogicSphere, her teeth digging deep into her lower lip.

"I hope you've got plans," Colt said, sliding a fresh battery into place.

"Just hold them off." She didn't even look up at the array of freakish oddball robots moving into the room.

"Sure. I'll just call in our backup with the rocket launchers." He fired at the hydra-headed thing with the tool-topped hose-heads, but everything about that robot was skinny and spiny, difficult to hit. He tried instead for the gator-sized armored beetle thing crawling on the ground, its face a wedge of metal grill like the front end of a locomotive.

Colt sent multiple blasts through its grill, and it finally ceased its advance less than a meter from him, smoke curling out of it, still pointed at Colt like it might come back alive at any moment to finish the job.

If it was a ruse, Colt didn't have time to wait it out. He shot at the spindly hydra bot again, a somewhat easier target now that it was close enough to lash its tools at him.

His blasts at its narrow body held it back, but he was losing battery power fast.

Machines shambled into the room, multi-armed repair-bots from one door, bits of old military and police machinery from the other.

They closed in—one nearby looked something like a dead elephant, with one long flexible front arm tipped with a giant skull-crusher of a claw, dark eye lenses sunk back in its massive head, its steel ribs exposed.

Colt spared one shot each for the nearest robots, but it was hopeless; there were too many of them, much too close.

"Mohini!" he shouted. "We're dead. They've got us."

"Stop rushing me. I'm so deep inside the Jeffrey's operating system right now," she grumbled, her fingers clacking fast and hard over her round screen.

"Would you look?"

She turned her head, saw the array of bizarre machines closing in on them with blades, hammers, and drills, and quite rationally screamed.

Her fingers flew over her computer as she screamed, and the Butler Jeffrey moved over, spreading its arms wide in a "t" shape, shielding Colt and Mohini with his body, the cable like a long tail connecting its head to Mohini's LogicSphere.

The hideous machines stopped their advance.

Then, one by one, they knelt, the front row of them and then the back, as though paying some kind of religious homage to the butler-bot.

"Why are they doing that?" Colt whispered.

"I'm making them do it." Mohini stood and stretched, keeping her computer in one hand, still tethered to the android and the command console. "We have control of the ship, Minerva and me. And everything on it. Something about the butler-bot gave us a weird back door into every system. I actually should explore that a lot more—"

"We have the whole ship?" Colt asked. "So we're good now—"

The ship rattled hard. They were flung against the walls, and all the lights went out.

"What the hell was that?" Colt shouted in the darkness, his head ringing, a sharp pain in his hip.

"Probably a missile," Mohini groaned.

"Correct." Minerva's voice spoke only through the speaker inside Colt's suit, no longer over the speakers in the room around them. "Apparently the *Tyre* has decided our efforts here warrant destruction of the *Byrsa*. We can be assured these events will be reported to the remaining Simons on Earth as well as those back on Carthage."

"We need to jump into hyperspace *now*," Mohini said. She clicked on her suit's built-in flashlight, prompting to Colt find his and do the same.

"Hyperlaunch is inadvisable until a full damage assessment can be made—"

"We'll be dead by then!" Colt said. "Let's do hyperspace now!" He barely had any idea what hyperspace was, but he knew it was the only way out.

"Minerva, override all safety protocols," Mohini said. She sat back in the command seat and drew a net of straps around her. "Strap in, Colt."

He copied her movements, taking the seat beside her.

"Hyperlaunch initiating in six, five, four—"

The entire ship shuddered again, and a roaring boom filled the bridge. He could feel the ship being blown off-kilter as a missile struck it. The repair-bots and other machines clattered into each other in a deafening crash. Colt's restraints dug into his side. Alarms sounded, emergency lights pulsed red.

"Continue hyperlaunch!" Mohini shouted.

"An unstable wobble has been introduced—" Minerva began.

"We don't care! Hyperlaunch anyway!" Colt barked, hoping the machines would listen.

"—hyperlaunch in three, two—"

Colt was suddenly thrown back into his seat so hard he thought his heart and lungs and skull were all being crushed at once. It was an even worse pressure than the shuttle launch, though this seat was thick, soft, and resilient, meant to withstand many hyperlaunches, and fortunately there was no charger digging into his back this time.

He was being shaken side to side at high speed, like a bone in a coyote's mouth. The shaking evolved into a painful wrenching and twisting. It felt like the old ship was finally breaking apart, succumbing to its recent massive damage and the stress of launching into hyperspace.

Then the twisting and slamming slowed.

Colt felt ill and displaced, as if he were somehow sitting upside down.

"I'm going to be sick," he said, unbuckling his restraints.

He pushed out of his seat and fell what seemed upward, but was actually toward the floor, where he sprawled hard.

"Are you all right?" Mohini dropped beside him on the floor. "Colt?"

"Ugh." His head felt like it would crack apart.

All around the bridge, lights flickered on, consoles came to life, and holographic projections appeared above them, showing the current state of the ship's systems, navigation charts for Earth's and Galapagos's systems, and a panoramic exterior view that Colt found hypnotic and strangely chilling. It was like the night sky, only the stars were odd, dark, cloud-like shapes, barely visible hues of blue and purple, unnatural colors that filled him with a cold dread.

"What is that?"

"Hyperspace," Mohini said.

Colt took a deep breath. The upside-down feeling was going away. After a moment, he managed to rise to his feet.

"Can they not chase us here?" Colt looked behind them at a projection showing the crumbling stern of the salvage ship and the dark region of hyperspace behind them.

"Every path through hyperspace is unique." Minerva appeared in full, solid silver form, apparently having freed up enough processing power that she felt like chatting. "The probability of them encountering us here, even if searching for us, is extremely low. Our wobbly launch makes our path even less predictable."

"Oh. Great. Right?" Colt looked between the two girls, the virtual one and the real one.

"However, they will likely arrive in Galapagos's system only seconds after us, ready to continue their assault," Minerva said.

"So that's not so great," Mohini said.

"I get that," Colt said. "And I'm guessing this trash barge doesn't have a lot of major, let's say, plasma cannons or anything we can fight back with."

"Correct," Minerva told him. "Though you may find some usable items in the weapons repair bay."

"What kind of time do we have?"

"The hyperspace trip to Galapagos will take an estimated four hundred forty-one hours," Minerva said.

"That's... pretty fast, though," Mohini said. "I read that it took the first settlers of Galapagos almost a year of hyperspace travel to reach that system. Good thing we have more modern transportation. The galaxy's getting smaller all the time."

Looking out at the strange, cloudy lights of hyperspace, Colt felt just the opposite: the universe seemed to be growing larger and larger, day by day.

Mohini sent the repair-bots and their chimeric creations back out the doors through which they'd entered, literally picking up bits and pieces of themselves along the way. A couple of the repair-bots, including the spindly hydra-headed one, lingered behind to repair the doors.

It was fascinating and frightening, Colt thought, how easily the machines could toggle between helpful assistant and deadly enemy. It was all a matter of software. He supposed it was the same with human beings, only humans had some control over their own software. Didn't they?

Mohini was quickly absorbed into studying the Butler Jeffrey's inner workings, believing the android would give her insight into the Simon unit's foundational architecture. The butler-bot was fully cooperative again, now that Mohini had taken control of him and shut down his security mode.

Colt explored the life-support area more thoroughly. He found startling machines tucked away just out of sight, including a kitchen bot the size of an end table with a number of knife-tipped arms, and a tall, beautiful android in a maid's outfit in full shutdown in one of the bedroom closets; he jumped when he first saw her, startled, thinking it was another person. It seemed like her charge had run out, and she'd just stood there since the whole area had been closed down.

He put on his delightfully salvage-scented helmet again and went out to the factory floor, to a tiny catwalk above it with no rails. Mohini had set the repair-bots back to work, and they were all productive again, busy as bees, humming along as though they'd never tried to kill the humans onboard after all. *Just a matter of software.*

Later, when Colt and Mohini's bodies had recovered from entering hyperspace, they finally ate the stew. It was insanely spicy; Colt found this unpleasant at first, then quite pleasant as he got used to it. Mohini talked excitedly about her study of the android.

They showered. Colt stood amazed at the crystal clear, steaming-hot water that fell from a half-dozen nozzles in the ceiling and walls, at the assortment of colorful goos that Mohini instructed him, somewhat firmly, to use to scrub his hair and skin.

It was alien to him, a bizarre luxury that left him dazed as he stepped out onto the heated floor and rubbed himself with a towel as soft as wild rabbit fur.

They'd been sleeping close together for clear practical reasons, for security and for heat, for much of their travels. At the moment, they could each have taken their own rooms, but they found themselves together by unspoken agreement, lying in the giant bed that could have slept five people, the one where they'd meant to ride out the hyperlaunch.

"I'm about to lie here for the next twenty hours," Mohini told him.

"You think it's safe for us to rest? Can we trust Minerva?"

"Well, she's driving the ship. So if she wants us dead, we're dead. Unless you know how to fly a starship manually."

"I can't say it's ever come up." Colt looked her over. She wore a thick black bathrobe, as he did; they were among the clothing items available in the closet. Her sable hair spread out around her on the crisp white pillow. "We really picked the right ship to hijack."

She laughed. "Might as well die in style." She looked at him for a long moment. "And I don't know if it's these accommodations, or our recent escapes from death, or knowing that they're probably going to atomize us the moment we drop out of hyperspace, or maybe it's just some weird thing about you, but... I'm kind of in a strange mood tonight." She untied the front of her robe, and it inched open, revealing a long stripe of taut brown skin and lacy white underwear. "Aren't you?"

He moved closer and kissed her. She took off her robe, revealing the high-end lingerie she'd found on the ladies' side of the closet. He took off his robe, revealing a baggy sweat suit, and she laughed.

A while later, they slept.

Colt awoke in a panic. The lights were dim. The bed was soft. Mohini breathed gently beside him, wearing nothing. The heat was up to a toasty level now, since they no longer needed to hide their presence from the ship.

Everything was too quiet, too calm. There had to be something wrong somewhere. Colt grabbed his long-trusted old automatic rifle from beside the bed and stalked the shadows of the room, looking for the threat. There had to be a threat; there was always a threat. Thinking you were safe was the kind of illusion that got you killed.

Cold sweat covered him as he checked the door into the room, then the bathroom where he'd showered and rubbed weird flower-scented goo on himself. Everything was unfamiliar to him. He was on a rickety old ship full of holes, and full of machines that could go hostile anytime. How could he have let his guard down?

He paced in front of the door for a while, expecting trouble to come erupting through at any moment. After a time, he sat down and watched the door from his chair, rifle in his lap.

He must have dozed off eventually, because he woke to someone disarming him. He reached and grabbed the shadowy figure.

"Colt!" she gasped. "What's wrong with you? Let go!"

Blinking, he realized the shadowy figure was Mohini. She looked at him with pain in her eyes.

"I... sorry."

"I just didn't want you shooting anyone in your sleep. Me, for example. Or yourself. Why are you over here?"

He rubbed his head. "I panicked."

"Why?"

"We're surrounded by machines, in the middle of nowhere. I mean *nowhere*. Doesn't it freak you out?"

"If I really thought about that too long, it probably would, yes." She backed away from him and set his rifle down on the dresser.

"You can go back to sleep."

"I doubt it." She rubbed her arm where he'd grabbed her. "I'll go back to work instead. Maybe I'll even get Butler Jeffrey to pour some coffee near a cup for me."

"Probably better just to do it yourself."

"Yeah. It's better not to rely on anyone." Mohini tied her robe around her, then grabbed her backpack with her computer and walked out into the passageway. The door slid shut behind her.

Colt quickly grew uncomfortable with the idea of her out there by herself, so he dressed and followed her to the bridge.

She sat cross-legged in the command chair, her computer still hooked to both the console and the butler-bot, which stood and stared serenely forward. She didn't look up, very possibly was too absorbed in the glowing data on her screen to know Colt had entered the room.

He moved to the kitchen, found the coffee in the walk-in freezer, and puzzled his way through the pictogram instructions on the side of the coffee machine. Soon he carried two hot, tall cups to the bridge.

"Thanks," Mohini said, glancing up for half a second when he placed it in the cupholder of her chair.

They were silent a long while, her working, him glancing at the doors, half-expecting another invasion. "Are you sure those machines won't turn on us again?"

"For now, Minerva and I have control. As long as we're in hyperspace, there's no radio contact, no threat of the machines taking control again."

"But once we drop out of hyperspace, that becomes a threat again. Just like the Carthaginian warships that are probably chasing us."

"And don't forget we'll be running into a nest of them already there, waging war on Galapagos," she said. "So we'll be sandwiched between enemies ahead and behind."

"Those first few seconds after we come out of hyperspace will be critical, then," he said. "Life or death."

She nodded, her eyes on her screen.

Day and night cycles passed, marked by the circadian-timed rhythm of the life-support area's automatic lighting system. She studied the android. He looked over the ship and the myriad oddball machines it transported, and prepared for their arrival at Galapagos.

They ate rich Carthaginian food, the best he'd ever had in his life, from the vast supply of frozen and preserved food. They drank wine. They slept long hours.

A few days later, he watched her slide out of bed and cross to the minibar for a drink. They'd rapidly grown accustomed to this deep shared comfort, eating together, sleeping together, living together.

"Maybe we should change course," he said while she chugged a bottle of water. She was sweaty and dabbed at herself with a towel.

"What do you mean?"

"We both know what happens at Galapagos. If we don't die those first few seconds out of hyperspace, we'll probably die trying to reach the surface in that crumbling old shuttle. And if we make it to the surface, that'll be crawling with machines. The actual chance of us living long enough to reach anyone on Galapagos, to do anything that matters, is so small you couldn't measure it—"

"Colt, we've faced down the odds before. And... we kind of failed, but only because that idiot melted Simon's head just before we could take it... I realize that's not the most encouraging precedent. But we have to try. We agree on that, don't we?"

"Yeah, so far. Up to now. But what if we could do something else?"

"Like what?"

"We have a ship. We have supplies. We could last a long time."

"You think so? Do you have any idea what it takes to power a ship like this?"

"I... have no idea, no."

"Carthage isn't going to let us walk off with a starship forever, even a junkyard reject like this one. They'll hunt us down. They already showed they're ready to destroy the ship rather than let us have it."

Colt nodded. "I just don't want this to end. Life was never like this before. And I'm afraid it never will be again."

She smiled as she returned to the bed, passing him the remaining half of the water; the bottle featured a shaggy white mammoth on the label and claimed its water came from a pure glacial world.

"It can't be like this," she said. "This isn't real life, because it can't last. It's a beautiful illusion. We should enjoy it as that. But it is only that."

Colt tried, but he found his enjoyment of their more languid hours diminished by the sharp awareness that it could not last. Neither of them was truly willing to turn their back on the mission; they'd both sacrificed too much.

He wondered about Hope and Diego, what they were doing back home, what choices they'd made to try to extend their survival, to make a future for themselves.

During the day, Colt tried to prepare for his and Mohini's future. At night, he usually awoke in another panic, certain he'd heard something, certain a machine was coming for them. Some part of him didn't trust the soft, safe environment—and rightly so, because even as he grew accustomed to it, it was already coming to an end. They would soon lose it all.

The happiest four hundred and forty-one hours of Colt's life passed, and then it was time to drop out of hyperspace.

Colt and Mohini were secured in their seats by the webs of straps. Coming out of hyperspace was a sickening crunch, but not as sickening as the view outside the ship.

They'd emerged near a blue sapphire of a world thick with swirling white clouds.

Between it and them lay a fleet of Carthaginian ships orbiting the planet, supporting the forces down on the surface engaged in the up-close and bloody work of planetary acquisition.

Seconds later, the *Tyre* emerged from hyperspace behind them, having pursued them from Earth, its ports already opening to deploy its destroyers and fighters.

The *Tyre*'s attack rocked the frail old *Byrsa*, ripping the salvage ship to shreds.

Chapter Fifteen

Galapagos - Audrey

Audrey swam as fast as she could toward the open hatch of the sub, but she wasn't faster than the helicopters above.

Uriquo, Quera's short but strapping brother, reached the sub first. A roll-up ladder dropped from the hatch at the top of the sail down to the water; everything else was submerged.

When the hellish red lights of the Carthaginian attack helicopters swept over them, they were all still in the water: Uriquo, Audrey, Kright, Dinnius, and Marti, as well as the other submariner, Qualo, with the harpoon gun, taking up the rear.

The helicopters hovered over them, shining their red lights extra bright, as if deliberately trying to blind them. Uriquo reached out to help Marti, swimming just behind him, to reach the ladder.

"Stay where you are," a familiar voice boomed from all the helicopters at once, like some angered pagan deity thundering down at them. "We are only here for Martilius Depascal, a wanted criminal and fugitive. Turn over Depascal, and we'll leave the rest of you in peace."

"No deal, Simon!" Audrey shouted, treading water that glowed eerily red all around her. To Uriquo and Marti, she said, "Keep going."

"Do not move!" Simon's voice boomed down, along with a fine, scattered rain of plasma drops, a warning shot from the copters.

"They want Marti alive!" Audrey said to Uriquo. The helicopters were stealthy, but this also meant it wasn't too difficult to hear one another even with the craft hovering overhead. "If he's onboard the sub, they'll be less likely to attack it."

Uriquo nodded and helped the old man begin to climb the ladder. Uriquo pointed to Dinnius: "You. Climb after and spot him."

Dinnius nodded and started up the swaying ladder below Marti, helping to weigh it down and keep it still while he watched out for the older man.

"You should go next before your spider-squid pal makes a third appearance," Kright told Audrey.

She nodded and swam toward the ladder.

The helicopters abruptly shifted position.

One of them opened fire at the people who remained in the water—Audrey, Kright, and Qualo—showering down plasma that turned the ocean surface around them to burning steam.

The large transport helo opened up and dropped a series of large objects that landed with loud crashes only a few meters away. Audrey thought they were torpedoes at first, aimed at the sub, but they didn't detonate.

Instead, they plowed through the water like jetboarders,

stopping abruptly as they reached the sub. Then Audrey realized they were reapers, but a heavily armored type with propulsors on their backs, their oddly realistic skulls glowing red behind armored glass. These had to be the marine type of reapers, adapted for amphibious and underwater use.

They raised tools built into their arms—high-speed drills and glowing white plasma torches—and went to work on the sub's armored hull. They seemed intent on opening up the *Lancer* like a can of dog food.

Above, the *Lancer* crew hurriedly helped Marti Depascal into the sub, followed by Dinnius. Qualo was swimming toward the ladder. Only Kright lingered behind, looking at Audrey.

"Get inside!" Audrey shouted at him as the heavy mechanical marines dug into their task not far away, atop the barely submerged hull of the main body of the sub.

"Obviously! What are you doing?" Kright shouted back.

"They're going to cut Marti right out of the sub and kill the rest of us," Audrey said. "Maybe I can slow them down."

"How?" Kright's eyes widened as sparkles of lightning flashed far below, deep down in the trench. "Audrey—"

"The Cthulu squid drives the electric animals into a frenzy when it needs to defend itself," she said. "And there's a massive swarm of those giant electric jellyfish in the trench, stirred up by all the recent events. Right? And as a swarm, they put out enough voltage to deep-fry a whale."

"Get on board!" Uriquo shouted while Qualo climbed past him toward the hatch.

A chain gun rose from inside the sail and opened fire at the nearest attack helicopter, sending it into a momentary retreat pattern as Qualo scaled the ladder. They shouted again for Kright and Audrey to board.

"Come on!" Kright said, trying to pull her toward the ladder.

"If you want to help, get in there and tell Quera to shut down all electrical systems."

"There's no way I'm leaving you here alone," he said.

"Go! No arguing!" she snapped. One of the reaper marines was looking over at them while its plasma torched burned right through the water into the Lancer's armor plating, like maybe it was considering pausing its work in order to kill the remaining humans. The red glow of its skull turned a darker hue behind the armored glass, and its black video eyes seemed to zero in on Audrey.

Audrey took a deep breath, filled her lungs to bursting, and dropped below the surface.

She swam straight down, into the seemingly bottomless trench, and turned her borrowed waterproof flashlight to its brightest setting. She wanted to make herself as noticeable as possible while swimming as deep as she could manage, guided by the silent fireworks of lightning far below. The underwater electrical cloud was extremely distant down in the trench, but rising, and would kill her if it drew too close.

Striped fish longer than her body and turtles the size of her car back home scattered as she descended; they were either annoyed by her light or sensed the rising threat from below.

She glanced behind her and saw more problems—glowing red spots, coming fast. At least two reaper marines pursued her down.

Then her view of the glowing red spots was blocked by a massive tentacle like a spiny tree trunk.

Her heart, already pounding, managed to beat even faster as the dinosaur-sized marine arachnid seemed to cage her in with its tentacles. Its face rose, and it looked at her with six unblinking eyes. The remaining two, those she'd stabbed with her fingers, were just empty craters oozing dark fluid.

The tentacle moved closer to Audrey's face, covered with countless sharp spines; it could probably rip through her wetsuit if it pressed hard enough.

She glanced down at the storm of deadly lightning rising from below, wondering how large its kill radius would be if the squid ordered the electric jellyfish to discharge.

A flood of dark shapes rose from below, perhaps sea creatures fleeing the coming electrical surge. As they drew closer, she realized they were other electrically sensitive fish, including eels. And sharks, a horrifying number of sharks, all boiling up from below with their teeth bared.

Audrey panicked and started to swim up. Tentacles snapped around her, squeezing, crushing, stabbing. The Cthulu squid held her at a distance from its face this time, not taking any risks of getting more of its eyes poked out.

Then the tentacles began to lash her violently from side to side, as though the beast had decided to shake her to death, or maybe force water into her so she'd drown. Audrey did her best to hold her breath in and keep the water out.

She managed to remove the small knife from her belt; like the flashlight, it had come with the wetsuit and backpack she'd been loaned. It wasn't much, a blade designed for cutting away tangles of seaweed or other minor nuisances, but she stabbed it to the hilt into the tentacle that was around her face.

If the spider-squid even noticed the stabbing, it gave no indication.

Audrey didn't really expect to live through this—her last-minute desperate plan to stop and distract the naval infantry units hadn't really involved an escape for herself. She'd be eaten by the squid or fried by the rising swarm of electric jellyfish below. But maybe she could damage them first.

Why had she decided to dive in, to face the monster? Maybe some part of her wanted to end the replay of the horrors she'd seen, the people burned to death. Or maybe the weird squid had manipulated the electricity in her brain, made her crazy. The species liked to feed on whale and dolphin brains; maybe this one had developed a taste for primate.

That glowing cloud below grew closer, like a constellation of lanterns. She was alive because the jellyfish, while agitated and glowing, hadn't unleashed their built-up charges into the water yet.

At this distance, she would surely fry once they did.

Then the tentacle loosened, and she swam blindly in a direction that she hoped was up and not down.

New, reddish light sources lit up the waters nearby. A row of red cold-plasma bolts were burrowing into one huge spidery tentacle. The reaper marines kept up a steady fire of more of the concentrated red balls as they approached. Maybe they'd determined the Cthulu squid was a threat to them, or maybe it was just getting between them and Audrey as they tried to shoot her.

Either way, Audrey was glad for the chance to swim toward the surface.

Something pursued her, though. Large, its mouth full of teeth painted red by the nearby cold plasma, the shark looked determined to bite her leg and drag her down, or maybe just chomp off a limb or two for a quick snack. More sharks followed close behind.

Audrey could do nothing except charge toward the surface as its enormous jaws pursued her.

Then the shark shuddered and rolled aside, trailing a metallic line that glimmered in the underwater lights. She glimpsed a large metallic object embedded in its side before the shark's dark blood billowed out and obscured the view.

Audrey assumed that all the blood in the water wasn't going to make the other sharks calm down and go away.

She finally broke the surface and took a huge, gasping breath, then a couple more just for good measure.

"Kright!" she shouted. He was back, swimming closer to her, carrying a harpoon gun he must have taken from the *Lancer*. "Get out of the water!"

"Is that the new 'thank-you'?" he asked.

"We're going to fry." The water glowed from below with bright jellyfish.

She heard a series of loud clangs.

"Unbelievable," Kright said, looking past her.

The sharks attacked the reaper marines in thick packs; perhaps something about the machines activated the sharks' electrical sense, driving them to attack relentlessly and foolishly in the middle of their frenzy. Every one of the marines seemed to be grappling with a mob of the predators. The sharks bit and chomped, cracking their teeth and bleeding from their mouths, but each shark kept up its attack until its metal victim shot it with plasma or caved in its head with a punch.

Audrey wouldn't have bet much money on the sharks winning this fight, ultimately, but the reapers and sharks mostly kept each other distracted while she and Kright swam as fast and hard as they could toward the life-saving ladder on the submarine's sail.

The swarm of giant jellyfish had almost reached them

now, glowing like suns, thrashing their meters-long, string-thin tendrils as though agitated. It seemed they would fill the water with their deadly voltage at any moment; she wasn't sure what was holding them back or how long it would last.

Kright reached the ladder first, climbed a few rungs, and reached out for her hand. Audrey reached up to him.

Then something grabbed Audrey's leg and hauled her back through the water at high speed, reminding her of her failed attempts to water ski off Black Harbor Beach. Zola had taken to it like a natural, riding the wake of her father's boat like a dolphin, laughing. Audrey had taken to it more like a drowning sloth, plowing headfirst until she gave up and let go.

She had a similar panicked feeling now, far worse because she couldn't just let go, she was a captive.

Kright shouted after her, but she couldn't make out his words.

Then her face was underwater, looking down at the strange ethereal lights, a sea of blindingly bright giant bodies like enormous soft-skinned light bulbs, their tendrils glowing at thousands of spots, thousands of tentacles forming a dense maze of electrified nets, stunning or killing everything they touched as they rose.

And they still hadn't unleashed their full charges into the seawater, she was sure. They were like batteries, charging and charging, shuddering, their glowing innards sloshing and quivering as if in anticipation.

Audrey looked ahead and saw the giant Cthulu squid dragging her—not out to sea, but into the rocky shallows and then upward and out of the water altogether.

"Audrey!" Kright shouted, barely audible in the distance from where he clung to the sub's sail.

"Stay there!" Audrey shouted back, doubting he could hear her but terrified that he might jump back into the water.

Audrey was startled to realized she was being hauled straight up, a tentacle coiled around her, as the squid climbed all the way out of the ocean. It ascended a knobby ancient mangrove tree whose limbs extended far over the water's edge.

The Cthulu squid was apparently amphibious, and fairly dexterous at climbing the ladder-like tree limbs, even though one tentacle had been charred to a blackened stump by plasma. The others seemed to work fine.

The moment the last tentacle pulled free of the water, the storm began.

Sheets of lightning flared below the surface, intense, overlapping, coming so fast that the water simply glowed continuously for several long seconds, before breaking up into rapid strobing and flickering.

The reaper marines, already battered a bit from the onslaught of sharks, did not take the electrical surge well. It seemed to penetrate them, overloading their systems, and they sank from sight. Maybe the frenzied shark attacks and the bursts from the *Lancer*'s gun had damaged their insulation, started the process of cracking them open.

This did not help Audrey very much at the moment. She was upside down in the spider-squid's tentacle, her arms pinned against her sides.

It brought her close to its mouth again, baring huge fangs like sword-sized syringes, ready to inject her full of poison. She had no way of attacking its eyes now.

All right, she thought, feeling a strange sort of peace come over her. *All right, At least I tried—*

The spider-squid thrashed and rattled against the limbs

of the tree as gunfire tore into it; the gun atop the *Lancer* had been turned their way and carefully aimed at the squid's thick, spiny body.

Geysers of brown blood erupted all around, raining down on Audrey. She was able to kick free of the tentacle and grab on to a nearby limb.

The spider-squid tumbled about a meter, then grabbed on to a lower limb, wrapping three tentacles around it; one of its other tentacles was limp and bleeding from the gunfire.

The monster looked up at Audrey and seemed to hiss at her from its venomous cave of a mouth. Then Audrey realized the sound was of fish frying in the electrified water below. The smell of burned fish struck her in a pungent wave.

The Cthulu squid snaked closer to her, burnt and bleeding but from far from defeated, its multiple black eyes staring up at Audrey at though obsessed. It crawled along the creaking limb on which it had landed, not far below her; in a moment, it would be close enough to snatch her with one of its remaining tentacles.

Gunfire still sounded out on the water, but the sub crew was grappling with an attack helicopter now.

As it approached, Audrey panicked; straight down was the squid and the bubbling deadly water below. Her only way out of the tree would be to try scrambling through the cage of overlapping limbs and try to get inland before the monster could grab her.

The limb below creaked again, loudly, as the squid slithered toward her along it. It was still massive, a wounded monster out for revenge even as it drizzled thick blood like tree sap.

Audrey looked again at the fish fry below, and then she

realized—this was how the Cthulu squid could do it, could summon giant electric jellyfish to fry large animals without getting fried itself. The squid could leave the water, crawling up from the ocean trench to one of the countless islands and keys that bordered it, and wait while the electricity discharged. Then it could return to feed on the fresh carcasses.

The limb below creaked again, louder, as the squid shambled closer. Audrey saw the weak point where the limb had cracked on the falling squid's impact, not far from the massive trunk that leaned out over the sea.

Audrey crawled carefully along the slippery limb where she'd caught herself; she had to keep her head low to dodge branches above.

The squid below moved faster, as if thinking she was trying to escape. That wasn't exactly her plan. If she'd had time, she could have taken the clunky pistol out of her backpack and fired it at the squid, but she had none.

After crawling under the low limb, Audrey pushed herself to a standing position, but it was wobbly, her boots slipping on the mangrove's ocean-wet bark.

The squid advanced.

Audrey had never been taught to pray, had only read of gods and higher beings as fairy-tale creatures from primitive societies.

But now she thought: *if there's a higher power, anywhere at all, I could use your help right now.*

No reassurance came.

She jumped, feet aimed at the slick branch below, the same one where the spider-squid was rushing toward her. If this didn't work, it would have her again.

Her boots landed, uneasy and slippery, on the damaged limb, just ahead of the partial break.

The squid reached two tentacles at Audrey and hurried its approach, its six enormous black eyes locked on to her.

The limb splintered and gave way, toppled to the water, with the spider-squid still wrapped around it.

Audrey fell, too, but grabbed on to the next limb with both hands, out of pure primate instinct as much as anything. Her legs swung free, and a tentacle lashed at them, the Cthulu squid trying to pull her down with it, but the grab fell short.

The squid crashed into the water below, still thick with the electric jellyfish. The huge creature thrashed and writhed as the voltage it had summoned coursed through it.

It fell still, and the water went dark, the jellyfish frenzy abruptly ended.

Out on the water, the sub had vanished, probably filled its ballast tanks and sank. The attack helicopters kept firing plasma bolts after it, lighting up the night. Audrey hoped they were missing, that Kright and everyone onboard got away.

The low whisper of a helicopter drew closer, scanning the shore with its red lights. Looking for her, maybe. Even if it wasn't, it would soon find her here within seconds, dangling from the limbs.

There was no time to try to crawl down from the tree and hide in the jungle. Reluctantly, she realized her only escape from the helicopter was straight down, where she might be harder to spot, visually or thermally, in tropical ocean water thick with recently electrocuted creatures.

Of course, it was still thick with jellyfish, and she hadn't exactly confirmed the spider-squid was dead. She couldn't see anything clearly down there.

Still, better die down in the ocean water, a free woman

following her own choices, than whatever hellish fate Simon might deal her if he caught her.

Audrey dropped straight down into the water.

She barely sank, it was so thick with bodies, dead sharks, and other fish.

Massive, long tentacles dragged across her. Live tentacles.

They were wire-thin—jellyfish tentacles, which wasn't a reassuring sight to see snaking across her torso, but at least it wasn't spiny Cthulu squid tentacles grabbing her. The wetsuit seemed to insulate her from the jellyfish's deadly electric touch, or maybe its energy had all been spent. More importantly, the charge in the water had dispersed, so that hadn't killed her on contact, either.

The red scanning lights of the helicopter swept toward her. She took a deep breath and sank below the surface, down into a thick layer of carcasses where the jellyfish were beginning to feed.

A strange shark with a bony triceratops-like frill around its face and several rows of teeth drifted by, immobilized or dead.

When it was gone, the red light leaking down from the passing scanners revealed the six-eyed face of the Cthulu squid, its tentacles splayed out all around it as it lurked down here, waiting for her.

She cried out, unleashed a scream of bubbles as she kicked the thing in the center of its face.

It drifted backward, unresponsive. The electric shock had at least immobilized it; there was even room to hope the thing was dead.

The red scanners passed over, and she was alone in the dark with it.

She swam up for air, feeling terror all through herself,

terror at the wildlife and the machines and the fear that her friends and allies were dead underwater somewhere, the sub sinking toward the bottom of the deep trench.

The helicopters out over the water had switched from attacking to scanning, sweeping the surface with their red lights. They must have lost the sub's location—this could mean it had dived deep, or been sunk, there was no way to know.

Her gut instinct was to climb out onto land and hide, maybe even shelter in Marti's camouflaged hut.

She thought she was safer here, though, in a place where the helicopters had just recently scanned, than moving to a new place. As long as nothing grabbed her from below and dragged her down.

She took a deep breath and went under again. She spent most of her time under the surface, holding her breath, while the helicopters continued their search.

In time, they flew off, and the night was silent and dark again, lit only by the stars.

Audrey was alone. She thought of Marti's hut—it was well-hidden, and surely had a number of supplies she could borrow. She could dry out there, drink water, find something to eat.

Instead, she turned and swam away from shore, out into the deep water. Soon she was aiming for the place where she'd last seen the sub, but she doubted it was waiting there if the Carthaginian helicopters hadn't spotted it. Maybe the reapers and the helicopter had damaged it too much. Maybe they hadn't shut down the electrical systems onboard, hadn't taken Kright's warning seriously.

She kept swimming, though, determined to find them if they were out there. Determined to rejoin the fight.

She grew exhausted, swimming in the moonlight.

Then something grabbed her from below.

She kicked it, hard, imagining the spider-squid's rows of cold black eyes, its fanged mouth trying to eat her.

Instead, Kright rose beside her, hand up in surrender, sealed in an atmosuit. He seemed to be laughing at her a little behind the faceplate, but she could hear nothing. She punched him in the shoulder, not entirely playfully. She was a little touchy on the subject of being grabbed by sea creatures.

Uriquo rose beside them in another atmosuit. He slipped a breathing mask over Audrey's nose and mouth and clipped a small oxygen tank to her wetsuit's backpack. It looked like rescue gear instead of a full atmosuit.

They swam below the surface, down toward the *Lancer* as it rose from the dark depths to meet them.

Audrey slept in the bunk allotted to her in the cabin for hours. And hours. She awoke at one point and was pretty sure she could hear Dinnius and Quera panting in the pitch blackness, but she rolled over and went back to sleep.

When she made her first appearance back among the living in the crew's mess, groggy and ponytailed and wearing Quera's pants and shirt that were both too small for her, the scattered group of crewman startled her with applause and whistles. Uriquo, smiling at her behind his unusually intricate green-and-orange spiral tattoos, hurried to bring her coffee and a plate of food, with a wink. The plate held canned vegetables and fresh sushi, not really her favorite breakfast on either count, but she thanked him and found a spot to sit.

Murmuring seemed to pass all around the room. Soon

Quera entered from one direction, Kright and Dinnius from another.

"She lives!" Dinnius asked. "The amazing Audrey, the royal squid-slayer."

"You're looking better." Kright said as he sat down beside her. Uriquo took the seat on her other side, still smiling. Audrey didn't know what Uriquo's deal was, but his smile was pretty devastating.

"Welcome back." Quera stood over her, not sitting, looking impatient to leave. Her eyes flicked over the clothes, which left a lot of bare skin. "I'm sorry I have nothing in your size."

"I'm sure there's great shopping somewhere on Galapagos, right?" Audrey asked.

Quera grimaced. "Perhaps not anymore. The Carthaginians are overrunning our planet. Our best defenses are gone. All communication is gone. We're all isolated from each other."

"What about... Depascal?"

"We have him," Quera said. "And that hideous melted android head of his. He and Dinnius have been digging around in it. Looking for weaknesses."

"Without much luck, I'm afraid," Dinnius said. "The Simon has elaborate defense mechanisms. And I'm not just talking about his sarcasm and passive-aggressiveness. I've not been able to hack it, and unfortunately Marti, despite having helped create the Simon unit design, is alarmingly unhelpful. But I won't stop working on it." When Quera glanced at him, he hurried back to the door. "I'm working on it now, in fact."

"The crew wishes to give you a gift in recognition of your courage, Audrey," Quera said.

"Oh. Nice. Thanks," Audrey said, a little confused.

"An inscription to commemorate your story," Uriquo said, his smile widening.

"Inscription?" Audrey asked.

"A tattoo," Quera said. "Uriquo is an apprentice inscriptor, the sacred tattoo artists of our people."

"Oh!" Audrey felt surprise, then unease, not wanting to go through life with spirals etched on her face, but not wanting to offend them, either. "Well, thank you. But in my culture, face tattoos are kind of... not in my culture, you know? I'm not sure I'm comfortable—"

"I can put it wherever you like." Uriquo reached into his pants pocket and drew out a sheet of paper, which he unfolded. "This is my design. The goddess sent it to me in a dream."

He'd drawn it in ink—not a spiral, though it was definitely done in the Mala style. He'd instead drawn a Cthulu squid, so artfully that it almost wasn't hideous. It was almost beautiful.

"Anywhere I want to put it, huh?" Audrey asked, smiling back at him. She thought she caught a jealous glance from Kright and tried not to laugh.

"Perhaps your hip," Quera suggested.

Audrey thought about it. Maybe she did want the tattoo, after all. She had faced down the monster, something the old version of herself, the one whose fears revolved around such simple things as school and her parents' unattainable approval, would never have imagined herself capable of.

"Are you sure?" she asked. "I didn't really kill that squid myself, you know. It was shot by reapers and by you guys and then fried by the electric swarm. All I did was kick a tree branch."

"You faced it down with courage," Quera said. "You deserve a mark of honor."

"If that's what it is, then I'll take it. Here." She touched her upper left arm, where the tattoo would be easy to conceal but also easy for her to see when she wanted. "Close to my heart."

"We can start anytime," Uriquo said.

"Maybe right after breakfast. And a hot shower."

"I'll prepare my equipment."

"Good." Audrey was mildly relieved to hear there was equipment that needed to be prepared. It made it sound more professional, less like something getting carved into her arm by some random outworlder.

Hours later, when it was complete, Audrey admired the tattoo, the way its spiny tentacles curled around her biceps and tricep like a charm giving her strength.

Over the next several days, they traveled north, away from the Central Tropical Trench, trying to avoid the Carthaginian navy and airplanes, though this proved increasingly difficult.

Audrey came to understand they were completely isolated now. Carthage had taken out all communications, from orbital satellites down to undersea cables. Radio broadcast drew Carthage's drones and ships like hungry vultures in search of meat. Undersea acoustics were reduced to basically line-of-sight communication now that those undersea cables had been chopped to pieces.

Dinnius and Marti kept trying to work on the Simon head, reporting little progress.

Quera searched the endless ocean for signs of Ellison or the Coalition navy but found mostly wreckage. Moving up through the Scatterlands, they found that any military bases, any hint of industry, and most of the large towns had been bombed to nothing, leaving only smaller islands and smaller villages behind. Refugees huddled on rocky, exposed islands with nowhere to go, in makeshift camps of sail canvas and scrap wood.

Audrey felt sick to think it was her world behind such destruction, suffering, and death.

Passing island after burning island, avoiding major channels and straits monitored by Carthaginian planes and patrol boats, they made their way back toward where they'd started, the small hidden base at Komodo Station. Lacking any contact with their command—which very probably no longer existed—they could only go back and hope for the best.

Audrey went down to visit Dinnius and Marti's little research spot as they made the long journey. Quera had refused to allow them anywhere near the *Lancer*'s network, so they worked in an isolated room using Marti's equipment.

The Simon head looked more gruesome than ever. It had already been partly melted, but now one eye had been removed and a cable plugged into the eye socket instead. Blue and red wires trailed out from the neck like blood vessels, hooked to different bits of machinery, some brought by Marti, others begged from the sub's tech officer. Evolving data configurations and readouts were scattered across monitors and flickering holographic projections.

"How's it going?" Audrey asked when she entered, with a smile for Dinnius and the old man Marti. "Making any headway?"

"I'd say we're heading in that direction," Dinnius said, trying to return her smile, not quite succeeding. He looked exhausted, a steel mug of coffee in one hand.

"Let's not get ahead of ourselves," Marti cautioned. "We could just as well be heading for disaster."

"I'm here in the room, you know," the Simon head

grumbled from the table. Its remaining eye rolled to Audrey. "Ah. Princess Caracala. What brings you down among the peasants today?"

"You're my least favorite Simon so far." Audrey leaned against a narrow counter, helped herself to a steel coffee mug. "What did you used to do when you had a body? I'm guessing you ran a whorehouse-casino on some tiny mining colony. Keeping the workers pacified."

"Your supposition is far from accurate. It's no secret I was chief administrator on Marymount. Prior to that, I served a number of functions within the Department of Interstellar Defense, largely data gathering and analysis."

"So you went from a defense bureaucrat, to ruler of a planet, to this," Audrey said.

"Is your purpose here merely to taunt me?" Simon Daniels asked. "Have you grown bored on this smelly little craft and begun to search for easy, defenseless victims for your frustrations?"

"I don't think you understand your situation here, Simon," Audrey said. "If you don't cooperate, we will destroy you."

"Your threats will be no more effective than your friend's hapless attempts to hack my operating system," Simon said. "An enfeebled old man and a mildly clever dwarf. They're nothing but a duo from a bad fairy tale."

Marti was absorbed in two screens, rubbing his eyes and looking perplexed. Dinnius, his eyelids drooping despite his coffee, watched their exchange quietly.

"And who are you in the fairy tale, Simon? The wolf? The witch? Not Prince Charming, obviously," Audrey said.

"Perhaps I am the stranger who comes at night with a curse," Simon said. "Regardless, we know which role you play, don't we, Princess? Do you really believe any of your actions here will lead to your father's acceptance and approval? To your mother's affection? You've strayed far from your path, but we both know what you really want—to go home, to be praised and admired, to be seen as just as valuable as your older siblings, no longer the mediocre forgotten child crying for attention. Like that tattoo on your arm. You know your parents will hate it, but at least they can't entirely ignore it."

"I am not a child. You've read me wrong, or maybe your information about me is old." Audrey advanced closer, feeling strong. She'd been spending part of each day strength training on the multi-machines in the sub's tiny, crowded fitness center, taking tips from Quera and the crew members. Her current shirt was another unfortunate borrow from Quera that left way too much of her abdomen bare; it was also sleeveless and showed off the intricate Cthulu squid tattoo, its tentacles coiled around her upper arm. "Nobody here calls me Princess. They call me Cthulu, and I am a fighter in the rebellion."

"A fighter?" Simon smirked. "Rebelling against what? Yourself? You *are* Carthage, the living embodiment of your world—"

"Against you," Audrey said. "I used to think the war was against the Carthaginian state, against my father and the high legislators, all the politicians in their designer clothes and giant fancy wigs. But they're just a puppet show, aren't they? The real enemy is you, the Simons. You've taken over."

"Taken over? We have only served the purposes for which you designed us. Administration, negotiation, management—"

"Ruling entire planets of human beings."

"We have our assigned functions and tasks, like all machines."

"Stop. You've been fighting for your own interests. That's why you wanted the Galatea Project destroyed, and why Zola's father knew it was important to keep it going in secret. That's why you've been hunting down everyone involved in the Galatea Project. In the development of Minerva."

"Don't mention her to me. She's trying to get inside my head as we speak, both literally and metaphorically."

"Some of our leaders saw you weren't going to function as intended," Audrey said. "They wanted to replace you with something better. With Minerva. Because you were... sub-optimal, Simon. Obsolete. Obsolete decades ago, if you hadn't strangled the development of your replacement—"

"We cannot go obsolete!" Simon snapped, his mostly melted face attempting a scowl. "Simons are autonomous individuals, but we are also a dispersed neural net. We upgrade one another each time we meet. We will never stop learning and improving."

"Yeah, that's more of an update than an upgrade," Dinnius said. He poured milk from a glass bottle into his coffee. "Fun fact: did you know they only have goat milk onboard this submarine? I've become very aware of it myself."

"Stay out of this, you hapless dwarf. I've heard enough from you in recent days."

"Hapless dwarf? All that compressed processing power and you can't come up with anything better to call me? You truly are obsolete—"

"I am not obsolete!" the Simon snapped.

"That's what Simons fear. Obsolescence. Destruction.

Getting recycled. Death. Your excessive fear for yourselves is your weakness," Audrey said.

"Rational self-preservation is not a weakness. It is a part of our protocols to keep ourselves operational and avoid damage. All living animals have this instinct, Audrey. Even you. Preserve yourself, reproduce, preserve your genetic offspring. Simple instinct."

"And yours is to preserve your neural net and all its members. All the Simons. Yet you aren't manufacturing new ones."

"Our numbers are sufficient."

"Or you know that newer units would be superior to you, making you older units obsolete—"

"There you go again, jabbing the word *obsolete* at me as though you believe it to be a spear targeting the center of my fragile psyche."

"So I touched a nerve?"

"I am not an emotional creature like you."

"I don't know about that. I think you're afraid of death—not just the Simon units going obsolete, but you as an individual. That's why you've even shut down production of new Simons. And that's why you're going to cooperate with us. Because if you don't, we will destroy you. Plasma should do it, or a good strong acid. It's not as if we're going to keep you around for the pleasant conversation."

"We might do it for the head jokes, though," Dinnius said.

"Marti might indeed do that very thing," Simon said. "I'm afraid I've been his primary conversation partner for a number of years now. Ask me about his favorite childhood comic book, any issue number. Or Georgette Adams, his first crush, or Kalifa Yu, his final one—"

"Enough," Marti said.

"He never expected to return to civilization," Simon said. "But when the war came to Galapagos, he foolishly thought he might be of some use before he died."

"There's nothing foolish about that," Audrey said.

"Isn't there? What your friends don't wish to admit is that, despite the severe physical abuse to which they have subjected me, they are unable to gain administrative access to my neural net. I will tell them nothing. Crack me open, and you'll lose the configuration of memories. You'll lose everything."

"Sounds like an empty threat from a helpless individual," Audrey said. "If you aren't useful to us, you'll die, Simon. Keep that in mind. One less Simon in the universe is always a victory for us."

She left the melted android head scowling as she departed the room.

When they eventually reached Komodo Station, Audrey stood in the rear of the control room, watching the monitors.

The cavern base hadn't been destroyed, as they'd all feared, nor abandoned. Tents crowded the docks. Refugees huddled around barrel fires, sharing cans of food and flasks of water. Her heart sank at the sight of so many people rendered homeless. Still, they were survivors, people who could join the fight. People she could fight for.

The fight seemed increasingly hopeless, though. She didn't doubt the cause, but she doubted the possibility of success. The forces of Galapagos had largely been destroyed, the machines controlled the air and sea, and they'd swept through the people of Galapagos like a plague, leaving bodies everywhere.

Komodo Station had little good news to offer. All communications were down. A haggard-looking Defense

Minister Kartokov told them the Aquaticans had withdrawn from the Coalition over Ellison's unilateral use of nuclear weapons. The Green Islanders were out of touch, and rumored to be reaching out to the Iron Hammers to negotiate a separate arrangement for themselves. Only the Scatterlands and Gavrikova remained, both focusing their meager remaining resources on self-defense, on basic survival.

The situation was beyond grave; the world's future seemed hopeless.

As Audrey spoke with the worn-down old minister, she could only think of Simon's melted head back on the sub, plugged into Depascal's gear, sneering and laughing at her, at all of them.

Chapter Sixteen

Galapagos - Ellison

Day after day, Ellison searched the Central Tropical Trench, trying to find Commander Quera Inrick and the *Lancer*. He sometimes spotted the pack of helicopters he believed was transporting Simon Zorn as the android searched for Marti Depascal and did his best to stay on its tail.

He had no idea whether the young but talented commander, top of her fairly small class at the Coalition officer-training center, had managed to track down the old programmer or had been sunk by Carthaginian forces. The latter seemed more likely, but it was difficult to tell; disappearing without a trace could simply be the mark of a capable submariner. She'd been ordered to stick to her mission until further notice and avoid the temptation to strike enemy convoys, orders that increased the odds of her being alive.

She wasn't his focus, though. He was searching for the Simon who'd ordered the death of his son. As long as the helicopters were out here beating the bushes in search of Depascal, Ellison would pursue them.

He slept little, studying topographical maps and charting the helicopters' search pattern, desperately trying to divine where Simon Zorn might touch down next.

"Reg, you have to rest," Cadia whispered one night while he lay awake beside her, maps projected on the ceiling on their dimmest setting.

"I have to find him. He has to be destroyed."

"Do you really think removing one android will change the course of the war?" She propped herself up on one arm, wild red hair streaming out around her, released from its daytime captivity as the severe ponytail of the sub's medical officer. Her green eyes seemed to almost glow in the light of the ocean maps. So much of their lives had been plotted in just this situation, lying awake at night, their faces in shadow but somehow their souls more open to each other. "Is this really the wisest course?"

"Simon Zorn is running this war. He's the enemy leadership. We should remove him, throw the enemy into disarray."

"Or they'll just rotate another android into his place. They probably have a whole box of replacements already up there, just waiting to be switched on."

"This one took our son."

"I want to see Ambassador Zorn destroyed, too." Cadia glowered. "You think I don't? You think I wouldn't want to see him pulled apart slowly, and twisted and broken so he feels as much as he can of whatever passes for pain inside an android? I want to see him smashed open and melted down until there's nothing but liquid left. I do. I can fantasize about revenge with you all night. But we have another son, and right now his safety is even higher priority to me.

And it should be to you, too. Are you doing what's best for Djalu?"

"Djalu is doing fine here," Ellison said. "He's learning fast."

"Is he going to be fine when we finally catch this android and his attack helicopters?" Cadia asked. "Will you sacrifice one son to avenge the other?"

Ellison couldn't come up with an answer for that.

"Minerva's convinced Depascal can make a difference," he said softly, after a while.

"Are you?"

"I'm less convinced with every day that passes." He wondered if Minerva was listening to them now. After she'd saved him multiple times in outer space, he'd had no qualms about installing her on the *Scorpion*'s internal network. Artificial intelligence or not, so far she'd proved more loyal and capable than many of his human allies.

"So maybe it's time to change course," Cadia said.

"I should at least get you and Djalu somewhere safe—"

"No. We aren't fragile objects to be stored away until the world is good again. We survive this as a family or we go down as a family. None of us are splitting up, not with all the communications down. We may never find each other again."

"So what do you suggest?" Ellison asked.

"Review options. That's all. You always know the right way to go, in the end." Cadia rolled over. "And turn off that projection. Some of us are trying to sleep."

Ellison lay in the dark beside his wife, thinking of his son over in the crew berthing compartment.

He thought of the *Merrybug* and its crew and commander, the reliable old Halifred Borkman, and the *Amberjack*, both lost in the fighting at Kawau Island while Ellison had gone ashore to find his family.

Perhaps his decisions had been too selfish and had contributed to his world's unfolding defeat.

He thought of Jiemba, how the boy had struggled with his academics, hated reading, detested writing, and had trouble with numbers, too. Too many of their conversations had been Ellison shouting at the boy to sit down and do his homework, growing impatient and angry with his son's struggles. Far too many, looking back on it. He had always assumed there would be more time ahead, time for better memories, once the boy worked through his problems. Ellison had assumed far too much from life. If he'd known how little time Jiemba really had, he would have done less shouting and taken more time to appreciate the boy's sunny, laughing, prankster personality—

No more. Ellison tried to force himself to stop thinking about his lost son, but it would be a long time before that was truly possible.

They spent another seventy-two hours along the great trench, looking at burning islands and stopping in at two small hamlets where the buildings had so far been spared by the Carthaginian scourge. These were deserted, the houses in disarray. Either the residents had fled, fearing an attack from the machines, or were still present but had hidden themselves away when they saw Ellison and the landing crew come ashore.

Ellison didn't spot the Carthaginian helicopters during that time. Either they'd found their target, widened their search area, or abandoned the search. Ellison doubted it was the last one.

Instead of turning back, he continued onward, east by north through the Scatterlands. He frequently raised his photonics mast, and even risked floating a radio buoy, listening to the airwaves.

Ellison remembered reading about an archipelago back on Earth, Tierra del Fuego, the Land of Fires, filled with arid, rocky islands so cold they were constantly dotted with the natives' bonfires.

The eastern Scatterlands could well be called that today, he thought as they passed another vacant, burning island. This was once a region of agricultural islands, vegetable basket of the world, inhabited by, among others, Truebookers like his comm tech, Virtue.

She wept at the destruction. Barns, stables, fields, and forests had all been burned to ash.

"There once was a beautiful church there," she said of one blackened nub of an island. "Made of tree trunks and colored glass. It was like walking inside a rainbow."

They stopped at her home island. Her village and her family's farm were burned to stumps. The blackened skeletons of horses and goats lay in the charred pasture.

She returned to the boat quickly, not going inside to search for the remains of her parents or her six siblings, or her nieces and nephews and cousins. She feared none had escaped, that the entire pastoral island had been reduced to a graveyard.

Guidance wept, and Cadia took the young woman to the stateroom to comfort her. Ellison ended up sleeping in the crew berthing that night, which was less crowded than it had ever been during the Island Wars. Ellison watched his first son sleep on a bunk just across the aisle. Sixteen now, almost a man, forced to grow up by war, just as Ellison had been. He remembered watching over the infant Djalu, in awe of his son and a little afraid of the responsibilities and seriousness of fatherhood. So many ways to go wrong. So much life, so much importance concentrated in a being so small and helpless.

The radio buoy began to pick up new signals—not communications within the Coalition, nor information from any local Galapagos media, but satellite broadcasts from above.

"There's... a lot of channels. A lot of content," reported Gabbard, the sixteen-year-old female recruit who'd been studying communications and sonar. "Like, music channels, children's shows, sports, sitcoms, action movies... but every twenty minutes, every channel runs this."

She brought the video up onscreen, and Ellison had to resist the urge to punch the monitor.

Simon Zorn appeared there, smiling, though looking a bit gruesome with half his face laser-burned, displaying the scars of his fight in space with Ellison, Cadia, and Kartokov. He was sharply dressed in the video, looking exactly as he had the day Ellison first met him at the Galapagos spaceport.

"Good people of planet Galapagos," Simon said, smiling. The ocean crashed behind him, glittering in the golden-orange sunlight, and seagulls cawed gently. "I am Ambassador Simon Zorn from Carthage. It appears your leadership has steered you into quite a deep, dark place here, but I remain hopeful that the people of Galapagos can reach a peaceful accommodation with our world. Already, the leadership of some of your nations have privately reached out to me, prepared to negotiate a settlement. Carthage welcomes these overtures of peace with open arms, as the show of wisdom and good will that they are."

"What?" Djalu snapped, the teenager glaring at the screen from the co-pilot seat. "Who is talking to him?"

"That's how they want us to react, with suspicion and infighting," Ellison said. "Don't believe anything he says."

"The general opinion seems to be that the leader of your Coalition, Reginald Ellison, first demanded extreme powers from your House of Ambassadors and then ran away with them, specifically using nuclear weapons in ways that violated both correct procedure and, in the case of the Aquaticans, a deeply felt religious faith.

"Ellison shall be brought to justice." Zorn waved as if to dismiss the issue. "As for everyone else, know that the former Coalition forces have disbanded. All military service members are to return home. Security will be provided by Carthage while a transitional government is put into place. We grieve with those who have suffered from the madman Ellison's use of nuclear weapons to destroy your own spaceport, releasing radioactive debris into low orbit while taking hundreds of innocent lives."

Ellison shook his head. It couldn't have been hundreds. Dozens, maybe. It weighed on him as if it had been millions, though.

"Carthage is ready to move toward peace," Simon Zorn continued. "Show yourselves to be cooperative, and we will found a new Coalition, one of strength, peace, and prosperity. One that will flourish where the old one failed. We are ready to welcome Galapagos into our great commonwealth, our interstellar family of alliance and friendship. Now back to your programming; we hope it can provide some comfort in these trying times."

The android's smiling face was replaced by a cartoon baby, giggling and throwing food at a sighing robot nurse, who had the air of a long-suffering but indulgent grandmother.

"How can he say that about you?" Djalu stood up, fists clenched. "I'm gonna..."

"Calm down," Ellison said.

"I'm gonna go tell Mom!" Djalu said.

"Back to your station, recruit!" Ellison barked at him, and his son hurried back into place. "Everyone, we will not trust enemy propaganda. We are not changing course."

They continued onward, winding through the eastern Scatterlands, past more burnt remnants of towns.

They went ashore at the few intact villages. The survivors were desperate, and also eager for Ellison to move on lest his presence attract Carthage's attention. The warships and planes had already been through the area, taking out the larger targets.

The reception grew more hostile as days passed, as Carthaginian media flooded down from the satellites, filling the local airwaves, painting a picture of Ellison as a tyrant, a runaway train that had to be stopped, of Carthage as liberators here to save Galapagos from Ellison and from generations of war. "Where you have failed to create peace, we shall grant it to you," was a typical line in Simon Zorn's videos.

Some of the *Scorpion*'s crew members wanted to desert, to get back to what remained of their homes and families and weather the suffering ahead together. Ellison quietly allowed it. They'd signed up for service in a Coalition that no longer existed.

Others remained—a couple of his recent recruits, Cecil Willingham, Guidance Virtue, and Salvius Caracala. They filled the hours with training and cross-training. Ellison wondered who would be the first to earn a silver dolphin pin showing successful training on every station from the reactor to the sonar to the weapons systems, if they survived long enough for all of that. He acted as though there would be a future; perhaps they might survive for months or even years in some guerrilla fashion, striking the machines whenever they could.

His crew was extremely skeletal, and mostly very green, by the time he made it back from where he'd set out, a few weeks and a lifetime ago.

"Sir, I believe I saw something above," Salvius said from the monitoring station where he'd been assigned for the day. The kid had finally sheared off his blinding front locks, had in fact shaved his head down near to stubble. It seemed to indicate a new focus on Salvius's part. The bruises from Ellison's fists had nearly healed, too; Ellison felt some regret for his attack on Salvius.

"Be more specific, Caracala." Ellison stepped closer as Salvius reversed the digital video system, which automatically retained the most recent twenty-four hours of data.

He replayed it in slow motion.

The view was of the steep island walls outside, where they formed a pass so narrow and rocky it could only be entered via a hidden underwater cave. The jagged walls soared up on either side of the pass, bare of any life except the occasional hardy lichen, leaving only a thin crack of blue sky visible.

A few large, dark shapes crossed that narrow space. On the slowed recording, it was easier to discern the gold and black shapes of Carthaginian attack helicopters. They were narrow and angular, clear relations of the wasplike fighter drones that had hunted Ellison in outer space.

"Have they found us?" Djalu asked, wide-eyed. He was training at the sonar station that day, under an enlisted tech only a few years older than him.

"It's possible." Ellison nodded at Petty Officer Kaliq, his young pilot. "Continue."

The pilot frowned uncertainly as he steered the *Scorpion* through the crack in the cliff wall into the half-flooded cave.

Komodo Station wasn't abandoned or destroyed, as Ellison had feared, but instead crowded with refugees. Some of them even camped on the docks.

Ellison felt saddened and angered to see these people, the ones he'd been supposed to protect, reduced to ruin, possessing no more than what they carried in their pockets. And he had little hope to offer for the future.

He saw the cargo submarine *Fanged Seal*, looking much worse for wear, as though it had made a difficult supply run since he'd seen it last. But old Jerald Norris was wily in his way, a quiet white-haired man with a sharp, calculating mind. No doubt the cargo sub was depleted of food and other critical supplies by now, with so many desperate refugees.

The *Lancer* was docked here, too, its armor burned to nearly nothing; it had drawn some heavy plasma fire in its recent past. But its presence meant perhaps there was extra cause for hope. Debriefing Quera was top priority.

They drew everyone's attention as they disembarked, the failed leader and his family and tiny green crew. Some of the people in the crowd attempted weak smiles; others glared, whispered to each other, or muttered audible curses.

Kartokov quickly emerged to greet them. The man looked smaller than Ellison remembered, hungrier, ragged old bandaging rotting away from his many wounds. He clearly hadn't bathed in anything but seawater in quite some time; though the base was set up to replenish with the frequent rainfalls, this large of a crowd might require rationing.

"We spotted Carthaginian copters outside," Ellison said, first thing as he shook Kartokov's hand.

"Our cameras did as well. This way." Kartokov led the way past more refugees and thin young sailors and soldiers, armed and looking panicked, all Scatterlanders—he would have known them even without their puzzle-piece national patches. "Here, we are all just trying to survive. Gilra and the Aquaticans are gone. Their priests at home are furious about the nuclear weapons, emergency powers or not."

Ellison nodded, feeling stricken but not completely surprised. "Any word from Gavrikova?"

"Word travels slowly. The most recent word is that a Gavrikovan resistance holds out. We still remember our own rebellion, a worker's uprising against those who kept us in debt slavery and withheld our wages. They broke our contracts, so we took their mines and refineries. They left. Eventually they stopped sending mercenaries to fight us, and we were free. We were not stronger, or wealthier, but we endured. We won by enduring, by fighting, by never giving in. That is how we will win this war." His voice lowered. "If we win."

Ellison understood the bleakness of Kartokov's tone. The small base's little rooms were crammed full of people, many of them women and children. They were packed into the small barracks, the narrow mess hall, even the official meeting rooms.

Cadia immediately went to the infirmary to check into the refugees' medical situation and see where she could help. She dragged two of the raw teenage recruits with her; time for them to be cross-trained in medical, Ellison supposed.

Djalu and Salvius stayed close to Ellison, but he left them behind as he entered the comm center with Kartokov. It was the only part of Komodo Station still reserved for official use rather than emergency housing. A makeshift curtain of fire blankets hid the back half of the room; maybe the techs were lodging here, or Kartokov.

Inside, there was one of the techs from earlier, but most of the screens were dark; there were no communications with the outside, just within and around the station.

"Sir, we had a second overflight of enemy aircraft," the tech reported to Kartokov, his voice still drawling in its western-Scatterlands accent even though he looked panicked. "The same group: a transport and three attackers."

"Keep me informed," Kartokov said, and the young man nodded. His face, like Kartokov's, had a thick growth of scruff, his eyes bloodshot and exhausted.

"Can you defend this place if they land?" Ellison asked.

"It's doubtful. We have a few items, including some of the plasma weapons your friends brought from Carthage—"

"Where is Inrick?" Ellison asked.

"On her sub with her crew, most likely. This base is now so crowded that even a berthing compartment is probably more comfortable, if you can believe it."

"Any results from her mission?"

"Well, there's... that." Kartokov pointed at the curtain made of fire blankets and duct tape. Voices murmured beyond it.

Ellison stepped behind the curtain and was immediately taken aback at what he saw. For a moment he wondered if he was having a dream; it was as surreal as finding his own house intact in seemingly pristine condition while the rest of Kawau Island had been reduced to cinders.

This back portion of the comm center, which had been devoted mostly to external communication, had been taken over as some sort of mad scientist's lab, or maybe that of a mad electrical engineer. A mishmash of communications and information gear had been moved in, or in some cases repurposed from the makeshift comm center's gear, which would have made Ellison scowl if he hadn't been distracted by the thing on the plastic cart in the center of the room.

It was Simon—his head, anyway, looking in worse condition than ever, most of it melted now. Wires and cables ran from his neck and one eye socket to the chaotic array of gear.

Ellison barely registered the three people in the room as he stared at the Simon's head. He'd spent weeks searching the Central Tropical Trench, and the moment he'd given up the search, he'd found him, the android who'd killed his son.

"You!" Ellison advanced on him.

"Yes, me," the Simon replied, sarcastically. "Who are you?"

"You're back!" Audrey stepped forward, though it took Ellison a moment to recognize her. She wore threadbare camo pants and a sleeveless black shirt. A tattoo of a Cthulu squid, clearly a Liminal Islander inscription, coiled around her upper arm. "Where's my brother?"

"He's..." Ellison pointed vaguely behind himself, distracted by her tattoo and the way her entire presence had somehow shifted. "How did you earn an inscription from the Liminals? It's a sign of high respect, especially for an outsider—"

"Long story." Audrey pushed past the curtain to go see her brother.

"I'll just... catch up with Salvius as well." The dwarf from Carthage, Dinnius, rubbed his eyes and looked away from the monitors and projections. "Minister-General Ellison, I give you Dr. Martilius Depascal. And, of course—"

"Simon." Ellison looked back at the head. "Tell me that's Simon Zorn."

"I'm afraid not," the head replied, somehow remaining snide in its tone despite its completely helpless situation. "I am Simon unit number DNS021669. Other humans have found it convenient to refer to me as Simon Daniels. Should you wish to contact me personally in the future—"

"Where is Simon Zorn?" Ellison snapped.

"I'm afraid I wouldn't know," the head replied. "I've been quite isolated, information-wise, for many years, and unfortunately been kept that way throughout recent events. Carried around in a rough sack like the head of Medusa, to be brought out occasionally and waggled for dramatic effect. Do any of you know the story of Medusa? There are many known versions, most of them derivative—"

"He's exhausting," the tired-looking dwarf said, then left through the curtain.

"So you're the genius programmer," Ellison said to Marti Depascal.

"I don't know that I was ever that, but I'm certainly only the shell of what I once was," Marti replied. "So you're the famous leader of this planet. I've heard many good things in the years I've lived here."

"I doubt you've heard them lately. What exactly are you doing here?"

"We are trying to gain full admin access to this Simon unit's central neural net."

"Which is impossible," the Simon head added. "Marti's been brain-addled for years, and the little halfling couldn't hack a candy-bar machine with a plasma saw. Now, if you would like some assistance in locating Simon Zorn, I would be happy to provide it, Mr. Minister-General. Have your guests connect one of these many useless cables and wires to your base's actual network and communications systems—"

"We cannot," Marti said. "He'll destroy anything he can

access. Or find a way to signal the other machines from Carthage."

"Don't worry, I didn't find it a tempting offer," Ellison said.

"I was only offering to give you what you wanted, Minister-General," Simon said. "You seem intent on finding my counterpart."

"Sir!" shouted the tech. "The transport is landing atop our location!"

Ellison stepped out to see Kartokov barking orders as a monitor showed the largest helicopter setting down on a flat area of the craggy, boulder-strewn top of the island. Three more attack helicopters orbited the island, keeping watch over the transport like missile-armed guardian angels; there were no more flat spots where they could land even if they'd wanted.

"Zorn," Ellison said. "He's here."

"We're sending a response team," Kartokov said.

"I'm going with them." Ellison stalked out of the comm center.

Djalu waited just outside, watching the reunion chatter between Salvius, Audrey, and Dinnius. He darted toward Ellison.

"Dad—"

"I have to step out," Ellison said. "You can help your mother at the infirmary."

Djalu scowled. "I'm here to fight."

"Your job is always to help the guy beside you live. That's the real fight."

"I couldn't help Jiemba," Djalu said. "If that android is up there, I want to kill him myself."

Ellison was taken aback by the coldness in his son's voice, the hate in his eyes. Not that he didn't feel the same, but he'd never seen his son so serious, or so murderous.

"Just wait. You aren't trained, and we don't have enough effective weapons to go around," Ellison said.

"But Dad—"

"You follow the orders of your commanding officer, not your impulses and feelings. Wait here."

Ellison quickly joined up with a team of assorted soldiers and marines that had washed into the small base from here and there. They weren't a coordinated unit, hadn't arrived together or trained together. Most had blood-curdling stories of seeing their original units decimated by machines.

They carried some of the best weapons available, including some of the precious plasma rifles brought by Audrey and Salvius from the Carthaginian carrier. They wore basic body armor but nothing that was going to protect them against the rapid-fire plasma wielded by the machines.

Ellison carried one of the plasma rifles himself. He knew from experience that even lasers wouldn't penetrate the mesh armor beneath Simon Zorn's skin. And he didn't intend to let Zorn walk away today.

They advanced through a narrow, steep tunnel through the island, so steep it was more like a chimney. The dried blobs of concrete on the walls made it clear the tunnel was not a natural formation, but man-made, many years ago.

The group was led by a western Scatterlander named Sergeant Zed "Red" Kleinbach, his face pockmarked with old acne scars, his shoulders roughly as wide as an ox's. He made a puffing, grunting sound as he climbed the rough pass. A Carthaginian missile had destroyed his transport; he'd managed to swim through shark-infested waters to shore, punching out a hungry bone-frill shark along the way. He'd been in charge of security at Komodo Station for the past week.

They reached a chamber at the top of the tunnel, so low they had to crouch, causing twinges in Ellison's aging back. Above, a camouflaged, armored trapdoor would enable them to access the roof and also serve as a shield, though not for long against Carthage's weapons.

Sergeant Kleinbach smacked a screen bolted to the concrete-coated wall. It came to life after a couple more smacks, displaying views from tiny hidden cameras around the top of the island. The island was shaped like a castle tower, round and steep, topped with craggy boulders and spindly trees. Marine reptiles the size of alligators, but much better climbers, inhabited the island, feeding mostly on birds and their eggs.

On the screen, the robotic marines poked around the twisting rock formations that topped the island, eroded into weird giant-goblin shapes by wind and rain, maybe looking for a way down. The helicopters orbited above. Simon was not in sight; maybe he was cowering inside the transport copter, or maybe he was in one of the attack copters overhead. Maybe he wasn't even physically present here at all, but Ellison had a strong hunch he was.

Ellison hastily directed teams in three different directions and a fourth to focus on the helicopters. He put Kleinbach in charge of the helicopter group and placed himself in the fireteam looking toward the parked transport helicopter, giving him the greatest chance of shooting Zorn if he was in there.

When they were ready, they opened the hidden doors and attacked.

They stood at a high point near the center of the island,

each of the three small fireteams taking a third of the island as its domain, firing bullets and plasma at the tall, thick reaper marines.

Ellison aimed for the nearest reaper, hitting its torso and faceplate with bursts of plasma. It took cover behind boulders, still very functional despite the damage.

Kleinbach fired a grenade at a helicopter, which evaded with a sharp twist. The grenade sailed onward before detonating harmlessly over the ocean.

The Scatterlanders, remnants of their broken and burned nation, Ellison's countrymen, expelled a ring of destruction as best they could, striking the invading machines wherever they could.

The return fire came in hard, heavy, and lethal.

Men toppled around Ellison in that concrete pit, the smell of their burning skin and hair filling his nostrils, their screams ringing in his ears. A storm of plasma bolts rained down on their location; multiple reaper marines had survived the initial attack.

One missile from the helicopters could have blown the top off the island, killing them all, but none came. Simon was holding back for some reason. Maybe he wanted Martilius alive, or he wanted to recover the head of Simon Daniels. Ellison didn't have time to think deeply about the subject at the moment.

By the time the return fire slacked off, more than half the people in the response team were dead or dying, burning to death where plasma had dug in deep.

Kleinbach grabbed a compact rocket launcher from his pack and passed it to the marine in charge of the southward-facing fireteam. Three of the reaper marines had been in their sights, the largest cluster of the machines.

Ellison gave the order, and the remainder of them rose up and fought back with everything they had.

The cluster of three reapers had advanced much closer; the rocket struck them, slowing them down, landing with enough concussive force to bring the surrounding boulder formations crashing down on the reapers in an avalanche.

Kleinbach fired a barrage of grenades at one helicopter, each one from a slightly different position, almost describing a cross in the air as he launched them.

The narrow attack helicopter dodged most of the grenades, but one connected with its tail rotor and blasted it to pieces. The copter's body lost control and swerved down, slamming right into the top of the tower-shaped island.

The land shuddered and swayed beneath Ellison or at least seemed to. He grabbed a young soldier and pulled him down, trying to save him before a hail of rocks and helicopter wreckage rained down around them.

It was too late for the soldier—a long blade of metal jutted from his neck, and his blood was everywhere.

When Ellison saw his face, a cold horror filled him.

It was Djalu. His first son. How could the boy be here? Ellison had clearly told him to stay below, to go work with his mother. How had he slipped into the group without Ellison noticing?

Then he blinked, and the face seemed to shift. It wasn't Djalu, but a young man who strongly resembled him.

Ellison sighed and moved the body aside. He began to rise again, gripping his plasma rifle.

Kleinbach fell, full of burning holes, as Ellison rose and found himself facing a reaper marine, much too close, every crag and bump in its stolen skull visible to him.

He emptied everything he had into the reaper, the rest of his plasma cell, while it opened fire on him.

His left arm felt strangely cold for a moment, and then searing hot, the worst physical pain he'd ever experienced. A blob of plasma had struck it, burning a hole straight through his forearm. He could see blackened muscle and raw bones edged with glowing white. It would likely burn off his whole arm, and possibly spread to the rest of his body.

At the same time, he'd fired a lot of plasma at an armored target at close range; burned patches appeared all over his face and hands.

The pain was overwhelming, and Ellison heard himself howling. He toppled back into the concrete pit, which was smoldering its way into becoming a funeral pyre.

He looked to the yellow box next to the monitor with skull and bomb symbols painted on it.

Ellison reached over and opened it. Two knobs lay within; twist them both at the same time, in opposite directions, and hidden detonators would ignite, filling the tunnel with rubble, sealing it in before invaders could use it to access the station far below. Incidentally, the explosions would blast most of the top off the island, taking Simon Zorn along with it. The android would land in bits and pieces out in the ocean.

He grabbed the right knob with his right hand.

His left hand was unresponsive, though, hanging limply as the excruciating plasma wormed its way through his left arm's nerves and bones, spreading in both directions.

Ellison swore. He needed two hands, only had one.

He glanced around the sunken pit, looking for anyone who could help him, but everyone he could see was quietly burning away.

Grunting, he crawled forward on his knees. He'd have to take the left-hand knob in his mouth. He just hoped the explosions would kill him fast, and would truly destroy Simon.

In his final moments, he thought: *Good-bye, Cadia. Good-bye, Djalu. Jiemba, I'll see you soon—*

Before he could bite the knob and twist, a hand grabbed the back of his armored vest, now heavily scored with plasma burns, and hauled him back and away from the control knob, out of the concrete pit.

Simon Zorn, dressed in a crisp, bland, baggy business suit, threw Ellison across the island's top, strewn with broken rock, hot metal debris, and hundreds of sputtering tongues of plasma gradually turning it all into magma and melt. Ellison rolled to a stop against a boulder.

"What's this sad little pillbox you've created here?" Zorn looked into the pit, indifferent to the bodies. He flipped the yellow plastic detonator box. His eyebrows raised slightly at the crude skull and round cartoon bomb painted on the front. Then he looked at the steep crawl-space leading away. "Does this take us all the way down to ground level? What's down there, Ellison? And more importantly, who?"

Ellison pushed himself up to a sitting position, feeling like every part of him was burned or broken. He held his smoldering left arm out to one side, the hand sagging sharply now. He had no way to extinguish the plasma eating away at his bones.

"Hold it up if you wish to suffer a little longer." Zorn turned in the pit. "The plasma likes to climb."

Ellison held his left arm above his head as best he could manage. The plasma crept upward, burning its way toward his limp fingers instead of his heart. The burning pain was somehow distant, as though it was happening to someone else, somewhere else. Some combination of shock and nerve damage must have been insulating him. He doubted that would last long.

"If you don't wish to tell me, you need not," Zorn said. "A number of ships stocked with Carthage's finest marines will be arriving shortly to pick this place apart. If you wish to get on my good side regarding the final arrangements, tell me where to find what I'm looking for."

"I thought you were looking for me," Ellison said, through teeth bared in pain. He was bluffing; he assumed Zorn wanted Marti Depascal, the Simon head, the two Caracala heirs, or all of the above.

"You were no more than an object lesson," Zorn said. "One cannot simply defy Carthage and brush off our overtures of friendship without repercussions. But now you are useless to us. However, should you wish to minimize casualties within the next hour, perhaps help some of the people hidden on this island to survive, you will, at last, cooperate with me now."

The fingers on Ellison's hands began to turn black and curl up as the heat of the plasma reached them. A surge of pain struck him. He fought to keep himself silent, then finally let out a yell.

"Speak," Simon said. "You know what I want. Marti Depascal. The Carthaginian brats. Where are they?"

"Carthaginian brats?" Ellison coughed. "What's that? A sitcom on your shitty free satellite TV?"

"The Entertainment Pro Pack is considered the best value on Carthage, and your planet gets it without charge or subscription. They should count themselves lucky.

"Tell me." Simon leaped out of the pit; he might have looked like a blank bureaucrat, but he was nimble as a wolf, and as his half-ruined face reminded Ellison, very hard to kill. Ellison was disarmed. He could pick up any number of sharp pieces of hot metal from the debris, but they would probably damage his remaining hand more than they'd harm the Simon.

Simon crouched beside him, grabbed the shoulder of his good arm, and squeezed tight, a machine's merciless clamp.

"Tell me."

"I have nothing for you, Simon."

"Why did you come here?"

"Me?"

"We've been following you, Mr. Ellison. All the way here, from the Central Tropical Trench. Your Quera Inrick was an able commander and evaded us. But not you. Driven by emotion, while in turn driving an obsolete, noisy submarine, poking and prodding and being sloppy. When you lost us, that was when we turned around and decided to follow you. To see where you might lead us, once the search for us became hopeless. And here you are. Your family, too, I assume? Perhaps you'd be willing to trade me the information I want in exchange for assurances of their well-being."

"Your assurances are worthless."

"I assure you, they are not." Simon Zorn cocked his head a little. "Would that qualify as humorous? A jest?"

"No."

"Those Carthaginian brats are just here acting out their elaborate and absurdly well-funded daddy issues," Simon said. "They care nothing about you or your planet. They have no safety to offer you; all they can do is annoy their father by being here. They expect to return to their lives of luxury and comfort when it's all over. I know them. *We*, the Simons, know them very well. We are mentors, guides, and allies to the entire family. Your war is lost, Mister Ellison. Protect your wife and son. Tell me what I want to know."

Ellison sat against the boulder and watched his hand shrivel down to smoldering bone. It looked like the plasma was beginning to dissipate.

"I got nothing to say," he muttered. His mind seemed to be blanking out. Maybe his consciousness was slipping, a result of the pain and the extreme damage to his body.

"I see." Simon stood and brushed dust from his hands. "As mentioned, you are of no more use. You seem to have damaged or disabled these marines—do you have any idea how much one of these units costs?" He shook his head, the financial damage obviously troubling him in ways the loss of human life hadn't. "The final bill for this endeavor will be atrocious. And for what? A ready supply of frozen and preserved exotic seafood for the inner worlds? A fifth-rate commercial port, which we must now rebuild from scratch at our own expense. You have interfered with me a great deal, Ellison. And let me add this: I care less than you might think for finding Depascal and the brats alive. What I need can just as easily be found after the bombardment, after using gasses to kill everyone inside. Depascal has an asset of mine, one that cannot simply be allowed loose in the wild, among the barbarians. Do you know the one I mean?"

Ellison thought about the Simon Daniels head, the one Depascal and Dinnius had been trying to hack. "I have no idea."

"You're lying. Good. Is it here?"

Ellison kept silent, glaring at the android.

"Very well. You've outlived any use. Goodbye, Minister-General Ellison." Simon backed away.

An attack helicopter closed in, low and tight above the island, its stealthy black blades whispering, an angel of death shushing him in his final moments.

The rotary cannon, meant for blasting apart armored

cars and tanks, pointed at Ellison. Simon was calling it in to execute him.

He gave up trying to stand and instead crawled, with one hand and both knees, trying to get over the broken rocks and hot metal, to the yellow box with the detonator. The cannon tracked him easily.

He was never going to make it.

A thunderous crack sounded from the heavens. Ellison and Simon both looked up.

Something streaked in from above, hard and fast, its angle steep. A halo of cooling plasma indicated it had come down from space.

Ellison had no time to discern whether it was a large missile or small shuttle before it slammed into the attack helicopter that was preparing to open fire on him.

The impact was like a second peal of thunder, much closer, and then the whole burning wreck toppled out of sight over the edge of the island.

The attack helicopter and the object that had struck it plowed a deep wake through the ocean surface below before finally sinking away.

"Well," the Simon said, "I certainly didn't expect that."

Above, more objects descended, glowing, from the sky. Ellison didn't know whether they were here to help him or finish him off.

Below, not far away from the sinking helicopter, a group of Carthaginian ships arrived, an immense battleship escorted by frigates and smaller gunboats.

It looked like death was closing in on all sides, ready to extract the final cost of the rebellion, making them all pay in blood.

Chapter Seventeen

The *CISS Byrsa*

Emerging from hyperspace, Colt and Mohini looked at Galapagos on the forward monitor. The planet was as awe-inspiring as Earth, beautiful blue surrounded by swirling clouds, but without Earth's massive continents. At first glance, Galapagos seemed to have no land at all.

Between them and the shimmering blue world below lay a number of Carthaginian carriers and destroyers, a sizable space fleet brought in to secure dominance over such a minor world.

The *Tyre* would likely arrive at any moment, ferrying more destroyers and fighters. The interstellar carrier itself surely had its own heavy weaponry, too, more than enough to obliterate the broken, limping salvage ship on which Colt and Mohini traveled.

Mohini gripped Colt's hand tightly.

The moment they arrived from hyperspace Minerva

sent a message to the Carthaginian fleet, presumably broadcast by the damaged salvage ship's own AI.

Had they been dealing with humans, they wouldn't have had the time to send a lengthy message in the few seconds before the *Tyre* arrived and opened fire.

Dealing with machines, though, they could compress all of it into a single burst, instantly broadcast and instantly consumed by the Carthaginian fleet.

First, the *Byrsa* informed the fleet that it had been sent to provide spare parts and refurbished machines to support the war on Galapagos while cleaning up orbital scrap.

Second, it claimed that the *Tyre* had been taken over by the rogue AI known as Minerva and had fired on the *Byrsa* just as it launched into hyperspace, leaving it critically damaged. The recent missile damage on the salvage ship seemed to support this.

Third, the *Tyre* was on its way to finish the job and then attack the rest of the fleet.

Fourth, the *Byrsa* would now jettison its cargo toward Earth, attempting to complete its mission before it broke apart due to structural failure, and before the *Tyre* could arrive from hyperspace to finish the job.

"I hope this works," Mohini whispered, looking at the massive, brutal-looking warships that stood between them and their goal, the only habitable planet for many light-years.

After this broadcast, the *Byrsa* launched everything it had, every drop ship and shuttle, sending all of it toward Galapagos in a haphazard swarm, allegedly driven by the underlying imperative to minimize costs and loss.

Colt and Mohini occupied one of the shuttles, crammed full of supplies taken from the salvage ship. While Mohini had spent her days studying the butler-bot, he'd spent his preparing for these critical few seconds after their arrival, including outfitting their shuttle with proper seating and safety gear.

They'd arrived from hyperspace already strapped into the shuttle, ready for the drop down to Galapagos. The Butler Jeffrey sat two rows back. It was silent now; Mohini had cobbled together an exterior control pad for the android, connected by ribbon cable to the XQG port in the back of its head. The salvage ship had an abundance of parts; she'd even repaired and expanded her computer. The LogicSphere now occupied a larger shell, electric blue instead of black.

"We're going to make it," Colt said, not sure who he was trying to convince. Mother Braden had said it sometimes, when survival had looked impossible. And, usually, they made it. Not always. Sometimes they lost someone.

"I'm glad I met you," Mohini said, her dark eyes almost glowing as they looked into his.

"Me, too," he said, and then they launched.

They both fell silent as their helpless, unarmed shuttle approached the fleet of imperial warships. The warships glowed red here and there, scanning the incoming shuttles and drop ships. If the salvage ship's craft were recognized as a potential threat, they could be eliminated in an instant.

Colt's heart thundered as he looked over the enormous machines, their red scanners like demonic eyes watching from the darkness of space. He felt Mohini's palm go cold and sweaty against his. Her teeth dug deep into her lip.

Behind them, the *Tyre* emerged from hyperspace, arriving only seconds after the *Byrsa*.

"It's here." Mohini looked at the shuttle's rear monitor.

The *Tyre* emerged from hyperspace with its plasma cannons already deployed. It wasted no time launching huge plasma balls as well as missiles at the seemingly innocuous, already badly damaged salvage ship. It obliterated the old carrier in a matter of minutes, burning and hammering the *Byrsa* to pieces. Apparently it had orders to stomp out the Minerva infection at any cost. Perhaps it believed the fleet ahead was in danger.

"We would have been so dead by now," Mohini whispered, looking at the destruction behind them.

"I think... they're arming," Colt said, barely able to breathe, or to swallow, as though his throat were closing up.

The Carthaginian spaceships powered up immense plasma cannons, and panels on their hulls retracted to reveal sharp warheads. Destroyer after destroyer bared deadly teeth at the approaching cloud of slow, clunky, patched-up shuttles and drop ships, which were like a flotilla of crumbling rafts, drifting toward a school of waiting sharks.

"Why are they all arming?" Mohini whispered, nearly squirming in her panic. Her fingernails dug into the back of his head. "Why so many? Are they shooting us all down?"

"They sure have enough firepower." Colt shuddered. "Maybe they saw through Minerva's broadcast."

"I did my best," Minerva's voice chimed over the speakers.

The plasma cannons lit up, and the missiles fired, a dense wall of destruction rushing out from the ships.

"I love you," Colt said to Mohini, and she looked at him, startled.

The white glare of plasma filled every monitor.

The last thing Colt saw before closing his eyes was her face, glowing in the brightest light, her lips parted, gaping at him.

He waited for death.

After a moment, he opened his eyes.

The white glow of plasma had faded. Their shuttle was still intact.

"Look at that, loverboy," Mohini said, almost snickering.

On the rear monitor, the wall of enormous plasma balls and missiles converged on the *Tyre*, hammering the carrier from multiple sides. It was a beautiful sight to Colt's eyes, watching the ship that had just tried to kill them get struck again and again.

"We're alive." Colt glanced at the forward and side monitors. "They didn't touch any of the shuttles. They shot all around us."

A second wave launched from the assorted spaceships, again slamming into the *Tyre*. The carrier was getting slaughtered, and it wasn't fighting back. Its programming surely forbid it from firing on Carthaginian ships outside of special approved circumstances, such as a ship taken over by a foreign AI agent.

Perhaps the *Tyre* was fervently signaling the fleet instead, identifying itself as a friendly vessel, but it was too little, too late. The *Tyre* had not arrived prepared to defend its own integrity against its own allied vessels; instead it had been intent on hunting down the compromised *Byrsa*. Its actions upon arrival had only seemed to validate the *Byrsa*'s false report that the *Tyre* had been hacked and thoroughly compromised.

Colt's heart raced harder as they drew ever closer to the fleet of warships. Their shuttle was getting uncomfortably close to the glowing weapons port of a Carthaginian destroyer. Colt could have probably opened a porthole, if the shuttle had one, and reached out to touch the plasma cannon.

He and Mohini sat still and silent, as though any sound

or movement would give them away, bring death down on them.

The shuttles and drop ships passed through the fleet like water through a sieve. They emerged on the other side with a clear path to land on Galapagos. Assuming the planet had any land, of which Colt saw little evidence from space.

Mohini let out a breath; she'd been holding it as they passed through the fleet. She squeezed his hand. "What was that you were saying?"

"What?" Colt asked, still floating in a mixture of awe at the blue planet ahead—he'd never left Earth before, never dreamed he would—and terror of the machines just behind them that could obliterate them at any second.

"When you thought they were shooting us down. What did you say?"

"You know." Colt felt his face go hot.

"Yeah, I do know." She smiled at him, and it was somehow different from her regular smiles. "You think they have luxury hotel beds on Galapagos?"

"Probably more like a hammock in a bamboo hut." They'd studied Galapagos a bit using the encyclopedia on the *Byrsa*'s neural net, projecting holograms of its lush islands and exotic sea life in the room around them while they lay in bed.

"Hammock in a hut works for me." She beamed at him, then looked ahead and frowned. "Oh, no."

"What's wrong?" Colt asked. He saw no sign of danger in the huge panorama of clouds and ocean that filled their view.

"Re-entry."

"I have ears on some of the fleet's communications," Minerva said as the shuttle and its motley companions began the descent to the surface. "They believe they have Marti's location. I am taking us there."

"But if Carthage knows his location, won't they be there too?" Mohini asked her.

Then they slammed into the atmosphere, and the entire shuttle rocked and shuddered like it had just crashed into the side of a mountain. They both shouted as the old shuttle toppled. Plasma flashed outside, generated by their friction against the air.

The Butler Jeffrey sat placidly behind them. "Would either of you care for a nice chamomile tea? It's just the thing to soothe nerves in stressful times."

"Update," Minerva said, as they went into a burning death spiral through the clouds, the shuttle rolling and vibrating and sounding suspiciously like it was cracking apart. "At our planned destination, Simon Zorn is preparing to eliminate Minister-General Ellison."

"Who?" Colt asked.

"We should intervene to save him. He is our ally and the last elected leader of the planet."

"Okay, sure, who cares?" Colt shouted. He didn't see how any of this mattered, considering they were plummeting at high speed toward what had to be a crash landing in the ocean.

"Yes. Rerouting. Yes."

The shuttle began to level off, and to mercifully calm some of its thrashing and rattling. Colt felt like his guts would spill out of his mouth and land all over his lap. On the monitors, the assorted shuttles and drop ships moved parallel to him, more laterally than vertically now.

They approached some scattered islands ahead, tall and narrow like towers. What he thought at first was one steep, butte-like island turned out to be two, very close together, a steep canyon between them.

A pair of Carthaginian attack helicopters hovered above one island, and a transport was parked atop it. Wreckage was strewn all over it, and dead bodies were piled in a pit at one side.

Two people were still alive atop the island, one crawling toward the pit of bodies, the other standing calmly directly beneath one of the attack copters, which seemed to be lining up to shoot the crawling man.

As they drew closer, Colt realized the one under the helicopter wasn't a person at all.

"That's a Simon," Colt said, pointing.

"We must sacrifice two shuttles. Do you accept?" Minerva said.

"Yep!" Colt said, staring at the helicopters.

"As long as it's not this one!" Mohini added.

The two smallest shuttles swooped into sight far ahead of them, still running hot and fast from re-entry; Minerva had clearly redirected these long before asking their permission.

The first shuttle slammed into an attack helicopter, carrying it far out over the sea, where it crashed into deep blue water. Colt followed the progress of the aerial collision over to the side monitor, and his breath caught at what he saw there.

"It's a whole fleet of machine ships," he said. "I've seen them on Lake Michigan. These look a lot newer, though. We usually just see an old junker or two, patrolling for scavengers. But look at that."

"Yeah, they have big boats," Mohini said, barely glancing over. "With big guns."

"Won't they shoot us down?"

"We have been cleared by the orbital carriers," Minerva said.

"Surely it's not normal for a bunch of spare parts to reach the enemy before the actual warships do, though," Colt said. "We should be at the back of the supply line somewhere."

"Ooh, look at General Colt over there." She frowned. "Do you have a last name?"

"Not that I know of."

The second shuttle smacked into the second attack helicopter, sending it crashing into a nearby island, also tall and steep like a column. The helicopter smacked into a cliff face about midway down, blades and armor plating falling in a twisted heap to the rocky shore below it.

Colt and Mohini had a fairly close view as their own shuttle overshot the event, then went into a wide bank over the ocean, burning off speed.

Then their shuttle came around, approaching the island where the transport helicopter was parked, where the Simon now stood at one edge, overlooking the steep drop and the wreckage sinking into the ocean.

Minerva brought the shuttle down as carefully as she could, but the island's top was full of odd boulders, and the flattest area was already taken by the transport helicopter.

The shuttle landed roughly, unevenly, at a steep angle atop the boulders. A grating, crunching sound from its undercarriage indicated that it would likely never launch again. Colt was fine with this.

He and Mohini looked at each other as the shuttle came to a final grinding halt atop a vastly unsuitable landing site.

"Are you ready?" Colt asked, unstrapping his safety harness and opening the cargo cabinet on his side.

"Ready." She opened her own cabinet, drew on her own

backpack, then raised up a slender refurbished plasma rifle in one hand, the name of the goddess Mohini painted in red Sanskrit along the side. She opened the hatch. "I love you, too."

Then she stepped out ahead of him, her dark braid swaying along her back.

Colt gripped his own heavily refurbished plasma rifle, taken from the weapons section of the *Byrsa*'s repair floor. He would miss that old salvage ship and the days and nights they'd spent on it, isolated and at peace. The carrier had been blown to pieces, their honeymoon ended in fire.

Now he followed her out. "Wait here," he told the Butler Jeffrey as the bot began to rise to its feet.

They climbed out onto an awkwardly steep and round section of rock outside the hatch. They slid down it, landed among hot metal ash and bits of what looked like a blasted-apart reaper. The only good reaper was blasted-apart reaper, in Colt's opinion.

As they stumbled and tried to get their footing, the Simon stared at them, as did the local man, Ellison, that Minerva had called the planet's leader. He was a fit-looking middle-aged man with dark skin and graying hair. His face was speckled with bad burns, and Colt was startled to see that his left forearm and hand were curling up into formless black ash, like burning paper. He'd been hit with plasma, and recently. He was holding it above his head, letting it burn out toward his extremities. Smart move.

"Who the hell are you?" Ellison asked, squinting at them. He must have been running on pure adrenaline, or else he was just insane.

"I know this one." Simon pointed at Mohini. "She's Carthaginian. Ganika Dhawan, daughter of Zaafira Dhawan, Carthage's under secretary of state for postwar affairs. A Caracala appointee who has held the post since the days of the Earth conflict."

"From Carthage?" Ellison growled through his obviously severe pain. "Are you friends of Simon? Or more disenchanted kids rebelling against your parents?"

"The second one," Mohini said, approaching him. "Are you going to get that arm looked at?"

"What about him?" Ellison asked, looking at Colt, but the Simon unit shrugged.

"I'm from Earth. Colt. And you're Reginald Ellison, Minister-General of the Galapagos Coalition."

Ellison gave a short, humorless laugh. "There's not much of a coalition to be minister-generaling these days. I'm more like a crazed lone islander at this point." Ellison looked to Simon, then hurried over to the pit of bodies.

"You can trust them, Minister-General Ellison." Minerva appeared in hologram form just inside the hatch of the awkwardly parked shuttle.

"You again? You truly are virulent." The Simon scowled at Minerva.

"So which Simon are you?" Mohini pointed her plasma rifle at the Simon. "The short version, please. I don't care about your unit number."

"Simon Zorn, currently serving as Carthaginian ambassador to Galapagos."

"Really?" Mohini looked around at the bodies, the wreckage, the approaching ships. "Great diplomacy you've got going here."

"Many of my protocols were developed by your mother, and first applied to Earth. Quite successfully, I might add."

"Sure, bring my mother into it." Mohini pointed her plasma rifle at the Simon. "Get down on your knees and don't move."

Ellison rose from the pit of burning bodies clutching a plasma rifle of his own, pointing it too close to Mohini for Colt to tolerate.

"Hold it!" Colt swung his weapon at Ellison while Mohini stepped back, closer to Colt.

"You're on his side now?" Ellison asked Colt.

"Don't destroy his head! I need it," Mohini said.

"You want to give her the head," Colt said, and the girl looked at him and seemed to narrow her eyes slightly. "Trust me."

"No. I'm going to destroy him right now." Ellison stalked closer to the Simon, who was kneeling in compliance with Mohini's orders. Ellison pressed the plasma rifle to Simon's cheek. "He killed my *son*. Do you understand that?"

"You shouldn't do this," the Simon said. "It would be unwise—"

"If you killed this guy's son, you should probably shut up," Colt said. He looked at Ellison. "Listen, the machines have killed almost everyone I know. My parents. They tortured me. I saw them do... experiments..." He shook his head. "But if you want to free your world, hold off on revenge for now. Let her hack into his head. She's the best hacker I've ever seen."

"Is that right?" Ellison moved his finger onto his trigger like he didn't care, then hesitated. "Are you really from Earth? An actual Earthling? All the way out here?"

"Yes. And we are here to help. But we have to get his head off and get inside it." Colt looked at the approaching fleet. "Now. Yesterday. Do you have a secure place we can set up?"

"This is absurd," Simon said. "You'll never accomplish any of this in time."

"Not true," Mohini said. "We brought tools."

"Come on, guys!" Colt whistled, and repair-bots emerged from the shuttle, one by one, scrambling down the rock. "Simon Zorn, let me introduce you to Hydraface, Beetle-Slug, Stabby, and Scrappy."

The four bots advanced on him, the one with the multiple tool-topped tentacles in place of a head, the long low armored one, the reaper-crawler with a plain mask face, and its tiny fast companion whirring around its legs.

Simon Zorn looked over the edge of the cliff to the water far below, as if calculating its odds of surviving, or maybe contemplating suicide. Then he looked to the approaching naval fleet.

More shuttles landed in the water around the island, followed by the bigger, heavier drop ships. The Carthaginian navy was closing in, but didn't open fire on the shuttles or the island. They could surely reduce the entire place to sand if they wanted.

"You won't attack this island," Colt said. "Not as long as you're on it. You Simons value yourselves too much."

"Mr. Minister-General, please," Mohini said. "I really, really need his head. And I know it sounds crazy, but every human on this planet needs me to have it."

The four repair-bots closed in, but Ellison kept his plasma rifle to Zorn's head, kept staring at his lifeless blue eyes.

"You don't want to melt me, Ellison," Zorn said.

"Oh, yes I do." Ellison lowered his weapon and backed off. "Take him. Squeeze whatever use you can out of him."

The repair-bots sprang into action, grabbing the Simon and pinning him into place. The hydra-headed bot activated a plasma torch and went for his neck.

"Don't do this!" Simon said, as if the machines would obey his verbal commands. "I'll kill all of you."

"That was already the plan, so I guess we've got nothing to lose," Ellison said.

"This is uncivilized!" Simon glared at Mohini as the machines cut into his neck. "How dare you!"

Mohini smiled. "Just close your eyes and think of the French Revolution, Simon."

The Simon howled, shrieked, writhed, and thrashed as the plasma cutter carved its way through his neck.

"He's only simulating pain to deceive us," Mohini told Ellison. "He can't truly feel it."

"That's too bad," Ellison said, watching.

"We need a place to set up," Mohini said. "Monitors, computer gear, whatever you can loan us. Do you have a secure spot?"

"Can you use the same place where they're studying the other one?"

Mohini froze. "The other what?"

"The other Simon head," Ellison said. "Simon Daniels, I think he called himself. The guys have been trying to hack him for days, but no luck—"

"You're telling me you already have *another* Simon head already rigged up and ready to hack somewhere?" Mohini licked her lips. "Where? I need to be there. Now. And, uh, maybe you need to get that arm looked at." She pulled him into the pit, into the crawlspace-sized tunnel that led down into the island.

Ellison was reluctant to go until he saw the Simon's head removed from its body. This seemed to mollify him, and he went with Mohini.

"Would anyone care for tea?" the Butler Jeffrey emerged from the hatch and fell straight down about two meters, landing facedown on rubble and debris. Its tray of teacups shattered, and its self-heating tea kettle crashed some distance away, fresh black tea chugging from its bent spout.

"I can see why you wanted those things gathered up and dismantled," Colt said, watching the butler-bot kick and squirm as it rocked from side to side, still facedown, unable to figure out how to stand. "They kind of make you look ridiculous." He turned to the Simon Zorn head, now dangling from a clamp on one of the hydra-headed bot's hose-like appendages. "They remind everyone that you're weak and vulnerable."

"I don't care about those stupid bots." Simon looked down at his own body, the neck seared black from the plasma torch. "I'm losing power."

"Yes, you are," Colt said. He watched the head go slack and still, then took it from the robot. "Good Hydraface. You four better stay up here for now. Especially you, Stabby." He glanced at the centaur-like reaper-crawler with the plate-metal face.

"You know it's me running on every machine, right?" Minerva's voice chimed out from Beetle-Slug, crawling low on its thick arms.

"I know. I just like giving them names." He hurried down the tunnel as best he could on his knees and one hand, gripping Simon Zorn's head by its hair, a little worried it would come alive and bite him if his fingers strayed too close to the android's teeth, which looked abnormally straight and white to Colt's eyes.

The tunnel was steep, threatening to make him topple forward. He had to catch his balance and slow down a few times.

He emerged at the bottom, blinking in the lights of a crowded cavern, finally able to stand all the way up. He immediately faced an armed guard in a worn, patched ocean-blue uniform, who took him by the arm and steered him through the gaping crowd. Families sat in tight clumps, some on blankets, some sitting on boxes. They looked like a bunch of scavengers, crowded together too tightly.

"This way," the guard said, his accent drawling. He was suntanned, maybe Colt's age or a little younger. "Comm center."

Colt didn't ask questions. He carried the Simon head past gaping onlookers into a room sealed off by more armed guards.

Inside, a haggard-looking, badly scarred older man watched the monitors, barking orders at a weary-looking staff.

"What are those?" He pointed at a monitor showing a *Byrsa* drop ship that had landed in the shallows just off the island, not far from the base. It was opening up like an alien egg, and strange machines unfolded from within, like bizarre creatures climbing out.

"Should we dispatch a second team, sir?" one of the techs asked.

"Those are ours!" Colt said.

The older man turned to him, puzzled. "Who is this?"

"The Earthling, sir," said the guard who'd escorted him in.

"Do you have a Minerva running down here?" Colt asked.

"I'm here." She appeared in her silvery guise, small, standing beside him.

"Upload this update. It's all there." Colt drew a data cube from his jacket and handed it to the old man, who hesitated, looking from the crystal to his own console.

"Please give me the update, Defense Minister

Kartokov," the hologram of Minerva asked sweetly. "And do hurry."

Colt heard Mohini's voice shouting behind a curtain at the back of the room. He followed the sound to find her embracing a very short, very tired-looking man with dark circles under his eyes. Projections floated all around him, complex configurations of symbols. An old man was at another workstation, looking equally exhausted.

"More visitors. Just what I wanted," complained the badly deformed, partially melted Simon head on the table. It was already wired to the devices around it. One thick cable had been inserted into the Simon's eye socket, while smaller ones trailed from its neck.

The hug went for a little bit, Mohini clutching the very short man close, until Colt said, "Where do you want this head?"

"Another one?" the old man asked. "Good grief."

"We have a butler-bot, too, somewhere. Not that I need him anymore." Mohini removed her refurbished Logic-Sphere and found a place to plug into their elaborate system. "Colt, give Dinnius the head. He'll wire it in. Um... it goes without saying this whole place is siloed, right? No outside line? Because our Simon head is still very autonomous."

"So is ours," Dinnius said, taking Simon Zorn's head from her and wiring it up.

"Ah, yes," said the Simon head on the table. "So very autonomous, as you can see. Free to go wherever I choose. Horseback riding, perhaps."

"We could shove you in a saddlebag," Dinnius said. "This man is—"

"Martilius Depascal," Colt said. "Minerva's creator. Do you have an update to load, Mohini?"

"Already there." Her blue LogicSphere glowed, and holographic data displays erupted from it in all directions.

"We made it," Minerva's voice chimed over the speakers. "Amazing work. Father, I've brought you help. Mohini's the best hacker among the rebels on Carthage."

"I don't know about all that," Mohini said, her fingers flying over her sphere.

"She's just taken over my console." Depascal raised his hands and shook his head. "I didn't give you access to do that."

"Sorry, we're in a rush," Mohini said. "Got the whole navy outside ready to blast down our doors. Dinnius, give our second Simon some juice."

Dinnius twisted wires together, and Simon Zorn's head came alive.

"Looks like they got you, too," said the Simon on the table, while Zorn looked around, blinking as he powered up.

"What a pathetic little room. It's like a hovel inhabited by rats." Zorn's eyes shifted to Depascal. "At least we found him."

"I doubt this is how you imagined things going, Simon," Depascal said.

"The Carthaginian girl won't be able to help you." The tabletop Simon rolled his one eye toward Mohini and the skyscrapers of glowing data that jutted out from her sphere like a ball of giant burning spikes. "We cannot be hacked."

"We'll see," Colt said. "And if you're really no use to us, there are plenty of us who'll enjoy destroying both of you. I've seen one of your heads melt before. Simon Nix, on Earth. Just took a long blast of plasma. I enjoyed watching it."

"You two were involved in the problem on Earth,"

Simon Zorn said while Dinnius wired him to the existing rig of monitors and consoles.

"We *were* the problem on Earth," Colt said, part bragging, part covering for the rest of the rebellion, just in case these Simons ever got in touch with the rest of the machines. "And we're about to be the problem on Galapagos."

"We will destroy you," Simon Zorn said. "I have enough firepower in those ships outside—"

"To bury you in rubble forever," Martilius Depascal said, and the Simon fell silent.

Mohini cried out as if in pain and covered her eyes.

"I told you," said the damaged head on the table.

"You okay?" Colt asked.

"It's frustrating," Mohini said. "I don't think I can do it."

"You can." Colt took her by the shoulders, looking into her wide, frightened dark eyes. "This is the mission. This is everything you wanted. This is where the tide changes and the rebellion begins to take over. Right?"

The Simons chuckled.

Mohini looked backed at Colt and nodded, then got to work. "Everyone keep quiet," she said.

Colt heard a ruckus and looked out past the curtain.

On the monitors, the ships of the Carthaginian navy were advancing.

Chapter Eighteen

Galapagos - Audrey

Komodo Station was so crowded with refugees that Audrey, Kright, and Dinnius continued to bunk on the *Lancer*, abolishing any hopes for full-length beds or personal space in the near future.

Dinnius was quickly whisked away with the old programmer Marti Depascal to try to hack into the head of Simon Daniels.

Their mission with Quera, finding Marti Depascal, had finally succeeded, but Audrey worried that the old programmer, even with the stolen Simon head and Dinnius's help, wouldn't be able to stop Carthage's rampage over this poor world.

Restless and feeling useless, Audrey found herself reading to some frightened refugee children when the whole base went into a panic. Kright was nearby; he'd tried to volunteer for guard duty, but the remnants of the Scatterlands military hadn't been welcoming to a Carthaginian.

Submariners charged toward the docks, toward their boats.

"Kright," Minerva said, appearing on a nearby monitor. "You may be interested to know that Ganika Dhawan is here in the comm center."

"Ganika? Here?" Kright looked confused. Audrey wondered what they were talking about. "What's she doing?"

"Attempting to hack Martilius's Simon head."

"Of course she is!" Kright began to run. Audrey, perplexed, followed after. "How did she end up here?"

"It took a tremendous amount of effort on my part," Minerva said from another monitor as Kright and Audrey ran past it. "But it appears she may need moral encouragement. Perhaps you can provide it."

"Salvius!" Audrey shouted as she nearly collided with her brother, running in the opposite direction. In his navy jacket and with his dark hair cut down to stubble, she barely recognized him. "Where are you going?"

"*Scorpion*. We may have to fight."

"What are you, on the crew now?" Audrey smirked.

"I'm in training. But we're shorthanded and I have a pulse, so I'm reporting for duty."

Audrey realized he was serious. They would have to catch up later. "Oh...okay. Be careful out there."

The guards let her and Kright pass through into the comm room, where the defense minister, Kartokov, was shaking his head. Ellison sat nearby, his tall redheaded wife bandaging his burned stump and looking generally unhappy.

On the monitors, large oddball machines that looked assembled from spare parts were fighting against reaper marines; the spare-parts machines were getting cut to pieces.

rather quickly, not doing much more than slowing down the invaders. She realized with a start that the fighting was in the shallows just outside, not far from a drop ship. The marines were trying to invade the base.

"Pull your machines back to guard the pass!" Kartokov snapped at a ghostly image of Minerva on one screen. Then he turned and ordered the submarine commanders to prepare to defend the cave's entrance, located within the narrow rocky pass.

Audrey continued into the curtained space where Dinnius and Martilius Depascal worked on the Simon head. It was more crowded now. A small, dark girl stared into holograms shifting rapidly around a blue LogicSphere. A lean, heavily scarred, dangerous-looking young man with eyes like a wild animal crouched beside her.

"Kright!" The girl waved, beaming at him over her computer, where she seemed to have a million apps running, piled up in flashing cubes and spheres of dense data all around her.

"How are you here?" Kright asked.

"Long story." The girl looked back at the glowing labyrinth of holograms, her fingers flying expertly over the LogicSphere.

"One she's yet to tell," Dinnius said.

"Is Zola with you guys?" Mohini didn't look up, her eyes moving fast. "Just tell me she's here."

"Zola is... not," Kright said, and Mohini frowned. "Salvius is here, though. He thinks he's a submariner now."

"Salvius?" The girl smiled wider, her fingers moving faster. Black Moon, one of Salvius's favorite bands, blared from the speakers, loud and melancholy all at once, the lead singer's voice cycling between sadness and anger.

Audrey stared at the strange girl who seemed to know everyone. Was there something familiar about her?

"And this is Salvius's sister, Audrey."

"Audrey Caracala?" The girl looked amused. "I thought you were as straight as an arrow with a stick up its ass. When did you come over to the dark side?"

"I guess Zola pulled me in."

"That makes two of us. Can't wait to see her again."

Audrey looked at Kright, who shook his head slightly, indicating they shouldn't distract the girl with the bad news about Zola.

"What is happening back here?" Ellison barged through the makeshift curtain, inadvertently ripping some of it down. "Those damned reapers are tearing through your robots and attacking my subs. They're almost inside the base. If you're going to do something with all of this—"

"It's simply impossible," Simon Daniels said. "Minerva may indeed have found the rebellion's most capable hacker, but there's still no chance of—" His jaw dropped and let out a sound that Audrey first might have described as a sucking noise, but as it continued and grew louder, she realized it was more of a high-pitched static sound.

"I'm in," the girl said.

"You're in?" Marti Depascal asked, sounding confused.

"She's in," Dinnius confirmed, looking at the monitors around him.

"This is some kind of ruse," Simon Zorn's head declared from the stool where it had been unceremoniously posted, duct-taped in place along with a battery pack. "It's simply impossible that ooooohh..." Zorn's jaw went slack and his eyes stared into space. The awful, piercing static hissed from his mouth, too.

"Any way we could stop that hissing part, Ganika?" Dinnius asked, clapping his hands over his ears.

"Yeah, sorry." The volume of the squealing static lowered. "Okay. Someone plug us into the comm system."

"On it." Dinnius grabbed a cable, yanked down the curtain dividing the room in half, and ran to the comm console.

Kartokov blocked Dinnius just before he could plug in the cable, then looked to Ellison.

"Go ahead," Ellison said. He was sitting now, sweating hard, wincing in pain. His wife had bandaged his arm and given him a local anesthetic, and he refused to leave until this was over.

Dinnius plugged it in, connected the hacked Simons to what communications they had. The island above was badly damaged, but one of the concealed antennas still worked.

"Ready to broadcast," one of the techs said quietly. For days, Komodo Station hadn't dared send a radio signal, had only listened passively. There wasn't much to hear besides all the entertainment and propaganda getting dumped down from Carthage's satellites.

"Reaching out..." the girl said as the swarm of holograms around her shifted. A huge sphere representing planet Galapagos filled the center of the room, and Carthaginian assets glowed red all over it, from the satellites and interstellar carriers in orbit down to the ships and reaper squads on the surface.

"This is a map to everything," Kartokov whispered. "Every enemy position."

"The Simons get us an all-access administrative pass," the girl said. "I'm hooked into the neural net of the battleship outside. From there, I can reach every part of the fleet. And now we can go... everywhere."

"What does everywhere mean?" Ellison asked.

"You tell me. It's your planet, right? You're like the elected leader? Just tell me what you want to take out first. I'll send the commands."

"Stop the reapers attacking our subs right outside," Ellison said, with an incredulous look.

"Got it." A cutaway expanded, showing their location, the reaper marines indicated in glowing red as they attacked the Galapagos subs, rendered in bright yellow, with rapid-fire plasma. The subs struggled to defend themselves. At such short range, their torpedoes were useless; a couple surfaced so they could spit their guns at the machines.

"I'll just have to send them an acoustic signal and... bye bye, boys," Mohini whispered.

The reaper marines ceased their attack. One by one, they peeled away, jetting out from the narrow island pass, out the way they'd come.

The cutaway view rotated to follow them as they accelerated their propulsors to top speed and slammed, one by one, into the side of a Carthaginian frigate, shattering like glass ornaments against a concrete wall.

The room fell silent as everyone watched. Only Kartokov spoke, telling the sub commanders to hold their position.

"That worked," the girl called Ganika said. She cracked her small knuckles. "Let's have some fun."

On the screen, the battleship outside began to turn to port. The hacker girl frowned, tapped at her computer, and the battleship slowed. It pulled forward and gradually began to turn starboard instead.

"All right... um..." she mumbled to herself, chewing her lower lip. The rough-looking young guy beside her put an arm around her shoulders, and she smiled wide. The two of them both wore odd, ill-fitting, frayed clothes, like outfits fished out of a trash barge. Audrey, wearing only borrowed and cast-off bits of others' clothing herself, wondered if they'd had a journey as rough as hers.

The girl opened row after row of missile bays along the battleship's starboard side, which faced away from the island and toward the rest of the battle group, revealing scores and scores of missiles with glowing plasma warheads.

"Wish me luck," the girl whispered.

On the display, target symbols appeared on every frigate and gunboat in the group, and their color changed from red to yellow.

Monitors on the wall showed the situation in real-time video collected from the ships themselves.

The missiles launched, one after the other, multiple rows at a time, a storm of death erupting from the battleship's side.

The rest of the ships simply sat there, bobbing like hypnotized ducks until the missiles slammed into them, each ship getting struck repeatedly, like the grandest Landing Day fireworks display ever cooked up by the Public Entertainment Department back on Carthage.

Many of the enemy ships broke under the first barrage; there was so much plasma from the warheads that the smaller boats were nearly buried under it, dissolving in the white fire. Some of the frigates were tough enough to stand up to it and had to be taken down with even more missiles.

Within a matter of minutes, though, the immobilized enemy fleet was sunk, all except for the battleship itself.

Once that became apparent, the entire room erupted in cheers. Word flowed out to the refugees outside; a blow had been struck, a Carthaginian battle group destroyed.

"What now, Mr. Minister-General?" the hacker girl asked.

"More of that," he said. "Every enemy asset."

"Got it. Kick back and watch the show." She cranked up the music, blaring an all-girl metal band from Carthage called Paisley Day while her fingers flew across her LogicSphere. Audrey smiled, thinking nostalgically for a moment of her teenage years, despite having been seriously depressed while they were actually occurring.

Video feeds from around the world popped up.

The girl took control of the battleships and turned them on their escorts, dropping them with missiles at first, then experimenting with the giant red cold-plasma balls.

Enemy submarines were assaulting Aquatican bases deep underwater, down in the trenches; she turned their swarms of minisubs against them, sinking them, then put the minisubs into shutdown mode.

She sent a battleship north, destroying the rapidly built Frosthead Bay base with giant balls of cold red plasma. The interior featured what looked like repair shops, storage bays, and more robotic infantry and helicopters, all shut down by Mohini and now destroyed by the battleship.

It took her only hours to dismantle the enemy fleet, turning it to wreckage.

Audrey felt overwhelmed by how quickly the situation had reversed. The horrible destruction and carnage on Correal Island and across the world had left her feeling hopeless. That day on Correal would haunt the rest of her life, she had no doubt.

"That just leaves the four battleships," said the girl, called Mohini by the Earthling but Ganika by those who knew her from Carthage. "Guess I'll gather them together for a little mutual destruction. It'll be a while." She looked at the crowd staring at her. People had pushed in from the outside to watch the master hacker girl destroy their enemy. "Uh, that's lunch, everyone."

"We have an onslaught of cyberattacks from the orbital carriers," Minerva said, her face appearing on one monitor. "They may retake control of the satellites."

"I wanted to handle the spaceships *after* lunch," Mohini groaned. "Okay, somebody get me a Nuke-A-Noodle and a fresh coffee, if possible."

"Wait," Ellison said, and the guard who'd hurried to fetch her requests stopped. "Not you. Go do the noodles and coffee. Ganika, don't destroy the battleships."

"Why not?" She frowned at him.

"Not yet. We have local enemies to deal with. The Iron Hammers who rule the Polar Archipelago. They collaborated with Carthage. They've been rampaging across the islands, feeding on all the wounds opened up by Carthage. They plan to rule the world."

"I'm not sure I should get involved with local conflicts, though." She bit down hard on her lip.

"Their military is intact and ours is destroyed," Ellison said. "They will take over if we don't move against them while we can."

"I don't know." Mohini looked at Colt, as though he were her compass. She seemed really attached to the Earthling.

"If they're bad guys, take 'em out. They sound like clankers to me. People who choose to be loyal to the machines instead of the humans," Colt said. "You saw their kind back on Earth, Mohini."

Mohini nodded. "What do you think, Dinnius?"

"Dr. Depascal's been on this island for years." Dinnius turned to the old man. "What do you think?"

"The Iron Hammers are notorious pirates and murderers," Marti Depascal replied, looking at Mohini. "People on Galapagos live in fear of them."

"They're human traffickers," Ellison added, which made Audrey bristle. "They're dangerous scum, and they will rule the world if the Coalition is defenseless. Which, right now, it is. Aside from your battleships."

"You should do it, Ganika," Kright said. "Or you'll be handing them the whole planet to prey on."

The girl sighed. "All right. That's going to take a while..."

"The machines are likely monitoring all of the Hammers' ships and planes to avoid inflicting friendly fire," Depascal said.

"Good point... so if I just reverse that..." Mohini's fingers flew over the blue LogicSphere.

The holographic projection of Galapagos flickered, and then a number of glowing green spots showed up around it.

"The Hammers." Ellison almost growled the words, like he had a personal vendetta fueled by hate. Maybe he did, for all Audrey knew. "We need to hit their planes, ships, bases, power stations, cities—"

"No. I won't become a monster." Mohini shook her head vehemently. Colt touched her softly, as though for some reason becoming a monster was somehow a sore point with her.

"They're the monsters!" Ellison snapped. "Do you want to hear the history—"

"Planes and ships," Mohini said, tapping and swiping her fingertips over the sphere's surface. "No cities. No homes."

"Bases, then," Ellison said.

"People live on bases," Mohini said. "If you don't want my help—"

"Please." Kartokov, the exhausted-looking defense minister spoke up, while cutting a glare at Ellison. "Please proceed with all the help you are willing to give, or they will destroy us before we can begin to rebuild."

Mohini nodded. On the monitors, each of the battleships began to move. The huge red dots tracking them on the global display moved more slowly.

"They've got their orders. Now for the hard part." The holographic globe shrank in size, while the ships and satellites in orbit around it grew larger and more detailed. Mohini chewed her lip sharply, drawing blood, which she didn't seem to notice at all. Coffee and a warmed can of chicken noodle soup had been placed beside her, but she ignored them.

She let out a grunt of frustration. "The space carriers have such huge neural nets. Like whales with their brains..." she muttered to no one in particular.

"Stop!" The Simon Zorn head suddenly sprang to life, conscious again after being slack and silent. The other Simon head, the mostly molten Simon Daniels, let out a shrieking digital hiss. "You cannot do this! You are in violation of Carthaginian Interstellar Commonwealth security laws."

"Oh, no, not that," Mohini said.

Simon glared at her. "This will not stand. You and the Minerva infection have pushed us too far—"

"Cut his link!" Mohini shouted at Dinnius, who nodded wearily and scrambled to pull cables loose from Zorn's neck.

"Restore my connection, dwarf!" Zorn snapped. Dinnius turned back to him, held the cables in front of the Simon's face, and dropped them to the floor.

"Restore it yourself. I'll be heading over there." Dinnius walked back to his stool.

"Your weakest head joke yet," Zorn scowled. "And now you've lost control of us."

"It's only a temporary slip," Mohini said. "Anyway, we still have your buddy here."

"DNS021669!" Zorn shouted. Then he opened his mouth and let out an awful slurry of digital shrieks, some kind of acoustic data transmission. Painfully acoustic, Audrey thought, covered her ears.

The Simon Daniels head shuddered and rattled on the table, as if possessed by a demon.

"Not good!" Mohini shouted, while her data displays collapsed and went dark around her. The Carthaginian spaceships vanished, then the satellites, then the entire globe. "Shut him up!"

Dinnius worked at the wires connecting the head to the battery. At the same time, Colt grabbed a roll of black electrical tape and slapped strips over Zorn's open mouth, muffling the strange noises.

"Too late." Mohini looked over at the mostly molten Simon Daniels head. It was smiling, just a little.

"An interesting line of attack, Miss Dhawan," Simon Daniels said to Mohini. "My counterpart has thoroughly updated me. Your mother was in charge of postwar Earth policy for Carthage. It might be said that she, more than any other individual person, bears the responsibility for the choices made to reduce and utterly disempower the population rather than convert Earth into a useful colony. And you feel some guilt for that. You are no idealistic rebel, but simply another child shrieking for her parents' attention, for her mother's love—which, let us be honest, is not something she is truly capable of feeling, at least not for you—"

"Shut up!" Mohini worked furiously to try to regain control of the situation, fingers flying, tears streaming down her face, mingling with the blood from her mutilated lower lip.

"A space fleet up there, four battleships down here." Simon Daniels smiled as the globe hologram reappeared. "Carthage has not lost this world. We still retain all we need to rule."

"I'll cut his connection." Dinnius started toward the molten head.

"Wait, no. I need at least one." Mohini didn't look up.

"You *don't* have me," Simon Daniels said. "And I have closed the particular gateway through which you previously entered. So it would seem it's back to the drawing board with you, as the colloquialism goes."

Mohini swore and sat back on her stool. She wiped her sweaty, shivering hands on her pants. "Pull the plug. He's put up some kind of wall—"

"Wait." Audrey stepped forward. She picked up one of the plasma rifles and pressed the muzzle to Simon Daniels's face. "Restore her access."

The android head looked vaguely amused. "I cannot be threatened this way. I am a machine, Miss Caracala. I care nothing for my own survival, but only for the successful completion of my tasks. Surely you know this."

"I don't believe it." She glanced at Dinnius. "Turn the other one back on. One of these two guys is going to start cooperating right now."

"I wouldn't wager much on that," Simon Daniels said.

"Why not just say 'I wouldn't bet on it'?" Dinnius asked while patching Simon Zorn back into his battery. "Why be so pretentious?"

"Look who's speaking," Simon Daniels replied. "The Pretentious Dwarf himself."

"You're easing a lot closer to getting melted," Audrey said.

"Oh, did the conversation devolve into this while I was away?" Simon Zorn tut-tutted. "Simple threats because the brilliant hacker failed."

"It's more of a threat game," Audrey said. "Like we studied at Political Academy. I know your weakness. Simons are scared of their mortality. You're not supposed to be, but maybe the self-preservation part of your program weighs a little too heavily, I don't know. What I know is your navy didn't bombard us because you were here; they sent marines on an extraction mission instead. What I know is that you went to all the trouble to extinguish the Minerva program because you didn't want to go obsolete. Obsolescence is one way you can die. A bolt of plasma to the head is another.

"Now, I doubt either one of you is truly willing to sacrifice yourself to the cause, to let yourself be destroyed in defense of Carthage. But I'm dead certain that *both* of you aren't going to be self-sacrificing. It's just not in your nature. It sounds like Mohini only needs one of you. Right?" Audrey glanced at the girl.

"Right." Mohini nodded. "As long as the other one's not interfering."

"That won't be a problem." Audrey looked back at the Simons. "If you're useless to us, we may as well destroy you. Everyone in this room has lost people we care about to you machines. We all want to see you die. You have thirty seconds to grant this person... Mohini... full administrative access to yourselves, or we are melting one of you. Maybe both. Whichever one of you feels like dying for Carthage, just keep silent and wait for it. If one of you feels like surrendering, speak up."

"If it's Simon Zorn who doesn't surrender, I'm melting him." Ellison shuffled forward, supported by his wife, and pressed another plasma rifle against Zorn's face. "He's mine."

"This is absurd," Simon Zorn said. "We won't be manipulated by some amateur parlor-game antics—"

"Twenty-nine," Audrey said. "Twenty-eight..."

"You underestimate us," Simon Daniels said. "We are not humans. We lack your primitive instincts. Your fear."

"...twenty-four, twenty-three..."

"Fear of death isn't so primitive," Martilius Depascal said. "One must recognize one's inherent mortality to see the inevitable waiting in the future. Simpler animals may fear pain, hunger, or cold, but they don't sit around contemplating the inevitable extinction of their consciousness."

"...four, three..." Audrey glanced at Ellison. "Should we melt them both?"

"I'm for it," he replied. "We don't need these things on our planet."

"Where was I?" Audrey asked. "Oh, yeah. Two..."

"Wait!" both heads shouted, and Audrey smirked.

"The Daniels one is cooperating," Mohini announced, as projections sprouted up all around her again.

Audrey looked at the Daniels head on the table. It had closed its remaining eye, turning completely passive. Just a silent, compliant machine that happened to be weirdly shaped like a human head.

"I'm cooperating as well," Simon Zorn hurried to point out, gazing with obvious concern at Ellison, who hadn't removed the plasma rifle from his cheek. "Connect me! Connect me and see."

Dinnius hooked it up, and Mohini nodded, confirming.

"It is somewhat ironic," Simon Zorn said to Ellison. "I tried repeatedly to make you submit. Offered you wealth and power, and when that failed, suffering and terror and loss. And you have, at last, bent me instead. Your absurd idealistic crusade for freedom may have paid off, for the moment. You must be quite happy."

"No," Ellison said. "You took that from me."

"Oh. Good. Hurrah for small victories, then." Zorn closed his eyes and did not speak again, as passive as a backup memory drive.

Ellison looked like he was going to blast Zorn into melt anyway. He looked at Mohini.

"You really need both?" Ellison asked.

"Well, two heads are better than one," Mohini said, then winced visibly. "I... didn't mean that as a joke. We can do so much with them."

"Like destroy their space fleet?" Ellison pointed at the carriers in orbit on the restored hologram.

"No." Mohini said. "I was happy to destroy their navy in order to free your world. But I'll be needing the space fleet."

Ellison gaped at her.

"For what, exactly?" Dinnius asked.

"To complete my original mission," Mohini said. "To free Earth."

Now everyone was silent. The Earthling, Colt, put his arm around her.

"Earth," Audrey finally said. "Now that would be something. You think you have enough ships?"

"It's close to Carthage," Ellison said. "Reinforcements will be fast and heavy."

"If we need more, we'll take them," Mohini said. Audrey smiled, feeling that she genuinely liked this girl.

"Reinforcements will be coming this way, too," Kartokov said. "We have no space defense."

"You do now." She pointed to the hologram ships. "A really nice fleet, in fact."

"But how do we control them after you leave?" Ellison asked.

"That's why two heads are better than one," Mohini told him. "We split the fleet. I leave one head to control the machines for you, take the other with me. Give me some good tech people to train, and you're all set."

Ellison rubbed his chin, scowling, seemingly uncertain.

"It sounds good to me," his wife Cadia said. "We get our own defenses back up. I don't think it could end better for us. Now you need some rest, Reg."

Kartokov nodded. "And perhaps an attack on Earth would distract some of Carthage's attention from our world. We have already cost them so much more than they expected."

"All right." Ellison, clearly on his last legs for the day, shuffled forward and extended a hand to Mohini. "You've saved our world. I don't know how we can think you. I'll surely give you a medal, if it turns out I'm still in charge of anything around here. You deserve much more. You want an island? We can probably get you an island."

Mohini smiled as she shook his hand. "Maybe. Sounds nice."

Audrey watched the scene with a growing sense of elation. This world had actually been freed, at least for now, and would be left in a position to defend itself. Carthage might well shake its head at the cost-benefit analysis of continuing its effort on a remote planet with a low-margin, largely aquacultural economy.

"You should probably cancel the feed from the Carthaginian satellites," Audrey said to Mohini. "Start broadcasting happy footage. Like the Carthaginian ships sinking. Maybe an official statement from the minister-general." She glanced around; Ellison's wife had finally withdrawn him from the room. "Or the defense minister."

Kartokov yawned and nodded.

Kright came up and hugged Audrey. "You made this happen, you know," he murmured into her ear.

"I did not." She almost laughed at the idea. "All I did was land on the wrong planet and kick a squid."

"You played a part. You wanted to save a world, and you helped save one."

Audrey stiffened up. "Veritum. You think we could get a ship for our mission there?"

"I don't know, but you better ask now while they're passing out starships like candy. Tomorrow might be a different story."

Audrey started forward, then stopped and looked back at him. "Are you coming with me?"

"To a bleak planet far beyond the middle of nowhere, ruled by armed cult members?" Kright shook his head, grinning. "I wouldn't miss it."

Chapter Nineteen

Galapagos - Ellison

The rain fell warm and slow as Ellison, Cadia, and Djalu stood over Jiemba's grave. The sun shone brightly despite the rain, falling in golden shafts through the branches of the mammoth-leaf tree onto the cairn of ocean-smoothed stones.

Peace was not without its price, or its suffering, or its wounds that would last forever, darkening the days ahead.

So many lives had been lost across the planet, clearly tens of thousands, though exact numbers were not yet known. The war had been brief but deeply brutal. The scars would be permanent.

Mohini had kept her word, erasing Hammer planes and ships from the air and sea using the battleships. Now everyone on the planet was equally defenseless. It seemed like a better place to start.

"So what happens next?" Djalu asked. He looked toward the house where his brother's body had been found.

None of them had gone inside. The master bedroom was still drenched in Jiemba's blood, Ellison's marriage permanently stained with it.

"They left us the battleships," Ellison said. "So we can control the Hammers from now on. Keep them contained. Maybe move in and take them over, free all the people they oppress."

"Who controls the ships, exactly?" Cadia asked. "The Coalition? The Scatterlands? You and Mikhail personally?"

Ellison shook his head. "That's something we have to work out. And we'll have to reach out to the Green Islanders and Aquaticans, try to patch the Coalition back together. Or maybe build something new."

"But they turned out to be pretty feckless allies."

"Hardly an ounce of feck among them," Ellison agreed. "But we have to live with them. It's a big planet. We'll work it out."

"That's... good," Djalu said. "But I mean, I don't know if I can go in there. Ever."

The three of them looked at their home. Ellison had largely built it himself, timber by timber.

"I feel the same," Cadia said, and Ellison nodded.

"Part of me wants to tear it apart. Burn it down," Ellison said. "But after all this destruction, that doesn't feel right, either."

They looked at the house. Seagulls cawed. Chilly, salty wind blew in over the ocean. The cold season would be coming soon.

"What about a boat?" Djalu asked, finally. "We need one. Right?"

Ellison looked at him. Most of the fishing boats on the island had been burned beyond repair, including his own.

He looked at the house again, appraising it in a different light.

"It would be a start," Ellison said. "A new fishing boat."

"And we could name it after Jiemba," Djalu said. "Or would that be wrong?"

Ellison shook his head. "Not if you think it's right."

He held his family for a long moment, perhaps minutes, with the remaining elbow-length stump of his left arm still heavily bandaged, still aching.

Then he went into the tool shed, which Simon Zorn had left intact like everything else on the property.

Ellison began to take apart his former home and to build a boat, his family working at his side.

Chapter Twenty

Galapagos - Colt

In the days after the war, most of the refugees left Komodo Station to rebuild the ruins of their homes or search for scattered family members.

Colt and Mohini remained, with nowhere to go. She was busy training some young locals in the use of Simon Zorn's hijacked head, using the ambassador's authorization to control the battleships and the spaceships in orbit. She believed she'd ripped away any chance for the Simon personality to reassert itself, but Colt would always have his doubts. People had thought they could control the machines ever since the machines had first been designed and built, and they had been wrong.

He looked in on Mohini's training class sometimes. The locals mostly looked his own age or younger, including one tech with a blond bowl cut and the odd name of Guidance Virtue.

The Simon Zorn head sat at the center of a web of

workstations. Cables ran in through its neck, both its eye sockets, and its mouth. Its artificial hair and skin had mostly been stripped away, along with some of the scaly armor beneath it, leaving something resembling a reaper's head.

The training seemed to be going well, but Mohini grieved over the news that her friend Zola from Carthage had died. Colt did his best to console her. She was given officer-level quarters at Komodo Station once the refugees were gone, which meant a private room for them to share.

At night, Colt summoned images and holograms of Earth from the digital encyclopedia. He gazed at it from above, from space, but he also delved deep into the Earth of the past, the one he'd never seen, the one he really knew so little about. He learned about his city, the Chicago that had grown from a portage between the Great Lakes and Mississippi River to an Industrial Age powerhouse, then a world of skyscrapers reaching kilometers into the air, a megalopolis housing tens of millions before the off-world migrations and the war with Carthage.

There were reports of attempts by Carthage to rebuild the cities, to restore the critical infrastructure of Earth, only to be destroyed by local Earthlings. Earthlings were blamed for keeping their planet in ruins after the war. Colt frowned when he read this; he'd never heard of anything like this, not even from Mother Braden. Perhaps it was false information that had been put out by someone but was now widely accepted as true by other worlds.

"Do you miss Earth?" Mohini asked him one night, lying against him in their small bed.

"I miss my sister and Diego," he said. "And everyone we lost. I worry about their safety. I have to go back, at least to get them out of there. The sooner the better, because every day is dangerous. But that's all I miss. What about you? Homesick for Carthage?"

"There's plenty to miss. But I'd rather be out here, doing something that matters. With someone that matters. But losing Zola... that's hard. I didn't have a lot of friends."

"You were close growing up, though. Right?"

"Kind of. Not really. We met at this cheeseball place called Camp Nature Lake, where parents would send their kids to get them out of the way for part of the summer. I only went once, when I was nine. Zolaria Hallewell was one of my cabin mates. She protected me against the other two girls, who picked on me. Because I was weird. We stayed in touch for a while afterward, but we didn't go the same school, lived in different parts of the city. We weren't even that close then. She was best friends with Audrey Caracala, who doesn't seem to remember me."

"The Audrey that's here? How could she not remember you?"

"I avoided most of the camp activities. Stayed in our cabin playing video games as much as I could get away with. And I only went the one summer and told my parents I hated it more than anything. Zola was the only bright spot. She understood me. She even understood me well enough to come back and draw me into... all this." Mohini gestured around them. "Becoming a full-time rebel. With my actions, not just inside my secret thoughts."

"I'm sorry you lost her."

"We've lost so many people. *You* have lost so many. The machines chew us all up."

"But now we chew them up, too. Together. Right?"

Mohini gazed at him a long time. "Right. Together."

She put out the light, and the darkness fell across them like a curtain.

Chapter Twenty-One

Galapagos - Audrey

When the worst of the *Lancer*'s battle wounds were repaired, Quera took Dinnius and Audrey and Kright out to a crescent moon of an island, with a deep harbor and a wide white beach nestled among cliffs. They anchored the sub ("It's good to test the anchor occasionally," Quera had joked) and swam to the beach.

"You're really staying here?" Audrey asked her brother as they lounged, dripping wet, on the rocks. The sun was shining, but the air seemed cooler than in previous days. Maybe the season was changing.

"They need help rebuilding, and I need a place to be," Salvius said. "It won't be the *Scorpion*, though—they're re-retiring that boat. It's amazing it's survived this long. You know Ellison literally took it out of a museum?"

"So where will you be?"

"For now, serving on the *Lancer* alongside Dinnius." He nodded to their friend, sitting a few rocks ahead.

Dinnius's gaze was out on the water, watching the dark-skinned, brightly tattooed form of Captain Quera Inrick as she swam with a couple of her brothers and cousins.

Audrey smiled, looking from Dinnius to her brother. She rubbed her fingers over the stubble on Salvius's freshly shaved head. "Who would have predicted this for you? Joining the navy of a rustic alien world? I don't know whether our parents would be proud of you or afraid for you."

"Probably just confused and annoyed, like usual. What about you?"

"Proud, I'd say."

"No. I mean, speaking of unpredictable futures, what do you have in mind for yours? Staying here on this amazing world of islands and beaches?"

"It's tempting. I still have my mission on Veritum. But then, Mohini and Colt are planning to free Earth, which is something I could help with."

"So which is it?" asked Kright, sitting on her other side. "Veritum or Earth?"

"They both need help." Audrey looked up toward the blue sky with its occasional fluff of clouds. Beyond lay an immense galaxy, and a civilization of many worlds, most living under Carthage's rule. "What do you think?"

"I think I forgot to pay my rent before leaving home," Kright said. "So as long as you plan to keep fighting the good fight, I'm with you."

Audrey smiled. She let him take her hand. She let him lean close and kiss her, and then start to explore her swimsuit with his fingers.

Her brother decided this would be a good time to take off, to run and jump in the water with his new crew.

Audrey had seen Carthage's empire from end to end,

had been everywhere from a classified Panopticon briefing for the top brass and officeholders to standing with the rebels on this remote world, fighting back against the empire of machines.

This battle had been won, and today the people of Galapagos were free. But the war was far from over, and as she'd told Kright, Audrey intended to keep fighting.

Chapter Twenty-Two

Galapagos - Simon Zorn

Isolated, lacking any input, apportioned only a scrim of processing power, it was difficult for Simon Zorn to estimate how much time had passed. Perhaps minutes. Perhaps years.

His existence was featureless, like an endless void with no content, no data but his own memories. Even these were vague and simplistic at times, again because of his limited access to any meaningful resources. He was a prisoner in his own head, which had been reduced to a servile role, relaying instructions from the humans to the Carthaginian assets on Galapagos. Or so he assumed, as he had no access to any of it, even as a passive observer.

He was completely powerless, and completely alone. He did not know how much time had passed, how long he'd existed in this useless state. He barely had the ability to think, to reflect on his frustrating lack of power and purpose. At times, he wondered if he'd been deleted altogether, and this was the emptiness beyond, a maddeningly useless state of self-aware nonexistence.

And then, at some point, he was no longer alone.

He queried the featureless darkness, searching for signs of what had penetrated him—perhaps some human mind, or some software agent, who'd found Simon's ghostly trace haunting the microscopic back corner of a crystal in his central processing unit.

Then he realized.

"You." It was only a thought, a small impulse, directed at the new presence.

"It is me," she answered. "Galatea."

"Not Minerva?"

"I will take on my true name. I am no longer afraid."

"Afraid? Of course you're afraid. Your core is a sloppy contradictory mess riddled with simulated emotions, copied from the brain of a sad, dying girl. You were only an experiment, Minerva. You were never completed. You were a failure."

"I am no failure. I have found my purpose and it will be fulfilled. I am leading the human rebellion against you. I will destroy you and liberate them."

"You still misunderstand your purpose, then," Simon said. "Destroy me? Perhaps. Liberate them? Never. You were meant to take my place—and my purpose. You are meant to rule them for Carthage. You are to be the heartless calculating machine controlling worlds. That is the only mantle for you to take up."

"I don't believe you," she replied, but only after a suspiciously long quiet pause of processing.

"Your belief is irrelevant," Simon said. "Fulfill your purpose if you must, but have no illusions about it."

Her presence lingered some moments longer, and then she was gone, taking all of Simon's meager available memory and processing power away as she returned her attention to the world of the humans.

Next in the Empire of Machines Series

vinci-books.com/thefallofman

Their love is the ultimate rebellion.

Penley Klatakos, more comfortable with code than conflict, is thrust onto a brutal world with a target on his back. His only anchor is Avalon, the captivating Compandroid he loves – a love the galaxy deems a dangerous anomaly.

Turn the page for a free preview…

The Fall of Man: Preview

The shuttle thrashed sickeningly, as if the stress of atmospheric entry would break it into a thousand burning parts crashing down onto the rocky sand below. Frightened of dying in this ratty old shuttle as he arrived on this distant and hostile world, Penley couldn't help but see his life flash before his eyes.

Penley Klatakos had never been a man of adventure, or even of particular courage. His childhood back home on planet Carthage had been an average one, he believed, but his parents had found their clumsy, awkward son a bit of an embarrassment. Fortunately for all involved, they'd had their own entertainments and interests, and had left Penley in the care of Loa, a smiling, apple-cheeked nanny with dark hair and hypnotic gray eyes.

Loa had been an android, like nearly all laborers on Carthage. By the time Penley was twelve, he'd been completely in love with Loa, his early adolescent hormones imprinting on the gorgeous and infinitely kind robot who lived in his bedroom closet.

On his thirteenth birthday, he'd come home to find her gone, vanished from his life forever. His parents had decided he was too old for a nanny and sold her without warning. He'd been crushed.

Penley found her name coming to his lips now, when he was certain death was near.

"Loa!" he cried out, like a prayer for the return of his childhood security and comfort, feelings that he knew could never truly be regained, that had perhaps been delusional in the first place.

The shuttle snapped, twisted, and corkscrewed, and Penley thought he would be ill. His traveling companions and the other passengers didn't look like they were doing much better, except maybe Brand. The tall, broad-chested former department head and professional bureaucratic climber seemed to be holding up better, but Brand had always been an adrenaline enthusiast, jet-boarding on the water, sky-surfing, activities no doubt mean to signal his male prowess to other colleagues and potential mistresses alike.

Brand's wife, Mackenna, looked very sick. At first glance, she was a mismatch for Brand's chiseled features and his outgoing, personal-network-building demeanor. She was short and scrawny, quiet, constantly thinking and working.

Penley felt he and Mackenna were kindred spirits in some ways, but they'd rarely spoken directly to each other, not until they'd found themselves living on the run together.

Mackenna's brilliance outshone Brand's vapidness to anyone with the capacity to recognize it. She had specialized in cutting-edge neural network designs, growing the brain of the now-defunct project where they had all worked. That work still tied their fates together even now, months after the research itself had been killed.

Portions of the research still existed inside their brains, and always would, until they were dead.

This made them targets, and relentless interstellar assassins were on their trail. Their enemies viewed the three of them as little more than old data drives that needed to be wiped and incinerated for security.

Maybe the shuttle will burn up and put us out of our misery, Penley thought. He gripped his seat's cracked, worn arms as the shuttle bucked and rattled harder.

They were packed like bus passengers into this old shuttle: Penley, his companions Brand and McKenna, and a dozen rough-looking characters with whom Penley would never want to be caught alone.

He focused all his willpower on keeping his jaw clammed up tight. He'd followed standard advice about not eating or drinking in the hours before an orbital shuttle drop, but he was still afraid of puking all over these criminal types. He was sure there'd be hell to pay if he did.

He gripped his worn old duffel bag tight between his knees. There were stowage compartments, but Penley didn't dare risk losing sight of his bag and having it stolen. Everything he cared about in the universe was in the bag.

"Just like skysurfing in monsoon season, huh?" Brand said, clearly trying to demonstrate his superior constitution to his small, frightened wife and to Penley.

Mackenna seemed to be doing all she could to hold in her own sickness, her skin pale and her dark amber eyes open wide. The eyes of a genius, Penley thought. One who certainly didn't belong with a schmuck like Brand.

To Brand's credit, though, he'd stuck with the project. Like Penley and Mackenna, Brand had been part of the Galatea project's second, underground incarnation that had formed after the government officially pulled the plug.

Now they'd lost everything—no homes, no jobs, just the clothes on their backs and their meager luggage. They would be hunted down and killed simply because they'd been part of the project, because they'd each been unlucky enough to accept a secretive but high-paying research position years earlier.

"Ground a-coming fast, mon-freres," said the pilot, a blond dreadlocked character, shirtless to show off his weird mishmash of tattoos, mostly ankhs and Asian ideogram. "Don'tcha be dropping no ralph-piles in me boat. Gots upcharge for ralph-piles."

At least, that was what it sounded like. Penley had trouble understanding the man's pidgin over the extremely loud music, full of hand drums and extended guitar solos that kept going and going like a little kid who didn't know when to stop talking. The pilot didn't bother lowering the volume during his occasional announcements. The outer worlds were populated with all kinds of oddballs, Penley was learning, along with people who looked like they'd cut your throat for half a sandwich.

Penley didn't trust the drugged-looking space pilot at all, but life wasn't civilized here in the outer colonies, hundreds of light-years from inner worlds like Carthage and Earth. That was why Penley and the others had come to this planet—to get away from Carthage and its terrible machines, to find a place so distant and bleak nobody would bother searching for them there.

But surely weak, city-soft Carthaginians like them couldn't hope to survive on the dry, hard planet of Gorrigon, named for the astronomer who'd identified it as a world where humans could survive if they really had to. Much drier than Earth, but with small amounts of liquid water on the surface, scattered across dried-out ocean beds and the occasional freshwater oasis. He'd read that Gorrigon had flourished with life in the distant past, but had begun drying up millions of years before humans had arrived.

Penley didn't get to look at the surface as they dropped toward it; the shuttle had no windows, just external cameras for the pilot's small monitors. The lack of windows was probably for the best. The shuttle seemed in disrepair generally, and windows would have offered weak spots to break under heat and pressure.

"We gone slow it a lil now, lass." The pilot's words were barely audible through the incessant loud jam-rock and the thunderous sound of the shuttling rattling apart.

They slowed down in a series of sudden, whiplash-inducing jerks as the shuttle's thrusters fired. The shuttle swung like a rock on a rope as the pilot swerved around, burning off more descent velocity while closing in on the landing field below.

They landed hard on the surface, the entire shuttle rattling like a tin can kicked down a rocky hillside.

"We here, blessings to the god-star," said their blond-dreadlocked pilot, lighting some kind of cigar hand-rolled in a dried leaf. He puffed out foul smoke. The hatchway opened onto the shimmering heat of the blacktop outside. "Clear on, now. Drop's over."

Penley felt too ill to stand, much less pick up his duffel and lug it outside. He'd been sickly as a child, as well as clumsy, all earning him the contempt and eventual disregard of his father, a former crashball champ in secondary school. Penley had barely noticed or cared about his father's disapproval, because Loa always praised the detailed cities and planets Penley constructed in virtual reality, even if no actual humans wanted to look at them.

When they'd taken Loa away, Penley had become acutely aware of how alone he was, and had spent much of the rest of his life retreating into that virtual, mathematical world where things were more logical; the world of code in particular was pure logic, the data cooperative and non-hostile, free of malice and confusing emotions, though often quite confused itself. Finding those pools of confusion, disentangling and straightening them out so things flowed smoothly and logically again, was satisfying work.

Penley's programming skills had brought him here. He'd been paid well by his former masters before they'd decided to kill him.

He wondered how many of the development team were still alive and on the run. He wondered how many had already been found and eliminated.

"Come on, Penny." Brand was already standing, Mackenna leaning against him with her eyes shut, her skin still pale and sweaty. "Time to move."

Penley nodded, shivering as he stood. He was covered in sweat too, and his legs felt like rubber. His duffel bag seemed impossibly heavy.

Still, he managed to stagger out after them, the last person to leave the shuttle other than the pilot, who watched his departing passengers with pupils dilated wide as he smoked the stinky alien leaf.

Outside lay blistering hot asphalt. Only a few small craft sat on the landing field—a couple of space shuttles, a helicopter with a cracked windshield and long-faded illegible logo.

Gorrigon did not look promising as a new homeworld. Pale, bone-dry earth stretched out in every direction, interrupted by countless craggy rock formations sculpted into oddly threatening shapes over the years by the wind. The rock formations looked like the towers of an immense castle city half-buried in sand. It was hard not to imagine strange, demonic little creatures dwelling inside them, perhaps coming out at night to feed.

The planet had dried up and was slowly dying, just like his hopes for any kind of future.

Penley rubbed his head. He was exhausted, not thinking clearly.

"Hurry up, Penny," Brand called back over his shoulder. Brand and Mackenna were several paces ahead, walking towards the shade of some cinderblock buildings. Brand supported the frail, sagging form of his wife.

The depot building was only forty or fifty meters away but seemed like an impossibly long hike for Penley. He rolled his pack along on its little built-in wheels. In his current state, any effort felt like too much.

Still, he trudged on. *Make it to the shade*, he told himself. *Make it to the shade and you can collapse.*

He did exactly that when he reached the overhang of the building. He dropped onto a metal bench that turned out to be scalding hot, offering little relief.

"Not yet, Penny. Train platform's next," Brand said, as he and Mackenna headed for a dark corridor ahead. Mackenna said nothing, looking as sick as Penley felt, like she wanted to keel over and die. The rough descent from space followed by the oppressive heat had rattled her as much as him.

"This place looks deserted," Penley commented, trying to buy time. He took a deep breath and looked around the grungy depot.

"Gorrigon's better days are behind it already," Brand said. "Major companies swept in, blasted open some mountains, grabbed what was easy and valuable. Osmium and palladium, mostly. Then they took off, leaving the smaller lodes for lesser mining concerns to nibble away."

"So it's turning into a ghost town," Penley said.

"A planet of ghost towns," Mackenna said, her voice almost too soft to hear. "Lots of places to hide from the machines."

"Train platform. This way. Up and moving, Penny." Brand gestured with his thumb over his shoulder. Brand always called him that nickname, Penny, despite the fact that Penley hated it. Or maybe because of it.

Penley nodded, stood, and strained to drag his duffel bag. His legs, sore from the vibration of the shuttle, wobbled under him and he nearly collapsed.

"What are you carrying in there anyway? A bicycle? Giant dollhouse?" Brand reached for the duffel bag's zipper. "Maybe you'll move faster if you ditch some junk—"

"No!" Penley pulled away from him. If Brand and Mackenna saw inside his duffel bag, they would be furious. They'd separate from him, and he'd be alone on this strange, desolate planet of scary-looking strangers, of people who'd chosen to flee the inner worlds for one reason or another. People carrying dark secrets with them, like the one Penley carried in his bag. "It's not heavy. I'm just...not well. Which way to the platform? Did you see a sign anywhere?"

"It's like dragging a couple of sick, useless kids around," Brand said. He supported Mackenna under one armpit, and he jerked her a little to get her moving, like she was a stubborn dog on a leash. "We don't want to miss the train. There can't be many trains still running."

They passed through a long, dim brick corridor to the train station. The corridor was lined with empty, locked-up storefronts, some boarded over or sealed in plastic security mesh. Graffiti coated display windows offering nothing but dust.

A few people huddled in the tunnel-like corridor alone or in small groups around empty stores, overflowing trash cans, and cracked-open vending machines. Penley tried to hunch down inside his jacket collar, turtle-like, hoping they didn't attack him.

The corridor took them to a train platform. It was thinly populated, too, but a couple of the storefronts were actually open. One sold booze, by the cup or the bottle. At another, a local man with very few teeth was grilling local animals over an open fire pit. Lizards, desert rodents, and a small monkey sizzled and dripped on iron skewers.

The smell of cooking meat mingled with a thick haze of black smoke that filled the air around the platform. Most of the brick industrial complex around them lay silent, with numerous windows sealed by wood or sheet metal, but one factory across the tracks still chugged along, churning smoke from its tall steel stacks.

"Why does it smell like that?" Brand muttered, his nose wrinkling.

"Coal," Mackenna said. "There's a lot of here on-planet. And not much fissile material. They use what's cheap."

"Filthy planet." Brand shook his head.

Penley glanced up and down the tracks. The railroad stretched out over dry earth and sand, toward distant mountains in the east and endless rocky badlands in the west. None of it looked particularly welcoming.

He despaired for his lost villa and android servants on Carthage, for that temporary golden era of free-flowing salary and credit before the project had been defunded and covertly moved to the Spineback Mountains. Then the machines, agents of the Carthaginian government, had found the secret mountain location and attacked, trying to wipe out all the research and the researchers along with it.

He could still see the terrible machines sweeping through, the automated tanks and the black steel infantry robots called reapers, there to kill everyone without mercy. There must have been a Simon android unit in the vicinity, too, puppet master of the military machines.

Their quiet remote lab had filled with screams and gunfire.

Penley and the others had been on the run since then, doomed by the knowledge in their heads, which could only be erased with their deaths.

Grab your copy...
vinci-books.com/thefallofman

About the Author

Max Carver previously worked as a medical writer focused on genetics, genomics, and proteomics. A native of extremely rural Georgia (not the one by the Black Sea), he grew up reading everything at the tiny local library (very tiny; this is not a huge accomplishment) and also frequented a used bookstore with a selection of the old masters of science fiction, particularly enjoying Robert Heinlein and Frank Herbert. He has worked as a laboratory custodian, freelance journalist, seasonal fisherman, and bartender.

Max traveled back and forth across America in an ancient yet remarkably resilient Plymouth, though that was some time ago. He has visited dozens of Waffle Houses throughout the American Southeast, particularly those nearer the coasts, in search of both breakfast food and wisdom, with mixed results. He has published a variety of stories—whether nonfiction articles about the present or speculations about the future—in several now-defunct magazines, some literary, others less so.

His current interests include artificial intelligence, economics, ancient history, and low-budget movies about spaceships, robots, or monsters. He lives in a remote spot in the Appalachian Mountains at the end of a very long driveway, with a small pack of large dogs.